FOSSIL CIRCUS

JOHN KAINE

THEY CALL IT SANITY.

THERE IS NO CURE

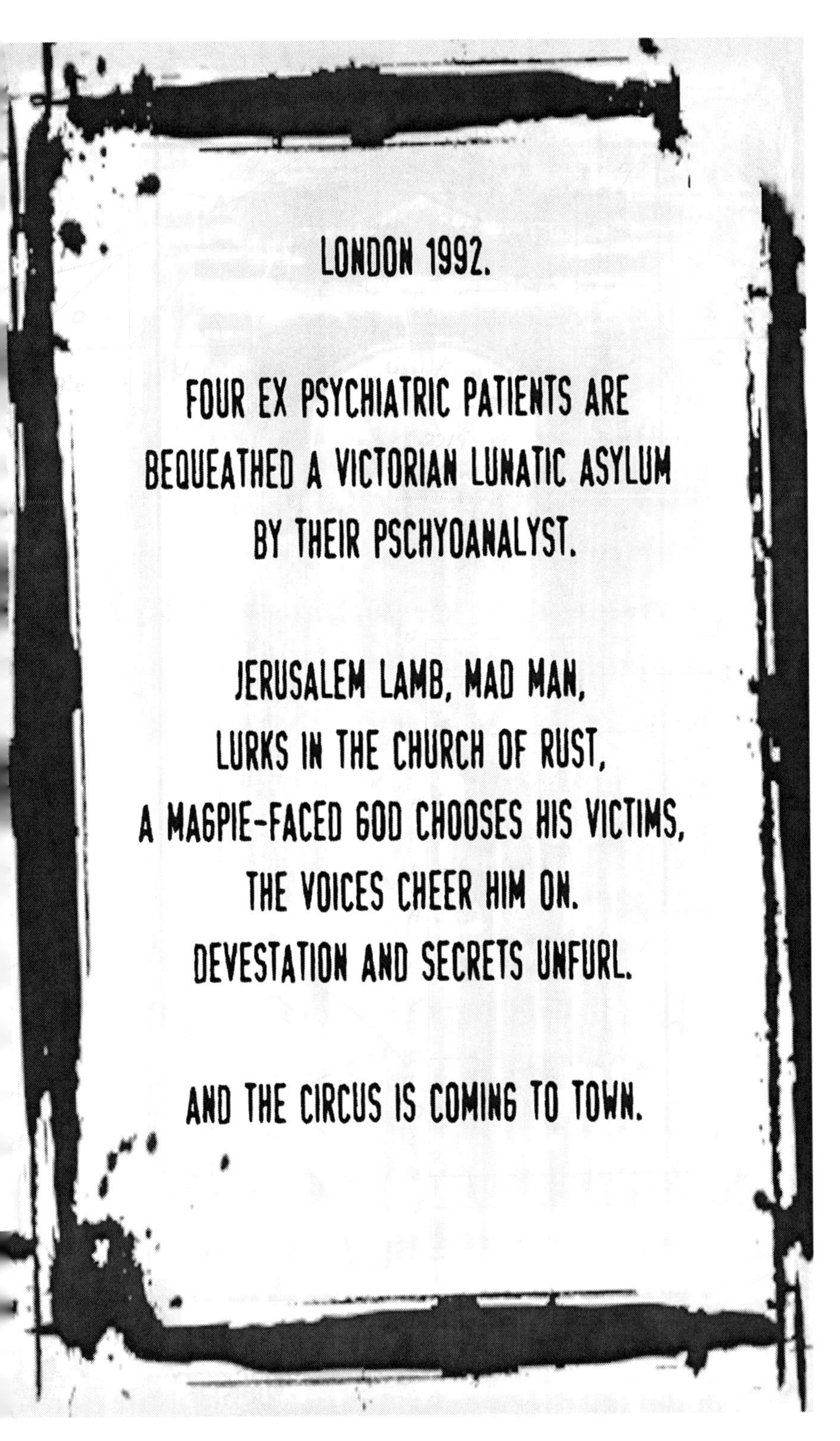
LONDON 1992.
FOUR EX PSYCHIATRIC PATIENTS ARE
BEQUEATHED A VICTORIAN LUNATIC ASYLUM
BY THEIR PSCHYOANALYST.
JERUSALEM LAMB, MAD MAN,
LURKS IN THE CHURCH OF RUST,
A MAGPIE-FACED GOD CHOOSES HIS VICTIMS,
THE VOICES CHEER HIM ON.
DEVESTATION AND SECRETS UNFURL.
AND THE CIRCUS IS COMING TO TOWN.

Freud was a great collector of antiquities…
…and once confessed to have read more archaeology than psychology.

Away to hcr right sprcads thc cold, cchoing hall, with thc pool of rain-drips spreading on the stone floor.
The drumming of the thick vertical rain on the roof is a background to everything that happens.

Titus Groan – Mervyn Peake

Fossil Circus

John Kaiine

Stafford England

Fossil Circus
By John Kaiine

This is a work of fiction. All the characters and events portrayed in this book are fictitious, and any resemblance to real events, or people, living, dead or dying, is just too bad.

Cover and all interior illustrations by John Kaiine
Author Photograph: Claire Doolan
Interior Layout by Storm Constantine
Editor: Storm Constantine

Set in Palatino Linotype

ISBN 978-1-907737-42-8

IP0112

An Immanion Press Edition
8 Rowley Grove
Stafford ST17 9BJ

http://www.immanion–press.com
info@immanion–press.com

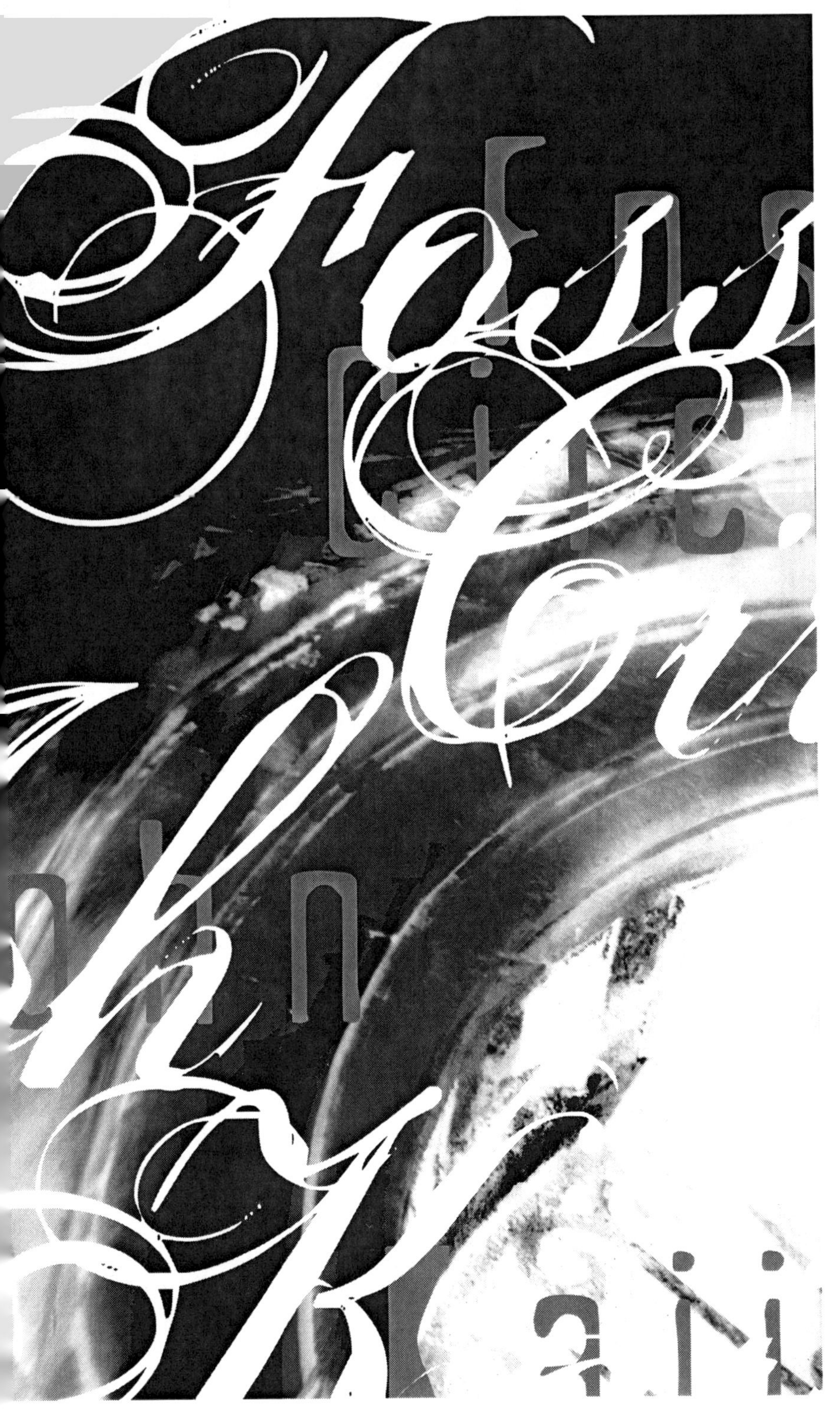

For Tanith Lee ~ with Love.
Without whom this circus
Would never have performed.

Special thanks to Storm Constantine and Immanion Press for enthusiasm and attention to detail in republishing this little horror

A fossil is a hidden thing
A replica preserved in time
And what are we
And what remains...

I

Untergehen

Man is quite insane.
He wouldn't know how to create a maggot,
and he creates Gods by the dozen.
Michel Eyde Montaigne

"Pipe a song about a lamb"
So I piped: he wept to hear.
***William Blake* - Songs of Innocence**

1

The insects whispered.

He could hear them lined up in the pews. Flies. Spiders. The many legged congregation, waiting.

He stood, arms outstretched, feeling at air filtered sepia through leaded, pale glass. Feeling aromas through fingers, dry scents: mothballs, damp church backrooms. Sensing the stink of new asylum.

Two hours he stood there, arms outstretched, the subconscious scarecrow, the unconscious Christ soaking up the shapes, sounds. Shadows chattered, coldness giggled, they told him of the church, its ruined state and failed history of fund raising. Jumble sales. Bring and buys. The bad joke of *Save St. Saviours*. Underfoot, discarded bodies of broken dolls and advanced Meccano sets. In the corner of the confessional a dead magpie wasted away.

Listening without ears, hearing dust motes shift, settle, hearing yellowing of Bible pages, here in the Church of Rust, he understood. He had escaped. Had run away through a field of corn in a suit two sizes too big, grain in his pockets, dead crickets in his shoes. Days ago, a different life. But here now, in London, this *quiet* town, he could begin again.

Jerusalem, muscled carcass in a baggy suit, blood slipping from his fingers, rigid in Calvary pose, allows dust the purchase on his shoulders, allows a crane-fly to land on a lapel.

Jerusalem Lamb: Mad man. Born awkward, pulled from the womb; forceps were used. An untimely movement leaving him with a dead mother and a hole in his head.

He could hear the crane-fly droning, could hear many

things. Cut his own ears off once to stop the sounds: The Voices. But it did not stop them, it only hurt. There are a lot of words for 'hurt' and Jerusalem knows them all. All the sounds, all the voices, every word he has *ever* heard, carried in the sack of his brain.

Every word.

All talking at once, telling him of right angles and rain and death-by-suspension. He could hear the crane-fly breathing, heard transparent bones floating in its gossamer blood.

He had broken into the church, found a window of easy glass depicting the Nativity. He had head butted it out, picked his way through. Now three wise men lay in shards upon the sandstone floor. A dried sanguinary seam inclined towards the nave. The crucifixion suit and the maniac just listening to insectoid contemplation.

The crane-fly shivered. Jerusalem heard the chill move through its fragile anatomy, heard parasitic ticks, *mites* gnawing at the invertebrate. Heard unicellular organisms on their bodies, heard microbacteria, sensed the very hexagonal shapes of viruses they bore.

In the Church of Rust his thirteenth summer screamed through the blood of memory, as he heard with clarity, the words, *"Swimming in pork"*. The crane-fly lifted, frisked in the air, a frail dance. Jerusalem spun, seized, swiftly rolled the flimsy thing between dry, raw fingers. The Voices screamed, *"Died! Died of clay and never coming back!"* He heard the synthetic machinery of the bug break down. Familiar lament. Observed the dead stain within his hand, crumbling limbs, tiny wreckage.

Beneath stone slabs of the altar, a thousand earwigs scuttle psalms, a solitary bluebottle greases its throat, joins in creepy crawly adorations.

Jerusalem hears their song, senses a cockroach scrape his soul.

2

And rain drowned rain. God's crocodile tears. In rain, a movement: walking shadow, draped in black, hands dug deep in coat pockets, collar turned, head down. A windswept old young man: Roane. In sodden duffle coat, workman's boots, pale skin, even his name mimicked drizzle. He walked towards the dim lit underpass, away from the cemetery and his work there. Cutting grass, tending graves, weeding out the living.

Rain trickled from the thin neon light tubes, crept through concrete, slid off wires, made electrics sweat, so neon fidgeted, sending blue shadows dancing through the underpass.

He walked on.

In blue light, Lurker followed. He had been there that afternoon, skulking in the cemetery with masonry angels, slipping between gravestones, trying not to be seen. And even now, his ineffectual stealth could be heard. Roane had heard the echo, had seen the man in suit lurking with angels.

Roane knew.

Rain fell all around like broken bottles let slip by drunken giants.

Roane kicked through the puddles, passing streets. Blurs for buildings. Rain bit his face, cut through to the bone. He kept his head down as he walked. His hair could not be seen, pulled back, tied, tucked into the coat. Rain filled his mouth, his nose, down into throat. He breathed rain.

He moved across the road to an alleyway. His eyes were raindrops now.

Rain followed Roane and Lurker followed after.

The house was a bed and breakfast accommodation where the council housed homeless families, unmarried mothers and psychiatrics; Outpatients undergoing rehabilitation. Roane, outpatient, walked in, went to reception, took his room key, climbed the thirteen stairs and locked himself in.

Lurker arrived soon after, stood looking up, saw something at the first floor window. Rain stung his eyes. Couldn't see. He *could* just make out the vague shape of a face, the followed man looking down. But rain ate the world, gobbled up vision. Lurker entered the hotel.

He stood at the reception desk and sneezed. Rain had claimed him, bleached skin pink, wilted his suit. He sneezed again, coughed up old rain, then Barkley appeared.

"What d'you want?"

But Lurker was weak, rain fatigued. He would be ill for months after this. He could not answer.

Barkley tried again. "Is it a room you're after? Well, ain't no rooms here."

Lurker was wheezing. He looked at Barkley, all peppery eyed. A nasal unpleasantry sounded: His voice - "My name is Slattery. I am here on a matter of some urgency. Legal business, you know."

"Do I?" jeered Barkley. Barkley was a Glaswegian and wore a brown cardigan.

"It would appear a Mr. Roane is resident here."

"So?"

"Well," - breathing heavily - "I would like to talk to him."

"Talk? To Roane? Ha, you'll be lucky. Cat's got his tongue."

"Cat? I know nothing of cats. It's an inheritance I'm here to inform him of."

"Cash is it?" Words spoken too quickly. Spoken as one word.

"Well, I've really no idea. I'm only here..." Slattery sneezed again, "...as an emissary."

Barkley did not respond. Just watched the puddle of Slattery staining his carpet.

"So, if you would be so kind as to inform Mr. Roane of my presence, I would be most grateful."

"Room fourteen. First floor."

"Oh." Slattery lurked to his left, found the stairs, and climbed.

Roane heard rain climb thirteen stairs and wait outside his door. Heard rain knock and try the handle.

Rain cleared its throat. "Ah, Mr. Roane...Mr. Roane, I know you're in there. My name's Slattery, I represent Messrs. Birch, Leigh and Frederick," he paused, adding, "...the solicitors. Perhaps you could let me in, Mr. Roane?"

Rain tattooed the roof. Re-echoed rhythm down the stairwell. Even here, outside room 14, Slattery stood in rain. Shoes full of puddles. Rain slid from his nose.

"Mr. Roane? Mr. Roane, if you're in there, I have some news for you. Rather good news." He sneezed. Rain sat in his pockets and moved the second hand on his watch. "You have been named a beneficiary in a will..."

Roane only listened. Heard rain.

"Mr. Roane?" Louder now, "If you're there, if you are here now, I work for Birch, Leigh and..." He sneezed twice. "Oh soddit." He took an envelope from his soggy breast pocket and slid it beneath Roane's door.

Slattery turned, unlurked down stairs, passed through unseen in reception and rushed out. He did not stop and stare upward, did not see Roane in his window. Just hurried off into the world and the rain of the world.

Roane watched him go. He heard Barkley below, hawking up phlegm, shouting at the television.

Roane sat at his window. A Dickensian angel scraped down off the astral, Narcissus in a broken mirror. The wet letter lay half under his door. Rain scraped at him through glass, tried to scratch his face, paw his eyes and tied, long black hair. Strong winds blew, shifting the window in its frame. Roane pressed his cold cheek to the pane, rain mauled the glass, cracked it. Thin lines of crooked symmetry spread across the glazing.

Rain pissed through the splinters, ran down and on to Roane's face.

He opened his mouth and let it enter.

3

It had rained the previous day. He had heard it. Heard the dawn, knew it was morning. Outside, a woman walked by. Voices told him, "*She puts sugar in her panties, makes her sweet.*" Jerusalem shrugged off their words.

He took the spanner, tightened the bolt. Screwing a nut into Christ's bronze head. The magpie carcass, wings broken, pushed to their sides and bolted to a Meccano cog, bolted onto Jesus' face. Erector set crucifixion. Thin wires held the magpie's beak open. Thick rope noose round Christ's neck, tied to the wood nave roof, hanging down. The bronze statue eight feet in height, suspended. Sacred suicide. Fly papers hang from Christ's arms. Right hand snapped when wrenched from the rood screen. Jerusalem had driven nails through bronze feet, renailed them, but into the floor. And stretching from the vestry, lengths of cable: A black fifties Bakelite telephone lay between Jesus' feet.

Lamb considered nothing. This new god was so much potential noise, little more.

Five books of used up colours, age stained, A-D, E-K, L-R, S-Z, and a barren yellowed Yellow Pages - telephone directories, 1971 editions, scattered, widdershins, round the fly paper deity. Three stained glass shards also on the floor. Three wise, sharp men.

Bugs moved around the fire on heat of burning pews, cassocks, bibles. Jerusalem built the fire not for warmth or light, but to entice insects. Naked, spanner in hand, caveman mechanic, Jerusalem Lamb strides toward flame, snatches at flies, catches two, takes them to the open wire mouth of the magpie, feeds them in. Where before, he had pushed a finger down inside the stiff bird throat, making it easier, wider.

"Shallow grave," taunted the Voices.

"Bollocks," dribbled Lamb.

"Our happy fracture, our icy heart. Stitched him up in a cat shroud…"

"Fuck off," Jerusalem's shouted whisper. He grabs at the spanner, sets it spinning into air and flame. "Fuck off." Louder. Screaming now. "Fuckoff." He knows nothing. He kicks walls, spits at thin air. Punches fire.

Diffused neon seeps through red orange stained glass, making Lamb and shadow, cave paintings; Devils chasing tails.

"Fucckofffuckofffuckkoffff"

Cassocks burn like trainee martyrs. Ashes grow cold in their own heat. Spiders piss on the night.

The madman continues.

4

Norman Fish farted and it smelled of egg. He didn't know which way to go. Confusion. Lost in the legal labyrinth. So many corridors, dark-oak panelled walls, brass names on doors - Messrs. Birch, Leigh and Frederick. The letter he held named him beneficiary in a will. Solicitors' letter: requesting, etc. Earliest convenience, yours etc. He had read it, reread it, folded it neatly, once, put it away. He had taken it out and read it again. Who had died? He didn't know any dead people.

A door opened; Fish turned, too quickly. Almost guilty, the letter in shreds, creased - nerve Origami, with words worn, type smudged, clutched in his sweaty palm like any grey rose. Mr. Frederick stopped, stared, spoke. "Yes, can I help you?"

"Oh, oh, I got a letter, yesterday, no, day before. Fish. Told me to come 'ere. Fish. Oooh! No, I don't *want* any fish, it's me name. Norman." There was a pause, "Norman Fish." He handed over the shreds of the letter. Frederick glanced at them, inhaled, coughed. Showed Norman to a side room, asked if he wouldn't mind waiting. Norman didn't mind.

He waited.

He fidgeted, paced the room, glanced from windows, picked fluff from the carpet. After an hour he thought they had forgotten him. He began to sob. He twitched through the room; Animated shock puppet, small time nobody. Pantophobic - afraid of everything. Afraid of being afraid. Breaking wind from fear. Stinking. Choking on his own words and smell.

"Never wanted to come... could've gone shopping,

could've bought me supper... nice bit o' hake... Matron said..."

Birch, Leigh and Frederick stood in the doorway. Fish unawares; "I... I *should've* come, maybe some money... M... Maybe enough for new curtains... new..."

"Ahem. Mr. Fish."

Bewildered, wiping tears from his eyes, Norman, innocent victim, stands facing them. "Oh, oh hullo," suddenly brighter, "Me name's Norman. Call me Norman, I do."

Wordless, three solicitors and 'Norman' wander off down corridors. Down stairs. Into offices. Into the past of Mr. Fish.

Ernie was sitting in reception. Nurse had brought along a jigsaw puzzle to keep him occupied. He toyed with pieces of India, Egypt, France; Map of the World. He put Russia into his mouth like a boiled sweet. No one saw.

Ernie. Ernest Wilson. Forty, with a six-year-old's intellect. Rusted brace on calcined teeth. Incontinence bag showing over top of trousers. Tiny eyes, cheeky grin. Tufts of sepia behind ears. A hand-me-down suit. A hand-me-down mind. Simple as sin.

Nurse had popped out to the chemist. Left him there playing with the world. He didn't know why he was here, didn't care. Nurse said he'd been left something in a will. But he didn't know what a will was. He heard voices, looked up.

Norman was almost screaming; "I 'ope it's not a dog. Don't like dogs. Filthy things, fur everywhere. If someone's left me a dog, I don't want it. Or a cat."

BirchLeighFrederick, push open the door, walk through. Fish follows.

"Oooh, is that you Ernie? What are *you* doing *here*? Oh, you're not in," *whisper,* "trouble, are you?" asks Norman.

"Mr. Wilson," Birch said, "is present as requested."

"Oooh, that's nice, Ernie. You've been 'requested'. Why's he been requested?"

No one answers. Ernie only grins, rocks to and fro sucking the Soviet Union.

Frederick opens the conference room door. "This way, gentlemen."

"Come on, Ernie. Oooh, put your tie straight." Fish fiddles with Ernie's clip-on bow-tie. Ernie slurps, white spittle tinged with rust. Fish wipes Ernie's chin, takes his hand, leads him into the room.

Birch starts. "Gentlemen, you are here today…"

Fish breaking in, "As requested."

"Hee hee," Ernie rocking on his leather chair.

"Stop it, Ernie." Fish gives his friend's wrist a little smack.

"You are both here, because you have been named in the last will and testament of Judith Anne Goldflame."

"Who?" squawks Fish. "Goldflame? Flame? I knew a Burns, once. Tommy. Wore a kilt, or were it a toupee?"

"Doctor Judith," dribbles Ernie.

Everyone looks. He doesn't talk much, but when he does, people mostly stare.

"Oh," says Fish. "I know."

Birch again. "Quite so. Doctor Goldflame passed away recently. She had named you both, along with two other *gentlemen*," the word stuck in his gullet, "in her will…"

"Is she dead, then?"

"Yes, Mr. Fish."

"What did she…"

"Cancer."

"Oh."

Frederick produces a document, clears his throat. Begins; Ernest Wilson, Norman Malcolm Fish, a Mr. Roane, and a Mr. Jackson are sole heirs to the Goldflame estate…"

"Estate? You mean house?"

Frederick, indignant. "Mr. Fish, please allow me to finish. You may ask all the questions you desire, afterward. Is that understood? Thank you."

Norman says nothing.

Frederick paraphrases from the paper. "The Goldflame estate, one Tookesbury Hall, Victorian sanatorium, situated in its own grounds, five acres, outskirts of London. To be divided equally among said four. Also, said four to receive ten thousand pounds each on proof of identity..."

Norman Fish farts loudly. Shouts, "Ten thousand pounds? Each?"

Wordless, Leigh opens a window.

Ernie giggles. Norman flaps around. Wealthy headless cockerel. "Ten, ten, are you sure it's not ten *pounds*?"

"Sit down, Mr. Fish," Frederick, red as pomegranate, shrieking. "Please just sit down!" Mops his brow with a square of William Morris. "We are still inquiring into the whereabouts of the fourth allottee, Jackson." His chosen words having no effect, the two just sit there, practised zombies.

Tempers lost, Birch, Leigh and Frederick nod as one. The subject of power of attorney firmly forgotten. Frederick shuffles papers, all three stand. Birch speaks. "Mr. Fish, your presence is required for an additional discussion. The finalisation of your proof of identity. My clerk will give you details."

"Oh yes, that's nice. Yes, yes." Fish not understanding.

"Mr. Wilson, here is your cheque for the previously stated amount, and your ID returned." He hands Ernie an envelope. Ernie beams. Corrosive rejoice.

Frederick and Birch have already gone. Leigh standing in the open doorway, gives Ernie and Norman a dry, 'Good day,' then turns, closing the door.

The two old acquaintances, amateur strangers, sit in the

room of dark wood. Legal books on every wall. Dust between the justice. Fish finally squeals, "Oooh, Ernie, we've got to share 'ouse with two people we don't even know. What if they're...well. You know, a bit, 'funny' like that Trevor was. Oooh," he puts bitten nails to pursed lips, "what if they're coloured?"

Ernie says only, "Blah," the sucked puzzle piece sitting on his tongue like some carcinogenic toad.

Fish took Ernie by the hand, led him from the room, back out, into reception, where Nurse was waiting.

" 'ello Ernie love, how'd you get on, then?" She was young, pyknic build. Brick blonde.

Fish darted in, "Well, I don't think that's any of your business, do you, young lady? Ernie's private affairs are his own concern, nothing to do with the likes of you." He broke wind. It sounded like Nietzsche's last breath. It smelled of onion.

Nurse laughed. Norman hunched suddenly over, mumbled, "Oooh, beg pardon."

Birch's clerk appeared. Lean like bacon with a polished carbon smile. She spoke to Fish. Arrangements were made for the following day. She didn't seem to notice the smell. Refined to the point of non-sense. Unseen, Ernie replaced the chewed puzzle portion.

Norman returns with the clerk. She admires the jigsaw, likes the fact that each piece is the shape of a country. Asks if she can put the last piece into place. No one objects.

She picks up Russia, but Russia is ill-shaped. Club footed, sticky. She tries to fit it in position, but it just won't go. She leaves it jutting out next to China. She says, "Goodbye," to Norman, Ernie and Nurse, and waits until they have left the building before inspecting her hand.

Unseen soggy jigsaw splinter.

5

The Fourth.

The Whitechapel swamp: Pre-primal, they wake. Shift from boxes, crawl from cardboard. Unfolding from hot water pipes, shedding blanket skins. Shivering from heat - hair like frozen lard. Tribes of One. Some begin coughing, others shake fists at things forgotten. The rituals of nothing. This habitual decay.

Looking like burnt clowns, failed exorcisms go tripping through puddles of clay, chasing the whiff of fried bread and hot milky tea. 7 a.m. soup kitchen breakfast. Ex dead men, their existence is some unwritten carnal act. But they are not here, look again, and they'll be gone.

These are the *real* Piltdown Men.

The Dwarf strolls up to the fridge-freezer box, kicks it, shouts, "Out White Meat!", strolls off to tea and burnt bacon.

Movement. Another shifting. The fridge-freezer box struggles, a cardboard worm giving birth. Gloves, mittens over them, reach out, dig into filth. Arms. Giant shirt-wrapped head pokes out. Massive body follows. Strange gymnastics occur. The front body pushes upward, struggles, finally stands. Swaying. Gloved hands deep in pockets. A dozen coats. Red checked shirt pulled over grease curls. Mud stained face lolling forward. Neck so muscular that he cannot turn his head. Serious bacteria graven in facial lines so thick, they have no shadow. He spits, and something grey slips down his grizzled beard, white and ginger hairs stubbing through. His left side jaw, squared off, pushed, through some accident, up, into his face, a permanent obscene leer. Conrad Veidt as *The Man Who Laughs,* but worse: Real. Left eye raised, both eyes popping. Static dewdrop. Tobacco canines. All the coats buttoned up to the very top of his bevelled jaw. Standing over seven feet high, teetering. Rag golem. Breughal overspill. Protohuman - **Mr Jackson**.

Dazed. A greatcoat dragging on the mud, a shepherd of flies heading northwest towards bacon. He stalks by an old geezer digging at a stump of charcoal that turns out to be his burnt leg.

Fires spit. Warmth fails. Cholera hides in a matchbox.

Jackson outside the soup kitchen, breathing rapidly. Enters.

The red brick building was originally a kosher slaughterhouse. Herds of salt-beef phantoms stampede through. No one sees, but Jackson - commonplace hallucination. *Pasul* vision. Only young ghosts haunt here, runaways, boys, girls. Missing persons.

The queue for the food is too long. He sits awkward at a table, waits. Coughs. Sweat runs *within* his skin, he can feel it. He is almost scared.

Suddenly, the Dwarf is sitting at the table, sucking on tea, eating a bacon bun. Crunching up rind with stolen dentures, both are lower sets. Small smile. Carnivore rabbit. Melted margarine trickles from his voice. "There's this rumour..."

Jackson does not look up. He doesn't know what direction that is. "Fuckin' rumours..."

"A suit's been askin' after youse..."

Jackson can't find strength enough to utter, "Fuckin' suit."

Never once letting go of the polystyrene cup, fed on possession, the Dwarf, following the giant's lead, says nothing more. Jackson slumps over the table, unconscious, dead maybe. No one really cares.

Later. Someone shouts, *"I'm not a Brazilian heavy, I shop at*

Habitat!" Jackson jolts back to *his* particular reality. The Dwarf is long gone, leaving only a solicitor's calling card in the puddle of Jackson's spit.

He pushes himself up, chair scraping, table toppling, clanging on its side. He strides out. Geriatric scarecrows watch him go.

Back at the fridge-freezer box, *Nephilim* tall Jackson drops to the ground, drags himself into cardboard, throws out bottles of mud, claws at carrier bags. Finally there is enough room. Unbuttoning his topcoat, he draws out a scimitar, it's real, no tourist shit. He pushes it through the top coat, and on then, in, through layers, then up. Buttons pop, zippers splinter. He is through to skin. Pulls off a dozen coats, tears off gloves, mitts, the rag wrapping his head. Naked now, but for cotton trousers, folded, pinned, up past thighs, or where thighs should have been. No legs. Severed in the same accident that angled his jaw: Double amputee.

Inside the coat are crutches. Stained titanium rods bound in tatters, tied by belts around armpits. To walk, he holds the crutches in his pockets, sways back and forth. Long practised.

He unbuckles belts, wriggles what's left of his body. Flexes arms, muscled like dead beef. Scratches at Niagara barrel chest. Calloused armpits, tattooed histories lost beneath dirt and sores, a rash of sorts, an allergic reaction to injecting *through* the coats. Hypodermics crunch beneath him. Syringes full of bluebottles. Injecting insects. Shooting up on flies. "Fuckin' fuck…" A broken needle jabs in his fist. Pulls it out, throws it off. Finally, through wriggling, he has found what he is looking for. Wrapped in a stolen shroud is a plastic carrier bag, in the carrier, is the money. Eight hundred in used fifties; the means of Escape. He could have gone long ago, out of this situation to another, instead of growing damp and fearful here. He *could* have, but there had been no other situation to get himself into. Until now.

The names on the solicitors' card are Birch, Leigh, Frederick.

Thrusting upward, the scimitar tears open the fridge-freezer box. Jackson pulls on a jersey, starts gagging, feels like he's swallowed wool. Saturn choking on the stone. Coughing, his hand upon the metal crutch, he coughs up something blue as Shiva, possibly blood. Possibly something more important.

There is a moment in which he wipes the spume from his lips, then an impatient rush of energy, lifting him on his crutches, steady. He searches pinned trouser pockets, finds a matchbox. Nods. The match is struck, the flame *singing*. He watches the fine fire, watches it drop, catch, devour.

Buttons. Drug flies combust. Old blood bubbles.

There's smoke in his eyes and a grin forming. The familiar stirrings of long dormant erection tugging at the cotton.

He had burnt the rumour.

Mr Jackson was gone.

6

What does a fish know about the water
in which it swims all its life?
Albert Einstein **- The World as I see it**

Norman Fish, frantic as a Benzedrine worm, hovering over the ID laden table, not knowing *which* piece of identification to take with him tomorrow. The solicitors' clerk had told him to bring a document with his name and address on it, and, if possible, a photograph. He only had one photograph of himself, which was on his bus-pass, and he wasn't sure if that counted 'legally' or not.

On returning home, (sheltered accommodation and a matron), he wasted no time in searching through his suitcase of papers. Medical records dating back to 1944; twelve bundles of ten held by elastic. His birth certificate. Ancient library tickets. Chiropodist, optician and dental appointment cards. Three black and white television licences. Forty diaries. A post office savings book. Small wad of letters. Calendars. Christmas cards. Book plates: *This book belongs to - Norman M Fish.* Tram tickets, raffle tickets. Dated receipts. Anything. He had even thought of cutting out the name tags stitched in his socks.

A decision claimed him. He had decided. He would take them all. Every paper, every last vestige of Norman Malcolm Fish.

Silently, he broke wind. He knew he shouldn't have eaten that last sausage.

7

Scrape the dermis off Stevenson's Id-Beast; boil down the Hyde bones, wrap them in clay, in hemp. Roll it in the dust of Esmerelda and Quasimodo, bake it in a Bergen-Belsen oven. Bury it in with Yorick and Ophelia, dig it up, shovel it all in a sack, lock it in Dr Caligari's cabinet, set it sailing down the Styx, down Haggard's Nile to port at Whitby. Crack open the box and you'll find Jerusalem Lamb.

He is bald, shaven as with glass. His eyes are like scars, weeping pus, and his nose has been pushed up into the skull. Bone, literally, *jags* out through his cheeks. His torn skin has never healed. E.C.T. burnt his temples. There is a hole in the head where the Voices crawl through. Sores. Broken stitches of mouth and lips expose gums and taxi black teeth. His blood-swilled eyes cannot blink. Cayman vision. Ice white skin.

Jerusalem Lamb slices up telephone directories with a splinter of Balthazar. Cross-legged on church floor, cutting beneath each entry. A million paper strips with a name and a number on either side. There is little logic in the arrangement of portioned directories: four heaps of names, numbers. Two million voices. Two million would-be victims.

He hears frost outside, crawling on its belly. Hears night shifting. He hears radio waves.

He is sucking blood off his thumb.

"Needed stitches in his hate," the Voices say.

He has the warmth of shadows. It can get no colder.

8

Somewhere off the Fulham Road, sash curtains are twitching with epileptic zeal. Twin-Sets peer from every Baroque orifice, jostling for *any* view possible of Birch, Leigh, and Frederick, solicitors to the oath. Phone lines buzz, an impromptu coffee morning commences at the house with the best view. Even the local celebs (voice-over hacks, TV vets' wives) have ventured out. No words exchanged, just looks of disdain and a feeling in the bones - *This will see our property prices drop.*

Ernie, chewing liquorice and gum, wandering the road, cannot find the legal house, but he *had* discovered he couldn't cash his cheque unless he had a bank account.

So, boarding a train at Caterham and remembering the number of stops counted on yesterday's journey, he arrived in London. Tubes next. Travelling the green District Line the counted thirteen, out at Putney Bridge. Onward. Followed trails, previous day's sweetie wrappings, discarded joys, toffee paving, and found himself shuffling along the very street which housed Birch, Leigh, and Frederick. Only trouble was, he couldn't find their offices. Couldn't read the numbers. Couldn't read at all.

Content now, just to smile at passersby, in *any* attempt at recognition. Somebody *had* to remember him and take him in. But whoever he smiled at either walked on a little quicker or simply crossed the street not believing what they had just seen. Surely such things didn't exist in S.W.6? Ernie slurps on sweetmeats. Sticky strands, liquorice oxide hanging from his mental metal grin. He had come for cash. He had no need for cheques.

The Twin-Sets are terrified. The 'funny little man' - *a stalker?* - had been sneaking about all morning, *smiling* at local people. They had seen him yesterday with a private nurse, perhaps he wasn't stable enough to be let out on his own, in public, let alone, God forbid, mixing with *real* people (Rodean old girls, Princess Margaret's colonic irrigator, etc). Perhaps the time had finally come to load the 4WD up and head off to the wilds of Surrey.

A whisper, the merest suggestion of thunder rolling in from over the river. The Twin-Sets shift, uneasy cross-legged. Somewhere, beyond the polyester, wisps of damp cling to M & S support garments. 24-hour girdles working overtime, condensation trickling through cotton undies or maybe it's just the rain they can feel. Rain slips across Queen Anne windows, mars for a second, the view of a young man walking along the road. But the young man stops and stares up at the Twin-Sets.

He wears any villain's colour - black. His hair, long, hangs around his shoulders, spirals down his back. Rain ghost. Roane.

He walks into the solicitors' chambers.

The Twin-Sets smile thinly. Hot flushes. Their eyes wander, as do their imaginations. Noses have to be powdered.

Rain expires on the pane. Waits between Lycra'd legs.

Norman Fish appears, dragging a suitcase by its broken handle. Visibly shaken, he's shaking an accusing finger at the case, cursing it. "Oooh, you're a naughty, naughty case. Fancy breaking on me like that… in public too. I were ever so embarrassed…"

Ernie strolls up, picking breakfast off teeth with tongue.

"'ello, Norman."

"Ernie! Oh, hullo, I'm glad to see you. Me case broke on bus, conductor called me ever," (fart) "such a rude name. What you doing 'ere, are you on your own?"

"Couldn't cash me cheque. Want money instead."

"Oooh, you poor thing. Never mind, we'll sort it out, Give us hand with this, would you, Ernie."

The two struggle with the case, finally lifting it, lugging it to the legal door. Twin-Sets view through opera glasses. They can smell something, possibly Norman, so get the Nepalese house maid to flit around with the air-freshener.

Ernie and Norman cannot both fit through the doorway with the case. Goonish movements and squeals from Fish, Ernie giggling. Roane stands in reception, watching, unvoiced.

In the street, something leather pulls up on a Norton, dismounts, strides toward the door, pushes between the baggy retards blocking his way.

The Hermes Motorbike messenger shoves Ernie and Norman inward, the case dropping to the floor, sprung open, scattering myriad ID all ways. Fish, floundering in a sea of paper, can only let off, "Me savings book… me letters…"

Birch's clerk arrives, receives the messenger's parcel, signs for it, stoops, picks up Norman's bus-pass, saying, "This will be fine, Mr Fish, if you wouldn't mind taking a seat. I'll be with you shortly.

"Oh," he says, as the messenger shoves him out of the way, "alright then."

The clerk turns to Roane. "How may I help you?"

At first he says nothing, just notes the clean bandage on her right hand covering a new rash of sorts. Pink blotches indicating infection spreading inward. Up her arm.

"My name's Roane."

"Oh yes, you are expected. Have you any identification?"

He hands over a medical card, this seems agreeable. He too is asked to take a seat. Fish, on the floor, hands and knees, drawing his papers together. Roane steps around him, sits on a chair. Ernie in the doorway, making an aeroplane out of Norman's birth certificate.

The clerk apologises for the extreme warmth. Apparently the central heating is broken.

Outside, a taxi pulls up. The Twin-Sets can only gawk, starch-eyed, as Mr Jackson emerges, tips with a twenty, throws off the stub of a Turkish cigar and strides *in*. He has a good feeling about this.

Mr Jackson doesn't need to make an entrance, he *is* an entrance. He has spent the last twelve hours and eighty quid on a shower/shave/haircut: Waterloo station. A new sports jacket, shirt, tie. He even stole some Brasso for his crutches. He knocks the door wide with a shined crutch, wades in. The prodigal son who's never been away.

But it's a clean Mr Jackson. A different person, another face. A 1950s face. Sid James uncast in the Lavender Hill Mob. He's almost charming, although suspended on steel. Then he speaks. You can hear all illusions shattering. "I like it sweaty!" A grating Northern accent.

Ernie and Norman stare. Roane, only indifferent. The clerk, half hesitant, offers a practised smile. Her professionalism useless, unused to such situations, she does the only thing she can do. She panics.

"And whom might you be then? Please? Sir?" Voice of old blackboard scrapings. She's reaching into her shoulder bag for a can of Mace.

"Name's Jackson. Mr Jackson." Deceased shark smile.

Norman and Ernie share a look of horror. The clerk's fingers tighten on the can of Mace, then there's recognition. Jackson, the fourth name in the Goldflame legacy. The penny, dropped, she straightens, asks for ID.

" 'ere's driving licence, lass."

The clerk shivers into corridors, through doors and offices, three identities clutched in rash hand.

Waiting, Jackson is as quiet as he can be, whistling a dry tune, eyes darting: addict of his own spontaneity. Three second-class rejects share his space.

Time, he bides.

Striding the two steps to the clerk's desk, he rummages through her open shoulderbag, picks out the can of Mace, sniffs the nozzle, grins, lifts an arm, sprays his armpit through the jacket. "Eeeeeee, beats a flannel and no mistake!"

Ernie lets slip a 'Hee hee'. Norman Fish feels faint, a ball of wind fermenting inside. Roane is elsewhere - on his chair, he has found a spider carcass folded in on itself, shrouded in its own making. He is happy enough.

Fish, words bubbling from his stomach, speaks to the back of the manic man with no legs. "Aah, 'scuse me, I couldn't help... overhearing... your name's Jackson, isn't it?"

Jackson sweating now. (Though not the usual whisky sweat.) What was this; Rat trap? Debt collectors? Too easy. Maybe some of Ronnie Bottle's boys come down to settle old scores, but not these Muppets, surely. He runs a finger under his nose. Sweat nail. There are exits: windows, nothing as complicated as doors. He could take these three and be long gone before the blood had time to stain the Axminster. He plays it cool. "Aye."

Wriggling, "Oooh, well, my name's Norman, and we're both here for the same thing..."

Mr Jackson leans down into Norman's face. Words come out. "Does it involve bodily fluids?"

Norman breaks wind, his very trousers move with the effort. "We've been left 'ouse. In Doctor Judith's will. Four of us, got to share it. You, me, Ernie 'ere, and ..."

"Me," says Roane.

"Well, bugger me sideways! The old Jew's croaked then. Hee hee, Good old Judith! House you say?" Jackson has grown visibly, not only in substance, but also at the groin. A lump bulges through his buttoned sports jacket.

Psychoplasm kicking from every pore.

Fish again. "The 'Goldflame Estate', it's ever such a big place, five acres. Somewhere in London… Oh, and ten thousand pounds… each."

Dry mouthed, Jackson lets slip his mask. Schemes burning out with every sub-thought. "Ten-fucking-grand!"

"Ooooh!" Fish squirms, pulls a face.

Jackson puts a finger to his mouth, making the 'quiet' sign, tapping finger on lips, pointing to Norman.

Clocks eat time and choke on the moments. Left waiting for half an hour. Blood-warm unwanted anger washes through them, even Roane. This has all gone on far too long. Explanations and money, sought. Jackson sniffs hard through his one *good* nostril, speaks to his right, but looks to his left. Snide, the sharp and schizophrenic vowel drawl of Dewsbury. "What t'fuck's 'appening, then? Could've fucken grown 'nother pair o'fucking legs, time I've fucken waited!" Louder, crutches slamming. Rattling a matchbox. "Bit cold in 'ere. Oughta-light-a-little-fire!"

Fish rushes to the lavatory. The clerk snuffles back into view. She's been crying. She's not alone. Nigel from accounts in tow. Nigel: a clever suit, the stripes going *up* as well as down. He wears the sacrifice - Ox-blood brogues. His face is almost Geminiacal, split by the purple slash of port wine birthmark; Map of Africa. Morocco as left eyebrow, the Cape of Good Hope arcing his chin.

"What seems to be the problem?" asks Nigel.

"Cairo," says Mr Jackson absentmindedly, looking at his face.

"I beg your pardon?"

Ignoring Nigel, Jackson charms at the clerk. "Eeeup, Flower. 'ave you got us cheques there?"

She shelters behind Nigel, shoots a thin, nervous arm out. Three cheques gripped in rash fingers. "T…T…Take them. Take them…."

Defying all laws, including that of gravity, Jackson leans forward, takes the cheques. Pockets his, hands one to Roane, holds onto Norman's.

Ernie's bottom lip sinks into his chin.

Mr Jackson, money secured, pleasant as July now, asks, for all four, the question, "Why did Judith leave *us* 'er house and why the money?"

Nigel answers. "According to Mr Birch, my uncle, there was very little detail to Dr Goldflame's will. She named the four of you as sole heirs to the estate, and fixed the sum of forty thousand pounds sterling to be divided equally amongst you. Oh, and you will be visited regularly by a registered social worker, to make certain you are all coping together. That's all. No further details."

Fish returns, stinking. The phone in reception rings, Nigel and the clerk are shocked into movement. She is far too scared to talk to another possible stranger.

Nigel picks it up, answers.

Apparently it's Mrs Slattery. Slattery's mother. He won't be in to work for the rest of the week, for what they had taken to be 'flu is, in fact, double pneumonia. He is to be hospitalised that very day. As Nigel replaces the receiver, down the wire, Roane hears a drowned man sneezing.

Nigel: "Well, gentlemen," (South Africa mouth), "that appears to be everything, does it not? Oh," he remembers, "here are your keys." There is some small ceremony of handing out the four sets of keys.

"Poo in a sock..." Boy voice. UnEarthed. Ernie.

Norman, fingering the seat of his trousers, digging at some caked on piece of cak. "Whatever is it, Ernie?"

Angry snail: Ernie whelps, "Want me money! "Want me money!"

"'ell fire!" Jackson steams in, everything falls apart. The clerk says nothing. Nigel suggests they all four open bank accounts. Jackson suggests he 'shut his purple gob," before

'Mr Fist meets Mr Throat.'

Ernie chews rust, something akin to burnt string bubbling on his lips. "Hee hee."

Roane has taken the spider relic and placed it on a radiator. He watches the dusty shroud blister, sees it sinking into itself, *fusing*. Becoming one.

Ernie, Norman, Roane and Mr Jackson leave. They become four bystanders out on the street waiting for a crime, four ex In-Patients waiting on a taxi. A trip into town, bank accounts to open.

Jackson with a smile as big as his fist, "Well, the world's our oyster!"

"Don't like oysters," chimes Ernie.

Jackson hails a cab.

Norman sniffs his fingers.

9

All that will be is the descendant of what is, just as what is comes from what has been, not from what might have been.
Salvadore Luria

Unreality:

Time festers. Inanna hung from the hook, left to rot, to jade with decay - the green of pus. Burst boil matter streams down Jerusalem's neck, descends over nipple, slips to the puddle of shit and piss in which he sits.

He has heard time discolouring. His neck wound had evolved. Colour screams, this is its noise. The lighter the colour, the higher the scream. White can deafen. Black is mute.

Days the madman has sat here, crowned by flies. Disconnected King, an icicle of waiting, back hunched, arms dead at sides, legs crossed: two broken logs. The penis shrivelled, ghost banana. A mayfly crawling across his face. *"Two sized piggy carcass,"* the Voices drift in and out offering useless words of charm, motivation. *"Pretty as nevermore!" "Oh, unshaved day!"*

Gone.

He is the seedling growing from rust church mulch. A Jerusalem tree sprouting up through metaphysical compost. Roots twice as thick as nothing, muscling down, fail to break through the sandstone floor, instead, go upward, inward, into Jerusalem, pushing with Vaseline ease along his internal soils, to that source of nourishment; that dunghill - Mind.

Jerusalem pitches forward, arms at sides, jerking, a

Parkinsons diseaser locked in an ice house. Inrush of memory - touch, taste. Licking hot wax off a candle, sucking razor blades. Recall: White flesh waiting under dressing gowns, knives wrapped in sackcloth buried beneath the river. A fat old woman in a polyester trouser suit. Sticks. Sticks.

Not enlightenment this. Endarkenment.

The Voices are lost. Unmade as a dead man's bed.

Only one sound - the church screaming.

Going back to nowhere. A blank page, an unwritten character. He is pre-living, embryonic, an egg of never floating in church womb.

Rain spits down upon Jerusalem. Loose roof tile.

He jolts, mouthing mucoid bubbles like some rabid saint.

Jerusalem Lamb is shedding his skin. Giving birth to himself. Birth memory deleted, a new darkness develops, aborting the future, a second chance for something that never existed.

Through this regressive alchemy he has created his own evilution.

He has become himself. The past has gone away. He is exempt from reality.

Flesh on the church floor, Jerusalem skin fidgeting, gasping for air. He spits out flecks of foam and blood. Has bitten the tip of his tongue off. Bile runs from his mouth. Eyes still unfocused, waving a heavy hand in air, he is snapped back into existence - and hears a raw sound, the diesel chug of a re-routed night bus, far away, the creaking of old bones in a bed, the moon howling, carrion crows calling out their goodnights. He is reborn as raw, unworshipped, *null*.

Fester. Scum. Holey Ghost.

He stands awkward, topples. Cramped limbs. Crawling through shit toward the magpie-faced-Jesus. All around, the paper chase of two million names and numbers, sliced telephone directories.

Hauling himself to the base of the bronze Christ, stiff-legged, drags himself up, face to face with the Redeemer. A mildewed magpie with maggots crawling from its wired beak. He had brought insects and grubs to this 'god' before, now they grew from it. *All the faith he can feel.* Muscled grey arms around bronze neck, Jerusalem's head on crucified shoulder. He has no use for this god anymore, it has served its purpose. For snagged on the flypapers are five strips. Five names, addresses, numbers.

Febrile, he remembers casting up the million strips, offering them to this god to choose. When was that? No time he knew of. It didn't matter.

Five names. Peeled from the flypapers, a small swarm of victims he holds in his hand. (Bluebottles, still alive, are kicking. Adhesive dronings cast underfoot.) Five names. He reads them slow, blood clicking from tongue tip.

"...K Shilling... M A Jones... P Tombs... A Ackroyd... J A Goldflame..."

Dizzy, facing forward, a thin light in his eyes, the merest suggestion of joy. The air is galvanised and cleaner. His feet twitch back into life, knocking the receiver from the Bakelite phone at the base of Christ. The receiver purrs: Reconnection.

Jerusalem only stares.

"Fuck almighty!" The Voices creep back. *"Flowers to burn!" "Clean young flesh!" "Trout look look!" "Stoney toads!"*

They are shriller than ever before. Screaming, an amphetamine choir. A million electric chairs left out in the rain. A billion masochists banging on an Auschwitz door, shouting, "Let me in!"

Jerusalem only.

"Letttttttttt meeeeeeeeee innnnnnnnnnn!"

Jerusalem stares beyond: Beyond the darkness, the abyss has a cellar.

II

Narrenschiff

Four weathered gravestones tilt against the wall
Of your Victorian asylum.
Out of bounds, you kneel in the long grass
Deciphering obliterated names:
Old lunatics who died here.
***Ian Hamilton* - Memorial**

Heads in profile are defined with a firm outline, eye-sockets are round, even hollow, and eye-lids often heavy; hair is straight, slightly wavy, or in simple ringlets, and nostrils usually open. Mouths are like slits or wide open in terror, often showing the teeth. The heads of both Devils and Damned achieve a maximum horror by the simplest means.

Hilary Wayment
The stained glass of the church of St Mary, Fairford, Gloucestershire.

1

There is expectation. Boundary high walls of Tookesbury Hall are sighted. Victorian white brick, up, all around. The tips of twisted holly trees peering over asylum ground walls. Roane had walked through the night, a pack slung over his shoulder. He had left his room, opened the windows, filled the room with rain. Drowned it. A handwritten note left at the gates of the cemetary where he had worked, he had quit his council job. Roane had moved on. Dawn dew washed his face. White clouds shelter the sun. Morning can be tolerated.

He pushes open black asylum gates and starts up gravel driveway, skeltering round and onward, a quarter mile long. The Hall in the distance, a stab of waiting. The madhouse called 'home' growing nearer with every step.

It is any white brick Victorian asylum. (A carved out hollow insect of arcs and stairs. The Egyptian bug god, Khepra, upturned, impaled on a square pyramid, exoskeleton left to be sun-stained, white bones showing, window eyes staring back at the starer.) There are added rooms protruding at odd angles, there are doors which do not belong. The graves in the grounds do not so much tilt, as slouch. There is the smell of burning and of time. Old fires had burnt here. The gravel underfoot is little more than chips off a mountain, grey as clay, hard as it is sharp. Ivy crusts the walls, strangling light from a rhododendron. Ivy choking ivy. Tookesbury Hall: an uneven body of time.

Roane, old shadow lover, staring at the doorway. Gargoyles standing sentry on either side. Above the door, a white stone arch with bronze face jutting forth. A face symbolising nothing, something forgotten, corroded and bottle blue-green. Its stain spread like hair on the white. It is unfeatured, smooth as a polished Greek tragedy mask. Unhidden, moth bones hang in webs of dark bidding. Roane turns his key in the lock. Enters.

It's like walking into a cheap dream. All the lobby walls, white as secret ice. Light bruises his eyes, he looks away, down at the marble floor radiating chill. Warmth falls with light, even the dust shines. Squinting through the glare, he sees a staircase, two corridors leading off to the left and right. There's a table and highbacked chair of dubious oakage. Above, spiders nesting in chandeliers. Broken bulb. Electric web.

Roane smells the dust and time of furniture left too long in unused rooms. Memory scent of any institution - staled semen stench. The simple stain of infinity. He does not like this brightness.

And how many more mornings like this have seen madmen secreted in, stick/skin bodies folded in blankets, the mouth open, drooling with thick hope. Thin eyes burnt by light, looking up, thinking they are inside a sandcastle. And two strong arms on both sides politely dragging the in-valid up many stairs.

Do not forget what this place was - a gothic madhouse, possibly full now of old mad ghosts. It hasn't changed since 1922, and Judith left it as it was for the twenty-two years she lived here. Even the air feels unused. The lobby seems made of breath or carved from a hard tear. Its time is bland, *unchanced.*

But nothing is this characterless. Sinister in its very wanting. It isn't even gaunt.

Bars on windows cut morning into squares. Roane moves across the floor. Dustmotes, nothing more than mocking spotlights. Moth bait. He cannot exist in such brightness. He closes his eyes, and there's the darkness - waiting.

Close-eyed. A black figure in a white house.

Stairs, he climbs.

New ghost Roane, on the first floor landing. Tall walls stretching on. A corridor, two bath-chairs wide, long and along. Doors on either side. Everything is grizzled white. Phone and light wires have been painted over, as have insects trapped on walls; flies and spiders, cobwebs and brush hairs from nineteen-nevermind, faint outlines of emulsion fossils.

Roane at the front door, tries the handle; stiff - it gives. Door hinges have been painted also. He ghosts in. It's a small white room, single bunk in the corner, iron-framed, the mattress sunk in on itself, nest of old dead things curled up inside of it. There are tiles on the floor, stains on the walls where shadows have lingered too long. From the window, the only view is grey. The window ledge is splintered, *peeling*. On it lies, yellow-black, a butterfly with a broken spine.

It's cold here and Roane breathes it in. Damp too. There's a strong yeasty smell. Things move behind the skirting, scrabbling, reverberating. At least *something* lives here.

These are the rooms where 'nurses' once slept.

Out in the corridor, and the quality of light like that of some anaemic virus stretches up. The corridors are arched, Roane had not noticed this until now. He moves on toward the stairs but the house invades his darkness. Somewhere, dustpores are burning on a lightbulb, a machine warmth chafes dull air. He isn't here alone. He smiles a morbid smile.

The last room in the corridor is occupied already. Roane opens its door, stands on the threshold. Something boils in an overheated kettle - an egg, bobbing. Steam lines the room. Thick black oxide, carrier bags, a small summit of take-away tinnies and last night's butts - props in this pit. Through the electric kettle cloud, a hammock suspended and there is no surprise to see Mr Jackson in it.

"Breakfast," Jackson indicates the egg. The kettle has a folded cigarette packet pressed into the 'on' switch. Unable to turn itself off, it boils mad. Jackson leans over, picks out the egg with Woodbine block fingers, pours boiled water into a red plastic mug and stuffs it with teabags. He eats the egg, shell and all. Condensation rolls down the window, but Roane is not taken in by it. Cheap tricks. The egg had cracked in the kettle, leaving white and yellow floating in the water. Jackson stirs the brew with a switchblade. Yolk tea. A nip of *Teachers,* quarter bottle. He drinks it down, still crunching as he launches into sloppy narrative. "Came last night. Cab from town. Coupla jars at local. 'Dog and Duck', real dead and alive hole. Pork scratchings, billiard table, still, their bitters' not bad, mind." He clears his throat, spits and it lands somewhere. "Hadda sniff round when I got 'ere. Not much doing. Bit o' silver in t' kitchen, forks and that. Bugger all worth having away."

His words have a brutal sentimentality, being threats, confessions, accusations all at once. He wears a string vest, wipes under his arms with a tea-towel. Thick, dark hairs poke out through holes in the vest. Sudatory ape. Tab ends are scabbed in his locks, a dry alcohol sheen claims his face. Fallow as a murderous sloth, wiping egg phlegm from his gob, it was not hard to believe that he had once firebombed one of the more 'Celtic' pubs in Kilburn: a bad barrel, apparently. But he is languid, the sun is not high enough yet, his psyche doesn't start kicking until opening time. One sniff of a publican though, and the 'manic' light is well and truly **on.**

" 'ere lad, does thee know where the shittery is? Only I 'ad to piss in 't sink and I don't much fancy crapping in it too."

Roane, spoken to, speaks. "No, no I don't."

Jackson's bowels trundle in response. He picks at a

sodden teabag and squeezes the content into his yawning throat.

Roane had gone. He was somewhere in the asylum, on some other level, wandering through white corridors, wondering what had scared Mr Jackson.

They are shabby shadows, war poem survivors. Norman Fish and Ernie, stragglers, straggling down asylum driveway.

"Oh, Ernie, it's ever so big. I 'ope I don't get lost," blubbers Fish. But Ernie is two seasons away, in imagination's autumn, under the massive horsechestnuts, picking up conkers and flying kites in September's breeze. He says nothing, just hurries on up the drive. Rust-mouthed and boy-boned. God's little joke.

Norman follows with curious reluctance, little 'poot-poot' noises coming from his trousers. Kipper breakfast. His stomach complaint is hereditary, as is his haircut. A savaged mix of pudding basin and short-back-and-sides, this cruel style had been passed down the Fish line of time and blood. A longevity conga of uneyed barbers and trigger happy intestines.

Ernie, uncomfortably still, kneels in the long grass. He's staring down at greyed graves. Sudden clouds overshadowing the sun.

"What does it say, Norman?"

"What does what say, Ernie?" Fish is shaking gravel from his Hush Puppy.

"This." Ernie points to the headstone.

"Ugh, come away, come away! Oh, graves, graves in garden. It's like living in undertaker's shrubbery."

"Is Doctor Judith buried here?" asks Ernie.

"I hope not. It gives me the shivers just thinking about it." Fish wipes grass from the headstone, moss has gathered in the indented name. Green mourning. "Basil something.

Valentine? ...Valentine, I think it is. Yes, that's it. Basil Valentine Junior. Oooh, queer name. Probably foreign." He nods in his own agreement.

They stand at the foot of the Hall and look up, but cannot see the sky. All view is swallowed by the mad white monolith. The asylum - Moby Dick's carcass, open-mouthed, beached, waiting to swallow them up, in.

At the base of the mountain all you can see is the mind's sky.

2

Tookesbury Hall is a bone-cathedral. Intended, first, to be a church, having been carved by an atheist mason who left the job half finished, undone: having long realised he was *creating* a temple for something which didn't exist. The mason downed tools, took his guilt and sacred disbelief, took his chisel and took his own life. Nuns found his body washed up at Hammersmith. The year was 1888.

Now rejected as a church, the building's potential for insanity was recognised. The minimalist architecture was ideal; arches, aisles, curves, lines. More white walls than a chromophobes's home. Soft walls were hastily installed, bars on windows. A name was needed for the establishment, something with moneyed clout. The headline in The Times that spring morning told news of Lord and Lady Tookesbury who had been tragically killed in a ballooning accident over the Pyrenees. Perfect. No need for advertisement. Lunatic asylums were like gold dust. After a swift gentlemen's club transaction, payment was arranged entirely in *krugerrands*. And in were moved the mad.

The instigators and 'owners' of Tookesbury Hall were never named. The Church of England? The Church of Rome? H*alf finished, undone:*

Time's asylum. History scabbed over with the growth of long erosion. Lightbulbs hang like dead electric bats within the monotonous madhouse white: Grey-milk cum colour on every side. Roane is on the second floor, in another corridor of original stone, checking locked cell doors. Role reversal - keeper, not inmate.

There is a different *mood* to the second floor. A thin

acuteness of light on the shadowed walkways. In any institution, unknowing violence hangs in the air (like heat breathing) and is only as far away as the first imagined insult or blunt instrument. But not here. There is a leisurely fear to this level. So many locked doors: Unkeyed, the warnings are inaccessible. Don't peer through the keyholes, for you might just be looking down the barrel of a 'What The Butler Saw' machine. But Roane *is* what the butler saw - Pale as Death's friend in his sackcloth attire. A walking ghost story.

The doors are wooden mirrors.

He kicks an empty beer can along the floor, it spirals, spilling out dregs of McEwans Export. Jackson had been here... Last night - *"Hadda sniff round when I got 'ere."* There is a door that has been kicked in, kicked in by steel metal legs. Crutches. Splinter wood and lock remains hang from the doorway. He has found the fear.

Rubber. The room has the Durex smell of old party balloons. The only light, a faint yellow glow drifting above the floor. Inside the room, Roane finds himself standing on uneven ground. Puddled ice, mud, slush underfoot. There are the stains of red all around and the stench of old blood, no, not blood, but poppies. The room is full of poppies. Opium breath, sticky breathing, overbearing. Roane stumbles forward, tripping on roots, slamming into a wall of what he thinks are rubber insects, but are in fact, gasmasks. He pushes his face into one, but cannot prise it from the wall. He sucks through the respirator, getting a mouthful of ice. He opens his eyes, and can see only the broken glass visor, frozen mirrors - his own eyes staring back at him. He breathes through frost, cold burns his throat, hits his lungs. Snowflakes fill his nose and mouth. He tears at the mask, rotten rubber beneath his nails. He spits ice. There are rents in the far wall where sometimes bad weather skulks in, to over winter, like wasps. There are sudden smells now of cow-shit and lard-fried bread. Summer farm smells. Roane turns. To his left there is a stained glass window, set into a black wall. The window depicts Hell in the form of a giant red devil, whose torso is like a second ravenous head, swallowing a shoal of the Damned. Judgement snack. Blood menu.

Ice melts on gasmasks hanging from the wall like fruits on a concrete tree. The Damned are reflected in a frozen puddle. That's little salvation.

The room is full of poppies.

And Roane, with frost in his hair.

...by the simplest means...

Stained glass minds. Broken. Broken.

Downstairs in the asylum, Norman Fish and Ernie scuttle about. A couple of homeless woodlice. Ernie, (smile like a car crash), snuffling around in every room, scurrying from door to door. Fish, with his angst, near screaming; "Look at the dirt, look at the dust. Soap and water, that's what it needs! A Hoover, beeswax..." He wipes a finger across the hall telephone, and something skitters out of reach. Fish farts, his dentures rattle with the effort. Blobs of BluTac hold them secure.

Up on the first floor, Mr Jackson, Space-Invader in self-inflicted string vest has finally discovered the bathroom. He flushes the toilet endlessly, gargles with soap and bath cleaner, shouts more than sings, "*We're all going on a summer holocaust*!" Skids and pyuria staining the bowl.

On the topmost floor, Roane has found Doctor Judith's room. It is small, almost a cell. Drained of light, tarantula brown, it is the colour of Anubis' unlicked arse. There is a small bed, table, books, notes: Mental histories. Blue prints of the Hall. A single window, grey light straining through. The cold is familiar, she did not like warmth. She was afraid of madness, so she lived in a madhouse - homeopathic magic - the use of darkness to ward off darkness. At the 'end' she was an old, scared woman who died virgin. Grim embryo of cancer curled in her womb. She made her decision to grow old here, with her locks and bolts, chains and keys. Enduring the long night's ending, she had sung and tapped her foot, making jolly, scaring off life with life, letting death slip through an open window. We go empty-handed into the unknown, knowing only that dying hurts and so does life.

Screams reverberate through the hall. Ernie's mouse banshee wailings, **"Where's television room?"**

Up in the roof beams, bats or birds are shifting. And at the window, Roane hears the sound of vertical grey, ever so softly hitting the glass. It is raining.

3

Muscled breath: Breathing through plastic. Heartbeat booming, blood aquatics drumming. Jerusalem drowning in the sound of his own life. Black plastic bin bags have been torn and taped around his body. A polythene *madd shirt*. He ties lampshade wire round his left wrist, fastening it, securing strips of black plastic, encasing arm and hand.

The bags were plentiful. In every stone corner, bundles of clothes, mothball fashions, rot in sacks. He had found the insulation tape in a cupboard in the choir boys' changing room. When he ran out, he used black ties, shoelaces, belts, then wire.

He ties his final knot. Flexes arm muscles, ripples fingers. He hears plastic shifting slightly, conforming to his shape. It resticks to his skin: sweat adhesive. He can no longer breathe, forgot to make airholes. Two fingers are pushed up and into the black mask where the eyes are. He could breath through these. Moth vision on either side of the eyeholes, giving a sepia tinge to all seen.

He stares at his wrapped hands, makes fists. A sound escapes his throat - voice-boxed sixth note of scale. Terrifying, he leaps, jumps from font to lectern, dives, rolls through ashes of pew fire, slams dramatic into walls, runs through air, punches holes in low-side windows. Dynamic, kicking over pulpit, stinking, all the sweat bubbling up inside. He sounds like fire.

Twilight ovens up the sky, streaks in through crimson stained glass. Light colours everything blood. Red has a sweet sound - like scalded gulls. Jerusalem hears this and rejoices, screams a scream of unforgotten *being,* and falls to his knees (cracked patella) before the Magpie-God-Nothing he had created. He stares at the black telephone beneath its nailed feet and five victims this worthless god has chosen for him. He lifts the receiver and dials. Awkward, wrapped fingers in number holes. Finally; noise of electrics spitting, wires embracing. **Connection**.

In Bermondsey, a red phone rings. Jerusalem, breathing heavily, holds the receiver at arm's length, stares at it through bag hole eyes. Polythene rising, falling on his face. In Bermondsey, the red phone rings eight times, is answered on the ninth. "Hello." Jerusalem stops breathing, his very blood ceases. The voice is Indian, female, cultured. Sound particles filter down the line. He can hear warmth, can hear undigested cardamom, gold teeth sheering together..."Hello, who is this?" He hears fear. She's scared. Behind her, possibly to her left, sits a clay jar full of Ganges water. He can smell it: Kerosene-sweat-ash...

She hangs up.

Fragments of noise continue to seep through. Memory sounds, comforting recalls of dream blue skies, (blue noise: Baby bone rasped on mirror glass), the thud of wood on wet laundry. He can now *see* the sounds. They spill limp from the earpiece like sugar grains. The sounds have a dappled quality of light as if seen through marble lattice work. A final miniscule beep of noise is that of decaying sandstone.

He slams the receiver down back in its cradle. Grinds dead teeth together, lifts himself, paces to the south aisle, picks up a manky demob coat, shakes it, and out falls a brass trench lighter. He knew it was there, could hear it. Brass sounds like lobster being boiled. He flicks its ignition twice and up comes the flame. Holding the lighter tight in his fist, a steady fire flowering up, melting black plastic on his hand. It burns through to the skin. It doesn't hurt. It is only pain.

Jerusalem had been given his *first* victim. So easy.

The lighter flame burns darker, smokes with charred plastic and blood and is choked off. The wound is cauterised and sealed by melted polythene. A second skin.

He stands for a while, contemplating the curious design of burnt sounds in his hand. It reminds him.

From far away, the Voices mutter of, *"Virgin stubble..."* He pays them no heed, for he is no longer trapped in with the Voices, they are now sealed in with him, in his twin skin of plastic.

Outside, and night is filling up the corners, snuffing out the sunbeams. *It reminds him.* He picks a dead thing from the floor, bites into it through polythene. Old bones crunched up, thin breakage of grey skin. He swallows it down, dry brain, tail and plastic. Mouth and teeth showing through bin bag mask. Grizzled fur snagged between incisors.

The quiet colour of black. The smell of mothballs. New sounds to consider.

4

The 'Hospital' at Caterham is built on a hill. Access to it is limited. Either chance the climb or take the bus. Best not to go there at all. This morning, Norman Fish and Ernie have risked the bus.

"Oooh, I wish you'd have put a vest on, Ernie. You'll catch your death."

"Don't want to wear a vest."

"Why ever not, Ernie?"

"I'm worried about global warming."

Opposite them sits a day-releaser clutching his worldly goods, a carrier bag full of bus-routes. He paws each one lovingly, strokes their corners, sniffs their folds. He sees that Fish is staring, and so with practised disregard, proceeds to unfold the biggest of the route charts. Voice like a creaking coffin lid, he addresses Norman "...The 264 goes to Croydon...goes all the way into the station, then it comes all the way back here again. Course, the 213B goes to Streatham via Norbury, whereas it *used* to follow the old Penge route. Ever been to Penge? A number 16 will get you there..."

Norman screws up his face, breaks winds. The day-releaser sticks his head in his carrier bag, mumbles, "I've got the timetable for the Guildford via Pinner Greenline here, somewhere..."

Ernie and Norman get off the bus three stops early. Decide to walk. As the bus pulls away from the kerb, the bus-route man thrusts thin arms through the protective rubber of the automatic door. Ernie notices that the hands are clutching torn, human-stained time-tables. Either spittle or something more dubious is wrung from them in the manic grip. From inside the bus, a screaming, scratced voice: "See! See! I told you... I told you it was here!" The screams die out as the bus gets further away.

Not all asylums are old white buildings. Some are big and red and have wheels.

The 'Hospital' at Caterham was originally a madhouse. Its instigators intended it to look gothic and menacing. However, funds were low, they couldn't afford gothic, so concrete was used in place of marble, guttering instead of gargoyles. A pebbledashed Bedlam. It looks like an unnamed concentration camp or Bauhaus mistake. Long arched windows set into concrete grey slabs. Blue steel walkways stretch from sector to sector, making unintentional H blocks. All of the plumbing is on the outside, white plastic pipes spread on and up forever. Tarmacadam wheelchair ramps lead into every rubber door. All of the roofs steam as if sweating.

Ernie lived here recently, away from the main wards, in a 'group home' along with several trusted others. He returns today for the last of his possessions. Norman also lived here once. He was transferred from Pontefract to a room in Ward 7. He met Ernie here, they became close friends until Norman was moved on again. And here they are, years later, an overcast morning, builders all around demolishing the old chronic wing; patients mingle with them, scrounging cigarettes. Ernie and Norman pass by an industrial skip full of broken wood and striplight tubing. On their right, up stalks one of the many 'Wanderers'; patients allowed to walk unattended about the grounds. This one looks like Nosferatu in a pac-a-mac. Suddenly another Wanderer appears with shouts of, "What? What?" and then they're gone, dived down an unseen turning to drown wasps in orange juice.

"It's all changed, Ernie," whines Fish. "Whatever happened to the conservatories?" He points to the little glass rooms, windows shattered, dripping shards.

"Conservatories all smashed out," answers Ernie bluntly.

No longer a privileged in-patient, Ernie finds himself in the uneasy guise of mere visitor, *not* a good role to be playing. Never stopping, turning here, there, taking the shortest route, dodging the 'Collectors': Pathological kleptomaniacs. Don't stand still! They'll take your dentures, braces, anything not screwed down. If it *is* screwed down, they'll take the screws. It is rumoured that a chap up in Ward 4 has a collection of stolen pocket fluff.

Up ahead, a boy with a beard. As they pass him, he mutters, "It's a shame about mother." Ernie bares rusted fangs at the youth and tugs Norman's sleeve, ushers him through rubber doors - short cut through speech therapy. Conversations all smashed out.

Inside, the smells are unmistakable. Industrial disinfectant, human waste. Graves smell sweeter. Even Fish wrinkles his nose. It is the stink of live bodies, the smell of semen, scent of frustrated sex and not knowing, which seeps through the pores, like a child smells of warmth or some pubescent girls smell faintly of sand. But this is more than mere smell, this can be tasted. That lingering pissy taste of unwashed sex. Unfulfilment mostly.

Scrubbed pink bodies come bobbing down the corridor in regulation blue pyjamas. Norman recognises a face. "Hullo, Grahame…"

Grahame skulks away covering his eyes.

Nurses appear, they don't wear uniforms, only jeans, jumpers or tracksuits, a white plastic badge fastened on secure with their names and status printed clearly on it. The nurses, Brenda and Eve, both smile at Ernie " 'allo, Ernie, love. We thought you'd left us."

Ernie just nods, rushes anxiously on.

"Ernie, don't be so rude. What's the matter with you today? Ernie?" yells Fish.

But Ernie has vanished. Norman dives off looking for him, ducking down corridors until he comes to rest outside his old ward. Ward 7. He grins, looks in and sees the back view of a man, unaged, standing at the window. The man either stares through it or *at* it. On the window ledge, a spider plant. A broken extractor fan hangs over the man's head: Decayed halo. It's a sketch Magritte threw away. In the far corner of the ward, an indentation where a man had sat so long in a chair, that he had made a solid dent in the plaster where his head usually came to rest. A Zimmer frame is partially hidden behind curtains.

Fish turns as all the lights in the corridor stutter and click. No doubt an old smoker attempting to light a roll-up by sparking an electric outlet. Once, a novice tried this method. He was carried out in an ashtray.

Up ahead, Fish sees Ernie, rushes after him. "Ernest Wilson, you just wait a minute!"

"Come on, come on," hisses Ernie.

Fish catches up with Ernie in the exercise corridor. The noise is reminiscent of the Bedlam aviaries. There are pretty murals on the walls and a guaranteed smattering of excitables. Today is no exception - a geriatric gent with unlined face, smooth, almost missing an unaccountable feature, strides along in an olive green raincoat. Two senile old dears wearing too much mascara and lipstick chitter by: Dementia Peacocks. An angle-faced man sits rolling an imaginary cigarette. Further down the corridor, an Indian with a pained smile strolls by occasionally inspecting the rubber insulated light switches.

Outside again. Free of the smells, Norman and Ernie hurrying on. They pass Bag o' Balls and try not to notice him. He's a short man with a twisted body, a burns-unit face and gnarled hands. Leg irons support his feet. He spends his days here at Caterham, pushing a shopping trolley full of plastic footballs around. A doctor once made the mistake of taking them away from him. The doctor still can't cough without bleeding.

Norman and Ernie finally reach the 'group home', the front door is already open. Workmen move in and out with rugs and rolls of green carpet. Ernie and Norman sprawl through the door, Alice, a relatively new-comer, greets them; "Ernie, Ernie, Ernie," she sings.

"What's happ'ning?" asks Ernie.

"We received a Government Grant. New carpet for every room and a rug for mine," answers hunchbacked Alice.

Ernie looks put out by this. There was never anything new when *he* lived there.

Fish dives off in search of a W.C.

Smiling, Alice asks, "Did you miss us then, Ernie?"

He shrugs. "Came back for the last of me stuff."

"Who's your friend?" asks Alice. "You didn't introduce us. He's nice."

That was *it* as far as Ernie was concerned. He disappeared into his old room, slamming the door.

Three of them shared the home now. Alice Child, John Awdely and Thomas Harman. John and Tommy - schizophrenics - worked in the nearby canning factory. They help put the jelly into tins of Spam.

Alice is sixty. She's been institutionalised for over forty years. When she was fourteen she was officially diagnosed as 'feeble-minded' under the Mental Deficiency Act of 1913. Her father had her put away when she refused to sleep with him. Kyphosis curved her spine, humped her back, the onset was gradual and pushed her face into her stomach. Yet she still sings.

Ernie in his old room, picking through possessions, placing them in a series of carrier bags. Playing cards, pocket radio, myriad betting slips, a broken yo-yo and a shiny

American comic: Red Raven - Issue 1. A toffee hammer, three polystyrene cups, feathers, coloured chalks, a ball of string and a postcard he had brought back with him from a happy daytrip to Hastings, long ago. The new carpet had already been laid in this room, he runs his hand over it, it feels warm, soft, it smells like new carpet smells. He walks out of the room, not bothering to close the door.

Norman is there in conversation with Alice. A burly man in overalls is coming through the front door carrying something big on his shoulder, shouts, "Mind ya backs!...oh, sorry love."

Alice just winks at him.

"Where d'you want this then, darling?" he asks indicating the twenty-seven inch television.

"Oh, just put it through there," says Alice.

Ernie's eyes are saucers now. A colour TV. A big, new colour TV. And new carpet. Soft green carpet.

Overalls shouts, "I'll leave the instruction booklet on the table, love. It's dead easy, just use the remote to turn it on and off, volume and that. Piece o' cake."

Remote control! Ernie thinks he's been a bit rash in deciding to move out, he's not even sure if he wants to go now. There's a knock on the door, Alice calls out, "Come in."

It's Mrs. Bryant, the head nurse, and with her, the grinning Indian from the exercise corridor. "Hello, Ernie," she says, "have you cleared out all that junk from your old room?"

Ernie nods.

"That's good, because Stanley Mosley, here, is moving in today."

Stanley beams. Ernie rushes out of the door, Fish follows.

Ernie moves like an overwound toy tortoise through the visitors' carpark. All around, unused rooms and the feeling of being watched. He storms out of the back gate, clutching carrier bags like they were Stanley's throat.

Norman is blubbing. He's never been so humiliated in all his life. He has, he just thinks he hasn't. He sees Ernie. "Ern…" He farts and follows through, stands shaking his leg.

Some old incurables are taking liberties with the builders' property. Hammers have vanished. An electrician catches a glimpse of a naked man disappearing around a corner with a length of his aluminium. A bricklayer looks up from his lunch to see a bald woman eating something blue. "That's my pullover!" he screams.

Up near the visitors' reception, Bag o' Balls is picking a daisy for Susan, the new receptionist. He leaves his ball-laden trolley and shuffles over to her window. He knocks once on the toughened glass, she's already seen him and is opening the window. He holds the daisy out to her: flower knuckles. She takes it, thanks him, puts it in a plastic cup of water. Bag goes away. Past his trolley and up, onto the lawn, where he pulls down his trousers and shits on the grass. He pulls his trousers back up, pushes with his clubbed fist, cotton trouser material, up in between the cracks of his arse, rubs it, seems satisfied, buttons and belts himself up.

Susan, watching from her window, is laughing. Someone who *isn't* laughing however, is Norman Fish. Leaning against Bag o' Ball shopping trolley, he's untucking his shirt tails, trying in vain to cover up the wet brown puddle seeping through his seat. "Ooooooh, ooooooh…" he simpers. Suddenly all is a blur. He feels the trolley moving and himself moving backwards, into it. "Aaaaargh!" He falls back, cushioned by the plastic balls. He grips the side of the trolley and squirms in terror. Nosferatu in a pac-a-mac has emerged from the shadows, and hi-jacked the shopping trolley. Norman Fish, an unintentional passenger/hostage.

Bag o' Balls looks up and screams. Susan pulls down her blinds, locks and bolts her door and rings for security.

Nosferatu - receding eyelashes, pencil thin moustache, pockets full of Velcro - screams also as he races out the back gate and down through Caterham High Street. He howls, "I'm impotent and I don't care!"

Norman Fish, legs akimbo, trousers soiled, grimly praying as they bump and grind towards yet another zebra crossing.

Bag o' Balls is tearing up the lawn, crying as he rips up the daisies, crushing each one under club flower fists.

5

There is no ancient gentlemen but gardeners...
William Shakespeare - Hamlet

The gardener at Tookesbury Hall is Mr Flint. He drops by once, maybe twice a month. Sees to the weeds, cuts the grass. The rest of his time is spent in the guise of medium. He also dabbles in more, illicit circles. This morning finds him, navvy positioned, leaning casual on a spade in the sprawling Tookesbury gardens. A clever man, hair like spaghetti hoops fried in bile, half a cheroot tucked behind an ear, furious eyebrows. He has the uncommon disorder of dyscoria; abnormally shaped pupils. His pupils are square. He wears a jersey of extinct wool, corduroy jeans stiff at the knees, string for shoelaces. He smells of tomato plants. A surviving character.

Flint watches a young man, Roane, moving around the garden. Both know the other is watching.

Flint begins singing, more of a chant. Gregorian tenor. *"Under the wide and starry sky, dig the grave and let me die: Glad did I live and gladly die, and I laid me down with a will. This be the verse you grave for me: Here he lies where he long'd to be…"*

Another voice is added. A Northern voice. Mr Jackson's. *"Home is the sailor, home from the sea…"*

Together now, voices joined, *"and the hunter home from the hill."*

Square pupils looking up, seeing a man with no legs and tall tin crutches.

Jackson seems pained. He wears a white dress shirt, the tails dragging on grass. Phantom limbs.

Flint risks conversation: "Good night was it?"

Jackson sighs, grins; "Dog and Duck, fishing trophies all 'round walls, 'orse brasses. Coupla shorts, like. Feeling lucky. Brandies." He wipes a heavy hand across his face, "Played the machines, won a few bob, landlord comes up, says, 'Mind someone don't plug *you* in, matey!' Ha, cunt-scab. Then in comes this bird, big girl…"

"Tina?" prompts Flint.

"Aye, that's the one. So I buy her a pint. Game o' pool. She likes me crutches, tongue int' ear job, y'know. Closing time. I'd 'ad a few. Starts slam dancing, me and this Tina. Up pops landlord, says, 'You're non-compos-bloody-mentis, Matey!'" Jackson sniffs hard.

"And?" asks Flint.

"Fishing trophies, like. Pike, salmon. Landlord gets swordfish up shitchute. Nasty, very nasty. I'm banned now. An' this Tina, big girl, up int' woods, fucked the stomach, y'know. Belly button full o' me mess. Woke up int' ditch. Walked 'ome.

"Who's the boy?" asks Flint.

"Ha, bloody weirdo. Just me luck to inherit house an' 'ave to shagging share with Nutty Norman, Little Ern an' Goldilocks over there."

"You own the place then?"

"Aye. Doctor Jew left it us. All used to be patients of 'ers, one time or t'other."

"Nice lady," says Flint.

"Aye," Jackson reverts to manic mode. "She buried 'ere them?" Nodding towards the graves. "Could dig 'er up, see if there's any meat left on't bones." He waggles a bruised obligatory tongue.

Flint wipes mud from muscled fingers, suddenly serious. "No. No one's buried here. All the graves are empty."

"Cremated, like?" prompts Jackson.

"All the patients disappeared, apparently."

"'ell fire!" It as if Jackson is a machine and something has just ticked over in his metal mind. He contemplates, rejects. "Still, who gives a toss. You the gardener, then?"

"Sometimes. Walked in one day, did a bit of weeding, been coming ever since. Find it relaxes me." He offers his hand. "Name's Flint."

"Jackson."

They shake.

Jackson muses, "Flint? Flinty? 'ere, didn't you used to work for that Sweet wallah?"

"Cornelius Sweet. That's right." Flint's words are measured, a mathematical quality to them. "Colour-blind he was. Crossed on green, met a lorry. What a mess; A puddle of frozen mince in a Moss Bros suit."

"Dead, then?" Jackson surprised.

"As a duck."

Jackson chances his luck, his question about more of the local London lowlife, lump hammer subtle. "What's news on Ronnie Bottles?"

"Ronnie Bottles is no longer with us. He's been recycled."

"By the cringe!" Jackson is now ecstatic. His very blood smiles.

Flint adds, "Mr Lampways saw to it."

"Lampways is it?" Jackson's eyes vibrating. "Tell ya what, Flinty, why don't you tell us about our Mr Lampways… Better still, talk over a drinky." He slides a bottle of Johnnie Walker's from his shirt. Flint produces a can of Mackesons.

Mr Jackson strides to a fallen tree, settles himself down.

Flint joins him, takes a swig and begins, "I first met Mr Lampways in the snug of the Bell and Compasses…"

While Jackson and Flint are drowning words, Roane drifts through the garden.

Beyond the potting shed, stands, triangular and whitewood, the broken greenhouse erected in 1888. Pampas grass and dusty air. The smell of old neglects. Grapes spread over the glasshouse roof, grapevine pushed up through the shards, preferring to be without. Roane lifts a boot to its door, locks creak, bolts snap. Fat smut spores rain dusty down all around.

Inside, corroded scaffolding holds up the internal structure, grapevine curls round it, bunches of purple black grapes draping down, some are pocked, spongy like piles. Others are pebble hard. All rotten.

On the floor, leaves and stones beyond death. Terracotta pots full of nothing. Plastic trays, upturned, discarded. Bracken and foxgloves sprouting up through cracked concrete base. Weed Eden.

Roane walks out.

Ahead, a row of clematis growing up dead apple trees. He walks through, under. A Black-in-the-Green. He had spent the previous day, the first at the Hall, in his room, pressed to the glass of his window, lost in the rain. Now he explores, free from the squeals of Ernie and Norman, who are this morning at Caterham, digging out possessions. Someone else's headache.

Roane is easy here, he likes gardens, cemeteries; knows graves, has dug enough. Tookesbury Hall is one big sepulchre: An insane asylum for the dead. But the garden here is different, Flint leaves it overgrown, as if the past has been left to die. Most of the flowers here have arrived carried on the wind as seeds, taken root, grown where they chanced to land. Flourished. The rest is dead, dying or deliberate. The topiary alchemical symbols of lion, dragon, toad and pelican have been neglected, misplaced their shapes, *become* other things.

Toppled topiary angels have lost their wings to weevils. Trimmed green goddesses now bloated, obese. New shapes have been made by Flint: Skeletons with penises, the crab shape of cancer cells, and lop-winged eagles, now extinct dodos.

On far boundary walls, century old horse chestnuts shiver with the passing of clouds. The trees are hollows.

The water-lily pond is now a swamp.

The main garden, situated at the rear of the asylum includes a waterlogged symmetrical mass of weeds and tangles; a maze once. Sunk in on itself . A statue of Cybele snagged in its inanition.

There are herbaceous borders of withered mint, over-ripe angelica. Feverfew, peonies, Chinese lanterns grow out of season. Flowering cacti thrive in green shadows. Bees don't come here.

Roane passes through a pergola of moss, its dead avenue bringing him to an arched gateway, gates long since swallowed by the garden's chalky clay. The arch was an entrance to the stables and the servants' quarters. This area was once, and still is, known as 'Round the back'.

Black ivy smothers the entirety of a broken stable wall. Roane looks closer; there is no wall, no brickwork to speak of. Mites ate the bricks in 1922, dark ivies took their place, growing tall, solid, replacing the wall with leaves as black as Annis.

Alongside - a burnt out section. Charred wood flaking on a stable door, a corrugated tin roof, fallen in, barring any way. Roane lifts the tin, heaves it overhead. It crashes behind him, breaking, *ashing,* its rust blown away by breeze. The stable is now only a charcoal husk, its gutted timbers creaking, cinders shimmying. Cremated time. Roane kicks through clinkers, hay and horse-dung heaped in kindling, there are burnt books with fire-licked brown writings, black pages which decay in the light.

It smells like November the Sixth.

Behind a charred cartwheel, he sees a bundle wrapped in horse blankets. He thinks it is a body. Some pre-war unfortunate tossed here to toast in the furnace. The cartwheel shudders to Roane's touch. He crouches, pulls back the blankets in anticipation; it's not a body, but strait-jackets. Ten or so Victorian strait-waistcoats. He lifts them out, one at a time, heavy, he holds them like one would a cripple or sheep and places each one far from the ashes.

There are nine in all. All folded, straps tucked neatly in. He unfolds one, it is stiff, cracking with movement, uninclined to the giving up of its secrets. Roane lays it out, a maniac's dress shirt. Insane Sunday best. There is a picture painted upon it. A scene of fear, many misshapen people, pregnant women, wretches being driven from their homes and fields, taken down to the sea. A ship waits in dock. Towers burn in the background. Strange hieroglyphics surround the borders. Runes?

He unfolds the second strait-jacket: Another painting, the story continued. The poor outcasts are caged, aboard ship, sailing out to sea. In one corner an ornate compass pointing North by North West.

Roane flattens out the remaining jackets. Seven pictures appear. The third is of a ship at sea. Night journey. A moon with face looks down over the voyage. Sea demons splash. No land in sight.

Something akin to voyeurism stirs through Roane at the sight of the fourth painting. Storm scene, ship whipped by tempest, sinking. Screaming faces drown in cages. Black skies throwing down golden lightning. In the far distance, an island.

The fifth. The cages washed up on the island. Misshapen men make a church from the ship wreckage. There are tropical trees painted in bright colours.

The sixth painting has been torn. The picture is all black

and reds. There are harsh slashes of white, square like teeth. Finger bone impasto. Roane recognises the red to be real blood. The small tears are bite marks.

The seventh is as calm as six is manic. A wooden raft adrift at sea. A sail of stitched pink skin is blowing in the wind. A lone figure crouched aboard. In the near distance, there is land; cities and towers, dogs watching from a broken stone pier. In fields, heavy horses chewing earthy-coloured grass. There are flat roofs, brown views. A burnt red sun. Horizons cutting in, in crooked lines of old geometry.

Eight is more difficult. There are angles, white needles reaching out of the sea; one appears to be a lighthouse. A mass of land looms up in the background. Another island. Grey sky. Holes in the skin sail. There are stains on the picture where the paint has not taken, faint smears where tears have fallen.

The ninth and last picture, the story complete: It is Tookesbury Hall drawn in thin lines of black. Tookesbury Hall before strange additions changed its shape, pushed it out of itself. Nostalgic green grasses and hollow horse chestnuts, majestic even then. And trotting up the driveway, a horse and carriage. Journey's end.

Noise. The unmistakable clatter of Mr Jackson. "I smelled ashes... Any luck?" he asks, striding eager forward, anticipating a sudden inferno.

Roane stooping over the nine mad shirts, spread neatly out - oil tarot or da Vinci's laundry. He almost snarls, moves a fraction too quickly. Animal almost. Flint sees this, Jackson only offers a pilfered Carlsberg.

" 'ere lad, get thee tonsils round that."

Jackson and Flint throw looks at the canvases. Jackson has gone quiet. He glances at the seventh shirt, at dogs on a broken stone pier.

Flint bends to inspect the quality of the creases. "Can't

get creases like that no more," he runs a finger over the folds. "1880s, easily."

Dated now. The journey has an age.

"They used painting as therapy." It is Flint who speaks. "I've heard tell of them, never seen them, until now. Used to stretch strait-jackets over easels, canvas after all, and let the patients get on with it. None of your ice baths or centrifugal treatments here, mate. The last doctor here, that is, the last doctor *practising* here, was a student of Freud's. Kept a dream diary of every patient. That's knocking about somewhere, maybe up in the Hall with some more paintings. Wouldn't know meself, never once set foot in the place. Too much like a bloody slaughterhouse, what with all them white walls."

Thunder rumbles like indigestion through an ashen milk sky. Rain threatens. The sleeves of the strait-jackets creak up, bending arm over arm across the pictures. Shutting themselves. Closing like flowers.

Roane with his Carlsberg, smiling. Flint scratches at his head - hedgehog flea. But Mr Jackson is forty odd years away, the sharks snapping at his heels, the name 'Mogador' unspoken on sour whisky breath.

6

There is an area of London, forgotten, unlisted, hidden from the world outside by bombsites, prefab facades and savage hyacinths veiling fly poster hoardings. No council dare admit ownership of it. If questions are asked, they are conveniently shredded. The area was to have been demolished once, but the plan fell through. No one wanted the trouble. Not worth its own dust. An A-Z reject. Unflagged, call it Doom Town.

The apprenticed foreshortened come here to learn, historians come here to die. Nobody leaves ungrateful.

There are no kerbs to crawl here, no 'Young model. Walk up'. Just old style infections, vintage disease. Canine blow-jobs, massage by flies.

Even the shadows have stretch marks.

Doom Town. Where Mother London miscarried.

And now, in black bin bag armour, pounding through the night, en route to Bermondsey, a voice to kill - the first of five - it is the shortcut of Jerusalem Lamb. Mad man.

From derelict doorways, those who are practising perversions as yet unnamed, catch glimpses of Jerusalem seething by. They bring blunt needles to their eyes, score out the scenario.

By now, word had spread, murmurs passed from greasy mouths - *something* is in Doom Town.

They watch. Gangrene gull eyes following him through the neon mud. Some brave the scene by fondling crowbars. The Horse Glue Boys, upon hearing the whispers, smack themselves up so high, they can't come down. They're buzzing on the apogee, burning up like Gagarin.

Jerusalem hears their noise, the internal sounds: Scratched wombs, farthings decaying in uteruses, rusted bars rent from a canary's cage. He hears it and rejects it. Commonplace evil. Second rate devils. He hears only one sound, the saffron voice moving down the phone line. *"Hello, who is this…"* His only motion is growth, every stride forward is another throat torn, one more unboned mouth of dead human noise.

(Ten thousand inches away, there is a *meating* of cleavers, a scuffling; violence amongst the scarecrows. Straw blood spilled.)

He walks on.

The end of Doom Town is marked by a colossal tombstone of its own making. A vast black wall - blitzed buildings, toppled, concertina'd together, strata upon strata, brick and bone, self monumental - jutting up, touching night. Beyond the wall is the real world. Jerusalem stands at its base, looking up to the very top: Odysseus before Polyphemus . The earth revolves, but he is still.

Amputees crawl from their holes to watch the bin bag golem. Mouths agape, they're eating dirt, sucking on moths, feeding necessary cravings. They do not know.

Jerusalem launches himself. Arms up, out, grabbing at the wall, securing a wrapped hand. He climbs, pulling sweat damp plastic legs up. A walnut tree grows from the wall, he throws an arm around it, pushes upward. Thirty feet up now, bricks splinter to the touch, he kicks out footholds, punches grips.

At the height of sixty feet, he shoulders the wall, butts it, loosens both hands and slams it hard. It's here the wall gives way, a hole opening, he falls forward, down.

The descent is diagonal. Crashing through old walls, a slated roof. An attic with dead pigeon water tank, down, slamming through floorboards, ceilings, nails spearing him, joists and joints of the derelict house splintering his ribs on impact. It is the carpet on the first floor that breaks his fall. Smashing through floorboards, hammocked in diseased brown shagpile…

He had fallen through the mouldy house, knocked holes in three floors. Tearing out of the carpet, dropping to the ground, foot slashing open on a brown beer bottle. Soft porn and bible pages semen-ted together and someone two breaths beyond death in the corner. Feathers and grainy underlay come spiralling down, all around. Grey confetti.

Somewhere, a Voice - *"Raped with Moses!"*

The spaces where once were a door and window, are now covered in scabrous lengths of corrugated iron, that Jerusalem peels back, squeezes through; vaults over crusty railings and is gone.

The history of Doom Town is chronicled in cave paintings. Tonight, a new tale will be told in spray paint effigy of how the plastic ghost walked through the world in surroundings of fire and seas of darkness and blood and of how he climbed the mountain and devoured the moon.

7

The Aztec god of twins, Xototl, has the shape of a deformed dog, a sort of autistic Pitbull with backward turned feet and a burst eye of endured austerities. It also has the honour of pushing down the curtain of night. An unearthly stagehand. The dark now, is unzipped: A sickly golden chill breaking on the horizon.

Dawn.

A west wind blowing, rustles polythene trash bags, jigs the flap of a torn cardboard box. In the Bermondsey backyard of Chattagee's newsagents, rubbish is stacked - vegetable scrapings, egg shell, fish bones. Beneath the bags, a plastic limb, an arm, flexed, concealed. He had walked through the night to be here, skirting streets of new decay, through Doom Town and beyond. Concealed now in refuse, *waiting*, toying with a brass trench lighter, hearing the sweet song of flame.

The shop had always been a newsagents, the Chattagees bought it from Ackroyd in 1976, touched palms over a five figure sum. Old man Ackroyd didn't mind selling to foreigners, had nothing against them. He was better off out of it, an early retirement. He had only lasted two weeks. Died of loss of newsprint, pined for the feeling of loose change greasing his thumbs. When they found his body, out on the Moors, it was wearing a newspaper hat, two handfuls of tanners clutched in oily rigor fingers. Pockets full of milk bottle tops.

The Chattagees, however, thrived. From their arrival the shop was a success. Licences granted for selling groceries, milk, wine and spirits. The family was well respected in the community, Mr Chattagee being official spokesperson of the Bermondsey Small Shopkeepers' Association. There were still the usual racist attacks, but these had subsided, just the odd threat or spit in the face. Sometimes they would say nasty things down the telephone line. Only last night, a call, no one there though. She had hung up.

Mrs Chattagee, graceful, waves her daughter, late, off to school. She has an easy pace, knows her own being. Likes this time of the morning, the rush hour over, paperboys been and gone, the navvies and labourers in for a pint of milk and the *Sun*. Just a few locals now. Her husband would be back from the retailers soon, restocked with biscuits, packet soups. Time enough to sort the Pools coupons and take a cup of tea.

The bin bags stand erect. Two arms, two legs, a head, the blazing lighter.

Jerusalem.

He plunges for the back door, it's open - in now, prowling through the kitchen. Assam leaves heating in the pot, clarified butter grease sticky on linoleum. He stinks of refuse, sweat and night. Smouldering incense masking its stench.

Sweeping through the kitchen door bead curtain, *"THEPRODUCTIONOFTHEWATERS"* screeching in his head. He hears another voice, the soapy twang of a Radio 2 DJ. 'My Way', playing on the transistor. He sees her, Mrs. Chattagee nodding her head to the rhythm, her back toward him, in oatmeal shawl, olive cardigan and sari the green of betting shop pens. A lifetime's hair, rice washed, scraped back, tailed in a long black spine. Rings on seven fingers, gold in her mouth, coal in her eyes. Jerusalem lunges, seizes a green shoulder, slamming her head into a glass cabinet, pipes and snuff smithereening in the base of her skull. Her screams are misplaced, Jerusalem hears, knows the pitch, hers are not cries of terror, they are howls of recognition.

Khali black Jerusalem smashes a red yellow fist in her face, stabs his hand towards her neck. She does not know why, but she covers her genitals. She can barely see, but sees him crashing into her, sees all detail in a freeze frame, the halted time of burning. Suddenly she is cold and there is the reek of pork, burnt wool, hair: She is on fire. Her fifty years of hair ghosting up into a searing blue light. Flame racing up tights, catching undergarments, bubbling up through her eyes, mouth, between her legs. Gold teeth melting. *Now* her screams are genuine.

Jerusalem too, is melting. His hands dripping thin slabs of fleshy plastic. The lighter, like Mrs Chattagee, sings its sweet song of flame. Sweet as sweet cakes.

She is still standing, spinning, catching *Independents* with her heat. Jerusalem lifts her and slings her across the counter. She lands on her ankles, and slams through the glass shop doorway. The white plastic OPEN sign melting. She crashes into the street, falls to her knees, slumps over. The Pools collector and a window cleaner look on, afraid to scurry up. She is pyre. Kindling limbs, veins baked, a scalded shadow. Her last spark of thought should be of Agni, the black-clad fire god with two red faces and seven long tongues, but it is not. Instead she thinks of packet soups and the scent of coal-tar soap. Jerusalem hears her final breath. It sounds like a horse breaking wind in fog.

Burning radio noise, barely audible now through the broken glass door. Sinatra crooning: He did it his way.

8

Before it's happened, it's old news: The Bermondsey Episode. Uneasy market banter - the Millwall boys checking their alibis. Old colonials in gentlemen's clubs.

"Can't see what all the bally fuss is about. In *my* day, they were throwing themselves on pyres, left right and centre..." High profile policing in the area for a fortnight. Dawn raids. Kicking down enough front doors of the 'Enfield connection' to make it look good. Two handless suspects held in custody, released through lack of evidence - no fingers to print.

The local news reports it with little emotion. The reporter with microphone and silk tie, laughing as he fluffs the victim's name. Telling his cameraman on the third take to, "Hurry up. I'm running out of sincerity." Jerusalem hears this, hears the words fragging on the ether. Can hardly remember the act, hears only thoughts: Sweet sound. Fire noise. Fog-horse fart. An Unvoice. A squashed bug.

He peels the sour strip of name, address, number of *A. Ackroyd, Newsagent, 47 Bermondsey High Road* from the waxy fly paper, listens to it, rolls it between burnt black polythene fingers and stuffs it down the rancid beak throat of the Meccano'ed magpie. Beneath its wings, ghost-thin grubs flicker in bubble pupae. He knows they are there.

"Wart correctional," utter the Voices. *"Ou est les marionettes du sang... Unknown spines she said she said she said she said she said..."*

A flock of stagnant starlings lift from the bird's nest that is his soul, break flight in his mind.

"Long Noise! Long Noise!" skirl the Voices.

Jerusalem Lamb in the Church of Rust, crouches, begins picking at, and off, the cracked, fused matting of polythene and skin from his charred right hand.

An Unvoice. A squashed bug.

Scars for jubilation.

9

One cold day.

On the corner of the main road, an old man is bent double, one hand clutches the wall, the other pressed to his ribs. He's coughing, hacking up bat-grey heavy phlegm; great gobs like jellyfish peppering his shoe, elastic snot hangs from his nose. Expectorate stretching down, springing back up as he wheezes in. Choking on a mucus yo-yo. He hits his chest, retches, bacon-coloured tongue sticking out, black grime falling from his mouth like flies. His swollen eyes roll back, just pink patches of sight. His pallor gone from drab to ghost. Bones convulse, a noise, call it a rattle, comes from deep inside. He stamps his foot, funeral fluid spilling through him. If he coughs any more he will surely break.

As they're waiting at the lights on the corner, Mr Jackson looks on enviously, thinks, *"Bastad. Some people really know how to enjoy themselves."*

The mini cab carrying Jackson, Fish, Ernie and Roane, pulls from the lights and turns the corner, heads east down Falcon Road towards Walters, a department store Flint had recommended. Electrical goods, clothing, kitchenware: relaxed terms on hire purchase, apparently. **This** had appealed to Jackson - goods for nothing, then split. Easy.

The cabbie has his head out of the window sucking in great gusts of fresh exhaust fumes, anything rather than take the air of the car; Jackson's sweat, Fish's flatulence and Ernie's crowded colostomy bag. Roane doesn't have a smell, just radiates chill.

Now they are liberated, free men with a home of their

own, they require objects of life previously unpossessed. Personal furnishings, clothes that actually fit. Norman wants new curtains.

"Ev'rybody out!" The cab has stopped. Street-works up ahead. The road blocked. "Have to walk from here, gents."

Jackson pays with two tens, and tips with a five. The driver, suspicious, says nothing. Reverses. Gone.

Left on the pavement, four lunatic orphans abandoned. Jackson lights up a smoke, purses crooked lips, *decides* not to belch, instead begins popping down strips of Nurofen, turns on his crutches, strides off. Ernie scurries after: a dog or loyal gnome. Fish, with his shopping lists, calling out, "Yes, yes, that's right, that's the way."

Roane follows up at the back. Reluctant shadow.

Straggling along, they pass new buildings, little Lego brick houses - day centres, hostels for the pre-senile and suicidal social workers. (*Their* promised social worker had yet to call.)

Workmen, that are not quite cretins, gawp up at the four, start with snorts and sniggers, but on seeing Mr Jackson, think better of it. There's something about the calm anger of his eyes, a certain hint in the nostalgia of his scars. (The soul of a warrior drowned in vinegar.) Black sheep of the mad family. The navvies, suddenly heliophobic, go underground, hide in holes they have dug, wait for the man with no legs to pass. They don't get paid enough danger money for the likes of *him*.

As they approach the store, Fish remains in a constant spasm of self. Quicksilver on the boil in the pot of his belly. Hectic, he is too expectant, jabbering about headboards, flannels and pants.

On entering the store, a cosmetics and perfume department greets them. Purple smells fill the air, heavy as honey. *Poison, Passion,* old blue bottles of *Midnight in Paris.* Jackson is reminded - the fragrance of a bra worn by a paraplegic contortionist he once encountered in Marrakesh. Norman Fish starts gagging, sure that the cosmetic air will bring on another allergy. Roane and Jackson wander off, separate directions. Between gasps, Norman calls out that they, "must all meet back here, by two."

Ernie rubs a Curly Wurly across his rusted brace, likes to tongue the toffee from it, enjoys the taste. He looks up and laughs, for on the ceiling are faded remains of 1950's Christmas paperchains hanging between the antique sprinkler system on smears of ghostly Sellotape.

Elsewhere…Mr Jackson is in the lift, heading up, going to get credit. He rocks to and fro, shaking the rickety lift, pitching the wheezing lift-boy into the depths of his very handkerchief.

Norman and Ernie - ground floor.

"Now then, Ernie, we must get you some socks and underwear. You could do with some new shoes. A thermal vest?"

"Want to find the toys," says Ernie.

"Ooh, you're too old for toys, not a little boy, now. Come on." Fish takes Ernie by the wrist, pulling him towards 'gents' outfitters.' "You can be measured for a nice new cap, now, won't that be nice?"

Ernie, as Niobe, full of tears, twists his wrist in Norman's grasp. Rusty restless bottom lip.

"Look, Ernie, ties, ooh cravats! Could never abide cravats meself. Much too…" he pulls a face of lemon biting, "vulgar."

"God poop," grizzles Ernie, snatching away from Norman, who breaks wind from shock.

Fish calling out, "Ernie!"

But Ernie is gone, strayed off in search of train sets.

"Everything seems to be in order, Doctor Edwards. If you'd

just like to sign here, and here, yes, that's fine, thank you. Well, I hope you find everything you could possibly need. If there's anything we can do, please just ask." The man in the suit rises, shakes Doctor Edwards by the muscled hand, passes him back his passport and documents. Mr Jackson pockets them, strides off to the electrical department.

Identities are easy to obtain. Jackson has many. Doctor Edwards is just one. Others include the Reverend Tobias Avenal, Arthur Pears, a pork butcher, and Tom Booth, a retired collier.

The scam is a simple one - provide enough positive ID, match the face to the photograph, forge any amount of signatures and it's done - Instant credit in an unlimited amount. Jackson calls it *H.P. Sauce.*

He purchases televisions, videos, a satellite dish, C.D. stereos, walkmans, angle-poise lighting, monster-sized speakers, and a nautical mile of extension leads. They are boxed, to be delivered that afternoon.

Down again, Jackson trundling the lift; lift-boy near unconscious on his stool.

In the toy department, Ernie has skipped through the Barbie dolls and boardgames, has found instead a hand held computer game - 'Hungerford' - the intention is to kill as many people on the tiny screen as possible. Ernie thumbs the controls, blasts away another byte by-stander.

Two young male assistants are laughing at the 'mong with the game.'

Jackson manifests before them, seems to sprout from the very floorboards. His crutches being titanic nails clawed out of the woodwork.

"Something funny?" It isn't a question, it's an invitation. He is tired of boys and their laughter; a bad joke no longer funny. The two stare at him, from his base which is not there, up to his blazered trunk, to his muscle bound face of scars and eyes. They are suddenly the invalidated, and skulk, with eunuch force, away.

'Walters' has only one in-house store detective and that is Mr Drowned. A lifelong glutton with the look of a northern train-spotter or Dr Who fan; two dead Brillo pads stapled to his head, a ginger Fu-Man-Chewed moustache, white silk shirt, pink leopard-spotted bow-tie, beer gut protruding. Proof that there is no God, or if He does exist, He has got a sense of *humour*.

Drowned, lacking only deerstalker and Inverness, moves from floor to floor, inconspicuous, blending in with the surroundings, striking fleeting glances at any unnatural movement or suspicious individual. He once almost caught a blind war widow stealing shoelaces. *Almost!* But right now he was in observation mode, squinting through the tie racks at a very suspicious individual indeed. The would-be pilferer had been handling the goods, suits, vests, at one point had even produced a tape measure. Now he looks around, nervous, taking up a pair of trousers; prowling towards the gents' changing room, he looks swiftly in all directions; dives behind the changing room curtain and pulls it across much too quickly. Drowned knows what the thief would be doing: stripping off *his* strides, tugging on the shop trousers, only to place the old pair on the sales rack and stroll out wearing the new ones. Drowned careers forward, ready to tear back the curtain, catching the thief with his pants down - literally!

Then it all happens. A second man closes in, striding to the changing room. They must be a team, one handing the other the goods. Drowned would wait until the pass was made, wait 'til the goods were in the bag, no mistakes *this* time, then he would pounce, blowing his whistle and waving fat arms. He wished he had a walkie-talkie for back up, or one of those Glock 22s, blow the thieving little shits clean away, like he'd seen on the telly. But unlike

Drowned's high power of imagination, his powers of observation are indeed sad. For he had failed to note that the second man had no legs, had two steel crutches, wore newly purchased Bermuda beach shorts, a T-shirt proclaiming. **PARTY ANIMAL!** and a pair of wrap-around sunglasses.

Mr Jackson stampedes up to the changing room, where, for the last five minutes, Norman has been trying to pull on a pair of slacks whilst also holding the curtain firmly closed, just in case someone should see him in his underwear. Jackson thrusts a tattooed ape arm through the curtaining, Norman screams; a girly squeal just high enough for no one to take any notice of it.

Jackson rips back the curtain, leans down on Fish, now sprawled and cataleptic. Teetering in garish shorts, whisky voice demanding, "What d'you think of me new outfit?"

"Ooooh. You look like a Butlins wreckage," reports Norman.

Jackson is impressed. "That good?"

As this happens, two little beeps from Mr Drowned's digital watch tell him it is one o'clock. Lunch time. After all, it was Wednesday, and Wednesdays meant veal and ham pie in the staff canteen. He would leave the villains to their own devices. Good luck to 'em. Sod the fucking store.

He had bought black shirts, thick black trousers, black pants, socks, and new black boots. Now Roane passed through the book department, scanning spines. He chooses Chekhov short stories. He will never look at it.

His goods secured, there is one more thing to purchase. The lingerie department is on the top floor. The lift only makes him think of falling. He decides to take the stairs.

Taking the signed route to the stairs through Kitchenware, he sees Mr Jackson dropping a steak knife into his Bermuda shorts. Even to Roane, the theft would be comical at any other time, but this just seemed tawdry.

Roane watches. Jackson sees him across the floor, does not like his personal leisure pursuits invaded. He snaps his boulder shoulders back, his face - a skinned bulldog - the sudden violence, obscene. "Fuck off! Fuck off ya fuckin' queer! Ya cunt! Fuck off!"

Roane just stands there.

An assistant, V Carking, (name badge)m witnesses the altercation. She doesn't mind the swearing, at least it's a distraction from pricing endless saucepans. She looks at the young man in black with the long hair, thinks she might have seen him somewhere, maybe one of those bands in a magazine.

"Arsy great fuckin' get! Ya fuckin' mental, fuckin' loony like rest of 'em! Fuckin' cocksucker!" Jackson bangs a finger to his temples, "...Round fuckin' twist y'are, fuckin' nancy boy!"

Roane walks past V Carking, takes the stairs.

Jackson, breathing heavy, runs tongue over top lip, knows *something* is wrong. The air has become near ice, almost electric. V Carking senses it too, touches troubled fingers to her crimson painted mouth, wipes at nothing.

Then it happens.

The antiquated sprinkler systems are vibrating, unscrewing from ancient ceiling mounts. At first, there is just a kiss of warm dew and the hiss of escaping liquid, next the tempest. Fifty sprinklers explode, water thunders down, shattering crystal goblets, denting frying pans, rustling cutlery.

Jackson drenched in Hawaiian décor.

V Carking is crying, her mascara peeling, lipstick bleeding. Hair colorant seeping out. Interior rain floods the floors, fills her mouth and ears, washes away her tears. Blues, greens, pinks stream through her soaken blouse, giving her the look of Dorian Grey washed in white spirit. Something Picasso threw up.

Sharp plumps of water sting at her nipples, now she is screaming, making tiny whistling sounds through the hole in her two front teeth. Saturated, Jackson stands over V Carking, engrossed. He ignores the metallic water, doesn't notice it. In his sodden shorts the outline of the twelve-inch steak knife, angled, pushing at macerated cotton. Another shape, a bigger one - his engorged dick strains up; A ravenous conger, muslin veiled. This is his sort of gig.

Her shrieks are piercing now, yet still no one comes. Just her and Jackson with steak knife erection. "Can ya scream a bit louder, luv?" He shouts hopefully through the spray.

There's some sort of commotion on the first floor, Norman Fish can hear it through the rickety old lift. He is loaded down with bags of clothes for himself and Ernie, towels, curtains and a new kettle. Maybe it was the combined weight of these, him *and* the lift-boy, that made the lift shudder to a halt.

"Ooooh, whatever's happened?" pleads Fish, but gets no answer. The lift-boy is too busy coughing. Then Fish recalls his cough, never saw his face; the lift 'boy' is the consumptive geriatric from the corner of the main road that very morning. Here now, lungs creaking like a door, crowing up great myxoid plops, breath bubbling out. It's all to much for Norman, squirmed in a corner of dead dried dribble, intestines shivering, pumping out an almost staccato rasp of gas; wind instrument. High fibre breakfast - Bel Paese, muesli, cold cabbage, wafting poisonous through the air. The confined shell of the broken lift is entrenched by stink. Fish, in between holding his nose, can only blub apologies, whine 'sorrys.' Whether the lift-boy notices the stench or not is debatable. Raw throated, fingers scratching in his nostrils, he's attempting to claw away the olfactory mucus membrane. He has no surviving senses, he had gobbed them all out, coughed up memory, brought the past through his throat. Hawked it into ashtrays, gutters. Letting life slaver by. A leisurely suicide. Death by self-secretion.

In the crowded lift, not much space, maybe just *rheum* for one more.

This snot has bones.

10

"Dear me," said Mr Grewgious, peeping in,
"it's like looking down the throat of Old Time."
***Charles Dickens* - Edwin Drood**

The Old Places are perhaps where Mrs Tombs inhabits. In the centre of the room, in a web canopied brass four poster, she lies.

The black bone of telephone resting on a table beside the bed. The name P. Tombs in the phone book, but P was dead these twenty years since.

For Mrs Tombs, old words were needed; frangible, marasmic. Her face parchment from which previous words have been erased. Ghostly Ouija board letterings - *Foxglove, Heart, God* - haunting her palimpsest features. Hair of old pencil scratchings, over-ripe teeth: dark smile. Big nose and jaw. Skeletal Punchinello. Old laughing eyes, but the windows to this soul are broken.

Her fingers, autumn bones, light as two feathers, clutch sepia sheets to dusty throat. If she speaks it is a sigh or a name. Sometimes it is the name of a sigh.

She has only pain and an absence about her which is almost a presence.

There is little here but the past, summer letters, lavender water, sands on the floor and daisies taken from the late Howard Carter's unkempt grave. All the colours of regret. There are spaces on the walls where pictures once died. Blackout material stretched across the windows, giving discarded tea-bag light. The bolted door keyhole, cramped with woodworm remains.

Staled time ticks here. Clocks hidden in a cupboard.

It is a room heavy with phantoms. Her existence is one of incidental exorcism. She eats ghosts in such a way, enough to shame the shadows. She knows her pain, employs it, so a sickly half memory of nothing can bring tears which she sips. Revenants and crumbs of tears, her food and water.

With a medical hunger she licks at her wedding ring, the brass curtain ring P had slipped on her finger. The ring has mouldered, fine levels of corrosion have grown there. Hot salt taste, like Penicillin.

On the table the telephone shivers into half life. Another whisper; dull pealing clunking out.

She idles her head left, grins, cackles at the phone. It would take a week, maybe more, to answer it.

The phone clunk-rings seventy three times. Stops.

Dead phone echo in hollow ears. She is hissing with joy now, the lavender fossil, with thoughts she can no longer call her own. Like Miss Haversham in spidery refinery, cobwebs between old legs, waiting, forever waiting. But Forever has little power here.

Old Mrs Tombs, a guilty moth impatient of light, carnivoring the dark damp whispers of 'forget' and laughing the laughter of a woman *paid* to forget.

Jerusalem had taken the second name - *P Tombs,* from the fly-paper god, dialled seven numbers and waited. Seventy three times the phone rang. All he heard were barren sounds; net curtain shrouds pushing against evening, *the creaking of old bones in a bed,* the sombre whistle of a bedbug, and three words like wrinkles or scars; *Foxglove, Heart, God.*

Angels? Never.

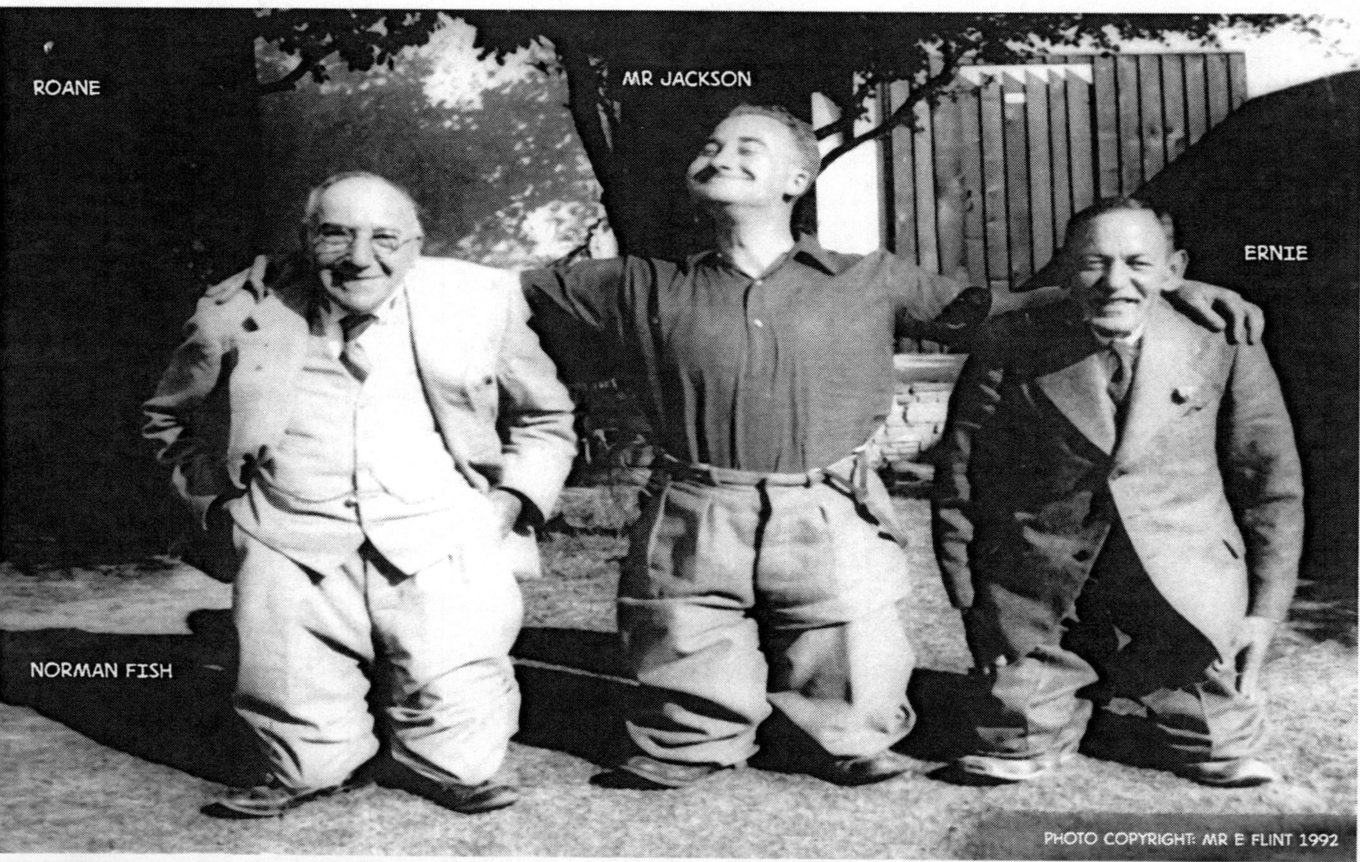
ROANE
MR JACKSON
ERNIE
NORMAN FISH
PHOTO COPYRIGHT: MR E FLINT 1992

11

King Kong didn't die at the foot of the Empire State building. He crept quietly away, found a respectable tree house above the snuff shop in Division Street, Manhattan, shaved off his fur, slimmed down to a comfortable two ton and took to 'entertaining' sailors in port off the East River.

OK, so it's what Mr Jackson would have *liked* to have happened. First film he ever saw - 1'3 at the Regent, Doncaster, wet Whit Monday, 1934. Funny, he often thought about it, caught glimpses of Fay Wray's stocking out of the corner of one eye, could see her now - wriggling in the giant paw, garters flashing. He takes a fourth and final swig from his flask: Pernod and Galloway's. He opens wide his bedroom window and begins slinging out the many cardboard boxes.

Shopping that morning had yielded no surprises; Running the credit scam past another sympathetic tit in a suit. No resistance anymore, no kickbacks - just a room listing beneath the weight of C.D., stereos, videos, teletext, speakers. A remote control midden.

Under Jackson's *insistence,* they had scrounged a lift back from the store delivery man. Ernie and Jackson up front, dazed Fish dumped in the rear with his parcels and smells. The boy, Roane, had pissed off. Probably, "down the 'Dilly, kissing lavatory seats."

Unpacked now, all the boxes slung from his window, Jackson with bath towel draped round still wet half body, crutch/stomps down one flight of stairs, nuts open the front door, out into garden evening.

Mr Flint had flown, leaving only phone numbers for Jackson's amusement; after hours card games at the Spencer.

Cheap genuine porn vids, the more *obscure* drinking clubs up west. All guaranteed. Legit. Apparently Flint has business overseas, a contact address given as Golden Lane, Prague.

Norman, new clothes folded neatly away in the chest of drawers, a new headboard and new sheets on the old bed, straightens out his new rug. Finished.

"Though I say it myself, it looks a proper picture. Don't you think so, Ernie?" He turns, turns again. "Ernie? Where have you gone?"

Ernie carries three of Norman's empty shop boxes down to the garden, unprompted, following Jackson's lead.

"Some more 'ere," offers Ernie.

"Good lad!" Jackson has assembled the boxes, five score of them, in towers of ten high. Unstable eyries.

"What ya doing?" Ernie asks.

Jackson answers. "Gonna 'ave us a little conflagration!"

Fish busies up. "There you are Ernie... Ooh, whatever's happening?"

"Con-frag-ration," explains Ernie.

Flowers to burn: lily roots, eucalypt sticks, a log of thorns. Flint's compost arranged, surgically precise, at the cardboard pillar's base.

Evening. No breeze. Still air. Burning weather.

Fish has made hot chocolate. Expectation runs high between them as Mr Jackson, arsonist artisan painting with colours of flame, touches a quarter split match (old gaol trick) to kindling.

Fire smoulders up in brown wisps. Soon the crackling noise, the folding in from heat. Styrofoam packing crimping into shapes like snail shit. Sparks catching. A sudden pyre worthy of any saint.

There are four degrees of fire. The first is slow, mild as fleece. The second is moderate, as of the sun in June. The third, great and strong, a calcined fire. The fourth, burning, vehement - a fusing flame.

Roane, back from wherever, strolls up, intrigued by the pyre. He is welcomed with wordless ease, offered cocoa and a view.

For Jackson, ithyphallic aggressor becalmed by flame, this is a staging of nostalgia; history, therefore the past, like books burning in Berlin's Franz Josef Platz; truth blaze erasure. It if doesn't exist, how can he believe in it?

Norman is glad the boxes are burning. Didn't want them cluttering up their nice new home. Thus, a cleansing.

Roane is cleansed already. Washed in rain, dried by shadows. The fire holds old meanings. Death is sacred, life is not. He sees her face in the flames, a girl with long red hair. Red as bright blood. It's easy to believe the Zoroastrians were right.

Ernie, cocoa cupped warm hands, rapt, watching green eucalyptus steam. Tracing embers in charry flight. Celebrating unknown ambivalence.

The four have come together with no argument, no chaos, in the grounds of their private asylum to witness burning, to see the hot colour of their flag; a red as red as frilled lizards. And the sky, bleeding, gashed through by twilight, a ghastly *madder*.

A preview of Hell?

12

Her feet go down to Death; Her steps take hold on Hell.
Proverbs.5:3

He had lifted her foot, positioned it on the footstool as he always did. The leg lifted, bent at the knee and ankle, as to allow himself the view up her skirt, of lilac panties, pale thighs. He ran a practised hand across her dusk yellow corns, lovingly pawed horny layers of hardened skin, grin-winced as the knotted shoelace tied around the stub of his penis tightened. With cold passion, Ken Schilling, chiropodist, MChS worked in from the thinnest piece of skin around a hard corn, cut away spongy dermic films, gradually worked towards the main firm mass: a long standing corn, too dark in colour to enucleate. Abluted then, in potash witch hazel solution, dried, powdered and padded. As with all his ladies, their toenail clippings, corn-pads, plasters, and foot scrapings are collected, sealed in airtight bags.

It is these and today's other spoils he toys with now.

Schilling clears away the dinner plate, boiled chicken, bland rice leftovers. And then he is at the cupboard, pulling out the black cloth. Silk. Laying it over the table, he empties out his treasures upon it - blister peelings, bursal squeezings, sero-pus, nail excavations, bunion scabs, septic heel infections and chilblain seepings taken with care from illustrious female clientele. He would never touch a male foot. Wasn't like *that*.

His hand then, arranging wet-white verrucae and toe fungi parings on dark silk. He likes to see the shape of pentagonal corns. He stoops to inspect them, sniffs at high Camembert mordancy. He can no longer eat Stilton in restaurants, it makes him discharge. The pleasingly painful shoelace restraint is cutting in now, cock like a lump of liquorice. Unwashed, uncircumcised, turgid through slacks. Clay in cotton.

On his way home he had collected the shoes of a local celebrity. She read the news on ITV. He had seen her in the park, jogging along. He had made it his business to acquaint and cultivate Sven, her cobbler. That morning, she had taken her worn at heel stiletto courts and fraying leather jogging pumps to be mended. A phone call, and for two bottles of Jamaican gin, Schilling had secured for one evening only, newsreader's shoes. He had yet to take them from the bag, had other things to prepare. Had first to take the foot from the fridge.

Once; a diabetic girl, feet like washboards, corns almost *veined*, came to him. Infected toes. Gangrene. *Beautiful*. Nothing he could do. Passed her on to a surgeon friend. Amputated foot. Schilling with Masonic handshake and book forward favours 'obtained' the foot, keeps it frozen, takes it out, twice, three times a year, special occasions, defrosts it. Uses it.

Underground 1940. Liverpool Street station. Air raids upstairs. Communities, families and friends down here, sheltering, tucked up in droves, terrified. Children sleeping head to toe. Top and tail. Fat Kenneth Schilling in a corner with his sister rubbing his willy with her bare, cheesy toes, making him kiss her corns beneath blankets. The stronger the smell of her feet, the harder he became. Strength breeding strength.

Passion gave way to deliberate fascination. An uncle - a

chiropodist: a grounding in the art. His first clumsy collections of ladies' toe nail clippings, D.K. glimpses. 1950, studying at the London Foot Hospital, Fitzroy Square. Soon he was lunching on the Ziggurat with cronies from the local lodge. At twenty-five he was the author of *The Mechanical Basis of Callous and Corns.* ("A tonic and stimulant to every practising chiropodist") and the widely acclaimed, *Hallux Valgus in the Adolescent Girl.* By thirty, his own private practice; Harley Street. Specialist in feminine foot care. Time has been kind: money, a house, the cars. But thankfully, for him, time and heels are not so kind on feminine tootsies.

The foot is a little grey, best warm it in the oven for a mo: brings out the piquancy.

He had only ever touched a woman, *any* woman, by her feet. Massaged the toes, kneaded heels. Thumbed arches. Tells his ladies not to wash their feet when coming to him, some lie concerning the idiosyncrasies of soap. On occasion, Schilling would pay a home visit to a valued patient, perform his own miracle, wash his hands afterwards in the bathroom and root through any convenient laundry basket for stockings, tights, sometimes socks. These would be secreted away, used later.

Now *is* later.

Trousers dropped, kicked off, does not notice the red light of the answer-machine mutely blipping. He tears down his pants: shoelace bound penis, grey as pumice - lack of circulation. He unties the knots and his gibbous stub goes hunching up. The foot has warmed through, reeking, placed gently on the table. Celebrity shoes ripped from the bag, scrutinized, eyelets licked, four inch heels tongued deep in throat, soles sniffed. Odour Eaters in both pairs, he extracts all four, runs them across his cheek, breathes them in, scalpels each into strips, gathers up his hoard of clippings, scrapings, encrusted corn pads and plasters and stuffs them savage into the foot piece of a stolen sweaty stocking. He adds sliced Odour Eaters, and cuts the leg of the stocking to the ankle, he then twists and ties the sliced nylon pieces together, making a ball of the collected foot ails, with two long stocking 'arms'. Mouth open, he jams the stocking ball in, loops 'arms' around his head and pulls tight the gag. Hands to the rear of head, ties another knot, securely tucking nylon behind ears. Toenail clippings pricking his upper lip.

Breathes it in...

Seated at table in shirt and socks, knowing better than to touch tongue to amputated foot (even *he* drew the line at gangrene). The foot then, positioned, rubbed between fub thighs, organ stubbing up, diseased toes stroking a rungless ladder, manipulating, gaining pressure, nudging ball sac with lifeless nails. Dead foot wanking in this room of clean shadows. Lapping through nylon, eating up EatenOdours, inhaling the chaste flame of infection. Schilling: old skin-sin-eater.

Jerusalem hears the curdled cumming as he kicks in the front door. Hears gangreney cells, flaking, falling from dead digits. Death has its own sound. A secret, secret sound.

Schilling - back to the door, spent. Breathless with soft-off, wiping spunk from thigh and amputation, tugs half violent at his cloy gag, then it hits him, smashing him from the chair.

Numb, his head poor-face down, powerless in near naked state; half born. Limbs, like the foot, without body, life. But another foot now, in plastic, black plastic, kicking in his mouth, teeth, blood souping up his throat, stopping the tongue, ending breath. Wishbones crunching underfoot.

Jerusalem called earlier. Down the phone the answer recording on worn tape hissing, boiled gull noise of red light flashing. But he knew there was someone there, heard the cheap breaths of lust, heard defrosting gangrene. All he

hears now are his toes breaking gums, jaw, life.
    The bad gravy of blood spilling from K Schilling.
    His head, stamped in. Voice taken.
    Secret, secret sounds.

13

Maudsley the parrot perches and craps upon Mr Jackson's terrible head. Jackson in his hammock, whistling Faust in his sleep: Mephistopheles on methedrine.

Belowstairs; breakfast. Bacon in a pop-up toaster. Norman making tea, spading in the sugars.

"There y'are, Ernie. Hot sweet milky tea, just the way ya like it."

"ThankoofNormun." Ernie is Tippexing his brace, whiting out the rust. He becomes elated with each new breath, senses heightened. The very patterns of his dressing-gown take on an entire new meaning. Palsied paisleys. Bright correction fluid hallucinations.

Outside, a cold wind blowing, a cold wind that would snap your neck in two. A delivery van fighting its way up the drive. Roane sees it from his window, the delivery man struggling to the door with hamper and then reversing out. Through the floors, Fish noise, logorrhoea whinings, talking through toast. Knowing nothing.

On Roane's wall, secured there now, the strait-jacket paintings. Nine mad canvas chapters. Was there ever a tenth?

"Aaaawk, gin and kipper!" squawks Maudsley the parrot.

Jackson stirs, scratches at hair: fingers full of bird shit. He sniffs, recognises Congo smell; cages full of feathers. He feels claws tug at his locks. He looks up, there is a parrot on his head, a black parrot, looking down.

"Fuckin' Ada," is all Jackson can say.

"Well, I don't know, Ernie, I mean, there's no one called 'Arthur Pears' lives 'ere. Must be a mistake, delivered to the wrong place. Ooh, whatever shall we do?" blathers Fish.

High as Heaven's attic, sitting, smiling white rust smile, Ernie falls face forward into the margarine. Fish farts suddenly as Mr Jackson marks his entrance with a resounding belch. Maudsley the parrot on shoulder; Longer John Silver.

"Right monkey! Let dog see rabbit!" Jackson lunges toward the Fortnum and Mason hamper, rips it open, proceeds removing dainties, delicacies: rattlesnake soup, sheep's eyes in brine, tinned locust, pike steaks, Sudanese coffee.

Fish, craning a thin neck, nosing at the foods. "Pears? Arthur Pears? Your name's not Arthur Pears..."

"It's an anagram..." explains Jackson. Goose eggs. Nettle tea.

Fish, pleasant. "Oh, that's nice. What's it an antigram of?"

"Mitts off. Tucker, *property* of Mr J."

"Oh, but..." Fish counting, "That's far too many letters!"

"Must be a misprint. Aah, 'ere we go." Jackson has unearthed a jar of floured chicken livers, roots out two garlic. The frying pan appears like a conjurer's dove. "Feeling exotic today!" He heats virgin olive oil, crushes in garlic, *sways* the pan, just touches chicken livers to the oil. Spoons them out. A bone china bowl. Pours the oil on. Egyptian coffee. Soured cream added.

Ernie is snoring in the Flora. Jackson, seated, eating with fingers, feeding Maudsley liver. Fish finally notices the bird.

"'allo, Mr Parrot." Nothing. Fish, persistent; "I said, 'allo, Mr Parrot."

Maudsley, unsquawked, ingesting offal.

"Is he a deaf 'n' dumb parrot, then?" asks Fish.

"Aaaawk, knob off cheesy!" says Maudsley.

"Well I never did!"

Mr Jackson spits with laughter. "Won 'im last night. Name's Maudsley. Maudsley the parrot."

Fish jerks like a Pathe newsreel soldier, blowing round the kitchen (A bill of sale, torn, left to the wind. Unelemental. Scared to be still in case he finds his true shape, then what would he do.) Mouth flapping. "Won? Won? You can't *win* a bird! However can you *win* a bird? Ya win money, ya win matchsticks! Not parrots!"

"Simmer down, laddie." Jackson, grease fingered, fed. Coffee voiced. "Cab into town, last night. Up west. Wardour Street. The Fox. *Drinking Schnapps from a dirty glass,* Tequila slammers. Throwing out time; coupla kebabs, sniffing round for a bit o' totty. No rush. Moon full as a cemetery. Nowt doing be midnight, slums it in St Moritz club. Place full of…"

"Quim," interrupts Maudsley.

Norman farts. Ernie glubs into the butter dish. Jackson nods sadly, continues. "Place is full of bed swervers, syphilitic cachinnation. Ponces in latex, leather. Sweaty walls. Hans 'n' Sweetie behind bar. Gins, blow. Music like, sounds; bit o' Sisters. Head banging to Stranglers. Bored be one. Had killed fatted calf, chewed the meat, sucked bones dry. Then I remembers Flint's numbers - Troy Club, Hanway Street. Poker game with film producer, a rag-head volcanologist an' a dealer in moths. Couple hands played, virgin faces - giving nowt away. Come three, just me an' the moth man, bluffs 'im, don't I? Hands down. *That little heart.* Bastad, 'ad no money. Pulls out laughing boy, 'ere. 'Called Maudsley', he says. Ha! Bloody good."

"Hairy arseholes," confirms Maudsley the parrot.

The room most hidden.

Roane, now in Doctor Judith's cell. Seated. On the table

side, books, records of patients that were once mad here. Victorian lunatics who disappeared, unburied in their graves. Other items also. Dream diaries, jotters, the original hall blueprint: a map of the madhouse. These are of no use to Roane. He seeks only keys. Keys to the locked rooms of the second floor. Maybe he will find other rooms thick with poppies and red glass devils. Maybe.

Nothing. No keys beneath the bed or pressed between brickwork. No keys tucked in book spines or down in her undies drawer. Nothing.

A sledge hammer, later. Take one of Flint's shovels, smash in the doors. Harsh entries. Find all the secrets. Roane, for now, content just to study the leather bound ledger of patients' names, dead mental histories. He takes all the books and the blueprint. From one, spills a scrap of grey paper; Brown words in a woman's hand - *It is enough to know that it is the past that imprisons*

Haemorrhoids had always plagued Norman Fish. Doctors had studied them, stronger/wiser men had measured them. His haemorrhoids had graced many a medical centre-fold, his fissures and occult blood have been, and still are, the subject of great debate. Once, a Swedish specialist… oh, never mind.

Rubber gloved, Norman dabs on his ointments, inserts his suppositories.

Mr Jackson peers through the bathroom keyhole. "'Ecky thump! They's hangin' down like a bag o' onions!"

Maudsley the parrot is picking a fight with an electric light bulb suspended from the ceiling. He butts it, breaks it. Glass in his feathers. 40 watt toothpicks.

From below, rust-margarine-high, Ernie, groaning, comes clomping up the stairs. Jackson with an invite: "'ere, Ernie, get an eyeful of them."

Ernie looks through the keyhole, screws up his nose,

says, "…Blibble…" and pukes yellow tea.

Roane walks by, heavy with books. He has no free hand to open his door. Jackson obliges, Roane says, "Thanks," and Jackson is in the room before Roane, his eyes darting, sucking in someone else's air.

Ernie piles in, staggering to the wall and the nine mad canvas pictures. "What's them, then?" he asks.

Roane looks to Jackson for an answer. *He holds him with his glittering eye… He cannot choose but hear…*

Near bitter: Jackson's words. "Ship of fools, that is, laddie." He 'reads' through each picture. Savage review. "Pirates dock. Any port. Paid to take the mad and deformed away. Unlocked *Tollhaus*. Beggars mostly, cripples. Caged, slung on board, to be sold in other ports. Sold as slaves, whores. The real loons chucked over the side. Sane towns left behind. Forty days in't wilderness, bobbing up. Down. Crackers as food. Wax in't water. Mad food. Sun, salt white. Nudging edge of compass, *spilling off world's edge…"* He brushes past the fourth scene. Self evident storm. For the fifth, he spits on his hands, rubs it in. "See coastline? Shape like a broken knuckle. Middle o' Nowhere that is. Unchartered. Cartographer's wet dream."

"What's it called?" asks Roane.

"Bastard Isles. That's what them's called. Still there, it is. Same bloody trees." Jackson, nostalgic?

"This is a funny one," chirps Ernie at the black/torn red/ bitten scene. Roane knew, or thought he did. Did Jackson?

"Them that survived, washed up, *truly* mad be now. Mortal after all. Built a church of flotsam. Blessed wreckage. Nowt to eat on Bastard Isles. Better off dead. Church? Eating host. Reddest wine."

Jackson knew (sacred, insane, cannibalism).

"Seventh," his jaw tightens, "one man ate all the meat. Used skins as sails. No bloody good, sea-gull food, ya see? This place, 'ere," he taps the scene: dogs on a broken stone pier, towers. Strait-jacket canvas feels no different to canvas galleon sails. "Dogs are sentinels, born with broken back legs, bred into 'em. Can't move. No running away. Sniffing one another's arses. Crouched up there all weathers, thick coats in't winter, shorn in spring. Looking out for reivers, howl like wolves if they see a corsair." He makes a noise, it's a laugh. "Eighth. Journeys broken. Too much sea for one man to paint. All same in end. Sea and sky. Blue night. These 'ere, these 'Needles' cutting out of sea, them's just that. *The* Needles. Isle o' Wight. Buggerlugs finally made it to England in his bone raft."

Jackson ignores the ninth painting. No air of salt spray to it.

Roane concludes, fishing for any one last spark from Jackson. "So the lunatic cannibal ended his days here in a rubber room, painting away his madness?"

"If ya like." Jackson leans against a wall.

"Maybe he ate the other patients?"

"Mabee." Jackson is not playing this game.

Roane tries. "Maybe he was locked in a room full of poppies?"

Jackson sparks! "You've seen it too, then? I don't mind tellin' ya lad, it nigh on 'ad me cackin' me pants. Too much 'Heavy' I thought, stick to meths in future I thought... Now you've seen it, must be real."

"It's real." Roane with his eyes of little abysses.

"Therapy d'you reckon? Indoor gardening, like?" Jackson is scared. Why?

"Maybe."

Maudsley the parrot - out in the hallway. Ernie stroking his tail feathers. Ernie did not remember seeing a parrot around the Hall. Not even a parrot who recited dark poetry, crowing, *"We were a ghastly crew..."*

The key came to him in a dream.

He had not read the notebooks, studied the blueprints. He had taken himself away for a walk in sudden rain. After, he slept. Two, maybe three hours later, the dream came.

In the company of darkness he watches over three glass coffins. Three dead girls lie in them. Skin and bone: Bergen-Belsen wallflowers. Their burnt-out faces painted by some sordid beautician. Bloated vinegar lips, red, crimson. Chic dead. The noise of a rusted creaking gate sounds all around him. Distracted, he looks from the coffins, looks upward. There ahead, through the gate, a long unlit corridor leading off. On the other side of the black passage white faces peer from the walls. Ghosts of white-faced clowns. Empty faces, they aren't wearing masks. And then they are laughing, severe hollow laughter, so strong and sharp that it shatters the fragile coffins. He can only watch as sudden pale men drag dead-as-mutton-dressed-as-lamb girls from their broken tombs, drag them, *dance* with them down the dark corridor. Their laughter is insufficient to banish him. Roane follows, follows them through long twisting passageways, watches as they Tarantella their way through, around and along corridors whose walls are falling in. Just edges now. Paths. He watches. There are more corpses, there is more dancing. He watches dead women lugging dead Astaires. Watches their Helldancing, the step-together-step. Three-four tempo, toe-heel, toe-heeling their way to the periphery. *Spilling off world's edge...* The path is suddenly no longer a path, it is crane bones held together by coagulated menstrual blood. Lost now, turning, like Theseus, forever left. He cannot move for their dancing and fucking in strange animal states. Zoophiliac humping, laughter and dance; Nonchalant damnation. Abruptly, the blood and bones give way and he is swallowed, fetching up (without falling) in a clearing of widened corridors. A massed space of nothing in this forever night. And then he sees her. There is a naked girl slouched on a petrified tree stump, her face, down, lost in hair, like drunkard's hair. Her skin, blue/pink. To touch she is dry as night, cold as day. Dead, but breathing. Up and down the breath, like the sun, the moon. *Dead, but breathing.* He crouches before her, opens her numb legs like some amorous mortician, wets a finger, parts her lips, slides one finger inside. All the eyes of Hell watching him. Two fingers now, next his hand, pushes it up, in, past the meat-melon-flesh of her cunt, his wrist in now, up, *touching inside her.* It is not his mother. He reaches in until he feels her ribs. Up to the elbow now, like climbing back inside...Her breastbone, heart bone, the ribbed cage. He snaps one off, drags it out through her. No blood. A clean white bone. A rib, no, not a rib, a boar's tusk and on it, spirals, Maori designs. Ammonite squirls.

When Roane woke, his very screams woke the clay-eared deaf, woke the dead of sight. Woke the shamans and the saints.

But did not, could not wake the dead girl.

First light drips through thin rain. Roane, dreamer of keys, is up, out. Past the greenhouse, past alchemical topiary, 'Round the back'. He barges through the toad-skull morass of the water-lily pond until he reaches the maze. The maze: waterlogged cemetery of symmetry. Time sunk in on itself. *A statue of Cybele snagged in its inanition.* Roane and his decision walk into it, sinking to his ankles, quag dragging at him. He wades in through dead liquid time. Tugged. Up to his knees now. Entering a world of meander, twists, turns; of coming back on oneself, a circuitous route to goal - Moving to the midriff of the broken labyrinth (a torque, a tension. No obsession, only obsession itself. He is dancing his dream awake).

Finally he *finds* the heart of the maze. The hidden pulse of unconscious sense: a seventh sense of rain. Rain has fallen here so hard, so long, it has washed away all mire, leaving just a waist deep pool of sky grey water. Roane slinks through it, towards the stone statue of Cybele, overgrown, congested with ivy. Kneeling in scum like some repressed priest before the fertility goddess. He tears away at the ivy, clearing his path.

Cybele's statue is seen in new light. Shaped from Lyme Regis lias; smoothed blue limestone rich in vertebra, taking her every form. Carved corn and poppies in her turreted crown, hair spilling around ample breasts, a necklace of lion fangs chiselled on her throat. One hand holds a whip, the other hand chipped off. Gone. Roane, crouching now, like he crouched in the dream, half baptised in old rain, looking down, past the tiny waist and big hips, down between her blue-spine-stone legs to where green pubis grows, to where moss has gathered. This, Roane brushes aside, her hole found, filled by yet more moss, this, fingered out. Hollowed now, the goddess of caverns.

One finger reaching in, *touching inside her*, tapping on smooth walls. Rain suddenly torrents down, dead thunder in flatulent skies. Rain like clay, clumping up the earth. Hailstones hammer him, precipitation scars his face. Half drowning in this very font, hail scratched fingers digging *in*, nudging at something, easing it out. Rain swollen fingers nearly dropping the *key?* Not a key. A fir cone between fossil legs.

Rain has coloured the blue stone black. Exchanged Ixtab's decomposed blue for the black of any Black Madonna. Rain has no respect for myth.

Roane's finger, in again, probing the goddess, tickling out a shape. Touching. Something scraping in a limestone vagina, something rusted. A key. The key to locked madhouse rooms. Key of secrets. He holds it tight, puts it in his moth, safe from rain. Then, a sudden voice. Psittacine: "Morning!"

Roane stares up. Black eyes piercing down at him. Not

Cybele eyes, he had kept them covered in ivy, had dared not look at them. No, these were the beady black eyes of a black African parrot.

Guilty, Roane stuffs fir cone, moss and ivy back into Cybele's hole.

Maudsley, in rain, perched on the statue's head. Half curious. "Aaawk... Bearded clam!"

Roane panics in the shitty rain, flailing, forcing against meander, twist, turn. Going back on himself. His dream, danced awake. Cannot undance it. Not now.

Like topiary, Roane has lost his shape, become nothing. Rain has exposed him for what he is. Not an angel, but an impostor. A rainy charlatan in easy black. Untruthed. A boy with rat tail hair, skinny in his darkness. He has never lived, so loves only death.

The pretender with key in mouth like toy in pocket, fights from the swamp, slips on a puddle, grazes the right wrist, bruises bone. He limps against hail. Stagger-runs through the mad river flooding up the garden. If he had a tail, it would be between his legs. A little boy running home to mummy.

But mummy is a madhouse.

Maudsley swoops off, gone to watch lightning.

Litter is thrown up in the tempest: torn circus posters, 'Coming attractions!' The faces of lions. Newspaper headlines - *CHIROPODIST KICKED TO DEATH.* Loveletters, blank cheques. Trash.

14

He who fights with monsters might take care
lest he thereby become a monster.
And if you gaze for long into an abyss,
the abyss gazes also into you.
Friedrich Nietzsche - **Jenseits von Gut und Bose**

Detective Sergeant Gregory, sitting in a newly painted office. Lights, *too* bright, too cold, burning out any warmth. The headache behind his eyes, at the base of the neck. The office is shared with three others. Their desks, empty. Chairs vacated. Out. Slouched in unmarked cars, watching, waiting. Marking up the overtime.

His desk is cluttered with files, coroners' reports, crank confessions. Someone else's earwax on his Bic pen lid.

Racists had been blamed for the first killing; Chattagee. Paki bashers for sure. But then, the chiropodist - with his head literally kicked in - had been found. (Bit odd that one, to say the least. There had been a severed foot there also. Had there been another murder?) Black polythene hooked between snapped molars. The lads at forensics had neglected to account for contact traces of burnt polythene at the Chattagee killing. Two murders in as many days and a psycho into black polythene. Red faces all round. Tonight all the dailys would have the leaked story - **LONDON SERIAL KILLER AT LARGE.** What would they call this one - the Bin Man? The Plastic Spastic?

Gregory rubs tired eyes. His ham roll sits in its wrapping, ham hanging out like ineffectual skin. The coffee, cold. On the table, black and white Polaroid mugshots: face on, left side. Maniac faces stare back at him. Escaped psychopaths, serial killers. Players who have given up the mental game. Seven known at the present time: Alistair Montgomery Judd, kills only pregnant women and children. There is 'Ambrose' and his breadknife, he calls 'Stanley.'

The 'Snapper', who dismembers women and leaves his calling card. A mouse trap in the vagina.

An unnamed woman who stabs to death with what she claims to be splinters from the cross at Calvary.

All section 8. Mad as fucking mad dogs.

This new one, 'the Bin Man', already had fifty-four pages of psychobabble written about him: M.O., psychological profile. *Painful headaches? Incurable. Highly intelligent, immensely strong like Bundy, Bianchi.* Notes of Edmund Emil Kemper and Henry Lee Lucas. *Sexual satisfaction? RANDOM? A creative psychopath.*

Fifty-four pages. Gregory's father got only two lines in the local obituaries.

He tosses the files on to his desk. Too much - Too many obsessions… *gazes also…* No thanks. What he needed was a nice point blank 'injury in the line of duty', that would suit him. Get him out of this fucking office, out of this fucking job. Early pension, limping round the golf course. Drinking himself into new oblivion. Maybe a walking cane (not a stick, not a cripple), distinguished, the girls like that. Or a kneecapping maybe? 'Touch and go' in intensive care. Nurses. Physio. No more paperwork. A commendation, maybe a medal. He'd be a hero, a celebrity. A cocktail bar named after him. Nice one. Maybe pay someone to do it. That little shit, Pellum, he'd do it. Would even enjoy it! Throw him a monkey, give him the gun. Pellum, yeah.

The idea of a shattered shinbone, bullets raked through pulped nerves and nicotine yellow powder-burn stinging round his would-be heroic leg-wound, makes him rigid, stiff with joy. He limps from the office (good practice), out across the corridor into the men's lavatory for a quick wank. If he had taken the time to look, the last but one file on his desk, is that of the newly escaped multi-psychotic Jerusalem Lumb. Mad misprint. The word **DECEASED** stamped over the facsimile of his face. He died recently (along with four hundred and ninety-nine others) in his ill-fated attempt to escape from Crowfields maximum security 'hospital'. Apparently.

Ectomorphic spiderplants over-photosynthesise on the cold window ledge. Lab reports yellow. The words, *hair fibre,* and *spittle* curl in on themselves from light. Shy murderous words.

15

Again, *progression* should not be confused with *development*
C.G. *Jung* - On Psychic Energy

3rd May. London – No sooner had I arrived, then I heard that Lady de Lucy had asked for a sheet of writing paper of a particular vellum. Eager only to impress, although unwashed and frowsy from my journey, I took the page personally to her room. Ascending to the second floor I was intrigued by the very silence of my new 'domain'. Reminiscent of Medvezhy. Melancholia even here.

Lady de Lucy received the paper and myself with wordless chill. I wore gloves. She did not look at my face. I am at least grateful for that. She took a stick of charcoal and began chalking out her words. And all the time, I, like Asklepius, standing before, my hand held out to heal her. She wrote only six words, I shall never forget them. They shall be forever forged upon my soul: **Montroy is not to be trusted.** She took the paper and ran it swiftly across her throat. Her blood *fleeting up my wrist, specking my heels. She had sliced away her life in an unfelt paper cut.*

Apparently, I vomited. Cannot remember. A nurse came and helped me to my room. Lady de Lucy's body has now gone. I heard horses.

This, may God forgive me, was my first glimpse of Tookesbury Hall.

The boy, Roane is on his bed pressed into a corner, arms cradling tucked up legs. He sucks the key: a mother's rusty nipple. Curtains drawn, storm petering out, occasional rain *mothing* at the window. No longer talismanic, the rain scares him now. Threatens. Denies.

All morning crouched there, dripping hateful rain, his bed soaking it up (a bandage or tampon) Excommunicated, this sad priest of old rains. Weak king self-assassinated. But he has his prize, the key of secrets.

Yet *he* is no longer a secret, not even to himself. Only *conscious* now, open, as any exhibit or broken window, all his secrets showing. Easy secrets of a dead girl on a mortician's slab.

He has achieved the easiest of alchemies - Loss.

The diary rests open on his knees, any pages before May 3rd, torn out. All life before the madhouse had not existed. Untime: the appletree childhood, schooling, Cambridge, the medical school in Kimmeridge. Rebecca and her betrayal. Joining the Tian Shan expedition without a second thought. The accident and the six month recovery. The voyage home. The arguments. Corresponding with Freud. Meeting Kellerman and accepting the position of senior doctor at

Tookesbury.

The diary, cast aside, dropped. He had only read the first entry; May 3rd. He will read it as it is written. One page a day. The name on the inner sleeve is that of *Doctor William Miles,* it is dated as *nineteen hundred and ten.* Before, the very age of the diary would have deepened his senses, changed even the half forgotten rooms into stormy shadows. Now all it had done was deteriorate beneath his thumbs. Old leather flecking his nails. Powerless as daylight shines in through curtaining, brightening his tiny morbid world of strait-jacket landscapes, blueprints, mad diaries.

The sun is only warm on his face. He cannot close his eyes, for the darkness will be waiting.

Crouched in his corner.

Later, he will creep out, draw a hot bath, steam away the rain and mud on his legs. Sneak down to the kitchen, pick at cheese, make a sandwich. A glass of milk or some of Jackson's beer. He swallows with hunger, key shifting in his mouth, the thought of opening doors, *discovering,* making him shudder. What else would he find? A room full of keys? Billions of them waiting to be turned… or empty rooms. Rooms full of old mad men from 1910. William Miles eating flies and spiders, his skin like wax melting in moonlight, bones through flesh like visible knives… The sound of horses.

Roane spits out the key. The rust sucked off. The key is black. Ebony.

On the wall nearest his bed, a game (unfinished) of Hangman in yellow chalk. Chalky yellow carcass dangling. Beneath the scaffold, a jumble of yellow chalk letters, none repeated. To the left of the game, four letters underlined, an empty space leaving one missing.

D E A _ H

Some of the digits have been quickly scribbled, missing intended underlines as if the game were played by only one man, who, on guessing a correct letter, looked away, hand covering eye, while chalking up another letter in its vacant space.

Almost deliberate, this solo game of Hangman.

Suicidal patience played with a loaded pack: Every card a joker.

They call it sanity.

There is no cure.

Second post. Lilac blue envelope addressed to E. Wilson Esq. Norman bustles up, takes the letter. "Oh, it's for *you*, Ernie."

Ernie receives it and opens it. A boy on Christmas morning.

Norman continues his tirade, "D'you think he's alright though? I mean, he looked like drowned rat this morning. He's been up there all day, could've caught his death! Damp clothes, rheumatism at least. I really do think we should..." Fish, interrupted. Ernie, taking no more, dives to the door, runs up stairs. Fish follows, hopefully asking, "Shall we go see 'im, then?"

Ernie locks himself in his room.

Norman, then, outside Roane's room, nervous at knocking.

Two taps on wood. No answer. Try again, swallow, speak; "It...It... It's me. Norman. Can I come in?"

Norman opens the door.

Fish screams. **"Ernie! Ernie! Come quick..."**

Blood from Roane's grazed wrist had seeped into his sheets and in flailing sleep had stained his face, painted the wall. Fish had screamed, waking Roane from wet sleep, a book half closed on his lap. The scene had the impression of an attempted suicide, but not. Just a muddy wrist wound. Ernie had come running, Norman instigated a bath. "Hot water, mind." Ernie had run the bath, squirting in Fairy Liquid.

Plenty of bubbles. Norman sat there with Roane for twenty minutes, fussing, flapping, mopping dry blood with a hanky. Roane took his bath, glad to be alive. Before he left his room, he threw Doctor Judith's notebooks in the bin. Threw out the unread histories of himself, Norman, Ernie and Mr Jackson: his new friends. His *only* friends, ever. The rain had truly shocked him, pulled him to his senses. What did he need with darkness? It had got him nowhere. Life was for the living, death was for the dead. Today, he would start afresh in his new home with his new family.

Overcoated, Mr Jackson, rolling a smoke, *seated* on his room floor. If he had legs, they would have been crossed. Massive headphones nestled on hard head. Head lolling rhythmic. The floor awash with newly acquired wires, extension leads, live cable, bare lines. Three cd stereos play at once, all wired to the single set of headphones. 48 inch television screens glare out pornographic savagery. No soundtrack. Two industrial fans sweep the air. Disco lights wired up.

Fish bangs on the door, no answer. Fear and trembling, entering electric Bedlam. "...H...Hullo,"

Jackson is away. Lost in the cacophany of Waltzinblack by The Stranglers, Photograph by Numan and Pink Floyd's Comfortably Numb, crooked eyes closed, head slamming. Fish, thinking him having a fit, almost goes into spasm himself. "Oooh, oooh." Brave in his foolishness, he approaches, touches Jackson by the shoulder...

A titanium crutch swings up, around, near taking Fish's head off. Jackson bounds up: a sudden tree. Headphones toppling, deafening bass, keyboards searing out.

"Wha' ya playin' at?" yells Jackson.

"It's young Roane..."

"He is dead?" Hopeful.

"Ooh no, no, not dead. Wet."

Jackson has been wet. Soul drowned. No need for 'wet'

boys. "Wha'did he do, piss 'imself?"

Norman pretends not to hear, "He's not been well, he's in the bath now. Cut 'imself. I thought we could 'ave a nice dinner tonight. All of us. Will ya be 'round?"

"Cooking is it? Aye, I'll be there. I'm a dab hand at the old *cuisine*. Black tie alright?"

"Oh, not Thai food, brings me out in a rash. Anything will do, as long as it's not foreign."

Five days. Five flipping days, that's all they'd known each other for. Not even a week. Two weekends and a bit, really. Ernie looks down at the wedding invitation sent him that morning. Couldn't read it. Saw the little blue bows and bells on it, knew what it was, could guess. Got Norman to read it to him:

Alice Child and Stanley Mosley

request your presence at their wedding at

The Old Church on the Hill

Caterham, Surrey

(Formal attire)

The date of the wedding and a small handwritten note were also enclosed.

Ernie, just a few lines, hope you can make it on the 14th, bring your friend Norman and anyone else who wants to come. Love Alice xxx

Wedding invitation firmly screwed, a blue ball to kick into infinity. Ernie thinks of Stanley with his fixed grin in *his* old room, sweet talking Alice over boil-in-the-bag fish. Swapping Steradents. Moonlit walks by the cremmie. Five days. "Bugger... bloody flippin' bloody flippin' poo bugger..."

Rusty tears.

Winged darkness glides through Tookesbury. A mobile shadow watches Mr Jackson stalk out, striding to the local shops, witnesses Norman cutting ox-eyed daisies from the garden, hears Ernie and his hate, knows Roane is in the bath. Maudsley the parrot swoops into Roane's room, lands on the waste bin, claws out three discarded notebooks of Doctor Judith's, tightens his grip, flies off with them. Scholarly bird. Black magpie.

Maudsley has made his own particular eyrie, a cubby above the madhouse library. Nest of first editions. He drops in the notebooks, positions them next to the Egyptian Book of the Dead. Will deal with them later. For now he had gone, off to shit on the plaster relief of Socrates.

The books are not nesting material. They are study. Not only can Maudsley talk, he can also read.

Shrimps, light fried in goose fat, simmered in stock: quail bones, black onion, garlic, sea-salt, mace, nutmeg. Water for stock, in which four pound of mushrooms have been washed. Fourteen minutes on a low light, sieved, returned to heat. Three egg yolks warmed in unguent, stirred into soup. Staled soda bread, egg whites brushed over it, fried, then toasted in the oven. Egg bread rested in bowls, soup poured over. The juice of one orange crushed in.

First course.

Five hours Mr Jackson toyed in the kitchen, popped out first; local shops, cab return - boot full of vegetables, butchers goods. He *hopped* about, sink to stove, chopping, peeling, hacking at sundries, sampling Slivovitz. Norman had been thrown bodily from the kitchen at least twice. *"Too many cooks..."* Ernie was allowed to scullion, venting anger on pots, pans. Jackson wore a chef's hat, soufflé shape of old white. Curious design unpicked on it; ghostly swastika.

Norman laid a white cloth, arranged daisies in a vase. Best cutlery, Victorian silver. Champagne flutes. Salt, pepper, red *and* brown sauces, napkins, candles.

Roane came down around six. His black, cast off, wearing a red check shirt of Jackson's. Norman's new grey cotton slacks, a blue (once white) vest of Ernie's. Hair tied back. *"We can all help each other."* Norman had said.

At seven they finally sat down.

Ernie pours the wine. A Californian Riesling from Jackson's personal hamper. Prefaceless, Norman spoons up, and in, the shellfish consommé, making tiny "Mmmmmm," noise. Jackson, tapping fork on glass, clears his throat like a landslide; Mock indignation - "Ahhemm... A little *prayer...*"

All eyes on Norman.

"Oh. Oh, alright, yes." Hands steepled, head bowed, "Dear Jesus...thank you for the food we eat and the drink we drink (pause) Amen."

"Right," commands Jackson, "tuck in!"

Clash of spoons, slurps of Riesling, peppery gasps. Jackson with a question; "Ay, Norman, what d'you think shrimps live on?"

Fish answers, neglecting to swallow, thin shrimp spit spat over white cloth. "You mean, (spit) what they eat, like?"

Jackson nods.

"Ooh, (chomp) I couldn't (spit) say."

Jackson drains his second glass. "Shit!" he says, "They's live on shit. Sewage and the like. You're probably eating ya own poo there now!"

Norman gacks up his starter. Most of it lands in his lap and/or in his wine.

Jackson, sham surprised, almost 'sorry'. "Nay lad, nay. I

was only joshing. Pulling ya leg, like."

Fish drips into the kitchen, mops himself down.

Jackson leans to Ernie. Evil whisper: "They eats babies, really." Ernie snaps in two at this, a folded bird, head down on the table, not needing to breathe, gugging in ulcerous laughter. The funniest thing he has *ever* heard. Roane only smiles.

Chablis is opened.

Five glasses. One for Maudsley. Wherever he is.

Wild rice. Pigeons braised in butter, marinated in Cognac. Artichoke puree. Casseroled broad beans, fennel salad, grilled mushrooms. More Chablis.

The four of them silent as the shadows. Then Fish half choking on a breastbone; rice, salad sprayed on the table. "Ooh...that's better... Hic!...Oh! Beg pardon... Hic!..." Hiccups.

"Hold ya breath, for God's sake," threatens Jackson, "that'll cure it."

Fish holds his nose, hiccups and brings sipped Chablis up through pinched nostrils.

Roane picks at his food, has the vegetables, rice, leaves the meat. Tries a glass.

More Chablis.

Ernie is already pissed, but doesn't let that stop him.

Mr J is feeling *pleasant* by now, belts loosened, burps behind a hand. Same hand rubbing over stubble; one day's growth of Weetabix. Chaos in the making. Fish is drawn in: the shortest straw.

"Could you pass the salt, please?" Ever polite Norman.

Uninvented, Jackson leaden-eyed, sipping butter/ Cognac from his plate.

Try again. "I say, could ya pass the salt, please?"

Wait for it.

Louder. Direct. "Pass salt please."

"What are ya, a fuckin' cripple? Get ya own fuckin' salt!

No, 'ang on," Jackson slings the salt pot (with velocity) across the table. Norman ducks just in time. Uncaught, the pot shatters against the wall. Taking this as his prompt, Jackson steams into an anecdote.

"See candles there, on't table?"

Fish snagged, drawn in. "Yes...yes..."

"Knew a girl once, young girl, six mabee seven, winter '52, Egypt..."

"Ooh, Egypt, yes, yes. That's right."

"Leperous she was, could take candles, lit candles mind, and stick one up 'er cunt, t'other up 'er arse, and they'd still come out alight." He burps, uncorks another bottle.

Fish mayhem: "Stop it stop it stop it! You always spoil things with ya swearing and ya stories and ya rude words and and..." Goose fat rich, the appetizer - Jackson knew this would happen - Fish farting like a locomotive fed on Semtex. Flustered, balatronic, letting off, stenching up the dinner table. Onion, shrimp stink. Mr Jackson holds his nose, makes wafting motions. Ernie, fennel mouthed, green root giggles. Eyes down, Roane takes another drink.

"You're rotten you are...Hic! Only wanted t'ave nice time for... young Roane..." Sobbing, he breaks wind again, long deep sound: bricks sieved through a didgeridoo.

"Baaaaa!" Jackson's response.

By dessert the altercation is forgotten. By dessert, crapulous, pissy-eyed, Ernie the named liability collapses from even a sideways glance from Mr Jackson.

Dessert wine, a sparkling burgundy. Sweetened chestnuts in a coffee/rum sauce. Iced buttered apples. The ice is frozen white Bordeaux. Black coffee, Norman *obviously* has white. Peach liqueur.

Jackson pours himself a second port, offers one to Roane.

"No thanks."

"Suit yaself."

He does. Roane uncaps a bottle of Mescal that Jackson

has dragged out. Gulps it down. Too sweet, not sweet enough. Another glass. Three.

Norman, tipsy on ice, "Oooh... there's awful lotta washing up to be done."

As if continuing the previous comment or adding to an existing, familiar conversation, Mr Jackson expresses: "Madagascar, 50s, eighth of day faster than rest of world. We'd scrounged float with **H.M.S. Swordfish**; *Athens, Said,* 'round *Aden, Zanzibar.* Turfed off at *Tullear,* made us ways to *St. Mary's.* Hell 'ole, piss for blood, hearts of coffee. Met this bloke Charlie, old Chazza, from t'other side of Halifax, working in't bazaar selling mucky postcards; girls, donkeys and the like. Get's talkin', coupla drags on Hookah, *hashish,* light-eyed, ash'd throated, gets a bit doolally does old Chazza, starts throwing 'is weight 'round, ends up taking this wog's 'ead off. Blood everywhere, like wedding night. Deported, old Chazza. No word of 'im for thirty year. Might as well be dead, prob'ly better off. Then, early 80s, Victoria coachstation, Sheffield day-return, sees old Chazza, no diff'rence, face like fried ginger still. He's waving as we goes by. So I waves back, recognition like. Turns out he's been waving to people nigh on fifteen year. 'pparently 'e can only say 'goodbye', now. Went back last year looking for 'im. Not there. Been gone five years since, di'nt even leave a puddle."

You could break the silence like a twig. Norman does. "Oh, ya poor thing."

Jackson burps as reply.

Ernie has dozed off. Roane has listened with near *surgical* interest. Black eyes carving up the detail. He had finished the Mescal, doesn't know he had swallowed the worm.

"Pity there's no cheese an' biscuits to finish with, eh, Norman?" offers Jackson.

"Ooh yes, cheese. Yes, yes. I like a bit o'cheddar."

Perfect; an unintentional double act. Jackson pushes himself up, unzips his fly, trawls out his manhood. Thirteen loose inches of phallus. Reminiscent of stitched greasy leather.

"Go on, Norman, give it a little lick! Cheesy enough for ya, is it?" His idea of an invitation.

Norman goes AWOL: a head that hangs like a broken gargoyle, immature fists. Someone else's words - *"Ooh yorra dirty man...You evil you are. Yorra dirty, dirty bastard. Your sort want a damn good hiding..."* Realisation, as any brick would, hits him. He had sworn. Cast assertions upon another mortal, stained a stained character. He collapses, hacks up his dentures through griefish tears: Gummy anguish. Self succubus. Stupid. He rushes off.

Jackson's only remark is, "Wanker."

Ernie, wine snooze woken by Norman's gnashings, is half under the table, weeping now in painstaking joy, threatening to break.

Roane excuses himself, saying, "Thank you."

Port live, Jackson in unnoticed cigar smoke shroud has decided this fine night: **Norman Fish must die.**

16

"Character is destiny."
George Eliot **- Scenes of Clerical Life**

Maudsley -

Shifting tail feathers from candlelight, positioning himself central to waxen light, two of Doctor Judith's notebooks opened out either side of him. Ambidextrous vision, can read two books at once. Picks at tidbits Jackson had prepared for him. Minced lamb. Weasel meat. The candles and matches were easy to locate - some kitchen drawer where he discovered paperclips, a small deposit of string and a rather elderly cleaver. The cleaver had proven, however, too cumbersome even for Maudsley to carry off.

Maudsley had found his previous 'owner' spiritually wanting. He kept moths, lived in a burnt out windmill. Used to *shroud* himself in second hand silk, liked the moths to nibble bits of the silk away, liked the feeling of being eaten, softly. Moth scarred. Liked Maudsley to walk over his naked body. Filthy. 'til Maudsley pecked a piece out of him. Didn't like that, too quick. He kept the bird in a duffel bag after that. A new keeper now: Jackson. A better proposition. Better food at least. The reason then, to check up on Mr J and those sharing his space. Weed out the weirdoes. Didn't fancy living in a carpet bag again. Decisions to make, stay or go.

Beak to the light. Begin.

He peels pages open, skims with either eye. There's the usual emotional detail; love, hope, hate. Drivel. There is a scribbled mental note. Judith's childhood remembered:

As a child visiting aunty Pat, all I could think of as we walked down the long white corridor of the sanitorium and heard and saw all the silly old women, was that I must never get mad when I grew up. Didn't want to live in a madhouse, didn't want to smell of wee and have my teeth in a bowl with all the other teeth, like strange fish. Didn't want to pull my skirt up, show my knickers, talk about keys behind clocks, take snuff and watch budgies in a cage.

Maudsley finishes that particular notebook. Casts it aside. No good. Pages of nothing. Things that go to make up a life. Irrelevance. Another book, positioned. Opened, read. The odd word ignored:

Norman Malcolm Fish, sexually abused as child by grandmother. Severe damage to emotional reasoning. Emotionally incontinent, hypochondriacal. Pantophobic. Compulsion to keep his environment neat and tidy, through this he himself feels 'clean'.

Maudsley clicks his beak. Contempt.

...Twenty one years in care. Transferred from Pontefract to Caterham, Dr Cassell believed change of scenery would do him good. New faces. The following, transcript of sitting: 14/3/79...

Too many words even for Maudsley. He rends at the pages, turning them swiftly.

...Truth... humiliated... Everyone looking, so many eyes...The Home... Ma Randall... Had to return to the school... children, boys and girls, uncaring to me, called me names, hurt me. Still, four o'clock soon came round, got to go home, and didn't have to come back until the next day.

"Uncaring to me..." says Maudsley, testing the words, swilling them round his mouth like a stone. The rest of the section, half full, scribbles, doodles, Doctor Judith's thoughts on Norman. Maudsley, content that Fish is just another defect and incapable of putting his own shoes on, let alone putting *him* in a bag, squawks, shits and wipes his feathery arse on pages of Fish history.

The second half of the book concerns Mr Jackson.

Fuckit. The candle's gone out. Maudsley scrabbles in the dark, opens a box of Swan with one claw, extracts, lights a match with the other. Flame popping again.

A mouthful of lamb pastry, chomping as he reads carefully.

It was my first day at Maida Vale and my very first patient was Mr Jackson (still don't know his first name, or indeed if that is his real name). Sitting in the day room, nervous, ill at ease in even my own presence and then in he strode. God, he had no legs, his dressing gown the nearest thing to the floor. Crutches holding him up. His face was like a terrible anger, eyes pushing out, that terrible scar, and then he smiled, loosened his gown, and there, between where his legs should *have been was the most enormous penis I had ever, and to this day still, seen. Fully erect - a hellish sausage! I burst out laughing, so did he. We became firm friends after that. He had never been institutionalised before, so I suppose we taught each other about 'madness'. He would never say how or where he had lost his legs. He had a compulsion to talk about foreign countries, Africa, Egypt and so on. He was remarkably well travelled. When asked about his childhood, he became elated, told me of a gang he was in and the initiations offered to prospective members; stealing from shops, jumping over factory walls. One test was to dive from a bridge into a canal and a newcomer was afraid. Kirby, Jackson's friend and also the gang leader, showed the boy how easy it was, and dived in from the bridge. Jackson's eyes became teary,* "'ard as nails, he was. Silly bugger though, couldn't swim. Gets caught on an old bike, stayed under. Nigger black when we brought 'im up." *Jackson had 'sagged' school, was put in an industrial school , having to do everything on the double, cleaning, sweeping, caring for a farmer's horse. They were allowed to play in fields near the school and he 'escaped' one day, ran and kept running, never went back, never stopped running until he was twice round the world. Joined the navy as Ship's cook. Claims to have once killed a man: an altercation over grave flowers. Tends to want the company of others just to have somebody there to be cruel to.* Doctor Judith had written in the margin, *'An undetermined animal'* and the word, *centuries.*

This is good enough for Maudsley. Jackson is O.K. A friend of scars. The remainder of the pocketbook is zinged through. Phrases graze out: *Sexual pyromaniac. Delirium tremors. Alcoholic hallucinosis.* Too easy an addiction. *Septicaemia?*

Down through the madhouse floors, the savage tinkle of silver on food. Norman choking on a breast bone, Jackson threatening with, "Hold ya breath, for God's sake." An old clock chiming eight.

One book left. Slim pasts of Ernie and Roane.

Maudsley whistles. Sharpens beak on sticky up nail, spits and starts.

Ernie, lovely Ernie, a boy in the world. Down's. Has the mentality of an unschooled six year old. Was left on the steps of Sheffield General a week after he was born. His mother had had twins. Two boys. One was 'normal', the other was Ernie. Brought up in a number of children's homes, shifted to Lees Hall and finally moved to Caterham in '72. Incontinent, illiterate, harmless. I pray he does not fall foul of disculturation.

'Disculturation' is a word Maudsley had never come across before. "Disculturation." He says it, finds and reads its meaning: *growing old in an asylum.* Remembered, stored within parrot memory. Dictionary cast aside. Continues -

...Donalds told me Ernie cried for days after I left Caterham for the new placement in Tooting. Poor Ernie.

Maudsley had learnt a new word. Right now, he needed an old word. Two words in fact, the words, "Silly bitch". Roane next. Ernie and his accountant brother forgotten.

It was June 1988 when Roane was admitted into my care. I had never encountered necrophilia before, though I had obviously heard of it - Jenks and Safer in the canteen exchanging grossities; those drunken student parties at the Farringdon cutting rooms. But, here was a young man, working as an apprentice mortician, his duty, the laying out of a dead young woman. He was alone with the body all night. He was discovered next morning, lying naked on a marble slab, his hand reached out, holding the hand of the corpse (apparently he had broken her fingers to acquire the shape for holding. I don't know if that is true or not). He was arrested, charged with gross indecency and within two days, transferred from Lambeth police station to my ward in Tooting…

"Toot toot!" says Maudsley.

…where he attempted suicide by slicing his wrist with a broken thermometer on the first day. In all my years of psychoanalogy, I have never encountered such a fascinating *example of morbidity. He expels a force of dark sensation, the sort of personal darkness found only in psychotic paedophiliacs and parousiamaniacs. He,*

This word is crossed out. She had written *Rain* instead of *Roane*. Soured spots of old rain speck the page. Bleached out Rorschach blots. A note in the margin; *Ask Flint to mend slates.*

Maudsley skips pages, looks for anything concerning 'fowl play', after all, there is more than one way to stuff a turkey.

Whenever Roane talked of any subject, his replies would be terse and ungiving. On school, he told me that after playtime was over, a teacher would come out, blow a whistle, signalling the end of play, and shout "freeze". The children had to stand still, a game of statues, until the teacher was satisfied that they were all static. Those who moved, twitched, or picked a nose, got slapped around the head. Roane would always remain motionless, never got whacked. After the teacher had administered her little punishment the children could return to their classes. The only time, he said, that they couldn't go out to play was when it was raining.

Maudsley yawns. *Emotional attachment, decay, Lovedeath.* Her words turn by. The last page, then, just in case:

...something I had never done before. Ever. Ethically impossible. Could not stay and endanger... Cannot think, so much to put down, can't think for the rain banging at the window, smashing on the roof.

There are no other words.

Maudsley closes the book, pushes it with the others. Three paper stones. He samples the pastry, chews on the lamb while musing the four scabby histories. They had all talked of childhood, babbled about hopes, dreams. And in all, no mention of locking birds in bags, not a trace of restraining parrots or goosy bondage. This was cool. Satisfied, Maudsley hooks up the notebooks, descends, glides, drops them atop the loftiest shelf available. Undiscoverable, even for a bloodhound on stilts.

Maudsley wings away, the promise of moonlight and leftover Chablis beckoning. Celebration of a passable new 'family'.

Three paper stones; Doctor Judith's books of reason. Mental fossils, tangible answers left behind; an informal bequest. Reasons: Norman Fish washing his life away with soap and water, cleansing the ghost of pegs on his penis, keeping down boyish erection. Abluting Grannie's enemas of tea and the nights in cotton gloves and rubber sheets. Repellent in his own fishy way, more than Mr Jackson. Reasons, like Ernie, the boy, a child she never had. And his twin walking about supposedly 'normal', both knowing something incomplete. The reason of Roane, like a thing under glass, wearing that mask: The Angel of the Rain shafting dead red-haired meat with Judith wanting it to be her. She had left Tooting hospital because of him. Ethics.

Mr Jackson and the base reason of sentimentality.

Sorrow. Posterity. Desire. Nostalgia. Her reasons for bequeathing a madhouse to her four favourite madmen.

But more than a madhouse. One last 'test', a Rorschach test in stone and lumber. They are the rats, the asylum - the maze, and the cheese is the **answer.** She had made it easy for them, left them all the clues, but locked the second floor doors. Floor of secrets. Hid the ebony key. She knew.

She wasn't mad, couldn't be. Wouldn't *allow* it. Couldn't become.

17

"I am the remedy and the medicine man.
I am the mushroom. I am the fresh mushroom.
I am the large mushroom. I am the fragrant mushroom.
I am the mushroom of the spirit."
Mazatec Indian Shaman Henry Munn.
The Mushrooms of Language

Fish was gutted. He had sworn. Tonight, a bad word had passed his lips. *Bastard.* A word foreign to him, like 'bonjour' or 'mort'.

Spinning circles in sight, vision out of synch. Hands clutching the wash basin, his dentures and regurgitated shrimp in pocket. His face in the mirror. Toothless, ill-fitting, he has already been sick. Mushroom, rice remnants scumming up the plughole. Teary, he secures the plug in its gooed hole, runs in the water, fills the basin. As he's rolling back his shirt sleeves, he hears or thinks he hears; a snatch of a song? The words a Blackpool fortune teller once whispered? Whatever. They are, he is sure, *not* his words: *"Here falls the heavenly dew, to lave the soiled black body in the grave."* Miniature suns of his eyes shine on in the mirror. He takes up the soap, splashes both hands, both arms, begins working the soap into lather, rubs it into the little finger of his left hand, abluting the impure body for a further counted minute. He plashes off soap with clean warm water, then continues the same sudden ritual for each finger, thumb - on the left hand, the entire left arm up to the elbow. The right hand next, fingers, thumb, each cleaned for sixty seconds. Lastly, the right forearm to elbow. Wet armed, *cleansed,* he loosens the plug from its hole: spinning circles only in the plughole. Running water, out of sink.

He had only been drunk once before: The Christmas Eve 'Do', Pontefract, 1962. That swine, Vitby, put formaldehyde in the fruit punch. But more than drunk, this. What he is feeling now, are the hallucinatory aspects of Mr Jackson's deliberate grilled mushrooms: *Psilocybin Mexicana.* The Sacred Mushroom.

Water dries on his wrist. He can *feel,* but momentarily. Most of the hallucinogen puked, washed down through copper pipes. He takes up the bar of soap, trembles it to his lips, opens out his tongued abyss, pops in the soap, begins sucking on it. Savage sweet.

He had never seen his eyes so bright before.

Swallowing, he speaks through suds, a word mispronounced? The soul-loosened word; "Albedo."

Siberian tigers strut commercial radio grasslands: Late night documentary, Andrew Sachs or Hywel Bennett narrating. Moon giving silver/white glare to the room. Ernie had laughed himself sober at the dinner table. Stretched out on the sofa now, only a curious lightness plays within him. A slight metaphysical mushroom calm. He dozes. A glass of milk half held.

He snores through the big cat stalking its prey, knows, although cannot consciously hear wireless words of Indian yogi, Tiger Swami: "You look upon tigers as tigers; I know them as pussy-cats."

He snores on through adverts. Lada cars. Roll-on deodorant. Out of season holidays in Hastings.

He snores through the late weather report, through national anthem, through the 'goodnights' and the high-pitched whine of shut down. Snores through his hallucinations and darkness, in sleep calling out softly. "Pussy... Pussy-Cat."

It has hit Roane hardest. Exhausted, pissed and tripping. Unknowing.

His skin (chameleon bone white) itches in his darkened room. Fingers twitching, stretched: an unconscious pianist with invisible Steinway. Bile rests in his throat. The room spins, his eyes close. He needs anchoring -

a hold, anything, something. Hands in air, brushing on wall, knocking the edge of a strait-jacket canvas, touching at the yellow chalk Hangman. Through darkness he sees the yellow's *colour* rubbed off on his fingertips: powdered golden glow (pestled moth). Reaction levels much too high. He doesn't want this, wants nothing more to do with darkness and its tempting thoughts. He reaches for any of the books - three missing now - taken from Doctor Judith's room; he knows where they are, can smell them. Centuried leather. Feels embossed initials on a cover: **W M.** Letters upturned, reflected, knowing not if either is true. The initials are the broken fertility rune *Inguz,* cast to its left, rent, split sideways long through its middle. Lowry's idea of the missionary position.

...this rune is akin to the moon... the need to share, the yearning to be desired, a search after similarities.

Roane, plunged on bed, frantically turning pages, reading diarised deeds in the dark. *"No need for ice pick psychology..." "Compassion as medicine."* Each line like an electric current, feeble Kirlian sparks. The aged words, unimmaculate, crumbling under sight like an orange under water. Roane watching old words of William Miles, like flies spilling up into night. *What* had Jackson put in the food? Dust now, he can *see* dust, his own skin subtly flaking off, dead cells flecking, *dry ashing,* folding away, chunnering in low small rasps. He can hear it as well. Each speck of dust, skin, word, takes a new shape; triangular shard, ribbed rhomboid, unequal circle. Each speck breaks, erodes into dust of new dust. A little universe of decay. Some spell out words, crack, fall into sparkling disregard. The sentence: *SOMETHING TO BE FERTILISED*. Some take new shapes, the bodies of reptiles, a spider. New and startling colours succeed them. Pre-Cambrian green, vomit orange. Raw jade, unborn chrome. Psychedelic creatures slither, *ooze,* like axle grease spilt on satin, shift sickly through pristine open sight. He chooses not to see, tries glancing away, to digress *now.* He stares at the diary, sees only his own hands, must have dropped the book, his fingers - the pages. Nail words: *...changing rooms... not need one. Hearts are... I do not believe...* If Roane screams, he cannot hear it. He stands and cannot feel his feet, remembers, "Movement involves danger" and topples face forward. If he could feel his feet/hands he would now know he was on all fours. Quadruped. Animal as any llama or boar. He doesn't care, seems to have lost more than just touch; he is readily decaying, visibly shrinking, sloughing the mythic envelope of self. Dead skin/live skin rots, slipping away: The dandruff of psychic time.

Somewhere, an ebony key...

Ten billion brain cells re-evoluting, synaptic bridges bending, barnacling, fusing, becoming one. D.N.A. uncodes itself. Jumbles of unwelded glucose chains snapping, flailing. Fat molecules fry, sizzling, doused in rickety rings of carbon, oxygen, (the smell of lightning). Self implosion. Darkness can be measured through each strand of hair. Proteins that pigment the iris quench heat: Gene colour erasure. Blood and skin are but sources of absent amusement. Muscle fibres, tissues and gristle divide, circle themselves, become tail-eating serpents, cannibalistic Uroborosi, suffering that same brown-mouthed fate as the Ouzelum bird. The heart, parched, a prune. Lungs: a bowl of corky fruit. His nervous system explodes: a tree of veins. Shifting now, drifting as on any sea, *untergehen*. Nucleotides washing out the unwound string of repeat proton, electron, neutron, atom. No ebb, just flow. Phosphate backbones unzipping, rupturing, uninspiralling. Cells burn. His tiny grave of existence is lost, the rhythm of time halts, rivers of life overflow. He is lumped electromagnetic meat sweating gutter sweat, spewing the hot broth of foetal waters. Sick as an S.S. dog fed on claret.

fusing, becoming one

Roane cheats time. Unpicks it. Pisses his molecules down a backward Mandela. Time's D.N.A. eroding, going back to nowhere. Pre-prehistoric. He sees himself as Pasteur would, peering at bacteria; some spore, a *crumb* of fur or scales. Gills or fern. Looks through compounded trilobite eyes, sheds air of the Coelacanth, is sealed as fly in amber.

Transcendentalised, etherised. The journey or 'trip' has taken Roane through himself, through what he only knows as 'time', to rub shoulders with Archaeopteryx, to shake hands (gone!) with eternity.

Onward.

Back to crawl through a shape gouged in energy. A shape with wings, long slender legs, an abdomen, and sharp tubular proboscis for piercing, for sucking. Stagnant muscles pushing through soul-soil/weak glacial ice, breaking time like toffee; the *anima* of Roane, ego-carnate, the femme soul beastie. A black mosquito. *Culex nigredo,* flying up, off into the madhouse.

In lightning illuminate, a tall man; a psychic ghost stalks the corridors, rattling the keys to his private mad zoo. Doctor William Miles, inebriated, brandy decanter pressed to his chest: A liquid heart. Without, the storm rattles, breaks the brain of calm, fractures night bones of 1922. An insect, a new gnat manifests, hums through, following Miles upstairs. A boned shadow skimming on Cognac fumes.

Doctor William Miles, king of the crazy castle, bumping on passageways, shouting at thunder. Greasy grey fingerprints touched on his brain. He drops his keys and the decanter, tears out bloody handfuls of hair, wanders on. Lightning exposing his ice burnt face. Pink skinned like a pig. 'Doctor Pig', 'Piggy Miles', 'Old Oink Oink'. Hands too, once scalded on ice. Moustache and eyebrows; yellow smears. Blue stubble. Icy scars. His eyes reflect the storm: syphilis eyes washed in silver nitrate, deposits have gathered, *pigmented,* corroded. Silver sighted, starry eyed, nova tear'd. The Tookesbury Basilisk. A nose, blackened, bruised. Lips coming apart. Last mental remains clinging like egg to the pan.

In lightning, Mosquito casts the longest shadow.

Miles on the second floor, *rooting* through his pockets. Looking. Only finding. Letters from Dr Freud are found, he tears these in pieces, casts them; so much fragmentary white - like masturbatory sperm. The confetti of bachelors. Searching for a key, an *ebony* key. Key of secrets. It rests round his neck on thin twine. The twine snapped, key in pink palm, in lock, in motion. *Turning...*

Mosquito slashes the psychic scene, cleaves air, *flies* through the keyhole, enters.

It is a room of words. Pictures: hieroglyphics documented in perfect walls of hard green schist. Figures kneeling, bowls, an ibex, squares, *scarabs,* owls. Twelfth Dynasty arid whispers on walls, ceiling, door. There are even inscriptions on the floor of the room, symbols hidden under thin sand; The dust of Khakheperre Sesotris II. Dust of secrets. Miles lurches through the room, stumbles, gathers himself into a corner, he takes the ebony key and begins whittling his own personal hieroglyph. Wailing. Human thunder.

This room had once housed a patient, an unnamed

admittant known only as 'the man out of Rosemary Lane'. He had no visitors, received no mail, was said to have died there, but no one came to mourn, even though he was known to have been a close friend and confidante of Major General Sir Charles Warren, the one time commissioner of the Metropolitan police, the man in charge, for a while, of the Whitechapel murders of 1888. The two men had been together at the beginning of archaeological work in Palestine itself. And later in Jerusalem, 1867-1870, tracing the foundations of Herod's temple wall, cutting through fallen stone, sinking shafts, burrowing, showing how the shape of the city had changed over the centuries.

A man can change in tunnels, under sand, breathing Poqer air. A man can trace his original heat, can touch the inner wall of himself and see and hear the red noise of life. Red screaming sounds of scalding gulls…

Any man, even a man out of Rosemary Lane.

A room of no windows. Room of new hieroglyphs: characters, one might say, shaped by the room's tenant. Words, indeed, made by a man leaden with secrets.

The room is an Egyptologist's confession.

Nuk pu nuk Xu ami Xu

Miles added his own word, the scratched word of questions, the word *Mystery.*

There is no mystery. He does not know this.

The room, departed, staggered from. Miles turns, looking back, but only behind him, as if he can't quite place an unseen ingredient of himself: the shadow of his shadow, or black mosquito fashioned from toadstool's psyche.

Mosquito, flown like a *Sopwith Camel,* down stormy hallway, followed a fragrance of blood. Hovered momentarily outside a closed door, swooped down under it and was *in.*

Blood and its history. Walls heavy with it. Mosquito feeds, sucking up the attraction. This room breathes blood.

Somme red, its corners are black, dark as punctured lungs. The room of the Angel of Maggots. The blood is at best, sweet.

"Forgive me!" Miles moans, slams hand to locked blood room door. Mosquito stirs, absorption jarred. The feast, for now, is postponed. **"Forgive me, Christ's harlot!"** Another confession?

Miles has shuffled on; the ghost of madness past. Thunder rattling in liquid bones. He boots open a new door - a room of poppies. Mosquito watches Miles tear up poppies from the remembered room floor, watches him rush off, laying the flowers outside yet another door in the corridor of doors, only to flee again, but his motion is descent now.

Down.

The poppies - one red, one an opium poppy - tokens, a second parting gift. Gift of dreams.

Slow raving, hissing, William Miles, a punctured soul with his face downstairs in a washroom mirror, a living ghost peering through filth, staring back at himself like some mockery. Like he wasn't really there at all. Inadequate skin pulled tight across the bone. Too thin to be natural, reminiscent of old **WANTED** posters. He wipes a heavy hand (waving goodbye) across the unclean looking glass and takes a pot of *Cherry Red* lip rouge, uncorks it, dips in a finger, daubs it on the mucky glass and draws it in the shape of a Valentine heart. Rose scented, oily, the base design of Love. A fat doodle of crimson curves. Cosmetic carrion.

Silver eyes reversed, an echo in glass framed by the heart; a voluntary inmate. Right palm (mirrored left) placed flat to the glass, fingers and hand trailing slowly down dirt/smoothness, dragging lines of sweaty scarlet sentimentality, leaving tears or tears. Leaving a bleeding heart. In aggressive mimicry, his fist slams the mirror, splinters glass, shatters skin, breaks the heart. Blood, dark and somehow thin, runs through patterns of lacerated lines, making new shapes, looking like the mark of Zorro or the mark of Cain. Blood spilling - the dew of mistakes.

Mosquito does not reflect in the broken mirror. Why should it?

The storm eats the night. Thunderjaws gluttonize. Tookesbury Hall shivers.

Elsewhere, now, an unnamed room, a gap with doors: Doctor William Miles knotting three silk handkerchiefs together, securing them to an overhead pipe. Around him, his diaries, records, **W M,** the initials on one; pages open, frantic words torn in paper as with a coffin nail: (Nail words) *I do not believe in Darkness. Darkness has no heart, it does not need one. Hearts are for the living. Darkness is a dead thing. Dead light. Ghost light. Light passed away. I shall exorcise this 'Darkness', I shall take night and make it morning, shall rewrite blackness...*

Thought madness was a darkness settling on the good light of minds. Miles was not the surgeon to abort lunacy. He wasn't even mad, though he *wanted* to be. He wrote books on the matter, near biblical text: **The New Laws of Madness,** which was never read, save by one: Doctor Judith. He saw himself as a true cleanser, the Divine Light. Brightest sun. In reality, just a moth.

And so, one dark and stormy, the last night of August '22, William Miles finally got death right - hanged himself with silk, found his light in a smooth noose; saw lightning through closed silver eyes.

Mosquito, the witness to ghosts, watches him hang there piss and cum spilling down his trousers. White at his mouth like mouth-organ spit.

The gnat is drawn to the dribble, sees it as a line of thanks, full of answers with no questions. A run in Time's stocking.

Mosquito climbs the dribble, skitters in, through the dead

man's mouth. **And is swallowed.**

Roane cannot scream. His throat is full of sick. Although it is dark, he can see clearly. He roars up wines, wild rice, *mushroom* and Mescal worm over his bed, the dream diaries, the key and Doctor Miles' journals. As he's heaving, knelt in the night's doings, his only thought is that the dream diaries are all blank.

18

Yes, tonight I am very sad... I slipped in blood, which is an evil omen,
and I heard, I am sure that I heard in the air,
the sound of wings beating, the beating of giant wings.
***Oscar Wilde* - Salome**

Brass monkeys.

Cold in the squat. Historically cold as the rain in Ireland. Anastasia fiddles with the gas meter, turns it on its long side, making gas run through old pipes of lead. The paddle wheel though, useless, unmeasuring illegal flow. She turns up the gas fire, lights another candle (the sixty seventh). The punter is undressing; folded trousers on the back of a chair. Civil servant socks. He eyes a stack of books, *Dickens. Conan Doyle, Kipling.*

"Do you like Kipling?" he asks.

"Wouldn't know," she answers, sniffing lighter fuel. "I've never Kipled."

Flea gourmet, Anastasia, pops a cold sore, kneels before the punter, a man called 'Symptoms', coaxing him with hand and mouth, making him hard with a £5 blow-job.

Anastasia: self-made anomaly in six-inch stilettos, torn latex top, and Oxfam mini skirt, washing-line fishnets, suspenders. Her breasts are two Durex filled with piss. Track mark arms. And on dry flat curls - that home-perm that didn't *quite* take, rests a black veil of mosquito netting, thankfully, covering her face. Boils, sores. The inclement skin of untreated parasitic acne: deep red abscesses, weeping scabs. Burnt crayon lipstick. Ashtray eyes. Rust brown rouge off a two-shilling piece.

The punter eats sugar, spoons out spoonfuls from a torn Tate & Lyle bag. She gobbles him, deep throating the unwashed brie-meat, rubs his testicles: heavy with ghosts. The inside of her mouth is salinated, preserved from a lifetime of drinking men's sperm. Salt-mouthed, her mouth is asylum. It is said, even her soul has an orifice.

The squat is by the river, a room on the old trading estate, four floors up. Fulham way - the beginning and end of the immutable trail - sex shops that are now estate agencies, Turk video rentals, weekend house boats and vandalised Land Rovers. The backside of the abdicated Kings Road.

Subterranean candlelight: their shadows on broken walls like shameful Hiroshima graffito. A picture of Jesus and a crucifix are nailed up too. A bare mattress lies stinking on the floor. At the table, rat rejects: half empty bottle of *Night Train,* tin of Argentinean corned-beef, the obligatory box of Swan and a nine inch vibrator weeping slow battery acids. Bare phone wires poke from the wall. All around, the wet ash smell of unwashed lace left too long in a carrier bag.

'Symptoms', ugly-buttocked, sweet-toothed, grunts, is cumming. Knees bent, penis prodding the back of her throat, ejaculating. "Swallowing your sons," Anastasia thinks, running her tongue round the phlegmy texture. Her mouth awash with the human fertilizer of poets, prophets and saints.

But saint is only an anagram of stain.

Bare phone wires poke from a wall

Puddles in gutters and the sound of rain. Laughing rain - that is its sound. Jerusalem hears this, words of sand in Sahara mentality. Soon forgotten.

He is squeezing in the head of a termite, dialling the fourth voice: *M.A. Jones, 88 Riverside, Fulham.* Receiver resting in hand, burnt fingers pushing round the dial. Each number has its own sound - 7 is the sound a child makes when it is choking. 6 has the noise of melting purple plastic. 3 like bells pealing for the last time.

Only nothing, just disconnection. Phone wire torn out of a derelict fourth floor room. Jerusalem has no need to listen, indeed, has no need for the smells and sights shat out down the earpiece. He can *touch* the noise now, feel contours of broken spirals - mattress springs, going nowhere, not even back on themselves. He knows the shapes of decades decayed, knows their stench, and the noise it makes is the noise of a face when it is torn from the head.

Blood thoughts well within, red words; *"Break skinny! Sodomize the feast!"* He is up, out, climbing through a stained glass window, down into night, gone to do the unwritten. Again.

The night is so full of Nigerian cab drivers, one can almost believe the static picked up on their Cameroonian Radio broadcasts is responsible for the darkness: some semi-forgotten *Sakarabru* entreaty called up, clogging up the air's waves.

The chimes of midnight are unheard, save by one. Rain slips from streetlights. This is the old fear circuit, Greyhound Road, Lillie Road - a little way off the wife-beaten track - the same redbrick houses as Kentish Town (now there's a recommendation!), down market yellow doors, a street called 'Star'. Jerusalem walks here, through rain, through cold, his mask of black polythene in ribbons, his 'working shroud' no more than plastic tats. Self made, unremembered. Tonight another voice sought, found, taken. Voided. But his acts are becoming banal, vulgar almost. The confession has become the sin. The vow of silence, deafening. Fuck the philosophy, do it anyhow.

Jerusalem shoulders in a butcher's shop window. Meat

hooks hang there, as does a steak knife. He leaps in and snatches up the blade, kicks his way out.

Rain laughs all around him, fizzing, pizzing in acid guffaws. Canine undertakers bury their bones. Puddles are *just* deep enough to drown children in. Car alarms buzzing. Jerusalem only exists: a map of himself. The knife sweats with rain. (12.5" of polished carbon steel)

On now, seething with inattention past tower blocks. Concrete ghosts that used to be the shape of things to come. Iron glass cuckoo tombs. Thin lights light rented rooms. Men and women and their habits of joy. He hears other people's dreams - burning mirrors, stiff sheets. Knuckle-dusters gathering dust, a grown man shitting cigarette butts - constipated time. Breaths, baited. Blood watered down. Incurable life. A spoonful of medicine to help the sugar go down.

Jerusalem falls, hammers his head against the road until something changes within him. He spits blood, rises, continues.

"Fallen from light!" the Voices sputter in the monstrous Munster Road. Streets stretching on like scars across a dowser's face.

On a long wall, 70's spray-paint angst, *Whatever happened to Slade?* Further along, the younger woe, *Whatever happened to Terry Waite?*

And further still - *Who cares?*

A blot on the landscape? The blot *is* the landscape.

The river approaches. Putney Bridge stretching from Fulham across. Lorries also approach. Circus lorries. Jerusalem hears - greasepaint, sawdust, cigar smoking midgets breaking wind. One other noise he hears as he vaults over the bridge, falling to water: The snore of a tiger.

God's crocodile tears.

Low tide. Jerusalem hits, dragged under like a bad soul to Hades. Muck water (the colour of migraine) floods through the bin bag seams, fills him up, making him a black plastic anchor. There is an insecure time, when one is drowning, life doesn't pass before one's eyes, it is death that makes the appearance. But death does not concern him. Hell cannot claim him, neither can the Thames. The one that got away. He slashes at himself with the knife, ripping polythene, exiting water. He cannot swim, doesn't need to. He *walks* his way out. Low tide after all.

Walking out of the water, up the shore. Inverted Moses. Wanders the strand down to Broomhouse Dock, climbs a mildewed ladder bolted to the side of the river wall and sniffs. Can sense the ache of an unloved crucifix and candles only half dead. *A nine inch vibrator weeping slow battery acids…*

88 Riverside. *An evil omen*

Uncle Strangewalk, (face of old vulture pains, long coat of dampness, Millwall scarf, cloth-cap, shoes full of rain water, shadow on his insides as big as a Yorkshire pudding. A coroner's court appointment card in one hand, a plain brown envelope of *Swedish Eroticas* in the other. Front two teeth knocked out on a gravestone. 'Winterlung' to his friends. Hee hee…), had first dressed Anastasia in her earlier childhood, sat her on his knee, telling her that she had nice hair and "wouldn't it look better if it had some pretty ribbons in it." He even gave her her name; Anastasia. Much better than Raymond. Her mother died. Winterlung, being the only guardian, took her in, taught her all she needed to know. Many an evening passed with Strangewalk and Elland Road (Peckham) acquaintances, watching 8mm *Sperma* films, little Anastasia taking it in turn to sit on their laps, giving them hand relief for a toffee each. Her skin diseases would come later. Puberty brought acne, a Moroccan docker brought herpes, sixteen stitches and a tropical rash. By thirteen she had parted company with

Uncle, taking to squats. Placed ads in *TV Friend, Translovelies:* ***MASSAGE BY LOVELY YOUNG THING. EXCELLENT 'A' AND 'O' LEVELS. BOUND TO PLEASE. YOU'VE TRIED THE REST NOW TRY THE BEST. (DISABLED WELCOME)*** This was squeezed, misspelt between *'Mouth slave with appetite for Greek classical' 'Higginson fans' 'Dentured males'* and those *'Open to ideas with A.B interests'.* She never used the word transvestite. Sometimes she was paid, but mostly not. But wallets were easy to ferret. Locks, like scabs, could be picked.

She is out tonight, down the Philbeach Hotel, Earls Court, securing custom. Jerusalem knows this. He can smell her absence.

A hand clutching a handle: a knife handle, then it was the door's turn. Jerusalem is in the building, half way up the stairs, stepping over strawberry-flavoured condoms stiff with old spillage. Strawberries and cream. The first and second floors are all burnt out: Greasy air. Dark time. Lice in the brickwork.

Third floor - sad and empty as a duck skull. Nothing here but an unwound clock, an unopened letter. Jerusalem hears its history: an old woman and her words... *"Confetti mouthed."* He shudders on.

Knived hand, standing, soaking up the fourth floor. His head slowly swaying left, right. Understanding. The room is crowded with suitable darkness like the inside of a brain scan machine. There is the faintest hiss, (the squeal of a rotten wheel on a rotten wheelchair), from a torn lead pipe: Gas spores popping. A hopeless 'klik klik' of an unmoving gas meter paddlewheel. The rising damp is tallest here. Dead candles, a king size mattress growing into mould of the floor. Naked phones wires hang from holes in holes. Up on the wall, Jesus in a nice frame, Jesus on the cross. Jerusalem grunts, brings a lump of something through his throat and spits it over the picture. A redeemed greenie.

"She does pigeons!" the Voices add. He kicks through the room, booting at bottles. (A sliver of Schilling tooth lodged between his toes from the last killing finally works itself free, drops, crushed underfoot) He hears sharp things, tiny tiny sharp sounds, faint tinklings, sweet ringings. He finds a sewing kit beneath a shabby copy of *The Jungle Book*, picks it up, listening to the needles: toy bells jingling.

The pores of the knife are sweating. Itching.

In the corner of the room, the mattress, and Lamb moving forward - the only way. He slices the mattress, top to bottom, pulls it open like a wound; horse hair stuffing, this drawn out with some of the broken springs, they crust, crumble, rusty from urine. Discarded. *Climbing* into the mattress now, shoving against springs, (dry stink of piss and years), knife held between teeth. He is stitching himself into the mattress. Entering. *Going back to nowhere...* Stitching himself *in* like a mediaeval lord's winter clothing.

The stitching takes a while. Needles, thread breaking. After an hour, just a hole left, a hole small enough for one thick finger to poke out and tease a scabby blanket over it.

The Voices squeaking of "*Ethereal errands.*"

Rain outside and close cheap laughter coming up the stairs. Anastasia and customer "Ha-Ha-ing" their entrance, dripping night onto parquet flooring. Cold air, mute light - an unclean rendezvous.

Anastasia is drunk or pretends to be. Washing her face in neat Dettol, scenting the flesh. No words spoken, no candles lit. They have full-moonlight. Romance for a price.

The customer, a male rumour, is skittle shape. Glandular troubles filling out his feet, thighs and stomach. The top half though, bony as Rosinate. Pinguid penguin. He wears a soiled anorak, both zipped and hooded up. Can't see his face, only smeared bifocal shine and the grey of his mouth: fillings in pawn shop teeth. Apparently he is one of the backroom boys on *The Saint and Greavsie Show.* Pear-shadowed, trundling over to the mattress, he loosens belt, trousers. Needs paint on his parts to keep himself stiff. His lucky night! Gonna clean up with the meat broom, gonna fuck her up the arse. A Bisto brown member. Lard as lubricant. *Yours to the backbone.* He was once married, a family somewhere. Now he only rents the shame.

Anastasia snorts crushed Palfium off an upturned chamber pot. Blue nostrils. Red eyes. Rolls up her rubber mini, and pulls down her knix. (The penis like so much forgotten wax.) She kisses her customer, tongues his fillings, probes his cavities.

Jesus in a nice frame. Easy loves and easier religions.

The unloving hand upon the thigh...

They fall on to the mattress, roll about, she's stroking his anorak, his dick. He fingers her arse. Jacobean statuettes. Wresting reptiles.

"Bed's a bit lumpy ain't..." The customer's words are unfinished. The mattress has changed shape. An arm and knife have punched up through it, slashing at them, these alchemical birds on a gory nest. Hacking the customer and tearing Anastasia's throat. The mattress *grows*, the death-bed stands. Another arm rips out, a torso, legs. The head of shattered plastic. Black phoenix rising. Jerusalem Lamb, madman, a terrible beauty with knife in hand, hell in head, begins -

The customer is gibbering, choking on fear and the stink of gas. The Lamb above him, killing his sounds, kicking, smashes, rending with blade. Left and right the knife. In. Out. Up. Down. **Forwards.** Red noise: scalded gulls screaming in the quiet dark, rain laughing, night applauding, bone smithereening.

Knife sweating, *itching*. The customer's body is slung around the room, stamped, crushed down, defiled, but the customer is still alive, not willing to let go 'just yet' -

wanting his money's worth, holding on for more. Jerusalem can smell his life, smells woodworm chewing on the crucifix, smell of sicky gas cloying up the room.

The gas...

Lamb lifting customer by blood neck, bare feet wiggling, bifocals nowhere, slams the knife through lips, tongue, gum to cut away his mouth. The blade hits a filling, sparks. Explosion is immediate. The room is blue and moving fast. Jerusalem smashed through lath/plaster walls, blown out, blown away, plunging four floors, burning in flight.

F
a
l
l
i
n
g.

The river has grown. High tide. Lamb hits, is sucked under. Swallowed. And for one dark, sparkling instant hears nothing at all.

Gobbled up

The Night has teeth.

III

Aedes Aegypti

Genius is one of the many forms of insanity.
***Cesare Lombroso,* Criminalogist (1836-1909)**

The gnat is of more ancient lineage than that of man
Proverb

1

Anastasia had bolted. High heels clopping down four storeys, out into night. Holding her throat together like an unhinged handbag, sealing in her internal graffiti. Was two streets away when the explosion knocked her over. False eyelashes broken, as is her wrist. Lovely blue flames reveal the sky. She remembers a picture she once saw as a child: The Blitz - scorched night, yellow air. Far away, sirens, engines. She wonders whatever happened to her customer and just for an instant she wants to laugh a sudden secret laugh, but doesn't. Carrion petals drip from her lips. Rain keeps her cool.

The customer fried. Just half a skull. Jerusalem unmade him. Claimed him. Took his noise away. And the things he did to him were very primitive indeed. He even tore his shadow.

It's three a.m. Deadly darkest time. Suicide hour when the drink wears off, when the joke seems funniest: prophetic.

Thunder phantoms scything greasy streets. Rain tearing paint off double yellow lines, knocking bats from sky, drowning spiders in their webs, and there's little Anastasia running through the streets like a redundant ghost. Her movements are a series of fallings. Picking herself up out of a backstreet 'garden', cider bottle glass torn at her kneecaps. Sweet smell of wet stinging nettles and burnt meat stink in her head. Blood weeping, scratching at her insides, the blue of her veins turning black. Overhead, lost in rain, the noise of helicopters. *Engines.*

Rag doll Anastasia, boyish as a Japanese drunk, giggling through blood, limping past condemned avenues, alleys, coughing up life. Light. Seeing all through rose tinted specs:

Blood clouding vision. Death staining life. Black rain, orange neon.

Night is lost. The rain is inherent.

Anastasia too is lost, bleeding her way onward to housing estates, multi storey Ararats. Eyeless stones squeezed of blood. Monuments of shit. *Other people's dreams.* Mud hits her, dirt, soil. She looks up. Rain hammers window boxes, contents uprooted, spuked out, late marigolds splatting twelve floors down. Floral suicide - even the plants are killing themselves. Now she *knows* the world is melting. It all merges - dog carcass, net curtaining, corrugated iron, rapist mask, bus-stop, betting slips, gutter sperm, all running together, fusing, matting like burnt polythene.

And then she sees the Church.

The Church of Rust - any Poe temple, brooding calm, white as drowned owls. A lighthouse, a Lamb white answer. Something sad in its comfort, like a decision to grow old. It is the house of God evicted. Holy Ghost exorcised.

She sees white through darkness. Scumbered alabaster. Smell of wet stone. Stained glass in white rain - she faints, falls, brambles and briars in her bloody face. Her body amongst glue bags, chip paper.

This used to be a forest. Torn down, stoned over. Up went the church - St. Saviours' - in went the windows, nativity, damnation. Wars came and went, prayers were just a way of remembering lines. Priests are only method actors. Candles were lit, the shadows warmed. Twice the font froze over. The Bibles all printed on sandpaper. Morning service was cancelled, replaced by pre-recorded Good Friday sermon. Resurrection always three days away. The tape broke, batteries corroded, rust kissed the aisle. Decay, like death, became a way of life. And selling, for fifty pence in the last church jumble, the Vatican's 'notice to quit'. Doors were bolted, locks sealed. Years withered on the outside.

Inside, the Church breathed again, flies had migrated in from Cuba, venomous reptiles crept in, slept by empty pews. Moulds and damp; spores with thought muscled in, preached disease. Time was measured in bacteria. Stagnation picked clean the bones of any intruder. No squatters/druggies here, too busy steering clear, not wanting *this much* absolution. The world forgot Church, and Church could do without, drifting through itself, shifting in warmth of self infection. No cure for Church. No vaccine. And then came Jerusalem, Knight of Nothing, as champion for Church. And tonight has come the body, the body of the half man on Church steps, in stilettos, in pain in blood and rain.

Anastasia wakes, broken teeth in her mouth, blood staining vision. She can still walk and does. Staggering up, on toward the church, pushing opens its doors, wandering in, dragging lapsed Catholicism and a broken high heel behind.

Inside: half light, light from pews' bonfire. Mothy ash smell, the tribal pissy stink of any gents' lavatory. *Inrush of memory* - Incense all around, steaming. Memories of a small boy pulling from his mother's hand, running down a shiny aisle on the first day of communion, sandals slipping, colliding with a table where remembrance candles stood. A scattering of sacred wax, child and dubious collection box coinage. She does not see the maggoty magpie Jesus. Can only see the confessional and a possible forgiveness.

From the ceiling, stag beetles watch her. Elder moths merely contemplate.

The confessional is a simple enough affair; purple velvet curtains stretched across skinny wooden strands. Hard seats of oak inside. Intricate leaden lattice designed to separate sinner from priest.

Anastasia tugs back the curtain, lurches in, sits, begins. Blood bubbling, coughed up, wiped away like spit; "Forgive me Father..." Her words, doubtful wishes, dead dreams, have a clean corruptibility to them; they are drunken ventriloquist words, mysterious, without guilt. Babbled pleasure. The word, 'sorry'. There is no sin here, only life and the will to live it. Her face hangs from her head, torn, sightless now, crowded with haemorrhage, snapped wrist at her side, burnt hair, scalded piss-filled breasts popped, washing her. Scented. She tips forward, slumping toward the lattice. Before her head hits she is dead.

Before her head hits, the lattice erupts, two lumps of melted blackness smash through, hands grabbing her by the ears, hair, hauling her forward, slamming her face through the lattice, forcing her head down, splitting her throat open on torn leady laths.

Jerusalem survived the explosion, survived the fall, was washed downstream, beached. Found the Church, followed its smell, found a Voice in the wooden box - like a coffin, just waiting. Heard its confession, heard more words, words heard before; bled over, screamed. Pain - the secret language. (Something you've never heard.)

Blood hangs like wool off jagged iron lattice. The body of the fourth voice, broken beneath it. Jerusalem, selfish redeemer sitting in the priest seat, breathing rust. He endured the gas blast/the Thames, that is to say he *lived*. The river quenched his blaze, the rain cheered him on. Night, like Harold, turned a blind eye. Polythene burnt into him, crisped his joints, fingers. The explosion *shortened* him like a snapped back. Some bones, a thigh, shattered. His face is a map of burnt black islands. Melted flesh plastic. What was left of his nose is no longer there. The polythene skin is solid, dull as sharp, dark clay. He cannot move his neck or turn his head. Something important internally no longer functions. Movement is fragile. He looks like something you wouldn't want to tell your children about: John Merrick's ugly brother. A walking mirror of ashes.

But the self-reflection is broken. Later, he will bring

together the pieces of himself: A gathering up of one, will remake the internal Jerusalem jigsaw. Stitch up the Lamb.

Later, not now. For now a voice lolls dead before him and Jerusalem laughs, loud, deep laughter and his laughter sounds like rain. Crocodile tears on a cold, cold night.

Pharaoh ants scatter. Weevils throw themselves headlong into vacant spider webs.

A Voice in the wooden box - like a coffin. Just waiting

Such dark business.

The blood hasn't had time to congeal, smoke to settle, yet already the photographs have been taken, headlines written, buzzing down wires. This morning the world would know: **SERIAL KILLER STRIKES AGAIN.**

Newspapers grating the mental cheese, squeezing Missing Red Heads and Brain Dead Boxers on to pages 7 and 13 respectively. There will be criminal 'experts' with their conclusions. *'Something in the water', 'Inner city deprivation', 'Satellite TV'.*

Tea break: tar-nosed navvies reading aloud, *Twenty things you never knew about psychopathic killers.* More words. Repeating nothing. Birthing new void. Chat show hosts making him the topic of sofa conversation. The psychopath that kills the mouth. "Better let 'im meet the mother-in-law!" The in-joke, the dropped unknown name. Celebritise him by proxy. Fly in Anthony Hopkins, make it look good with dim lighting, grey clothing, the hushed voice, manic stare. Nervous round of applause. Richard and Judy asking, "What kind of mind could be capable of such acts?"

It's no act. Mad needs no rehearsal. No prompting.

Tomorrow, or the next day, there'll be a rash of sudden books springing up under *Real Life Crime,* criminologists in cardies out to out detail one another, comparing notes on contemporary and historical 'serial killers'. The theories will fly: morbid birds, all overlooking Jerusalem's preliminaries, the oblation: the deadened whine. An uncommunion, a selfish sharing. The exconsecration, unholy, pseudo sacred. The simple conclusion of one less voice, a mouthless head. Torn beetle.

In churches, congregations listening to sermons on forgiveness: the corrupt text of the living. How many know that the congregation *is* a sacrificial gift?

And of course, doing lunch, restaurant crews of endless suits, proof readers, reviewers and first novel Cambridge chappies bleating of *"the brutal precision of the blows, the simplicity of will taken to create such force."* They may even note the *"sacrificial element, the pure offering. Something akin to the Zosimos visions"* in all of the slayings. Unknowing men bandying other men's words. Warm consciences. Warm beds. All of them wrong, all wrong, all making their own noise: The noise of seeds spat from a decomposed pomegranate.

In Harley Street tepees, medicine men's leather couches are collapsing under the weight of psychoanalysts' professional jealousy. Somewhere beyond locked doors and white corridors there *had to be* a manila file on a loon who likes to dress in black polythene and kill 'innocent' (ha!) people - mouth first. The strait-jackets are waiting, as are the injections, isolation rooms, beatings, book deals. *Somewhere,* (Romford? Richmond? Nowhere that matters), there is a room, probably an old gymnasium full of Rorschach tests, Xeroxed to within an inch of their invention, faded, enlarged, cut, joined, just waiting for a lunatic to dribble over and nod and yes and confess by word association. Papers blotted, folded, meaning only what they mean: a spilled mass of ink. A blob of black thought. Ink blot tests are only mirrors.

(Every minute, every day, there are loons in rooms, with no will of their own, tissue paper in their slippers, butterscotch on the brain, who are shown continuous catalogues of Rorschach tests, not *knowing* their significance, value, just shapes on paper. *"Now then Johnny, which is the prettiest? The two headed eagle, the cow with its face caved in or the flowers in a vase of cunts?"* They are bombarded with ink blots to help jog a false memory, to enable them to 'confess' to anything from shoplifting to genocide. Did you know that? It's called Confessional Therapy. The 'patient' is given a longer sojourn, stronger medication. It saves the government thousands every day on policing revenues, sole leather and man hours.)

Only mirrors. And Jerusalem does not reflect.

Jerusalem *is* the mirror. A correct mistake. Jung's warning. Kant's promise. Jerusalem: The Sacred Joke.

Late night, and grieving relatives of his victims tuning in; World Service red eye, unsleepen, shaking their heads, looking down at imaginary grass, asking "Why?"

There is no explanation. No *mystery.*

just Mad.

2

The mad are innocent, and can do no wrong.
***H.G.Woodley* (Certified 1947)**

Saturday morning. Black Saturday. The 14th. Alice's wedding day. Ernie, already washed and suited, kicking heel at scrubbed kitchen table, scrunched wedding invite smoothed before him. He's waiting for someone to tell him what to do. He doesn't know.

Norman taps on young Roane's door, asks if he'd like to come along to the wedding. A conversation though wood. Roane declines, knowing the scene: Fish and Ernie scuffling off, Jackson tagging along. Taxi cabs. Leg irons chewing pews, top hats and stump socks. Ernie eating his buttonhole carnation and Norman getting hay fever from his, sneezing over the person in front of him. The inevitable moment when Mr Jackson wants a slash in the church and pisses in a carrier bag. Ernie heckling the vicar, "*...or forever hold thy piece...*" Jackson pulling his dick out in the wedding photographs. Carnation mouth'd Ernie spitting in the punchbowl. Jackson picking fights with the best man, vicar, catering staff. Too much marzipan on the wedding cake. Jackson *insisting* he make a speech about, "How glad I am me old mate Stan's finally got hitched, cos for years now I thought 'e were a fuckin' sodomist!" The obvious greasy pocket - dodgy doggy-bag of cold roast chicken legs, vol-au-vents, trifle. Jackson and Ernie hijacking the mobile disco, playing nonstop Carter, Killing Joke and Numan. Jackson slipping a luminous condom over the bridegroom's drunken head. Norman catching the bride's bouquet and Jackson in a phone box making an anonymous call to the police: details of a stolen car..."Easy to spot. Big 'Just Married' sign int' back window..."

"No thanks," Roane's voice, sheepish beyond the door. He will sit out the Ghost Dance.

"Oh well, suit ya self." Fish, electric ferret, darts off, thoughts full of wedding bells, pressed seams. Cake.

Mr Jackson, on the other hand, has only murder in mind. The old killing habit with Norman as pale target. He could be stomached at first - the squeals, the fussiness, the hypochondriacal whines almost a perfect foil to Jackson's sledgehammer sophistry, but then he became a disadvantage. Mental luggage on too long a journey, made to be jettisoned, preferably from a great speeding height. Just a case of forging Fish's signature on his own will and Mr J would be sole heir to what was left of Nutty Norman's legacy. Coupla thousand, better than nowt. Pin money.

Besides, no easier way of settling his betting debts. Four grand lost in that one poker hand. Maudsley, the only thing won that night. At least he had another twelve days' grace. Mr Rind being good enough to take an IOU.

Murder

But how to do it?

Jackson had connections with most people: Hoodlums, defrocked papal hitmen, dubious 'insurance' salesman, but bullets cost. Low-life like death does not come cheap.

How then? A DIY job? There was always the possibility of an OD. Switch his pile cream for a tube of Deep Heat Muscle Rub. Kaboom! Ha Ha! Nah, too messy. He did know a squadron leader, RAF wallah with kickstart moustache, who owed him a favour (choirboy Polaroids). One quick phone call, rustle up a small nuclear strike. A "Bucket of Sunshine" to land square on Fishy's head. A *real* S.M.A.R.T.

weapon. But there could be complications, think of the fallout… Much too much to explain away even as dandruff. A helicopter gunship then, the SuperCobra, p'raps a Bomber, a B52! Any Desert Storm leftover, any 'coalition' oversight.

There's a rap on the door. Would-be-victim, Fish, calling out, "I say… Me an' Ernie's of to wedding. Would ya like to come?"

Jackson is adamant. "Fuck off, I dan't wanta go nah fuckin' wedding…" But where there's a wedding, there's possible mayhem, fist-fuckable bridesmaids, free drink, chance of a ruck… It's settled then. Mr J, mind changed, yelling, "Aye, 'ang on. I'm for that! I'll just *Brylcreem* me pubes."

Murder could wait. Free drink most certainly couldn't.

What now?

Late morning. Roane all alone in sprawling asylum. Another brooding scene of corridor, key, second floor doors. The situation almost post-coital in convenience. There is sick on his shirt, last night's sick, nightmare on his breath and the question, "What replaces death?" on his lips.

Only yesterday he had decided that he would forsake darkness and all its deeper meanings, he had binned his black clothing along with Doctor Judith's journals and taken the first steps to 'normalcy' with his new found friends, but last night - Jackson had spiked the food or drink, and he found himself taken out of himself, seeing the past of Tookesbury Hall through the eyes of a psychic dream mosquito. He had puked, slept. Upon waking he knew he was still a child of darkness, knew what he must do. The black clothing removed from the bin, the sombre thoughts of shadow reinstated. Easy isn't it?

Roane throws off his shirt. Naked now in his fear. Scared, shivering in skin. He holds the key to all the doors between thumb, forefinger, turning it round, scrutinizing: an ebony clue.

He gets up, walks out, new stiff movements climbing stairs to the second, secret floor. Arsenic white walls, whore grey doors. The stairs are the Past, an abandoned cave. Above the stairs, an arched window bleached in light. Birds outside, winging by, their shadows - glimpses of shade cast upon corridor's floor and the barefoot Roane. As the birds move, so it seems does the corridor. A flickering Super 8 scene, sacred cinematic time.

Roane, driven by instinct, not quite conscious, strolls through the empty eternity of the second floor, his shade leading the way and him falling behind as if *he* were the shadow.

The floor is cold, icy shivers like shame stake through him, stiffen him, making his hackles and penis rise.

He stands outside a door, key of power breathing in his paw. He had dreamt of a room of blood, an Egyptian room…

The key fits the lock, it turns. He enters.

All is suddenly slower, the world given too much Fentazin. The door wides open, he is unsure what he will find. He can feel the light warm on his face, chest. He opens his eyes.

The room is empty.

Bare white walls on every side. A single wide window. No lights. A plain white marble floor. The air, cool, peanut sweet. There's something unnerving to the room, its void almost carries a character. A simplicity bordering on pretentious.

"Bollocks." He never swore, it just seemed apt. Only a room after all, nothing more. A Victorian cell. What of the others? All the same, with just the Poppy Room different? Some trick of Flint's? Jackson's suggestion of "Indoor gardening"?

The room is left open, *abandoned*. He tries another.

Dust. Webs line the doorway, he walks through them, snagging them, pulled to his body. Something unfolds, tumbles on his head, something dead lying above the door. A skeleton. Small bones, a rat or pigeon maybe. It rests unfelt in his hair, giving him horns. Dead diadem. The room is suffocated under books. Paper dust swamps the floor, some of the books have decayed, others are only half there, deteriorating slackly. It is a scene from Gormenghast, lacking only owl nest and mice. Roane treads carefully, picks the way through, chooses at random one of ten thousand books, attempts to lift it, but it crumbles with soft resistance: a dictionary of dust. Another and another, all the same. Not books, volumes of dust. A tomb to tomes. He turns, brushing the books that ash to compost. Sepia air, tea-bag light warm in its age, drifting up, powdery dirt sticking to his sweat, colouring him the brown of baby bears. The webs in which he stands run alive with spiders popping free from yellow white eggs. The bones on his head have cut into his temples. Skull teeth pricking the simple sacrifice of blood trickling over cheeks, nipples, thighs and feet. The spider touch tickles, he laughs, but the thought of the room fills him with sudden grief. Then there are tears. The walls are a cheap brown, but he can't *see* walls, only towers of dust with the shape of books. Beneath feet in dust shingle, three quarters of a shoe print seventy years there. Half a dust novel lies in crumbs on the floor, ghostly fingerprint touched into its cover. The ceiling is difficult to see, not knowing what lies beyond the dust in the air. Roane licks the dust from his fingers, spits it out violently, toy choking. It tastes like pork.

He feels sick again, wants to sneeze, but to sneeze would make the room fall in.

Out in the hallway he sneezes twice. Two stupid sneezes. And the world does not crumble.

The third room. Another desired entry.

Key *turned*, door pushed wide.

Right angles.

The room literally *jags* out at him. He falls back. Jagged steel shards zagger the room. A room full of bayonets, razor blades, needles. A room of hurts. Great sharp sheets lacerating other sharper accuracies. The violence shines like greasy skin. Steel gleaming smiles, angular white serrations, shatters of cold. *A shiver in metal.* New malign light slashing off every corner. A sea of stabs. Myriad reflections off steel give impressions of movement, as if the room beckons, just willing to accept a new soft occupant.

Roane slams shut the door, locks it, hurries on.

Something is wrong at the fourth door. It is open, pushed almost closed. Tiny slivers of metal, iron filings, chipped lumps of wood, line its threshold.

Something is wrong

Is this where the mad kept their pain, tucked away in some hateful cupboard? What if the mad hadn't yet died, what if they were all still in this room, waiting, sharpening long teeth on the bones of time...

He inches the door further open, can see no dusty old loons or fangs. He sees roots. Tree roots, growing *up*, out of the wooden floor. In one corner, a black thing stirs.

"Aaawk, 'allo big boy!" - Maudsley.

Maudsley is perched on the furthest root bough. Small bag of cashews in his claws. Lunch. Tinny curls snagged on his beak: iron filings. The bird had picked the lock, found a seat on a backward tree and fed.

Roane chances the roots, their very shape giving them the *appearance* of a skinny, uneven tree. Dirty earth-caked limbs. Potato skin texture. Jonah's oak.

Maudsley flies off.

The tree reminds Roane of an eight legged horse. Something not quite Roman - an unhoused equine taken to wandering the world in search of a place to die.

Below, on the first floor, there must be a room without doors, windows, where the crown of the upside down tree grows out. Its roots stay here in the North. Place of wisdom.

An upper and under world.

...myself and offering to myself - knotted to that tree, no man knows whither the roots of it run.

After the fire, all that grows is *ash.*

After-noon. Light deepens, shadows stretching like Lycra. Maudsley, the black African parrot, sitting on Roane's shoulder. A tail feather falling to the floor. Intelligence at his head, memory at his feet. The Well, the Will. Roane, pathologically Bohemian in webs, bones, running alive with young spiders. Blood brown at his cheeks and chest. Horns on his head, the phallic horn erect, willing. *As mad as mad may be...* Standing outside door five awaiting the necessary invocation. Ignorant in his knowing. Maudsley burps, (do parrots burp? Maudsley does), wipes beak in Roane's hair. "Manners," says the bird.

In with the key.

In.

Maudsley has smelled it. Familiarity, nostalgia. He swoops first in. The stink of furs, dried grasslands. There is sand on the floor, paintings on rough walls, of bison, bears. Across the only window, spread like skin, a parchment map. Continents, reefs, previously un-noted lands. *The Bastard Isles?* Maudsley smiles down at an aboriginal frog totem. Small rodents scamper in African sands between an Aztec vase and a Slavic mask.

The room is suddenly hot, not warm. Sweat air, tropical. Too much. Roane backs out. Maudsley rolls in sand, chirping, "T'was on the good ship Venus..."

Sand on his feet, walking on glass-paper. What next? A room made of cockroaches, a cubby full of phlegm? He doesn't want to chance the next door, decides to peer through its keyhole. Stooping, a blind voyeur brushing cobwebs from his eye. All he can see is another door. The door is near, near enough to see *its* keyhole, only to see *another* door.

A room of doors.

Doors within doors. A barren landscape of brown doors like hills. A locked view.

Mindless in ritual, Roane moves down the hallway to yet another door. It seems familiar, different from the rest, but the same. A vague quality of guilt, a masturbatory shame to it.

something from a dream?

The door to which Doctor William Miles bestowed poppies, 31st August 1922. Blue incarnadine stain on the floor. Poppy revenant. Ghost 'romance' souvenir.

In an illegal movement - any bailiff's greeting - Roane kicks down the door. Inside, bare blank. Sterilised, walls, floor, roof. In the centre of the room is another, smaller room, something more than a cupboard, it has no door, no handle or space for key. Unformed.

He walks around it. It cannot be more than four feet in height, width: An abandoned packing case of stone.

Brushing a shaky finger to its texture...

He touches, briefly, snatching his hand away.

The dough of echoes, the sound of breathing. Heartbeats.

He has the feeling that he is being watched. Something protective not wanting him there. Unseen eyes of clay scooped from Mother Earth's belly. Old tears dew damp on the pristine floor.

breathing

heartbeats

eyes of clay

He races off, the Angel of Shames, running fast like he was racing ambulances to Elysium.

3

...did I solicit thee from darkness to promote me?
***John Milton* - Paradise Lost**

Jerusalem.

Slept away a night, a day, down on the ground like a frozen foot soldier. Dreams of drowning in a biblical river, dreams of landing without first falling. Impotent prophecies: Thankless phantoms.

His bones are broken, a finger missing. Old scars blossom, newer, darker damage has been done. He is burnt. Blood singed, charred of heart. A brain turned black. The gas explosion served only to roughen already rough edges. Unmade the unreal, reset bones by breaking them. Cured by the disease.

One-eyed waking.

One eye peering up, a murderous astronomer's eye. The eye of Horus, opened, turned away from dreaming. In the corner, the body of Anastasia, dead in the confessional. A dead truth. In pews ash bonfire, a black thing, stirring, and now a noise, a buzzing. Some bug breaking wind: Fffzzzz Fffizzzzn Fizzzznd Finzzzned... Finizzzed? Finishhhzed? Finished? Finishedzzzzd?"

"Finishedzzzzd?"

"Finished?"

"Finished?"

"Finished?"

Burnt muscle shifting; Dark Lamb, stands, shedding sleep like a second skin, kicking off the night. Lurching now, on through the church, chasing nothing, snorting absence. Hearing **all.** All the little Saturday night happenings. Outside - the World: a slick of Neasden boys, loading, unloading. Haggling price over a Nessan-Dorma-bil chock full of Pavarotti vids. Knife blade negotiations. No sale. A street, two streets away, a cider party and dead virginity. Newspaper ageing in the base of a canary cage.

"Finished?" the 'father' asked.

The boy nodded, was glanced a blow to his head, tied, gagged and shut back in the cupboard.

The boy was taken out six times daily, ungagged, unbound, made to kneel, to utter reverence. To pray.

The mother had been no good, got herself filled by the local air force base. Bloody Americans. Six months it was, before she started to show. Fell down the backstairs, she did, tried to get rid of it, but brought it on early. And the Doctor, Hopkins, pissed as a sod. Saturday night in the kitchen, the girl up on the table, a towel in her mouth, legs spread, pushing. Too tight, babe round the wrong way, used the forceps did Hopkins, stuck them in, twisted them round, got a good grip. Too bloody tight. Squeezing, and the girl screaming, pulled the little bugger out, great bloody hole in its head. The girl, dead. Died of fear. Can't blame her. Mopped the blood, cut the cord with a corkscrew. Hopkins filled the hole in the baby's head with a cork, put it in a pail, covered with cloth, left out back. Thoughts of flushing it down the khazi. But the woman, the dead girl's mother, couldn't face it. Too much Catholic left in her. She took the baby to her sister in the hills, pleaded with her and her husband to keep it safe, bring it up right. Sunday dawn: Hopkins and the dead girl's father had drunk themselves sober. Had dug a big hole, slung in the girl and covered bucket. Did not, could not peer inside the pail for fear that the babe be still alive. Still breathing.

Matthew and Mary were good God-fearing folk. They

called the child Jerusalem Lamb. 'Jerusalem' as a guide, a goal to strive for. 'Lamb' as he was a gift, as was Abel's gift to the Lord. And as a reminder of his own mortality. He was but another sacrifice. An unburnt offering. Having no children of their own, (they had not been blessed), they set about shaping his young life along pious lines, instilling in him the dread fact that his mother had gone to Hell and would burn there for eternity in a fiery lake of damnation, and *he* was of his mother's flesh, making him impure, soiled. For this he must be all the more virtuous if he were to strive for a golden place in Paradise. This, sermoned to a crying week-old baby. And the tears did not stop.

When Hopkins pulled him from the dead womb, the forceps cracked his skull, setting minor cerebral arteries popping, scraping his mind, sealing his fate: A tangerine in the paw of Kong. The tiny damage of brain spitting wrong signals to all the wrong receivers. Jerusalem heard only static, severe tinnitus aureum flooded his life, clogged the senses. All he heard were his own screams. Vicious lullabies to sing him insane.

The new 'parents' did not take to tears, so took a strap and beat belief into little Jerusalem. The lesson of pain was soon learnt, the child became impervious and the tears were kept cried inside.

Childhood was a series of biblical scriptures and darkened rooms. At the age of five he was chained in a backroom for daubing, in nosebleed blood, the number 6 on each of the three faces of Jesus upon the 'family' triptych. After the thrashing he received for this, he no longer mistook pain for affection.

Eight times daily, 'father' preached to him Numbers, Judges, John, Revelations and Nehemiah but never Lamentations. Stood, reading by candlelight, shadow on the wall like a plague locust. The words droning out. Repetitious, boring, *boring* into his skull, crawling through the hole in his head, each word cancelling itself, becoming blur. Ecclesiastical echoes. Gibbled glory.

Three years Jerusalem was locked in the room, fed, beaten, prayed at. (The first inkling to desire shadows.) A backroom furnished in darkness and stinking candle wax. The only light coming through five stained-glass windows. Victorian windows depicting biblical scenes: The Temptation, Nativity, Noah's Ark, Crucifixion, Judgement Day. Birds nested in alcoves outside the room. Jerusalem heard them, cooing, purring, making nice soft squishy shitting noises. And down one window, they had crapped so much, it changed the image: Noah and the ark, the olive-branched dove flying overhead. The bird shit trailing down the window from the dove's glass arse, giving image that the dove shat deliberately over the ark. Noah and his boat interred in shit. And on that day, the boy, Jerusalem, like Balaam's donkey, found his voice, screamed **"Hallelujah!"** and began laughing, laughed so much he laughed himself into a fit. The 'parents' knew nothing of epilepsy but knew about demons and their master Beelzebub. Quoting Revelations 26: 13-14 and 18: 2, 'father' beat the Devil from the boy with the poker until it broke. When Jerusalem finished convulsing, he was tied, chained, shut in a cupboard.

Three years in the room, ten more in the cupboard. Prayed at through a crack in the door. He had learnt darkness, knew a whisper from a sigh. Had 'voices' in his head, companions in the dark, praising him. The 'family' did not exist, had lost any meaning. 'Mother and father' were just sound. There was only noise.

It was his thirteenth summer and the sun came scorching the house, filling Jerusalem's cupboard with sweat and the scent of escape. He was taken out to pray, but something was wrong. He had bitten through his bonds, swallowed steel chain. All there was, was a noise and a mouth where it existed. Jerusalem slammed the 'father's' crucifix into the 'father's' mouth, filled up the noise hole, choked him on holy. He killed the 'mother's' sound; reached in, tore her throat inside out. He killed the noise. The Voices cheered him on.

Blinded by light, Jerusalem escaped into a new world of sound. Night found him in a forgotten farmhouse, where he took a stick and rammed it in his ear to stop the Voices. When he came to, he could not move. The stick had caused additional brain damage. He lay there in a pool of his own blood for three days, passing in and out of consciousness, many hundreds of insects gathered around him, played in the blood, sucked at the gaping ear wound. Spiders spun webs on him, moths, beetles, ants, all were ensnared, cocooned, left to rest on his eyes and mouth. He hated insects, for they made little chirping, scuttly noises. *Droning on and on…* He was Gulliver to the bugs' Lilliputians. He should have died on the fourth day, but he didn't. For birds through a broken window flew. Fat pigeons, magpies, jays, swooped in and down, chewed down on the bugs, feasted on the sounds. Birds were salvation. Insects, the noise.

He was discovered that afternoon, taken to town, a hospital.

When the bodies of 'mother and father' were finally found, questions were asked. Fingerprints taken, blood samples too. Within a week, Jerusalem had been transferred. A psychiatric unit in Dyfed.

Month after month of treatment brought him back to 'normality'. He remained tranquillised, strapped down for his own good: violent tendencies. Kept on an intravenous sedative cocktail of 50mg Sparine/100mg Pethidine. Given the usual tests: Rorschach, thematic apperception and in the drawing of self-concept; he drew a broken cross and ate the crayon. Heard new words from other patients; 'cunt', 'motherfucker', 'lobotomy'. Mind-altering drugs served only to intensify the sounds he could hear: watches screaming out the seconds, hairs growing, colours evolving. He cut off his own ears to stop the sounds. It only hurt.

New doctors came and went. Jerusalem was more than an enigma, he was for real. Once, in an extreme drugged state, he was allowed to mix with other tranquillised patients in an experiment of 'free association'. He killed them all, five doctors, fourteen nurses and the ladies that cleaned the corridors. He escaped, was at large three days. Killing and killing again. Was finally recaptured by an SIS D17 unit. They used tear gas and HK semi automatics. The whole operation was hushed up, given the government blanket. It never happened. The body count stopped at thirteen. Reality holds the score at seventy-seven. An entire farming community slaughtered. The village has got a new name now: *Pant Corlan yr Wyn.* It means 'The Valley of the Sheepfold'. The psychiatric unit no longer exists. No roads lead there now. It does not appear on any map made after 1988.

On the night of his recapture, Jerusalem was taken under armed guard, (eight of them), by Chinook helicopter to *the* maximum security 'hospital' for the criminally insane: Crowfields. Where they locked away the snake-brained, the child eaters and mad dogs. An Edwardian black brick construction, surrounded on all sides by dry river beds and field upon field of vivid corn cracking up through the slate and stone.

Here his treatment was as savage as the wounds he had left on seventy-seven dead heads. Kept under *constant* multi-video surveillance, bolted into *two* strait jackets, screwed into the soft floor of the smallest cell up on the Solitary wing. The ECT was brought to *him*. By now he didn't legally exist, so it didn't matter if he "got a bit burnt up". He was known amongst the head doctors at Crowfields as 'Playtime'.

Jerusalem was subjected to many experiments. One in sensory deprivation. He was shut, (handcuffed and chained), in the Tank, a sub chamber filled with liquid similar in texture to watery glucose. Shut in for days, weeks at a time. Once even face down. The Tank was meant to take away, erase. It was only dark. Full of quiet blackness, a breeding ground for perfect silence. Darkness rubbing his skull, massaging the death bone, fuelling the hate engine.

Four years in solitary. Coprophagous: eating his own shit. Doctors grew tired of him, beatings and burnings no longer fun. Took away the strait jacket as a form of punishment. Apparently, he had used it to sharpen his teeth on. Only the newer guards would peer frightful at him through surveillance cameras, viewing the whispered myth. That is how he finally escaped.

There were originally twelve cameras built into the solitary soft cell, ringing the ceiling, taking in every view of old mad Lamb. Only a pair of cameras viewed the forgotten patient now. A new guard watched, taking in the two views. Left and right. Beyond the rubber wall of the cell was the internal generator for the entire building. An ugly structure, stuck away up on the solitary wing. The main feed pipe led from the generator, through the floors, walls, ceilings. The pipe fed the madhouse with power straight off the grid. The pipe was arm thick, armour plating protecting four sets of cable, each having ten thousand copper wires woven in an industrial weave, carrying 1100 volts. The pipe ran directly behind the soft rubber walls of Jerusalem Lamb's solitary cell.

(Since dawn that day, spiders had broken their webs, found suitable high corners in the cell to sulk within. In the surrounding fields, blackbirds and woodpeckers were unusually shrill. Rooks had not left their nests all morning. He knew it was approaching, had sensed it before, but it had never promised to be so near.)

Jerusalem had heard the power, sensed the dry stink of electricity. Head pressed to rubber walls, listening without ears, hearing, he had followed the dry line of noise around the room, knew where it led. *Knew.* The surveillance camera with its little whirrs and clicks, videoing him for the files, for overseas seminars, for wardens to take home weekends to watch with the wife when all the *Freddy Kruger* films were out at the local video store. Whirring and clicking, watching him, the cameras moving quickly, scanning the soft scene. Too quickly. Operated by some new boy, scared even sitting four floors away. Watching.

viewing the whispered myth

The safety lighting and the surveillance cameras were the only items wired through a safety fuse box - maniacs and electricity do not an easy union make - but the bulk of the wiring, by virtue of the age of the building being used in that 'mental health kinda way', was quite old. The sprinkler system was not wired to the safety trip. It alone had its own protected supply. Jerusalem knew this. He heard the wires. Knew what the noisy water knew.

It took Jerusalem twenty two minutes to bite through the nine inches of padded rubber and reach the concrete wall. In an hour he had scraped five inches of that away, (pausing only to walk toward the cameras and out stare the starer), and there, in a blue-painted alcove was the conduit. The pipe. Square steel panelled, buzzing with invisible sound. Jerusalem could hear it. Like hated wasps in a hot house. Could hear cracks, weaknesses in steel armour piping. Dug at these, peeled away poor armour, stripped the red plastic sheath covering woven copper wires, exposed the *Power.*

Had sensed it before: complex tracks, internal spiralling movements. Cumulonimbus. Darkness, clouds. The storm.

He tore great sheets of padded rubber from the walls, threw them in a corner. The new guard watched. Two television screens of mad Lamb peeling away his soft walls, digging, biting, chewing. Stripping away outer wrappings of the old black negative circuit. The new guard watched, stone still, afeared to the bone, his only movement the constant pressing of the 'scan' button. The new guard watched Lamb, *insulated,* wrapped in rubber, begin climbing the wall toward the camera, watched him wrench out soft screws holding the camera together, watched as he tore the camera from the wall and watched the mad man hold his face to the lens and stare back at him. Face to face with the Lamb. Like staring at the skull of Christ through grey electric milk. (The new guard was already dead. Heart attack. Death spasm twitching rigory fingers on the 'freeze frame' button. A clattering machine printing out a grainy black and white of Lamb's terrible head.)

Blue black, nice, new fresh wires exposed; the safety lights and security cameras.

He exposed the inner copper cores of all four sets of cable, bundling the newer cables together, thick wiring of the heavily fused sprinkler system, touching, tapping them on the old neutral circuits. 'Playtime' was playing. Too much power in short bursts. The safety lights stuttered on and off, every surveillance camera whirring uncontrollably, resulting in the newer circuitry activating its own cut out. No safe light. No camera.

The air was momentarily intensely electrified.

Sound travels slower than light. He heard it, knew it was coming.

He waited, wrapped in rubber, cables held in hands.

He heard far enough away, the sound, fury and nothingness of thunder - an old bearded, (slowly dying), man wet-farting.

Darkness, clouds...

When the lightning struck the building he slammed the cables together, breaching neutral to earth for the lightning bolt to *use* the neutral circuit to rip through each light, socket and every old wire throughout the institution.

Snug in rubber, the lightning was not interested in him, *he* wasn't the way home. Lightning, like water, is lazy, it will take the easiest route.

Down, through, *along...*

Lightning looking for earth. Fuse boxes exploded, wires overheated causing sparks, fire. *Too much power.* Another old gothic madhouse up in flames. Oak, pine, dark, dark engineering bricks.

The sprinkler system melted.

Until, running amok, the lightning hit a small copper pipe in a toilet. Gone to ground. A complete circuit.

The force of the explosion tore the cell apart, blew a hole clean through four floors. Jerusalem would have been blinded by the flash had he not been shrouded in padded rubber. Ten seconds after the lightning strike, the thunder made its little rumble. Long enough for the deed to be done, the walls rent wide, and the mad man to be bounced literally through the flames, out, down and away.

Passing insects and spiders were sucked into the building by the torrential rush of oxygen through air bricks. Their silly screams and the screams of men blended, howling, *whistling* as the movement of burning air turned Crowfields into a giant wind instrument. Flutes, tubas, sax. Fire sounds like song. That is its noise. Burst into flames. Burst into song. Mad music. Insane opus. Big loony tunes played out to the singing flame. How satisfying.

Crowfields was powered entirely by electricity. Two hundred and eighty eight security doors opened wide. Alarm bells could not ring. The fire soon spread. So did the smoke. No lights in the madhouse. No one could see their way to the emergency generator. Most of the inmates suffocated. Others burnt. The warders who were not murdered by crazed inmates, either choked or were electrocuted. The dead, excluding jailors and jailed, numbered doctors, nurses, cleaning staff, engineers, social workers, clerical, personnel, gardening staff, the chaplain, telephonists and a surprise visiting delegation from Whitehall, investigating unofficial reports of brutality. There weren't enough body bags in six counties for them all.

And in the ashes of Crowfields, there lay a torn picture. A grainy black and white freeze frame. Half the picture crisped away. One edge ripped. Half a face. Half a man.

Jerusalem had escaped. Left an asylum in flames behind him. Tabloids told of **500 DEAD IN BUGHOUSE HOLOCAUST**. He ran away through a field of corn, stole a scarecrow's baggy suit and shoes. Fed on rats, found and followed train tracks. He knew where they led. Somewhere gone bad. He could hear the decay seething through the lines. Within a week he was in London. The outskirts and the Church of Rust beckoned.

"Finished?"

"Finzzzzzzzzd?"

"Fzzzzzzzzzz."

The noise came from a dust mite. Jerusalem could not see it, had no need to. Could hear it. The mite crawled across a desert of paper. A torn Bible page. Exodus .3. Crawling across the **H** of the phrase, **I AM THAT I AM.** Jerusalem takes the page, crushes it, tosses it on the fire. Watches it crack, shrivel.

"Finished?" asked the Voices.

"No," replied the Lamb.

4

...a duller spectacle this earth of ours has not to show than a rainy day in London.
***Thomas de Quincey* - The Pleasures of Opium**

Television? The word is half Latin and half Greek. No good can come of it.
C.P. Scott

"Bored," insists Ernie. "Bored."

Norman sits at the kitchen table knitting furiously. Ernie stares at drizzle through the window. Four gas rings burn fierce on the oven. There are no lights turned on. Rain gloom colours the kitchen cider bottle brown. Two half mugs of tea on the table. An orgy of inactivity punctuated only by klik klak of number 8 knitting needles, the odd thud of thunder and Ernie's protests.

"Bored, Norman. Bored."

Fish drops a stitch as well as his bowels. "Oooh, now look what you've made me do..."

"Norman?" whines Ernie.

Fish opens his mouth as if to speak, but he has forgotten his lines.

Finally: "What?"

"I'm bored."

There's rain on the window like painted harpoon scratches. Gulls are tossed by invisible terrors. Grey-sienna lightning. The coldness is almost theatrical.

Storms crowd the clouds. Cue taken, Roane walks on.

He's re-dressed in villainous black, a blanket wrapped about him: a drink-hungry *Carry On Cowboy* Indian. He wants to talk, to *ask*, but he can't, not knowing how, as if talking was painful. He takes a seat at the table. Norman is too busy for looking up, lost in woolly labyrinth. Ernie, a stork with cramp, shifting weight from one foot to another, stiff with boredom, trying to outstare the tempest.

Neither saw Roane enter, or knew he was among them. He was not there, so could speak freely.

"Where's Jackson?" he asks.

Ernie answers, thinking the voice to be Norman's. "Went to a club last night, after the wedding."

"When will he be back?"

Fish answers this time. Overacting as usual: "Ooh, I don't rightly know, Ernie. Hope he's back in time for dinner. Roast beef tonight."

Jackson could be anywhere, might never return. Roane needs all three of them together. Must show them all the rooms, no use one or two of them at a time. They were all four left the madhouse, bequeathed the secret rooms of the second floor, it was only fair all four have at least one chance to see them, to *know*.

They did not see him come. They do not see him go.

After a minute, Norman looks up, shivers, turns to Ernie, but Ernie has not moved since the scene started. He stands, face to rain-window-audience, dumb in his tears. Unprompted. A role of stone.

Rain has clogged radio waves. Fish in the kitchen, bleating over boiling sprouts, half ignoring a fluke Radio Suffolk(?), Tasmania(?) transmission. Some nasal ponce 'talking' to a comic book 'expert'. The 'expert' says "absolutely," a lot. Drops a lot of unimportant names, grows fat on the fact that he knows 'personally' the 'Mexican' who dotted the 'I's on the speech balloons for issue one of *Angel and the Ape*. He's a git, posing as a poseur and getting it wrong. He cannot even masquerade. Even Norman cannot stomach the continuous insignificance of it all. He flicks channels. Radio 4. A documentary on the rising infant mortality rate in Bradford due to cancer. Anything is preferable.

Roane sits in his room, Tookesbury Hall blueprint curled in his lap. Curtain drawn, hiding from the rain.

Face slung down, a 'looking for me lost season ticket' look of near anguish in the eyes. Mouth like a cup of fish hooks, near pursed, sharp, *featured* and blue. Tree trunk arms slow in their action. Coal in the pockets of a big black coat filling out his top half. There is no bottom half. No legs. Mr Jackson strides languid up the rain gravel driveway. An almost edible sadness to his aura. He does not see the rain.

He finds Norman and Ernie sitting in the kitchen for warmth. Ernie yelps with relief, asks a mass of questions.

"Where'd you go after the wedding?"

Jackson's reply is too swift. Practiced: "Remembered Saturday night eight to nine were happy hour at the Drink 'Til U Drool Bar, Isleworth way. Bailey's Irish Cream night, couldn't miss that!" Bravado. Tired lies. There is no joy in the violence of his words. He has the (scarred) look of a man scared by the beggars down on the South Bank. Mouth tight as a St. Trinian's suspender belt. His temporary colours of favour have faded. He becomes suddenly distracted by small nothings, lifts the kettle, shakes it, fills it from the tap. Roots through his pockets, does not know where the pockets are. A newly 'acquired' coat. He tugs out last Thursday's copy of the Sporting Life, tosses it on the table.

Norman finishes knitting, proudly holding up a lopsy green grey mohair effort, "There, finished."

Ernie looking at pictures of Sporting Life horses.

Jackson investigates the sugar bowl.

"Well, don't ya want to know what it is?" Fish asks,

hopeful. "It's for Ernie's (whisper) *bag*." Norman points to the baggy lump of colostomy bag in Ernie's slacks.

"Oh," says Jackson. "Oh."

Dinner: the usual pantomime. Roast beef tasting like Fairy Liquid - Snot sweet. Potatoes, peas, sprouts, grey as ashes on the hearth. Winter on a plate. Fish however, is self sufficient in praise. "I thought that were right lovely. Very tasty."

Mr Jackson, mouth screwed up, pulling a face like Popeye snorting spinach, burps, spits out a sliver. It lands on Norman's plate. There's a sudden (but expected) outburst from Norman's bottom. "Aaaaay, eeeeeee, iiiiiiii, ooooh, uuuuuuu!" Five rasps of ruinous wind: bowel vowels. And no one speaks for twenty minutes.

Mr J and Ernie sit around picking tomorrow's winners from the Sporting Life. Seven nags, a Yankee. A fifty pence stake. Ernie is unsure about parting with such cash. He asks Jackson if Ladbrokes would take a cheque.

Six o'clock: Ernie calling out, "There's an Arab at the front door!"

Mr J investigates, mistrusting arrivals of any unknown. Arabs, especially, were to be avoided particularly after that episode in *El Harik* with the camels.

But it's a false alarm. It's no Arab, but an Indian. Imram Poones, the hedonophobic manic depressive. Accompanying him, the Reverend Syd Dacy, his dog collar pulled tight around a surgical neck support. And standing in the exterior shadows, in pyjamas, dressing gown and damp slippers, the white-haired wonder: Nelson Browne. It is the Reverend Dacy who speaks: "Let us bastard in, me knob's turning into a fuckin' ice cube."

"Stab me sideways," says Mr J, "it's a fucken' party!"

Mayhem.

The three arrivals ensconce themselves savage in the gothic splendour of the Hall. "Brought some tinnies," offers the Reverend, rattling a carrier. Imram asks if it would be OK to call the Samaritans. Nelson Browne squelches in circles, smirking with moist slippery comfort.

Norman pops up, waving arms, legs. Premature gesticulation on an imaginary unicycle. "Oooh, 'ello, glad ya could make it..." He turns to Nelson, "Ooh, come sit by the fire, dry yaself off, must be frozen..." Grim, not wanting warmth, Nelson whips out a Swiss Army penknife, officers-only corkscrew attachment swinging to and fro in Norman's general direction. "Oh, thank you," says Norman, calmly accepting the corkscrew, heading off to the kitchen and Jackson's unopened wine.

Poones, Nelson and the Reverend were encountered yesterday; the wedding. Friends neither of the bride and groom, but a loose collection of inadequate individuals drawn to gatherings of abnormal nature: fatal séances, ratcatchers' funerals, Satanistic coffee mornings. Travelling the world in a hot-wired hearse, they are the blameless bystanders who can never be found. Those three fleeting faces on burnt-out Evening Standard front pages (late edition). Some call them freaks or miscreations; call them what you will, but they do *know* how to have a good time.

Jackson had invited them yesterday. Jackson had done a lot of things yesterday, most of them to Norman. Attempted murder it's called. Death by Karaoke was far in a way the most original. Other attempts were more straight forward. Setting fire to his trouser cuffs, tying him to the bridal car with a strong rope etc.

"Where's the totty, then?" winks the Reverend.

Imram slams down the receiver. "Bloody engaged!"

"Hooooooooooooo!" simpers Nelson Browne, pouring a bottle of stout over his already drenched slimy slippers.

Fish with wine; "Well, here we all are then."

Ernie runs up, loud, showing off with Maudsley. "'e can talk, can bird." Maudsley says nothing. "Say 'ello, birdy, 'ello." Maudsley is unimpressed.

"What happened to ya neck, then, Rev?" asks Mr J.

"A number four iron." His only answer.

What follows are stories, reminiscences of older reminiscings: tall and taller tales, all true. Self-censored phantasmagoria told in vicious pick-axe-aresque: escapes and alibis from La Rochelle to Bodmin Moor, Ibiza to the Norfolk Broads, that 'incident' in the Vatican. The chickens! The trio are bathed in a warm golden glow, it looks like the light of a late summer's afternoon; kind, giving, but it's not. The 'glow' originates from Imram Poones' mouth. Brutish dental work and newly 'inherited' gold-filled teeth pliared from corpse cousin. Priceless incisors, Midas-mouthed. All he will say on the matter is, "Cousin Smiley owed me money."

Dacy asks if there's a television, wants to see the news, something about a 'suspicious death'.

"Aye," says Jackson. In quick minutes a 52 inch colour television dominates the sitting room. "Latest thing from Japan, that is." Mr J nods toward the telly.

Nelson growls at the country's name, but Poones is at hand, comforts Browne, does not need to see the blank spaces on the old man's hands where fingernails once grew, he knows the POW story.

Jackson, Fish, Poones, Browne, Ernie, and the Reverend shoved together on an overstuffed settee. Six of them: an unhinged pentacle. Mr J has the remote, flicks *ON* to scenes of carnage, the human sushi bar of a derailed bullet train. Landslides in Azerbaijan. Flash floods in Senegal. Kate Adie. A war everyone thought had finished. Close ups, always close ups. Ethiopians watching *Neighbours* as they starve. Cannibals with microwaves. The milk of human kindness curdled. Closer to home: *another* IRA incendiary device. Rabies. Shallow graves. A gas explosion in Fulham and finally, *"the dismembered remains of a promising young radio playwright were today found inside several Harrods carrier bags outside the Victoria and Albert museum, South Kensington..."* A publicity photograph is flashed up on screen. Poones, Browne and Dacy give a little cheer. The picture is that of an oriental male, late twenties, with a face spottier than Jeffrey Archer's 'supposed' back. You can smell the halitosis through the screen. You can hear the stutter like an Uzi clogged with clay. The name is unpronounceable - seven silly syllables. *"...almost unrecognisable... ceremoniously hacked to pieces...police wish to contact a man...eliminate him from their..."* a photo-fit flashed on screen. *"...enquiries."* The computer image has the same grim cardboard features as the In Jail prisoner on the tenth square of any Monopoly board. The face, albeit a bastard of suspects, is remarkably similar to that of the Reverend Sydmond Dacy. All it lacks are the surgical collar and the scar-like bite marks on his lower grey lip: savage kiss. No one on the sofa says a word. Norman and Ernie clutch at one another. Shivering siblings.

Poones asks for a pen and some paper, time for an abridged suicide note. Maudsley sits on Poones' turban, pecking bits out. Jackson, channel zapping with the remote: religious programme. Scars on Sunday. Lots of new hats and cut shaved faces miming Blake's words. Self appointed angels. Haloes in hock.

"Cunts," says Dacy. "Cunts with a small 'c'. Self righteous wankers." He's making the sign of self abuse: greasing an invisible cattle-prod. "Father, Son an' Holy Ghost? Fuckin' troilism, mate." He nudges Jackson's arm, winks. "Little bastards!"

Televisual glare fuelling pub climate: cigarette smoke ghosting above the sofa, sour brown air of canned lager, the smell of old men and wee. The warm heat of impending vehemence.

Channel zapping:

"Fucking aristocracy," growls Dacy as the credits roll at

the end of a documentary about the royal family. "'ere," - he nudges Norman - "ever noticed the remarkable facial similarity between Princess Diana, there, and Myra Hindley?"

Norman can only dribble.

Brian Ferry's face appears on the screen – "Fox hunting Cunt!" and then some applause.

Zap. Channel 4. An African charity appeal - the familiar calm voice-over segued between a desolate landscape, fly-eaten natives, green fields, running water and smiling brown-skinned children. The voice-over celebrity appears on screen, serious; white t-shirt, no makeup, pale Chinos. Jackson and the others are unsure who it may be. From the distance of the sofa to the television it's hard to tell the difference, it could be any one of the Dream Tickets - Jonathan Ross - Paula Yates - Lenny Henry - Barbara 'Babs' Windsor - David Mellor - Nigel Kennedy - Damien Hirst - Terry Wogan – Katie (Jordan) Price - Alan Titchmarsh - Chris Evans – Gyles Fucking Brandreth - or any other waste of oxygen 'personality'.

Mr Jackson decides he has been too quiet, too long and belches majestically.

Zap. A re-run of The Tube or is it The Word? "Rat's knackers!" spits Jackson. Dacy attacks him bodily, a small skirmish takes place for control of the zapper. "I'm not watching that crap!"

Dacy rabbit punches Jackson below the belt, follows up by nutting him, but misses.

Ernie and Norman are visibly shaken.

The zapper is stabbed at. Finger after vicious finger. Channels blip...

It's all a blur.

Another face invades the screen. Who's that? Could be anyone - a swallowing bi RADA reject or permed 'unmarried' comedian - any one of endless smiley glad hands or life-sized cardboard cut-out clones with plastic tits, hair pieces: another well scrubbed soap star, perma-tanned to the bone, blinded by sorbeted angel photofloods, fixed-grinning like a cunt to camera, coked-up on sincerity, autocuing rewritten ad-libs. Famous-for-nothing - singing?, dancing? - *proper* stars. Shit wrapped in ribbons. The studio audience - a glut of fractious Afro-Carribeans - subliminal celebs - fifteen seconds of (edited out) Mexican Wave fame. (And there, waiting in the wings - the liggerati, hospitality feeders, hopeless hacks, pro-nobodies, *another* fucking transsexual.) Television - the world in a bubble. Life cappuccino'd down to thirty minute instalments of froth: makeovers, game shows, life-style shows, talk shows, phoney phone-ins, reality TV and emotional studio debates. Ten million years of evolution had led to this - effortless immortality, lipsynched spontaneity. Old rope.

"Behold also, the gallows fifty cubits high." quotes Poones.

"Eh?"

The insults fly as do fists. All a blur...

Screams of "Fat old ringworm!" when a celebrity chef, her father's daughter, appears on screen.

Dacy joins in, "Yeah, cunt like a horse's neck!"

"Tits like terriers!"shouts Poones, completing the triad.

They watch as she sucks sour cream off her fingers.

Even Norman crosses his legs.

"I 'eard she's got a cunt like a torn out fireplace!"

Mr J with a laughing mouth of knuckles: "Dyke! Wouldn't put me finger in it!"

"I wouldn't touch 'er with yours!" from Dacy.

Zap. It's the South Bank Show.

"Big fat elephant's fanny!" But Poones is a zap too late.

It's Melvyn Bragg and, as Nelson Browne so eloquently puts it, 'some silly bitch' who has apparently written a book. It's quite a surprise, as she looks as if she would have difficulty in remembering her own name, let alone writing it. She sits there, in turn pursing her lips and sucking in cheekbones, as if sucking off a ghost. She says, "yah" a lot. One of the characters on the sofa - any one of them, even Ernie - comments that it seems anyone can write a book these days, just as long as they are related to Clement Freud. Surely there must be some 'supernatural' connection somewhere, what with all those ghost writers, ghost agents and ghost readers. For it seems spooky how much is paid for in advance, then written, finally published, the prizes automatic.

"Fuck that."

Jackson zaps channels.

BBC2. *Call My Bluff.* Robert Robinson.

Sue Lawley is a team captain this week. Poones is not impressed.

Robinson pings his bell, up comes the word CAFARD.

Jackson offers, "Great big green cheesy helmet flakes!" No one's sure if it's an insult or an answer.

Ten minutes of solid abuse.

Shouts of "Papist!" when Ned Sherrin appears.

PING!

The new word is HYSTERESIS.

"Chickenshit," gums Nelson Browne.

Zap. BBC2. Something arty with Kenneth Brannagh. "Who?" asks the sofa. Jackson lobs his beer can at him.

"Go on J, chin the bastard," invites Dacy.

Jackson gobs, it hits the screen. The screen dents.

Poones roots round for a bogey, hooks one, a nice greasy ball of snot, rolls it dry, flicks it, landing in the dent of the screen, giving it a dimple. "Ha! Kirk Douglas!" Laughter like Armageddon. Not a dry seat in the house.

Zap. A party political broadcast. Nelson Browne loosens his dressing gown. Around his waist, a toy cowboy holster, he pulls out two guns, left and right, plastic yellow water pistols. "You jug of farts!" he yelps, squirting the pistols first at the telly, then, thinking better of it, he turns them on his slippers. "Ooooh," is all he has to say, satisfied as the only living man with a damp slipper fetish can be.

ZAP!

The endless self applause of back-slapping actors, politicians, artists, critics. The noise isn't clapping, it's the sound of spines snapping. Zap between classical and soap, sitcom and newsflash, it's all the same face, just a different mask. Lear on top, Bilko underneath. Groucho Marx *is* Hamlet: *To be or not to be? Ah, to hell with it, I'll have the soup."*

Some people consider art a four letter word. It isn't. 'Fart', however, *is*.

Stiff Fish. Norman, near narcoleptic, starched of cheek, cannot keep his bum quiet. Great fruity rasps are threatening to detonate the sitting room. With unknown power he holds the others in a juicy *possession,* they're going nowhere if there is a chance of an explosion.

Zap and zap again...

"The man is a bucket of badger spunk!"

"Motherfucker!"

"White trash!"

"Minge-piece throwback!"

"Slag," agrees Jackson.

"Vile Festilug!" adds Maudsley.

Even Ernie has a go: "Poo baggage!"

"Chutney ferret!"

"Tosser!"

"Nonce!"

"Bedsore!"

"Tatty-bollocked goat-fucker!"

"Cunts! Cunts! They're all cunts!"

The Reverend Dacy lobs a conveniently empty Valpolicella bottle through the television screen. A small flash and loud bang happen. Silence for a moment, then they collapse, weep in untameable joy, forgotten who, or what they were shouting at. Even Maudsley admits a stupid tear. Fish though, an anchor, stony still as an Easter Island head. Static in his fear, poo in his pants.

The wine and beer all gone. Spirits now. Jackson and Poones talk together on death. Poones is a strange one. Phobic on fun, manic depressive too, talk to him long enough about dying and he gets giggly, silly as a schoolboy. See, depression is also a mania. Too much of one triggers off the other. A fine line between fun and fun-eral.

The Reverend teaches Ernie to play poker. In the background a country and western tune. Willy Nelson's *Gypsy Woman.*

Death and poker. *A fine line…*

Midnight: Nelson Browne announces he wants the toilet. Returning after forty minutes, dank of slipper. "Laid a big brown sausage…"

"Ooooh, I hope ya flushed it," shivers Fish.

Browne reports: "Couldn't flush. No chain to pull. Couldn't find the bathroom."

"Well, where did ya go, then?" screams Norman.

"I did it in *your* bed. Wiped me bum on ya pillow case. Nice an' soft it were too,"

A one man apocalypse ensues. Fish invents a new energy: foul bowels and fright propelling him seemingly through the ceiling. How anything human could move so fast is beyond debate. Howls, wails. Fishy lamentation. A bawled flat threat.

A curious sober interlude finds Poones, Browne, and Dacy gathering their things. Departing. Nelson Browne feet first, carried out. Led to a puddle and lowered into it. Grin like a broken flea comb. Collars turned up, unspoken, the three climb into their hearse. Poones in the back, lying flat, arms crossed over chest: practicing. Through rain, Dacy gives a nod. Jackson acknowledges.

Then they are gone.

The rain is addictive now. Without it there is no night, no ending, just senseless repetition of ritual, like Ernie's morning mantra: "Bored, bored. *Bored.*" The sweary evening had been the same, though instrumental in its savageness. For every 'shit' 'piss' 'wank' 'fuck' 'cunt' 'bollocks' 'bastard' spoken was a plea. Primal screams. Brutal self exorcisms. Integral convocations of the devil named 'Change'? (Nah, just old men swearing.) Or maybe they *had* purged continuum, left it broken like a bombed Mormon church. Surely *something* must happen soon.

Jackson knew all about it, knew the reasons, but it's taken its toll. He takes himself off, locks himself in. Ernie calling out, "Night night." Jackson answers, trying hard to be nice, as if he'd done something wrong.

Elsewhere -

Roane, asleep, self-wrapped in painted strait jacket. Oil colour night sea journey, sea serpents, a craft of mad men. *No land in sight.* Head pressed to his stomach, balled up, wriggling in shadow as if swallowed and in the belly of a whale, fish or dragon. Drowning all he knows in thoughts of his own. New thoughts as dark as the wild, driving rain.

Fold. Fold again. Dripping wax off a greasy candle. Waterproof the beast. Mr Jackson building a newspaper sailboat: **HMS SPORTING LIFE.** Yesterday, the wedding, after breaking the DJ's only copy of '*We are Sailing…*', he had fled, jumped the last train to Portsmouth, had wanted to see the sea. England's an island, Jackson's the shipwreck. Half a castaway with itchy feet. Thoughts of escape: water, blue as a whaler. Becalming diesel chug of engines running on the swell. The familiarity of any foreign tongue. *Maps.* Drowned men buried below the tidemark. He toyed with taking a row boat, it would probably have sunk. Plastic pleasure boats only an industry, not a life. Gone the days of 'she oak' and cold iron. No bloody good. Can't sail sand. Still on dry land.

He had mistaken his wants. It's no use *seeing* the sea from land, it's seeing the land *from* sea, that matters. *Knowing* that you are on your way. Never arriving. Departure is **all.**

Jackson, like a figurehead, bereft of legs. Naked women, anchors, Christ tattooed on his spine. Leaning from his window, newspaper boat tossed to the tempest. It floats away, *departing,* full winds to the sail in rain-washed gutter oceans.

There is the sudden smell of spice. He remembers rum on bruised gums.

Cloudward, gulls killing over bacon rind.

"Bastads," whispers Jackson.

Inside, there's a barometer kicking zero. He looks out and all he can see is land.

"Bastads."

And just how does a man with no legs outrun his nightmares?

5

...nothing is random to a man of knowledge:
everything he sees or hears is just there at that time to be seen or heard.
Don Juan

Day hits like some punch-drunk southpaw. Night's shadow lost. Slow time, new light licking at artificial life. Ever watch the sun come up? Like someone left the lid off God's paint box: tandoori reds, golds. A blue as blue as blue jeans.

Six a.m. Caton's Bar, New Billingsgate Fish Market: The Isle of Dogs. Mr Jackson sharing Bavarian vodka with old man Caton himself. Shot glasses, one swallow, gone.

Monday morning, nothing happening, the place as empty as a bottle. There's no Sunday fishing worth talking about, so there's no fresh fish on Monday.

"Not like the past, uh?" sighs Caton. "Church could wait, then. Sea was the only goddess. Nets, *ice,* muscle. None of that now, all mechanised. Businessmen now, suits, ties. Watches still on New York time. Five hours slow! Time marches on mate, for some."

But Jackson is comfortable here: the Grecian leather perfume of ice skin fish. *Hull, Grimsby, Aberdeen.* Oil on cobblestones. The memory of *running.* He downs three bottles of brown.

Behind the bar, Caton works wonders with an iron frying pan. In goes the egg and up pops Wally. Wally Todman: one of Billingsgate's few surviving Scats. *Scats?* Methos, who scrounged wage pulling barrows up Fish Street Hill. Turps ghosts, who don't know they've forgotten how to die. Wally is a sad case: no buttocks, anorchid too. He can't sit down, if he does, he slips off the chair. Sleeps on a diving board. He falls over a lot, no centre of balance, so he wears a full laden leather/cork 'Bobbin' hat originally worn by Agincourt archers, and later used for carrying crates of fish on head in the *old* market. On a 'fragile' day he's weighed down with a hammerhead, a more 'stable' day will find him light with dab. His gravity is a dead fish. This Monday morning finds him hammerheaded and hungry, not for sausage, egg and beans, but for the detritus left scumming up Caton's frying pan. Sizzly lumps of charred lard resembling truffles or black bees. Wally takes a straw, sucks it up. A diet of grease.

Behind the bar, amidst Sun bingo cards, is the skull of a horse. Between slavers of bacon, Mr Jackson is curious.

Caton explains: "Found it. Washed up it was, down by Cherry Garden Pier."

"A lucky token, then?" suggests Jackson.

"Not as such." Caton takes a swig of tea, swills it round; begins. "The horse is worshipped, at least in skull form - the Mari Lwyd - a Hobby-Horse, and there's already a clue in the name, 'Hobby', a pastime, strictly amateur ritual. Anyhow," he continues, only half knowing, "at a knacker's yard the skull is bought by well-meaning but ecologically sound fools. The skull's then garlanded and pulled out at Christmas time, taken door to door, the idea being it has to gain entry to each house visited by means of a riddling song. Anyway, if the occupants of the house can't finish the song, and none of them bloody well can, they must let the Mari in and give it a drink. Why not? Season of goodwill after all. Some *real* Christmas spirit; Glenfiddich, Dutch Gin. Now, after a time, the fools with the Mari get well tanked up, pissed as farts, and they're banging on doors, crapping through letterboxes, kicking in faces of plaster gnomes, no one wants to know, they'd rather invite a Jehovah's Witness in. Y'see, the Mari Lwyd was turfed out of the stable in which Christ was born, and now has to wander the land in search of somewhere to stay, so in a way, the fools have got it right! No one wants to know them, *or* the Mari. Ha! They've drowned in their own realities, finished off the dregs of Christmas punch, put away the festive skull for another year. Old films are watched, mince pies eaten. Morecambe and Wise or Joseph and Mary, it's all symbiotic."

Two more sips, forks in some cold beans. Caton continues, "Here's another one - hack hooves off a horse, boil them up and you've got yourself glue. Now, skinheads purchase the glue, skulk off, sniff it out of a crisp packet, get high, see hallucinations, visual riddles this time. Strange urban visions. They charge at one another like bulls, canter along motorways. This way, the horse reincarnates, albeit temporarily, living through the thoughts of the glue-minded. Do the skins see what *they* are seeing, or what the **horse** is seeing? The horse remembers: equine eternity - Annual Rhodian sun sacrifices. Driven off a cliff with chariot and spear. The skins jump from bridges, choke on white thoughts, swollen bodies washed up on shores, the sun can rise for another year. The horse belies order. Remakes chaos."

"Glue ya say?" chomps Mr J, "I tried Evo-Stik once, didn't rate it."

Cautious, Caton produces a funerary urn from below the bar's counter, handles it careful, like it was the head of Bran. "Know who's in here?" he asks.

"Nope." Jackson sucking rind.

"These are the ashes of the *late* Charles Walton, Horse Whisperer, claimed, like the Celts, that the beasts were clairvoyant, vulnerable to enchantment."

"That so?" asks Jackson, "How'd he die?"

Murdered.

"Horse Whisperers held power over horses, could

command a response on the wind with a, *Sic jubeo* "I command thus". Most feared of the Whisperers was Walton. Know how it was done? How he could 'talk' to horses?"

Jackson is agog. Tongue like a canoe fighting the rapids of ale and egg.

Caton, palms spread, all smiles and answers, enjoying the role: "Hoof glue again. Walton mixing it up in a stable, gristle and hooves in a pot, partaking of the flesh of horses - *inhaled* it, he did. Don't you see? He *too* got stoned. Intoxicated. It's not just skins who can sniff. Ha, he had a horse in his bloody head, *knew* what the horse was thinking, they could sit and chat for hours, days on end."

"Well fuck my old boots." Mr Jackson, clearly impressed, can't let go of this one, it may be profitable. More ale and an eroded continuance: digressions, sub-plots. Wally Todman has heard none of it, ears clogged with scales, he snatches now the odd dark whisper from Caton and Mr J - "The thirteenth God... Horse sense... **Hayagriva**... *Sacrifice...* Frog bones... Godiva..."

Wally is suddenly coherent. He stops for a second, looking down to his hands, bony ashtray fingers, some missing, pawned like his wedding ring. There is a taste of rotting metal in his mouth. Mental squalor in his head. And in that immediate instant, he screams and screams and screams a scream of what *was*.

She was waiting for him, knew he would come. She had laughed, laughed as he bit her throat open. A fear greedy laugh.

Like Minotaur, he tore through floor, climbed, smashed way up from the lower stinking levels of Old Mrs Tomb's rotting labyrinth. Laughter and the words, "Unclean! Unclean!" spilling from her dusty mouth. One bite, bit through skin, gullet. Sound of bones breaking, the same noise as guilt. Tight loose flesh on fragile neck. Snapped. He had bitten her head off. Ex-sounded her. There was no blood; it had all dried within her.

Stuffed in her bed; stained fifty's porn - air brushed genitals, lipsticked aureola, oiled greasy goddesses. Sepia snapshots of a crucified horse. Embryo bones. Defaced happy endings in a bed of bad secrets.

He kicked her head round the room 'til it broke.

Jerusalem takes the fourth name: P. Tombs, from the fly paper deity. Drops it. Forgotten now, like reason.

He peels away the fifth and last name: J.A. Goldflame. There is a telephone number, an address given as Tookesbury Hall, London. The strip of paper disintegrates. The numbers are remembered.

Elsewhere; noise. Whooping Cough spores. Smeared beef grease on an oval mirror. Blisters on a heel.

"Unclean! Unclean!"

Looking suddenly up, through stained glass shards, at the festering orange scab of the sun. It weeps warmth, the magnetic star. *Weeps.* He would put a noose around the sun, hang it, watch it kick, like a cow on the gallows. Would put the Earth in a box and drown it in carrion. Would, and probably will.

6

Norman Fish still hadn't found his missing Hush-Puppy. Stupidly tragic, *hopping,* wearing the surviving shoe; the hunt for his comfortable slip-on had taken him from the depths of his chamber pot to the very ends of what he considered to be the Earth - his room, Ernie's room, the bathroom, the kitchen. He had hopped round them all, *hoping.* Eager for activity, Ernie joined the search, in the presence of, rather than *with,* Norman. Find them now, poking nose, craning neck, on the second floor. Floor of secrets.

"'ave ya got a screwdriver on ya, Norman?"

"Screwdriver? Screwdriver? What would *I* be doing with a screwdriver on me, eh? *Me* of all persons!" Screaming now. "A SCREWDRIVER!... Oh, 'ang on..." Fish, from his pocket, produces the Swiss Army penknife Nelson Browne attacked him with last night. He hands it over. Ernie accepts, kneeling, not praying, before the first of the many locked doors.

"Whatever are ya doing, Ernie?"

"Pickin' lock." An old skill. At Caterham, nurse had put a padlock on the fridge door, guarding the toffee ration: most things can be bested with a sweet tooth and a ratchet screwdriver.

Klik. "There," says Ernie. The first door opens.

"What are you doing?" The voice is Roane's.

Norman and Ernie leap in sudden fright: Jump-leads on a welcome-mat. "Oooh, ya scared the life out of us..."

Roane, unmoved, repeats, "What are you doing?"

Ernie *explains.* "Looking for Norman's Hush-Puppy."

Burnt Bible black, he stands there, had given up any hope of ever getting them to view these secret rooms, and here they were, the first room opened, looking for a fucking Hush-Puppy. Roane sighs. His hand, a gesture - "Walk on in," and they do.

The room - it *is* a room; walls, ceiling, door, but that's where any similarity to normalcy ends. A light bulb hangs from the room's ceiling, hanging from *it* are smooth transparent tendrils, too numerous to record. The tendrils weave off, cross-crissing, *webbing* themselves, cohering to walls, ceiling, floor, with no visible marks of connection. It's as if the bulb had melted, dripped, spreading fine glass limbs to embrace the room. Suddenly someone, (later, and still no one will confess who), flicks on the light switch. Perfect white light floods the room. Light *pulses* through the tendrils but fades when it meets the walls, floor. Could it have been some form of light-show for Victorian madmen?

None of your ice baths or centrifugal treatments 'ere mate.

Too simple.

"Well," blithers Norman, "I can't see me Hush-Puppy in there. Let's try the next room."

Ernie had been there already, has run from door to door, *tickling* on knee, unpicking, opening wide many secret doors. Guide Ernie scuttles up, takes Norman by the cuff, Roane by the will, hurries them along, ushers them in: the second secret room - baggy canvas walls spittered in dry puddles of darkness. The room has the appearance of a deflated hot-air balloon: the manky yellow brown of a bad summer. On the floor lie six inch lumps of exploded metal. Wrist-thick holes in the wall. Behind the door, (hidden), the stone gnomic face of a fiercely-bearded gargoyle; horns growing through a visor, *three* rows of vertical teeth. The broken grin of something hastily defaced in a Templar church. Only Roane notices the word painted on its forehead. The word *Emeth.*

There is the annoying sound of dry whistling and the sudden aroma of old coldness. The blunt scrape of metal, and poking round door's corner - the crooked face of Mr Jackson showing only instant innocence. (That 'laughing inside' look, threatening your doubt, insisting the answer. 'Asking' "Do I *honestly* look like the sort of bloke who'd go to pet shop, steal a frog, sacrifice it and invoke the *horse-necked demon* with promises of bull blood and bottled breath of a sleeping cat, just to get seven horses to win seven races?")

"Bullets, them are," he says.

"What are?" asks Roane.

Jackson swoops, scoops a fist of buckled metal. Shrapnel. Tosses one to Roane. "'oles int' wall, there. Bullet 'oles. 1940, *Blitzkrieg,* Asylum? Rubber walls. Exploded, burst like a Johnny." With this he turns, gobs, takes himself off, *intends* to leave. But doesn't. And for an instant, there's a pout like a broken tea-pot, and a light in his eyes; a twinkle of grisly Bremen nostalgia? Some favourite regret? "Nothing," he says to no one. "Nothing" not "nowt". Slow as Guinness pourings, shrugging it off, shaking his head. And the shine to his eye is a piece of broken glass.

Norman by now is physically rattling, bounding room to room on his quiet-dog quest. He hops to a room of hieroglyphics from a room of doors, hops from a room of gas masks and poppies to a room with a tree, upside down like Benito Mussolini.

Slouching, finally defeated through bland blend of exhaustion and hectic bunions - dry swallowing tranqs, gagging on the chalky taste - his future does not look good: a cracked crystal ball, a dyslectic Ouija board. *Unbegun,* he begins, "Shall I call the police?"

The response is exclusively violent: sound of a divine dictate - **"NO!"** (although Ernie was sure he heard Roane shout, "Know!")

The debate is halted. Mr Jackson, snake smooth, with his arm round Norman's shoulder, drags him up, friendly like Judas; "No need for rozzers, Fishy. Tell us what ya looking for, an' we'll find it."

Blubbing. "'ush-Puppy..."

Jackson had forgotten. Silly really, might have known this would happen: that morning, before leaving for Billingsgate, he had taken Norman's Hush-Puppy to his room, where he had connected it up to the mains. It was a plan he had made in the night. A couple of words spoken via a dream angel's tongue: *"Hush-Puppys equal death."*

"Waaaaaaaaaaah!" The scream is Ernie's. Murder and its methods are for the moment forgotten.

Ernie in the hallway, crouched, folded, a broken chocolate soldier. His arms wrapped round legs, thumbs pushed in bent rust mouth. Fish, Roane, Mr J gather to him, striking dramatic poses, (three discoverers of Elizabeth Stride, Berner Street 1888 or a trio of yellow card Gazzas, Italia 1990). Norman and his belly let rip. Roane's watch stops. For down the corridor, blue black gold, an apparition in feathers, dried sunflowers heads, a shroud with eyes: Chas Addams' Aztec or cartoon Carmelite, (religion stops at Disney), comes *drifting* toward them, moaning. Is *this* the secret of the asylum - a mad ghost? Something left over from a bad dream doomed to wander the corridors of the second floor? A mad *blue* ghost?

Hardly.

"'ang about," says Jackson, sniffing hard through his one 'good' nostril, head moving with the effort of his s(c)arcastic greeting of, "'ow do, Flinty!"

The apparition pulls off its face. Sure enough, there's Mr Flint beneath it, smiling, voicing his return. "You bugger!"

Calm stampedes through.

Ernie busies himself with the mask. Flint in ceremonial long robe, blue/black design of open hand and eye of Horus,

(Cabbalistic keepsake), has *changed,* sporting a beard now, grisly hair cropped, two more teeth missing, a rope burnt neck, a *new* limp. A sudden lighter aspect to him. Grateful for life, willing to give without repercussion. And just for now, the winter within has thawed. He and Jackson exchange words - shared routes, travellers' secrets. When asked by Ernie of his appearance and journey, the square pupils dilate, the truth lying just out of reach, an 'answer' offered, (which had nothing to do with aborting preparations for Agrippa's 53rd Homunculus with colleagues, a man called Clay, a man called DoubleHead). How long had he been gone? A week? No more than two. But he talks of no time. He had gone from inner to outer time, skimmed the days like stones on a lake. He takes a package from his robes, tosses it to Roane.

Brown paper, string. Torn open - a book. *The Broken Equator: a slender biography of the life and travels of Doctor William Miles* by Mrs Rebecca Hope. Fumbling with pages and words, Roane saying, "Thank you."

"Picked it up in Prague. Might be of interest. It's about a doctor who used to work here. I often heard Judith talking about this bloke. It's written by the girl he was going to marry, but didn't." Flint, shrugging off self-knowledge with a "what's all this then?", dives into an open room. After all, this is the very first time he has set foot in the Hall. Not the first time however, that he had ever set foot in *any* asylum. For he was born in one. Childhood visits to grim old institutions can leave a life-long aversion. Sometimes though, years can tilt the perspective. The threshold not always so intimidating. In height as well as psychically he had grown: a different *physical* view.

In the room - there are bones leaning from a far wall of rock, not of an ape, no *homo diluvii testis,* but the perfect skeleton of a man impacted. A fossilised man caught in a static jump of joy, legs bent, upraised behind him, thigh bones crossed like the number 4. The ribs and spine squashed down, matted together, spine tip poking through giving him a tiny tail. Arms making the semaphore letter **Q.** Grey mud outlines him; a smudged shadow. To his left, and lower, the fossil remains of a small winged reptile. Further, and up to the right, the partially uncovered bones of something huge. Something jawed, fanged. A lightning eater, something from Earth's nightmares. A piece of walking night.

"'ell fire!" announces Jackson, steaming greed first into another room. The others follow. Jackson 'stands' in the centre of the floor. For once he is quiet. He has seen many things, but nothing quite like this: walls, floor, ceiling thick with blood. *Clotted.* On a wall, a picture in a frame, on a small shelf sits a broken clock. The clock is awash with blood, the picture and its frame are painted in blood. There is a window but the only view is scarlet.

"The Angel of Maggots," says Roane, beneath his breath.

Silently they leave the room, close and lock its door.

There are many more rooms. A room of ice, a room of doors within doors, an Egyptian room, sultry and dry to breathe in. A book room, books of dust. A room housing a smaller room. A sharp room. A room thick with melted tin soldiers. A plain room, all white walls. A room like a room in a doll's house, everything perfect in miniature, stools, tables, a bed. The tiny mirror.

There is a room where an angel has been sculpted from its dark marble walls.

A room of pastel shades with decorative holes in the walls. Outside, and the wind blowing, blowing tunes through the holes, like a wondrous recorder or enchanted clarinet.

Poppy room. Turvy tree room. Room of cave paintings and sand. A room with the numeral II pawed into the floor, nothing more. A room full of party balloons and on its walls, in an Art Nouveau surround, a mirror, another mirror, but looked at close, *revealed,* it is secretly frozen Champagne with a polished silver backing.

Ernie has been here before them - the door wide - Inside the room, a hangman's noose swinging to and fro. Flint and Roane take a closer look - the noose is human hair, fifty, sixty brunette years, tailed down and around. Knotted. The floor of driftwood. Through the shabby window, a fall of dirty light. The smell of burnt paper. Even Flint shivers.

Rooms of wonder. Rooms of dread.

Madhouse rooms full of answers with no questions.

Jackson can see the potential; Elstree, Boreham Wood. He could have the new Pinewood here. Hire out the Hall to Dicky Attenborough, use each room as a different set. *Mother of Frankenstein* one day, *Love's Secret Heart* the next. The British film industry would never be the same again. He knows where to lay his hands on cheap Korean monster movie scenery... This could mean serious cash. But stuff that, he's never forgiving Dicky for that 'accent' in *Brighton Rock.* "Great git." No, a different kind of exploitation was needed. Get the Japs over with their Nikons, call it a 'stately home', entry fees, souvenirs, *exit fees!* Top yen.

Mr Flint and Roane investigate the Egyptian room. It all seems painfully familiar to young Roane. Dream *déjà vu.* He has the strongest sense that he can hear buzzing, like that of a fly or some such insect.

Ernie is frolicking, purring through rust, leaping from room to room in joyous wonder; one moment a cowboy, next a spy or superhero. Maudsley has arrived and is perched on the wing of the carved angel in the room of marble walls. He mouths the words to 'Rawhide'.

Norman however, is not so chipper. Smelling salts in one hand, hanky in the other, mopping up his river of sweat. He has no need for hopping anymore; he can just *slide* from A to B in the hunt for his lost shoe. Perspiration propulsion carrying him downstairs to re-search kitchen, bedrooms, loo. He did not find the rooms in the least fascinating, rather the contrary: didn't like the way they were *all* different. It would have been fine if all the rooms were covered in blood or were full of dolly furniture, but not all individual. There is no order to the rooms, they are 'wrong'. No, they did not please him. In fact he found them most distasteful, like the sight of other people's feet.

Mr Flint, curious: "OK. We know the place was an asylum but what," indicating the rooms, "were these? And what, if any, was their purpose?"

Roane in the doorway of the doll's house room. "And who lived *here?"*

"Couldn't give a tuppenny vomit, meself," says Jackson, making mental inventory of everything worth melting down. Films and tourists forgotten, it was scrap now: mad salvage. Could make a few bob out of totalling the place. There's that junk metal dealer down in Camberwell, near the old Greek church... and if that failed, then there's enough here to fill a Lada in a car boot sale, easy.

Just then a phone rings. Thick shivers lick through Roane, Jackson, and Flint. Five a.m. feelings, the news of a death or worse.

"I'll go," says Ernie.

But Fish is already there. Impatient. "Who? Who? Yes, yes... Hang on!" He drops the receiver, yells to Jackson that the call's for him.

It's the nearest thing to nervous that anyone's seen Mr J for a long while. "Fishy, Fishy," hisses Jackson, "who were it? What d'they want? Money?"

"Money? No. It's an accountant called Hill."

"Accountancy? Hill? What ya bloody talkin' about, man?"

"William Hill. A turf accountant," screeches Norman.

Jackson almost jumps down the stairs, within seconds he

is *at* the phone, receiver gulletward, devouring words, numbers, "Ascot...Yankee... *Uncle Tangie* first past the post at 50/1... *Nonios Boy* first at 33/1... Ha Ha!... *Young Etasa* by a nose, 7/1... 20/1... photo finish... rank outsiders... romped home... 'ow much? **'OW MUCH!** Haaaaaaa!" Mr J kisses the phone, bangs it down, picks it back up, yells in the mouthpiece, "I'll be right over, I want it in tens and twenties, untraceable if poss."

That morning after breakfasting at Billingsgate, he'd laid a fifty pence each way Yankee on for Ernie and a little side bet of his own, (there was of course the small matter of a sacrifice and a promised offering...). He'd forgotten about it, until now. Jackson's horse was still running but all of Ernie's seven horses had won. **WON!** His winnings being roughly twelve grand. But this worries Jackson; that's a lot of cash for Ernie to be carrying around, with so many unscrupulous types about... work-shy morticians, beasts with pretty faces, all dodgy as Babylonian astronomy. And what would Ernie *do* with an extra twelve K? He hasn't spent any of his inheritance yet. No, best make it easy for him, don't give him so much, he'd be grateful, anything over a thousand was strictly off limits, Ernie couldn't pronounce it, let alone count it, he'd get a headache trying. Five hundred? Still too much, he'd want it in pennies. Bollocks to it, he can have his 50p back, least that way he hasn't lost anything. Jackson would pocket the rest.

"Twelve fuckin' grand... **TWELVE THOUSAND SMACKEROONIES!"** Mr J *pirouettes* around the hallway, light in his violence. Smile akin to something from a Valium-induced sexual fantasy. Thinking - fuck Mr Rind, he can have his four grand with interest. Fuck 'em all. Fuck killing Fishy for his measly little legacy; still it were fun trying. Good old Caton, good old Charles Walton. Must remember to unplug Fish's Hush-Puppy from the mains..."

"Everything alright?" Flint calls down the stairs.

Purse-lipped, blowing a kiss to God, Jackson shouts up, "*Sic jubeo*! Ha Ha!"

"Oh, I see," confirms Flint.

Jackson is gone. Off for a celebratory crap. Off to pay thanks to a horse-necked god and a willing toad.

J.A.Goldflame. There is a telephone number, an address given as Tookesbury Hall, London.

The candle of his soul, flickering - Jerusalem Lamb, shapeless in garment of ash; a cremated monk, stands face to face with magpie skulled used-up god. Maggots have picked clean feathers, flesh, eyes. The maggots were impaled on a pin and burned.

Face to face. Skull to skull.

Lamb begins kicking at the base of the non-god, kicking at the bronze feet of Christ, kicking out six inch nails, kicking away the floor until the suspended statue gives way, spinning on its rope.

Sacred suicide.

Jerusalem slams out, smashing the bronze, sending it swinging back, forth, slamming the bronze gut like it was an open mouth or punch bag. Fly-paper arms 'flying', the dead magpie wings flapping with motion - the face wanting to leave the body. A body of bronze boned over in damp, change and decay; the head of a bird, a body of a man. Egyptian sun god. Horus (Horrors) swinging to, fro, like Poe's pendulum. Back, forth.

Rhythm and flow. Energy and matter filling a momentary space. Lamb steps back, watches. The thick rope tied to wood nave roof. To. Fro.

The noise, a *swyyyyyeeeeeeeeeeeee,* is a noise of time, like a whistling grave. Time is only noise.

Crouched, his hand, a slab of black pork, hovering over the Bakelite telephone, hell in head, and the skulled pendulum sway above him...

"A bilious mystery," crow the Voices.

Too many words.

It means nothing: time - the edge of a circle, the squared route of reason.

Measurements in quantum bullshit.

DO IT!

"Fifty pee! Fifty pee! Yippee! Ernie gives a tiny jump.

Mr Jackson has broken the news of Ernie's *little* win.

"Norman, Norman, I've won fifty pee!"

But Norman can't stop. No time, see? Tearful, spiteful. Pushing Ernie to one side, darting floor to floor, going off on so many tangents he's a geometrist's golden boy, squeezing into crannies, nooks, in his eternal Hush-Puppy undertaking.

"Well done, lad. What you gonna spend it on?" asks Flint in the Explorer's room, touching fingers to cave painting paint.

Easy. Ernie has already decided: "Cuttlefish for Maudsley."

"Nice one," says Flint.

And then it happens, the sound. Like some deep sea beastie roaring: familiar sound distorted. Fearful.

The telephone is ringing.

Again

A kind of seminal shorthand telepathy raps through Roane and Mr Flint. The message is there, they just don't know what it is: braille without the bumps. Night with no stars. For the first time, their eyes meet, the tableau frozen: soft panic. Slo mo, *waiting for time,* Roane turns his head, watching Ernie making his way down, just in case there's another 50p in the offing. Jackson is *nowhere.* Norman is in every room, blurring the edges. And then Flint has moved, getting smaller, far away, but it is Roane who moves, running down the stairs, looking up, stairwell giving secret pattern of a square ammonite, Flint's face peering over one side. But Flint has changed. Cave paint trailed across face: billiard chalk blue, Incan red. Like something twice born. Like a warning.

"I'll go," chirps Ernie, hand on receiver, but suddenly Roane is there, a shadow with a name, pushing Ernie out of the way, taking up the bone of receiver. Listening. He does not talk, he breathes. Breathes down the mouth-piece, the sounds spiral though the line like an unwound turban: history sounds - daft rasp of dragging lace across a sheep skull. The icy shrill of a playtime whistle, the pale sounds of marble. A dead girl, any of Klimt's red heads. The tender crunch of breaking finger bones. Cold hand, blue heart. Dug graves, crows and roses. The words, *"not enough belief..."* Past life arrangements made in rain. And all the time, the laughing *sound* of rain through the wire, taunting Lamb like he was a comedian or disgraced priest.

Jerusalem understands.

The phone has gone dead. All that Roane heard down the line was the sound of a nod. An agreement.

Ernie has picked himself up, dusted himself down. Looks at Roane like a child looks at a drunken stranger.

"Sorry," says Roane, but not to Ernie.

Messrs Flint and Jackson appear. Flint is only subdued, wiping cave colours from face, as if it too were an apology.

Jackson bruises the quiet, "What's the matter wi' you's all? Like wet weekend at Whitley Bay. Seen more life in a bag o' nutty slack. I'm off up west, any takers?"

There is an explosion and a sudden scream.

Smoke billows from an upstairs room. The downstairs lights flicker and stutter off.

"Ooh bugger," says Mr J.

Flint, Roane, Ernie, dash upstairs, find Norman face down in Jackson's room, smouldering. The lost Hush-Puppy clasped in his fist, burnt to a crisp, only the rubber sole intact. It had been attached to the mains: two bare wires and a Bulldog clip. Jackson had forgotten to disconnect it. Silly really.

An ambulance arrives, takes Fish away. The others follow, leaving a madhouse without power: electric power.

The damage done, all Maudsley can offer is a prudent, "Cheerio."

Celebration, rooms, drink, destiny - postponed.

7

Let no one enter who does not know geometry
Inscription on Plato's door

Driving in my car
Madness

The car is parked on top of a hill. It is light metallic blue in colour. The salesman once called it 'Trojan Blue'. The noise it makes is that of a scorpion willingly stinging itself to death. Jerusalem can hear this, considers it. Acts.

The door is unlocked, waiting. He tears it off, needs no invitation.

Inside now. It's a metal cage with padded interior. No bars at the windows: careless. Above him first, something flimsy, giving. He rips through it, the sun roof. Above him now, through the vinyl rent, he sees only sky. Cinder grey dusk clouds full of laughter and rain. Clouds in shapes of hearts, fists. *Leaping,* he punches out, arms pounding, denting roof, smashing right side window, kicks at steering wheel - jamming gears in fourth. Breaking space like limbs, possessing empty with his necessary conflict - the mad man.

Biting through yellow black wires, sparking, fusing. Wires that kiss together with static *slizzz* of joy. Ignition wires melted, joined, smoking. Hand-break snapping, car trembling, rocking into 'life', lurching suddenly forward, floating down hill, cruising slow like falling over. Then it **bursts** with power, ramming Lamb back, slamming his brown-bound rags of feet into the accelerator. Something mechanical fails, locks. Downhill at fifty. Sixty.

It's a very high hill. The scenery blurs, detail is molten.

Seventy when **Car** hits the straight. Engine sustained, *eighty-five, ninety* when **Car** hits the child. Something shears off. Sparks.

Dynamic, dramatic, Jerusalem; king on a moving throne, stands, screaming out of sun-roof abyss, screaming at Earth, screaming at sounds of grease and speeeeeeeeed. Sounds of **Car** radio kicking in: words, words - *"...curious Roman tradition, which has apparently been preserved in parts of the English Fens, is that of using a toad as a primitive compass. The Romans used to place a dagger blade on a toad's back; it is said that the creature would move around slowly until the dagger pointed due north and then stop..."* He leans in, rips it out, throws it off.

Car carves into a Daimler, spins off left, clipping a cyclist. She falls under the wheels of an oncoming bus.

Traffic lights screaming red noise. A pedestrian, a louder scream: foetal canticles.

It's after rush hour. Late hour. Eight o'clock.

Here comes the main road.

Ninety-five...

Jerusalem butts out the rear window. The steering wheel left right, right left. Turn. Collide, shearing chrome and skin.

Faster.

This road is wrong.

There are two lanes of traffic. Renaults, Austins, a Jag. **Car** breaks through them like a bull through ice.

Blood and oil. Painting with steel on a crowded canvas.

FASTER!

There's a man in a Triumph Dolomite in the middle of the road. He wants to turn right, he's waiting. The traffic is a little too heavy to turn just yet. His rear indicator lights aren't working, he's got his arm out of the window, patiently signalling: a lacklustre Nazi salute. He looks in his wing mirror, cannot see **Car** coming, it is moving too fast. **Car** flashes past, smashing away his arm and most of a shoulder. Damage as red as a flag.

Car moves with a Force, driven, *literally,* by a nature raw as age, by the power of the spiral made straight. Guided, directed. Jerusalem is oblivious, cracking open the windscreen, biting glass. *Ley*-ed back.

Another car here - a mini-cab. Everton, the driver. He carries his sawn-off in the passenger seat. No fucker gonna short change him, no white trash gonna pull no blade on Everton.

"Fuckin' rain, tcch." He sucks his teeth, turns up the heater. The radio crackling, he picks it up, turns it on; "Base to Two-Zero, come in, man..."

"Two-Zero here, wha's occurin'?"

"Everton, you gotta pickup at de Oval, man. Take 'em up to Brockley. Over..."

"Ten four, my man. O an' O..." He turns left, eases out. Something blue and travelling fast storms his car, sending it spinning off, trashing a stationary VW.

The power of the spiral

Everton is shaking, has swallowed thunder. Blood on his mouth and dreads. Facial bruising. Tinny taste of warm tears and fear. A broken bone. Head stinging hot: a hat full of wax. Grey focus, cheeks burning, numb like too much rum.

He sees his face in the wing mirror. Is *he* cracked, or is it the glass? The drum of blood, beating. Can't walk away from this thing. Must finish what he didn't start. He only knows what he's been told. He takes his gun - a splash of consciousness; he blinks it away. The windscreen wipers are waving back and forth although there is no longer a windscreen. The engine still chugging over, he mashes down the accelerator and is gone.

Rain is falling heavy now: rabid stones. The police are ahead, clearing a stretch of road, blocking it off with their Rover 3.5s. Hem the bastard in. Hammer the bastard joy-rider.

Already there's the noise of engines. The police helicopter above him, Jerusalem knows the noise: the talking blades, the wishing steel. He looks up at it, the black machine, spinning, buzzing,

like…

like it was an insect.

He remembers rain of another year. He can hear their radio, knows of the blockade ahead. The speed engulfs him, **Car** ploughs down a wino on the pavement, Lamb *likes* the feeling of impact jolting his brain on his skull casement. Memories on wheels, just like ECT, but not as much fun: no sparks.

Everton is crying. Powered by wisdom, warned by memory, he had learned how to talk, he could learn how to die. He'd seen it on a re-run of *Starsky and Hutch.* Foot down, flying at ninety; low gear, running bumper to bumper with that Blue Fuck. He throws the wheel right, rhinoing **Car's** boot. *No fucker gonna short change him…* Migraine brightness filling up vision. Brute rain/words filling up mouth. Shitty mantra; "…Yuh favour me bummer, rass clart…" Everton aims the sawn-off, fires. Kick of the shot forcing him backward, falling, his arm remains stiff, rigid. Locked in total paralysis. Sin quick, swerving right, bringing the car level, wheel to wheel, Hell to Hell: Everton sees the other driver, neither black nor white, *something else.* The eyes, symmetrical cemeteries. The 'face', or what was left, the skull of a scarecrow. Words, words. "Fuckin' Dread, mon!" The front wheels of both cars have locked, metal scrunching together, like knuckles on tongues. **Car** moves of its own accord. No steering wheel now. Jerusalem leans over, stretching through torn away door, (is reminded of the confessional), and reaches in through Everton's broken windscreen. Everton, frozen with shock, stopped like a clock. The rhyme is unintentional as are his screams. His fingers pumping, bullets blasting, raking, taking something away - like subtraction.

Trigger-nomitry.

Jerusalem plucks the gullet. Removes the sound.

O an' O...

Fleshy rain, black road. The police can't see through the rain. It bubbles, hisses, their minds shiver and the thought explodes through all of them - They've waited all their lives for *this*.

Waited for something quick and bad.

dangerous Saracen magic...

And then they hear it. It is a noise to bruise stones.

The blur approaches, they don't know it won't stop.

It doesn't.

Car hits the blockade. All that follows is noise and the uncomfortable miracle of death.

Everton's car is in pieces, as are the policemen. Their cars arranged in wreckage, steel upon steel, like stones on a plate. Bones in a pocket. Confusion: A voice on the police car radio. "What happened? What happened?" Above, the helicopter circling low. On the ground, limbs, rain, movement, a policeman crawling like a lizard in a desert, face down with flies and gravel. **Whomp whomp** of 'copter blades, ripples in a puddle. Petrol slooping out into mouths and wounds. Something is melting, dripping, *snaking* along with flame. Brief smell, like someone's just blown a candle out.

"WHATHAPPENED?WHATHAP

Everton's car explodes. Angry furnace engine burst. **Upward.** Up. Through easy glass, skin, blade, police helicopter, pilot. Life.

The explosion grows - an instant tree of volume,

substance. Fruit of fire, leaf of heat. Black season.

Car continues, no, the *route* continues, is constant, strong as a blacksmith's heart. Gorged on lines that have been drawn and erased; the web is broken, but *remains.* And there is fear in the lines.

Crashing through a roundabout now, the casual crunch of man and moped.

Sirens, red noise. More 'copters.

The very speed of **Car** and driving rain, like coal, smudges up the scenario. The sky; sicky yellow, electric concrete grey. No form or straight line out there - chaos, unshaped as thought. No angle, number, tibia, rib. No butcher's van with its load of Silverside, or rep in Sierra, (backseat crowded with reject globes - printer's error, no England). Boot full of Ken and Barbies. Laughter and screams. Red and rain. Jerusalem is immune.

Burnt offerings.

Beef and Barbie dolls.

A lung speared by spine.

Three cop cars collide in the wreckage. Broken taste, stale tears. The young PCs gurning with panic, death-vacant, that sick feeling like red wine on an empty stomach. Blackened blood on mind and lips. Explosions follow thunder.

But **Car** is exhausted. The chariot pulp - it is dying. One headlight snuffed out, the other ablaze, lit up like Balor's eye. Exhaust pipe gone; banging out throaty roars. Tyre pyres, thawing rubber, Daggered rags of radiator. Overheating, steaming. Boiling oil bubbling, *pealing* with heat. White molten metal. Pistons and friction. Burnt brakes, break lines broken, wheel brace shattered, scraping, sparking -

- a flame in rain...

Car combusts.

Smoke, white hot, hot as faith. Steam spitting a howl. Pain. Metal cracking like midnight frost. Jerusalem's eyeballs are vibrating. The fire is frying. His limbs bend inward involuntarily.

The fire sings, that is the sound - Song.

A machine requiem.

Jerusalem steps from **Car.**

No one sees the comet coming. **Car** meets the heavy goods vehicle head on. The plumber's truck ploughs into its back.

The HGV load is **Corrosive Substance:** lithium hydroxide - ten liquid tonnes of car battery acid. The plumber carries two tanks of oxy-acetylene.

Tumble.

Shudder.

A small holocaust.

Commuters off home for the weekend, now screaming, crying, mortal freights caged in wreckage, snagged in a metal net. Fingernails scratching at windscreens. Metal sound of army boots kicking in the roof (possible rescue?) but it's only rain.

The survivors, bubbling, buckling. The skin turns to soap.

The acid comes in waves.

Like the sea.

The sky is blackened by smoke. A horizon of crows take wing with their carrion crooning, "Kaaar Kaaar!"

Ka; the Egyptian soul.

Car.

"No comment," announce the Voices.

Jerusalem had left the ghost to die. It would be dead now, rotting. Not a comet, not great bones of some great beast. Just a car. A burnt out Ford.

8

"I want a cigarette."

"But Norman, ya don't smoke."

"I know, I know. But I *want* a cigarette."

Ernie unknows.

"Go on, Ernie, go an' get us one. Please."

"Alright then." Ernie wanders off, peeling back the curtain of the next cubicle. There sits a man with his face caved in; face like the Devil's bum, black in the red. A square of gauze covering one eye. He smokes a cigarette, looks up, sees Ernie staring.

"Awright mate?"

Ernie nods.

The man continues, "Sitting there this afternoon watching the box, me best mate walks in, starts bashing me with a baseball bat. Dunno why."

"Can I 'ave cigarette?" asks Ernie.

"Yeah, sure, 'ere are." The man hands Ernie the packet. "Help yaself."

Ernie takes one, hands back the box. "Thank you."

The man nods, looks down, shakes his head.

Ernie returns. "'Ere are, Norman."

"Oh, yorra good lad, Ernie," says Fish rattling his emergency box of matches. "Light up."

Norman takes the cigarette, puffs, swallows, coughs. Ernie pats him on the back. "I'm alright… I'm alright…"

"'ow's your hand, Norman? What did it feel like, all that power?"

"What power? I 'ad a fall, that's all. Nothing special." Fish takes another puff. "Funny, though, I dreamt I saw flashes, colours, ever so pretty, but weird…"

"What d'you mean, 'weird'?" Ernie is concerned.

"Queer like. Odd, y'know. In me dream I was lying on terraces at football stadium and all these people in animal masks were pouring pots of Dulux all over me…"

Ernie interrupts. "Shall I get doctor?"

"No, no. Listen right, and all this paint, it were all over me, moving like..." He pauses. "I want a cigarette."

"But you've already got one, Norman."

"Finished. I want another one. Go an' get us one." Norman sits up on the bed, pulling on his cardigan.

Ernie heads off towards the waiting room and Mr. Jackson.

Out in the casualty waiting room, among the out-patients, sits Mr J, thick in the gravy of reality. Wrapped in the sorryish self pity of giants. He'd done it this time, no escape, no get-out. Murder for sure. *Death by Hush-Puppy*. Death by electrocution: fried fish. Well, it was Friday. Maybe he'd get away with manslaughter, a 3 to 4 stretch, but even so, the thought of slopping out, lights out, dicks out, did **not** appeal to him. A plea of diminished responsibilities, then: insanity. Easy, just check the records, count the blunted needles. But if prison wasn't top of his list, neither was Rampton. Fuckit, luck, like the money, had to run out sooner than later. So what was the option? Split. Runaway, just like always. Life fugitive. Purgatory truant. He looks down at his cup of dead coffee. Mr Flint had gone in search of food long since, still hasn't returned. Ernie or a nurse would come out soon with the news of Norman's death. Nothing to do 'til then, but listen to the rain and watch the wounded.

Over near the taxi-phone, a man crying. A boy and his mother. A Jew in a knotted handkerchief hat constantly coughing, clicking. Children underfoot. An anxious shell suit girl sweating out a vicious trip. And in the corner there's Deborah. She's worried. She's heard the rumours. When she wakes of a morning, her knickers are crawling off her of their own accord. *She's heard the rumours.* One business lunch too many. One overseas publishing seminar too much. Wanted to take the easy route up the business ladder. Funny, she can't seem to shake that cold...

There's an uneven clatter of hospital trolley wheels coming. Ambulance men charge through with a swollen skinny kid in lycra shorts and velvet vest. Oxygen mask touched to his lifeless lips. Crisp puke and 'E' tab remains skukking up his throat and lungs. They rush him through, through rubber doors and beyond. An ambulance is a stupid place to die.

Then it hits Jackson - what it is about this place? - the drab smell of cleanliness, the urgent sloth of it all - it's like a bloody church! Plastic pews, row upon row of bowed heads sitting there: a field of grey wheat. Incomplete strangers licking at fond pain, worshipping the slow death of life. There was nothing *really* wrong with these people, they've come here to bide time, to watch and learn. Maybe even be jealous. Ghosts in waiting for the grave. The new generation of the Dead.

Not a hospital: A Losing Ground.

He looks up through sweat, sees the shape of Ernie coming toward him. This is it. This is the end. Outside, he can hear the sirens. Should he put up a fight, go out kicking? Nah, no fun kicking without boots on.

The sirens grow louder, send red/blue light spinning through rain glass windows. Sirens, not siren, too many cops even for nicking Mr Jackson. Something is wrong. Not only cop cars, but ambulances too.

Ernie comes over. For a second everyone is silent. Looking up, a noise, motion, shaking. *Is this it?*

Door bursts open, trolleys race through. Police, police with guns, nurses and the near dead.

Soldiers.

Army lads steaming through with a body in a bubble. Another. Two more.

More bodies, wounded. The dead, the dying.

The noise is blinding. Sirens and army helicopter blades grating dark rain.

A policeman in pieces, still breathing, you can see the bubbles at his nostrils. Someone, or some*thing*, carried in, covered in a blanket, the blanket slips. It's not a pretty sight to see the insides without the outsides holding them in.

Ernie presses his face into Jackson. Jackson is wanting to be lost. Police pouring in; gunmetal blue. Is this an aftermath? A consequence?

Police women burdened with walking men, women in blankets: shock victims. White as lies, weak as truth, staring onward, staring *north*.

The khaki departs. The big army boys are out, running through the hospital grounds, past the ornamental pond and century old willow. In, up and off. The helicopter, a blur in rain. Gone.

A doctor, an Indian, comes out: "Please, there has been an accident, a very serious accident and a lot of people have lost a lot of blood. Please, we need volunteers to give blood. If you could line up at reception, the nurse will take your details. Thank you."

Ernie asks Jackson if he has a cigarette.

"Ya what?"

"'ave ya got a cigarette? Norman wants one."

It's no use. Jackson's clearly lost the plot. "What the fuck are y'on about?"

"I know, it's Norman, 'e wants a cigarette."

"He wants… He's alive, then?!"

Ernie nods, "I think so."

Beyond a rubber door someone screams.

"Ahay!" Near tearful in rejoice, Jackson tugs out an Old Holborn tin, hands it over: the gift of fire.

"Ta." Ernie is about to scuttle off, when a new noise is heard - a Victorian noise - *hooting.* Lolloping through the rubber doors comes a clown in full motley and slap, honking an antique car horn and handing out leaflets. He honks his way around the bewildered circuit of waiting room, giving out colourful circus flyers, gets to Ernie, pats him on the head, slips something in his pocket, grins, honks and lopes out tooting.

"What the fuck were that?" enquires Mr J.

"Clown! Clown!" reports Ernie, digging out that which was placed in his pocket. He looks but cannot read the words.

Mr J takes over. "Tickets, lad. Free tickets to circus next weekend. Ahay! Well done!"

"Circus! Circus! We're going to the circus! Heeeeeee! Norman, Norman..."

Ernie scuttles off. A boy in the world. As he leaves, so Su arrives. She teeters out of casualty on five inch heels, a buttoned black 'crombie, lump of cotton pressed to broken nose like a half eaten plum. Mutton dressed as Spam.

She sits next to Jackson, rakes out a lipstick and a mirror, but the mirror is cracked and the lipstick blunt. "Soddit."

Mr J leans over, offers her a hip flask. She smiles, accepts, tips him a wink, takes a swig.

"Cheers luv. Brandy innit?"

"Aye. Sixty year old and Spanish at that. Jackson's the name. *Mr* Jackson."

"Su. Pleased to meet ya. Ohh..." Pain - she's wincing. Mr J. says nothing. She smells of ashes, fresh fire. His erection flaming up.

She sniffs. "This bloody Arab picked us up, me and me mate, Meg. He says he wants a good time, three in a bed, y'know. He was driving us down to Epping, short cut he said, ends up in this bloody crash, cars, bodies everywhere. We was hit behind. Pile up. Some poor sods got acid all over 'em. Army brought 'em in. Burns unit. Poor bastards. Couldn't get no ambulance down there for ages, road's all blocked off. We had to walk, me and Meg."

"Where's Meg, then?"

"Emergency. She might lose an eye. Her right one."

"What about the Arab?"

"Him! The dirty cunt." She takes another swig, "We left *him* at the wheel."

"Dead?" Jackson knows already.

"I should bloody 'ope so. Bloody great side of beef hit him on the head. Silverside it was. Quite funny really. Still we this got out of it." She pulls out a plastic bag full of dull white powder. "Grade A smack," she whispers, loudly. Dips in the nose cotton offal bandage, brings it up, white on red, sugar on a doughnut, pressed to broken nose. Breathes it in.

Jackson sinks a finger, scoops it out, touches it to tongue, tastes. Bitter: burnt feather. "Not bad," he says.

Su is talking. He hasn't heard. "You live near here, then?"

Jackson experiences a dangerous feeling, no, not dangerous - immoral. They giggle up, cackle out.

Out in the rain a taxi is waiting. They clamber in, sit back. Puddles in the seat.

"Cabby, take us to Fez, I've a mood for figs!"

"Certainly, sir. The airport is it?

Jackson says nothing, uncomfortable in the presence of a machine-generated warmth. The engine chugs. Rain beats down.

"You can go now Mr Earthburn, everything's all right." It's a young nurse, pulling back the cubicle curtain; rugged pallor, long tied hair. She's been crying. Norman and Ernie stare at her. "I said go, we need the room."

Fish rolling a roll up: "Are ya talking to me?"

"Yes." There is fresh blood on her uniform.

"Earthburn? Earthburn?" Norman looks to Ernie.

Ernie knows: forgotten. When Norman was brought in to emergency, Mr Jackson, fearing the worst, had registered

Fish as, **Jupiter S. Earthburn.** He had 'explained' to Ernie, "Ya can't be too careful."

"Well," says the nurse, "go."

Rizla mouth Fish looks her in the eye. Malign Baccy/hash voice: "You're a dozy mare."

But she's gone. They've brought in another stranger, another burnt stranger with a heartbeat outlived by moths. And hers will be the last face she ever sees.

Molten night. Black and cold as old silver. Rain like chains. The storm rages on. Fire noise, ash smell - miles off, carried in the wind. Jerusalem had stepped from destruction, glanced crows and bones, heard engines, tears. Walked away. Walked here.

In the distance, through lightning bright sky, he sees it - the building. A slab of white waiting. Deafening white, a dead museum. A ghost with windows.

Nearer. Beneath Lamb's shadow, worms root up from drowning earth. He moves on. Thunder on lightning. (The slamming of Doom's door). It is a cloudburst. Rain like rivets and diamonds, a tide in drops, like the sea. A shard of lightning cracks open a centuried oak. The ground shivers, opens. Lamb is swallowed into a clogged, empty grave. There are worms in a blank coffin. He kicks from it, out. A fist slammed on stone. He holds a punched off chunk of tombstone. A lump of false mourning: the 'B' of Basil Valentine Jnr.

He looks up...

It's the **Church of Rust:** *brooding calm, white as drowned owls*. How could it be? His journey has brought him 'back'. Full circle. A return to savage.

But no.

He stands in the grounds of what was once to be a temple, a church, a church turned mental. An asylum. Time's asylum: Tookesbury Hall.

Burnt time. Dead time. The reek of fox and the lightning-blasted oak.

He has returned. To nowhere.

The taxi driver is a born again Christian. 'Born again' - resurrected. Once dead. He wears a cross, he wears a truss; both give him support. He is talking, but his passengers do not hear. He is saying something about the road ahead being blocked, an earlier accident. Police, rain. "I'm afraid we'll have to go the long way round to the airport, sir. What time is your flight, sir? Sir?" The driver looks up through steamy partition, pulls it back. "Sir? Sir?" Su is bent over Mr Jackson's stomach; she has something white in her mouth, makes a noise like she's choking on a wish-bone. She had dipped Jackson's erect monster in the smack, sucks it off: gagging on a pillar of salt.

"What are you doing back there?" The driver is not happy. "No, no. I don't like this. Not in my cab. No." He pulls over, gets out, yanks wide the door, doesn't like what he sees: a man stretched out with no legs and a scar for a smile. Metal crutches poking through an open window and a girl on the floor vomiting white vomit. "Out, come on, out, you filthy things!"

Mr J looks up; there's a man looking into the taxi with no eyes, just gold light in the sockets. Jackson only laughs the question, *"Florentine?"* then tells the driver to "Fuck off." He's sweating crazily, it's *pouring* out of him. Self rain. The storm's a few miles off, but he can feel it here. A dull, fierce ache. A feeling of twisted wire in the bones. Bloated gums. *What* fiendish thing had he stuck up his nose?

Suddenly there are two cops. Su is being hauled out, thrown off. The bag of heroin dropping to the wet ground, splitting, spilling loose, souping into erratic stains - Australian coastlines, dogs with no spines. White in the dark night, rained away. A good time turned bad. Su is warned.

She is gone. They can't be bothered with her, not at her age. Bruises only look good on a young girl's skin.

Jackson laughs, announcing, "I'm a swinging guy!" His erection is almost spectacular: cheesy as a stump sock, stiff as stone. The cops only see his crutches - 'deadly weapons' 'possession' 'intent'. Jackson is pulled out, the driver told to go. The taxi rolls away - black in the blackness - *joined.*

And they stand there, holding a swaying Mr J. Three men in the rain and the night. Beneath one star. He knows what's going to happen, can feel it - a knot of white hot shit in his stomach. Face to face to face: Jackson spitting: "Go on, flat-foot."

They kick away his crutches, knock him to the ground, start booting, slamming him with their truncheons, this crowd of two.

The ground's as greasy as a sheep's eye. Jackson doesn't notice the rain, face down in a puddle, he knows enough to *roll* himself into what he can of a ball. One arm covering his head, the other pressed over his kidneys: Three quarter embryo. He finds it funny, can't help but laugh; wouldn't be the first time a good day had ended in a serious beating. Shit happens. It was happening now. Coupla tuppenny cunts working off some 'executive stress' - on his spleen. He's hot, furnace hot, and thirsty. Skull on stone, laughing. Pain like the bite of a horse.

The blows do not diminish, do not weaken. Just bore. He finds it funny - their despair. Poor sods. He sees rain in the cops' headlights and wonders how much longer this will last. This rude reality, this smeared dream. Acid's fiction, fact's steel toe cap.

Jackson, roaring like a camel. Weeping like a wound.

Rain. Rain like chains. Rain to wash the blood away.

And then it happens. He is at the door and it is open. Above him, bronze green, the head of a human figure with a terrifying face, full of threats, wrath. Terror to witness trespass, then. And he is in, through the door of the big white house.

Jerusalem is in the Hall.

Dark. No lights, all the power gone. Dry stink, brown air, sepia smell of burnt electrics. He moves through it, the darkness, the *wanting* darkness, sticky as newsprint pressed to the mouth of a dying man. Alchemickly dark, (like something mindless and ancient persuaded out from a vault). He likes it, the quiet. Somewhere, the chiming of a clock, the rustling of feathers - *"Hey Ho! Whoop Whoop! Make sense..."* chirp the Voices.

Jerusalem moving up the stairs, movement like the folding of old carpet.

The noise of nothing and the night inside. Alone and floating in this workable darkness, he can hear voices, history sounds, but muffled, far away, like the cries of a bride shut in an attic trunk. Memories through muslin. Confessions whispered down sleeves caked with clay. He knows the noisessssssssss.

it reminds him

But no.

Now he hears it: the breath of death, like the rattle of a stick in an old tin tub. Stiff black lace on smooth white bone. The sound of dead red hair, open graves and shut mouths. The noise of thorns raked through sand. The Fifth Voice found, and Lamb in ascent with all the elation of stones.

Maudsley had been taking a nap when he heard the burnt man enter. Now he watches him, trailing him from floor to floor, the burnt man, breathing like a bulldog, sniffing at the perfume of sounds. Maudsley knew, he wasn't stupid, *he* read the papers, this was obviously a psycho-killer. Just look at his eyes. Like two wells. Pain wells. But there's a problem; with a murderer in the Hall toting a hefty lump of rock intent on doing something nasty, the question is - should he raise the alarm? Ring the law? Have a quick word with Jackson, if he was in? And who *was* in? Had they even bothered to tell him they were going out? Nah, fuck 'em. He'd take it easy, see what happened. Better than the telly, this.

Jerusalem on the second floor, which is darker still. Dark as ravens eating burnt toast. As dark as that. Darker. He finds the way along corridors, to the room, the door...

Unquiet blood bubbling within.

Something, somewhere... the noisesssssssss.

And then it happens. He is at the door and it is open. There is a figure in the bed, beneath one sheet, long hair spilling out. Without warning, the chunk of tombstone is stabbing down, hacking the bone of mouth, skull of sound. Jerusalem, taking away life with the evidence of death.

Thunder. Lightning lights up the room and Lamb. Nine painted strait-jackets on the wall. And on the bed, a skull with hair, no eyes - a pink body all less of life, in grey silk lingerie.

Something

Somewhere...

Something was wrong. There is no sound. No 'voice'.

Screaming white, the lights jump back on. Power humming through madhouse walls. Dead air hissing through ripped rubber 'skin'.

He does not know, the mad man.

Does not know it's an inflatable doll. Roane's love, dead rubber love in plastic skull mask. Wig of cheap redness. Love death done up in silk. Breath of lust seeping out of the cadaver fuck balloon. Skull asunder, mask split open, dead face bare, and there it is, the hollow ruby wound of lips, the 'inviting love tunnel' of mouth and throat. Stretched circle set in silent scream. Like the 'o' in the name of God. *The mouth, the throat.* Not his victim. Not skin, but breath. No, can't kill breath.

He cannot move.

He does not know.

He stares death in the face. Rubber death. A buyable skull.

He holds the moss-engraved stone. The 'B' of Basil Valentine Jnr...

And then it happens.

He turns, whipped around, slammed into recollection - There's rain on the window, thunder at the Earth's ear. The noise of night and the mind inside. He knows the noisesss; they are the sounds of ghosts in pain, the sounds a machine would make if it were trying to pray. They are the sounds of madness, and he, the mad man had walked willingly into a Mad-House. The tall white walls like a pit, a grave: the white abyss of asylum. House of mad men. Home to Hell.

And the Lamb starts screaming. Night isn't listening, but Maudsley is. Winging way down, teasing the mad man, squawking, "Aaaawk, welcome home! Welcome home!"

A burnt black hand punches up. The fist behind the face, the mind inside the pain, ripping at tail feathers, failing. Here is a voice with wings! A talking bird, but birds are his salvation, chewing down bugs of voices, nibbling at noise, but now...

Jerusalem falls off the cliff of self, and erupts.

"Nice Dragoman! Awwk nice Dragoman!" warbles Maudsley.

The mad man roars. The door to Roane's room, torn, slung off. Fists in the brickwork. A grazing of air. Rage. Unwordable rage. No 'need', just 'act'. Amok down corridors, Jerusalem cannoning after the voice of wing, mouth of flight. Noise of madness all around - different rooms drawing primal breath. Impossible sounds: blood thawing on walls of blood. Gasmasks melting. Light pulsing through limbs of lines.

Impossible, familiar, sounds.

Little truths and poppies.

Cannoning after - he does not see the stairs, does not stop, smashes through banisters, falling two floors, kicking, twisting, landing on his back, rising on impact. Maudsley swoops above him, darts off down darkened routes through kitchens toward the cellar. Jerusalem watches, *listens*, follows.

The flooded cellar is as black as his feathers. Maudsley snorts in the damp, he will surely sneeze, but mustn't - for the mad man will hear him. He's here now, at the open door, stalking down the steps up to his knees in the bacon brown water, *wading* in. There are wires on the walls which resemble veins. White spats of light shimmering on the water, like late winter flowers. The cellar doesn't smell right, Maudsley knows, so does the mad man, walking through the water; salt sea water. The stinks of skin and herring gulls. Old electricity and fear.

Maudsley sneezes. The mad man lunges.

The sneeze echoes in screeches around the hard, dark walls. Crashing 'Choooooo chooooooo' noise. Crows eating a locomotive.

Maudsley has gone. Out the door, shut and bolted it.

Jerusalem emerges. Up to his waist in cellar ocean, slowly turning the powerful bone of head, listening…

Something was in there with him.

Something in the stagnant, mucky waters…

moving

in the air now, all around, a new noise, *buzzzing*, crawling up guano-hard walls of stitched human skin.

Crawling.

Something as thin as damp Bible paper.

A soul ghost anima. A black mosquito left over from a dream of 1922. It skits, lands on Jerusalem's bare burnt arm and bites him. Like kissing diamond. Like scratching slate.

Jerusalem slaps the bug. Through darkness he sees it has left a smear on his arm, which quickly vanishes, leaving the bad black stain of a headless cross.

Far away the thunder rumbles.

Jerusalem, bone golem, falls to his knees, as if praying, slumps over, arms outstretched as a crucified man, falls forward and floats away.

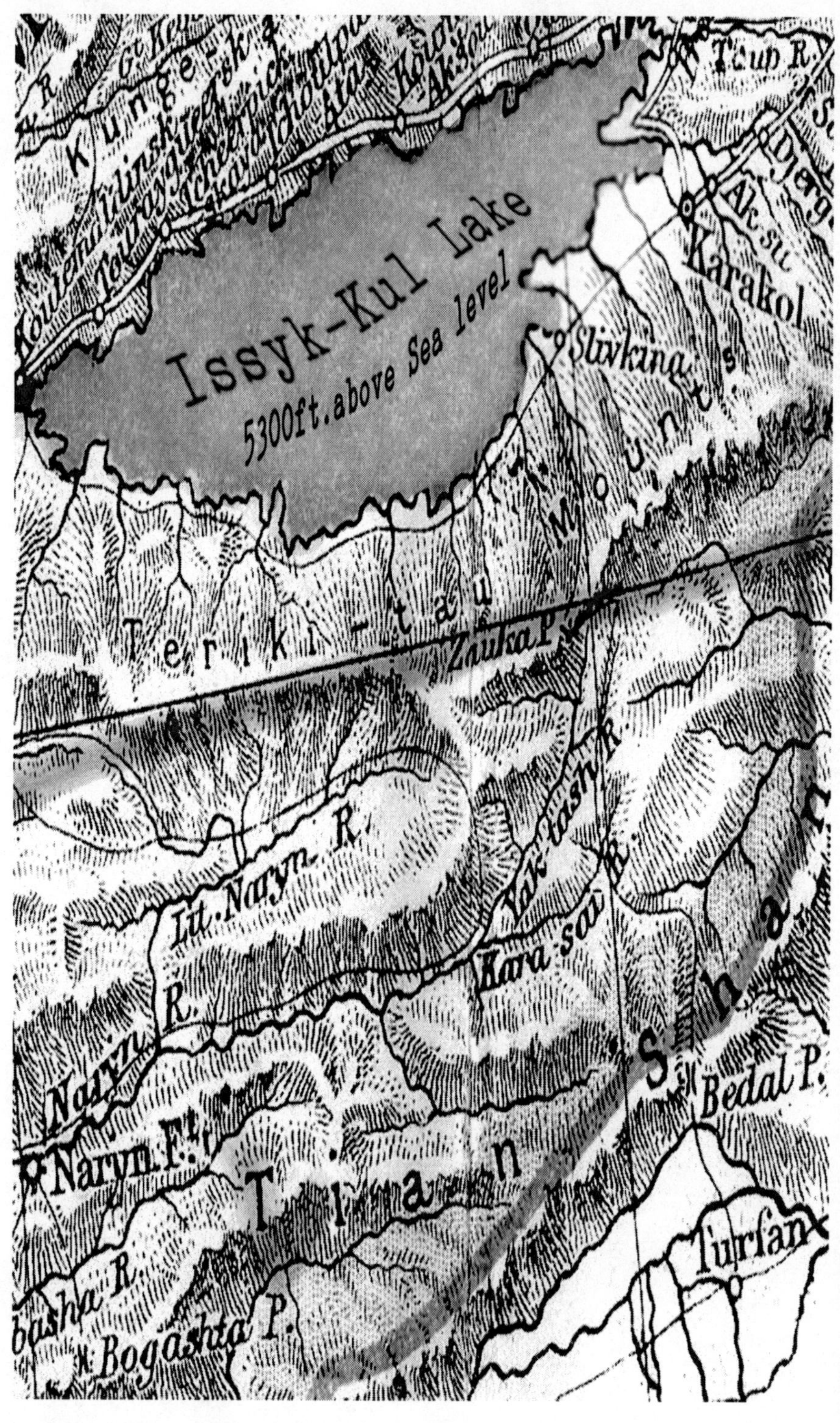
Issyk-Kul Lake
5300ft. above Sea level
Karakol
Ak su
Slivkina
Teriki-tau
Zauka P.
Lit. Naryn R.
Naryn R.
Naryn F.t
Kara sai
Bedal P.
Turfan
Bogashta P.
Thian Shan Mounts

9

Art is not a handicraft,
it is the transmission of feeling the artist has experienced.
***Leo Tolstoy (1898)* - What is Art?**

"I've a hankering for painting shards of glass in matt black paint." These are new words Fish speaks. He is using, now, words like 'montage' and 'extraction', words maybe always known, put aside, caught up with. His hair is suddenly longer, unfurled from Brylcreem. Dark sacks under eyes green as olive stones. Stubble waits at his face like some dark reason. Like the shadow within. His world had been black and white - industry black, institution white and the horizon, grey, like a funeral in the distance. Now Fish has evolved - grown limbs, crawled from the sediment, climbed the trees, grown wings. Flown away. It was the shock received - *Death by Hush-Puppy.* Electricity. It can do that. Medical men call it ECT.

Brick smoke voice. His collar turned, face like torn paper: angry young old man with a rewritten life. A gull outrunning winter.

Ernie is worried. Can't quite recognise this new chain-smoking Fish, who's not slept since his return from hospital, last night. Who's been out since dawn, coming back with mud on his shoes and talking of the mud *as the journey.* No, Ernie doesn't realise. Doesn't want to. Happy enough to keep his distance, toy with his circus tickets. Play games, play safe.

Mr Jackson, beaten, bruised black, slumped on a chaise longue, a hot water bottle steaming on his head. Flint sits before him, crosslegged, manipulating with thin, fine hands, the ghosts of feet. Reflexology.

"Owwwh! 'ell fire, Flinty, mind what ya doin'…" wails Jackson.

"Sorry mate. Nearly done." Flint is precise, kneading, rolling. He had found Jackson bleeding on the doorstep that morning - a police beating - it would be taken care of: favours owed from friends in low places. He had found Fish too, retuning, paint spattered, a different person, two stolen tins of industrial undercoat under his coat. They had lugged Jackson in, set him down, had been talking ever since - a sudden double act: *the old Barker and Johnson routine.*

"I want to cough into jelly moulds. Not subtle, don't want subtle. I want the disease made tangible…"

"Shapes," says Flint, "you want definition. Solids."

Fish can't stop. Manic, *diving* now. "Coal in a wine glass! Right! Painting the skull as portrait…"

"X-rays of miners' lungs as the canvas," compliments Flint.

Ernie and Jackson are both superfluous to this exchange. They too have shared the same basic beginnings as North-Man Norman - the scar of Yorkshire, taken for granted. The industrial landscape, psychic doom pumped from factories, mills, and mouths. Early graves of black stone school houses. Pit disasters. Sweat. Hearts. A chill remembered. They knew. Their ambiguities are necessary. It needed the outsider of the London-born Flint to see the other, more hidden, possibilities. A secondary adrenaline.

The boy Roane appears with rolled Hall blueprint. Sulky, lurid in a red shirt. Shallow as a grave. He's not saying where he was last night. Not at the hospital, not in the Hall. No one's asking, couldn't care less. He *had* been out, for on returning he found banisters broken, his room trashed and love torn - the rubber doll with skull asunder. He has his suspicions: Jackson on the sofa, wrecked like the room.

Coincidence, heavy as coins on a lily-pad. Roane says nothing.

Fish is off again, stubbing dead roll-up on sole of shoe. "I want to sweat onto maps. Make lands of my actions. Want to dig up a mosaic, run it through a washing machine. Erase. Rediscover. Flatten someone else's hill. I want to..."

"Ya want to shut ya mouth for five minutes! Good God, man, gi' it a rest, can't ya!" Jackson unheard, Fish darts off, gone. *Looking for.* **Doing.**

Flint has finished, wipes his hands and clears his throat. The subject changed: "What you got there then, lad, blueprints are they?"

Roane hands over the rolled sheet. They clear a space, straighten it out. The prints - wax white detail on a yard of midnight blue.

Flint casts an eye. "Don't say who built it or who was the draughtsman. What's this in the corner, a date? 1888! Ha! The Ripper year!"

"Sutcliffe?" from Jackson.

"No, the other one."

"Oh."

Roane knew there was something wrong with the blueprints. Rooms undrawn, seemingly out of place. The rooms of the second floor, floor of secrets, mad rooms. Rooms of lights and poppies, pain and tiny. No master mason or artisan had shaped *those* walls.

Nobody's ghost, Ernie, appears with a tray of coffee and biscuits.

"Good lad." Flint is intrigued now. "This second floor," he taps the print, "where those freaky rooms are, says 'ere they're patients' quarters."

"Fuckin' weird patients, even for fuckin' madmen," muses Jackson.

"I have a record of the patients and all their histories," says Roane. "It belonged to Doctor Goldflame."

"Well let's have a look-see! See what loony went in that room."

Roane goes. Fish streaks in with a can of 'Trojan Blue' spray-paint. The obvious synapses must be crackling, the connection made, he sprays the blue paint all over the blueprints before anyone can stop him. He stands for a moment, regarding his action, his re-creation, and rejects it. "Too flat," is all he says.

Roane returns with a brown leather ledger and finds Flint, Jackson, Ernie and Fish, coated, buttoned up, shuffling out. He does not see the blueprint.

Implicated: Flint with an invitation. "Come on, I'll buy you a pint."

The pub is full of empties. Flint had brought them here, could not get service at the *Dog and Duck*, Jackson was barred, the landlord still limping.

Flint gets the drinks, the others settling at tiny tables. He had been here once before, it hadn't changed. The barmaid still looking like a Reader's Wife; face painted an inch thick, lipstick on her upper plate. The old men in the corner, smoking, sharing pints and memories. The tide mark of years, brown on walls, skin, and thought. The smell of liniment. Sounds of laughter in a raincoat.

Jackson is bothered, shifting limbs juicy with pain. Enjoying it. "Good God, Flinty, is this the best ya could do? Barmaid's nipples could curdle me ale!"

"I dunno," says Flint, "I like it."

Ernie sips his shandy.

The strip of damp peeling wallpaper catches Fish's attention; he tears it off, savage, quick. Starts sketching the old men, rubbing cigarette ash into the new page of grey.

Roane produces two books, clears a space, lays them down. One a ledger; a mad history book of names and manias. The other, *The Broken Equator: A slender biography of the life and travels of Doctor William Miles.* Flint picks one up, thumbs through it.

"Where's the blueprint?" asks Roane.

All eyes on Fish.

"Errrrr, must've left it behind," says Flint. "Right," he says with genuine noncommittal, "who's for another pint?"

There's a man lurking near the 'gents' with a Thermos flask.

A West Indian pays for a black and tan and sits under a grey window.

The barmaid laughs: a sound like breaking.

Flint returns laden with light and mild. Armagnac chasers. Empty glasses are shifted, new ones thumbed with thirsty love.

"Boip!" reports Jackson, wiping his mouth. He screws up a beermat and throws it at an old man. It bounces off his cap. No one seems to notice.

"What's...?" starts Ernie, but thinks better of it.

A man with a moustache orders a cheese roll. His fifth. The barmaid laughs another laugh. She is not impressed.

Outside the rain is gently falling. The windows of the pub darken slowly. A comfortable chill settles in between glass and mouth, shiver and stomach.

The old men in the corner are like ghosts in a Pinter play. Their lives stopped long since, they're like mice; constant. Abject. Their horror is existence. One of them lights up a Woodbine and a moth flies into it. Another old man gathers it up, careful, and pops it in his breast pocket. A pocket full of moths. Brittle and ash over the heartbone.

"It's your shout, you tight-fisted bastad!" Jackson gives Ernie a fifty, tells him to, "Get them in, large ones mind."

They grow drunk with drinking, their bodies are joyful, they shout aloud, their hearts exult.

"Says 'ere," begins Flint taking up the ledger, "that a young man, known as 'Wires', the only son of a parson from the Parish of St. Mary Cray, was *confined to Tookesbury Hall on this the fourteenth day of October, eighteen hundred and ninety-nine. The case, possessing of a nefarious pulse and curious lack of bodily hair, has been vehemently ecclesiophobic,* ("afraid of churches," explains Flint), *since having been struck by lightning in late childhood. From said day he has suffered the worsening delusion because of which he claims that electricity is the 'only true religion' and that the 'real' God is nought but a machine driven by electro-magnetic fluids'. The Case is inflicted also with hallucinatory delirium of so-called 'Electroplasm', a liquid electricity with metamorphic properties. Apocalyptic visions of snakes and angels. Further physical examination proceeded exposure of myriad fine white scars of a small 'star' design, speckled about his body, particularly to the upper left torso, thighs and genitals. The scars he has confessed to be self inflicted..."*

Flint has stopped talking, takes a swig, laughs, swallows. "Ha! He plugged himself in! Straight into the ring mains!"

"I don't understand," says Roane.

"*Fine white scars?* He was frazzin' himself off the main current! 'Course, he should've burnt himself to crackling, but he'd already been immunised by lightning. *DC.* Direct Current. He was a living dynamo. Got his thrills 'shooting up' off the light sockets!"

"Fuckin' weirdo," Jackson, informal. Waving an empty glass.

Fish is up, off. An altercation at the bar. Voices raised in threats and aggression. He comes back, a bottle of Walkers and five glasses secured.

"Good lad."

Hungry, Ernie wants a cheese roll. They're all gone. He tries the menu, a plastic effort that hasn't changed since 1963. Never been wiped. There are no words, just stains. You point to the stain you want and it's brought to you on a plate. The menu is a meal in itself. Blotto. Ernie tries to eat it. Five mutton tikkas are ordered. Pissy smells of cooking lamb waft in from the back room.

Flint is skimming through the ledger with open abandon. Pages of names, dates, frantic scribblings as the years go by: Dennis Poulting, Basil Valentine Jnr, 1913, Rydal Bowtell, *Wake,* Mr Eke. Some pages stuck together by splashes of ghostly silver, peeled carefully apart. Flint sniffs it, touches it to his tongue, spits "Silver nitrate. 'orrible stuff!"

"Compound 606," reveals Jackson. "Eye wash. Stopped ya going blind, supposedly. The French disease. Syphilis."

The barmaid serves them up five steaming plates of thick grey gravy.

"'orrible stuff," repeats Flint.

Jackson groans.

Fish suddenly starts randomly quoting great chunks of *The Broken Equator, the life of Dr William Miles,* boiled down between mouthfuls. *"Kimmeridge... Some fellows at St. August's off exploring 'unknown lands'... talk of following Semyonov's route... The eve of departure... Disagreeable Cologne... Express to Berlin... Easter in St. Petersburg... zavtra... fish soups... Russian ice... The Hebrew's melody... Webb's letter of credit... Tea money... A trade in shawls... A devout but unwashed peddler... Exiles burnt alive... The new meat... A monument of stones... Przhevalsky's grave at Lake Issyk-kul..."*

Jackson looks up in recognition, "Nearly lost it on the Caspian, once. Course, we were 'eading south. Persia. Murzanabhad."

Fish cuts him short with a coughing fit. He spits out a bone.

Roane takes up the reading, *"Beyond the Lake, stretching to the very Heavens, lay the unbroken snowy chain of the Tian Shan. The Mountains of the Spirits. Solemn in sunlight against the mirror of the sky."* He skips a page, continues feverish, slurring sometimes. *"Crossing the Tian Shan range... crossing rivers... the broken bridge... filing down river gorges overgrown with Honeysuckle, Sweetbriar and Clematis. Further on, the narrow trail steepening... thin air... bodies of local tribesmen, camels, horses and rams preserved by the icy air... Frostbite... Snowblind... Kyrgyz guides calling aloud to Allah for help..."* He takes a drink, spills more than he swallows. *"Solid streams of ice... a glacial valley. The avalanche... rope and bones broken by the frost... Falling... a muddy lake of meltwater... sediment... 'Just like hell'... A flotilla of ice chunks... Human flotsam... hands burnt onto ice... The first waterfall. Under ice... The second waterfall... Beached."*

He can read no more. New Fish is all eyes. Piercing, seeing the scene, plotting its progression to capture it on steel or mirrors.

Jackson shrouded in black nostalgia.

Their plates empty, save for shadow. The rain is audible now, outside, like the scratching of ravens.

Ernie asks, "Did 'e fall in, then?"

Jaw blindly falling, Flint, wide eyed: "Fall in? Did he fall in? 'Course he fuckin' fell in!"

Ernie, smug and stupid with drink, smiling rusted smile.

"Give's it 'ere." Flint snatches up the book and wipes a muttony hand across his cropped skull. His mouth a little hidden by the cloud of his jawbone: his beard. He speaks with the loose memory of a witness. A voice like autumn: "Miles fled England at the unfaithfulness of his beloved Rebecca. He joined explorers, travelled through Europe and Russia, climbed the mountain and fell from the mountain. Like Lucifer heavy with rope and frostbite. One thousand feet into a river of white shit. His hands, through sheepskin, scorched onto ice. His face, burnt away by ice. He was washed downriver, buffeted along like a stick. His heart stopped, frozen in a coldness like a red-hot iron. Swept over waterfalls, pushed under ice, beached on a bank of nothing. Listen," he quotes from the book. "Miles' own words - *Upon waking, I did not know where I was. I was wrapped with a blanket of dark furs. I could not feel my arms. My breathing was laboured, bruised. A taste akin to copper upon my tongue. I opened my eyes and saw the sky and the sky was red and I truly believed that I had been received into Hell. And by God, the red sky was moving; Clamorous. The air around me was alive with a swarm of insect life. An infestation of moths streaked with brilliant scarlet, vivid crimson beetles, blood red flying ants, &c. the noise was disgusting. I begun to feel buried alive, when suddenly the sky darkened, and another noise angered the elements, a noise of rushing. Wings. Birds. A murmuration of starlings. Pink starlings devouring red insects. The birds were smoothing me, boiling the air with their sour unctuosity. And in that very moment I knew that I was still alive, for only a scene as atrocious as this could be acted out in the land of the living. Oh, by Christ, it was terrible. I could bear to watch no more, but I could not shut my eyes, for red-bellied moths had settled there. And so I chose to scream, but no sound would come, save for a hard crack. Mercifully unconsciousness struck me. Later, and I chanced light once again, only to find a tall, swarthy man dressed in a long black coat and grey sheepskin cap covering the bone of his head, leaning over me, grinning. The sky was no longer red but a curious blue, cold with starlight. I could smell wood burning. A pheasant was roasting over an open fire. No speech could I make as four old men gathered round me. The Elders, one by one telling me that 'night was only day turned upside down'."*

Flint, drunk with his psychic high, lays the book face down, places hands upon it: psychometry. He stares forward and begins: "Miles was found washed up by the Rom..."

"Russian Gypsies," sighs Jackson.

"His heart had stopped from the freezing waters. They had their own potions and experiences. They reset his busted bones, kept him warm, dry, and fed him their secrets and soup for six long months. They took him through the desert to British India. He was brought back to England by a one-eyed captain. Miles would hallucinate: feverdreams of an eagle soaring, vultures too. The golden bones of a good man had been spilled. The birds fought over the flesh and leftovers, ripping at one another in a savage ballet of violin and guitar, tambourine and drum. A dance of death in the midst of death. Their battle lasted half a year, in which time the bones had knitted themselves back together, formed a skeleton, regrown insides and skin. Only the face and hands burnt pink, the nose and lips, black, bruised. The moustache and eyebrows just yellow scars. A burning man of ice. Hungry, he awoke with a ladle to his lips and ate the remains of the eagle and vultures. As he ate, four old men told him that 'the desert was as warm as a prayer and dry as a curse'." Flint stops, sniffs, blunders off to the toilet. Full bladder, overflowing psyche.

The whisky bottle empty. Roane, Fish, Ernie, and Jackson slumped at their tables, reticent, feeling somehow *judged* by the history of a dead man.

The barmaid teeters over, removes their plates and glasses. Roane roots out a twenty; she takes it and pulls them another five pints. A stylus-scratched tattoo (an eagle or vulture) now visible on the vast expanse of her powerful white bosom. As she's leaning over them serving up their drinks, Jackson tells her, "My God, you're ugly."

She only laughs, punching him lightly on the shoulder.

"I think you're on to a winner there…" burbles Ernie.

A nodding uncomfortability settles in.

Staggering, Flint returns and swiftly drains his pint.

Fish scratches out an idea on the pub table. Adrenalin and a Swiss Army penknife producing cross-hatched harshness. He rolls a cigarette, careful, lighting it from the dying butt in his lips. "I want metal. Padlocks, chains raked from the river. Right angles. New shrapnel. I want to weld nails into shapes of hammers…"

"Oh Christ, he's off again," moans Mr J.

"There's a place down Wimbledon way, does welding - torches cheap, good. We can go there this afternoon, if you want."

Fish accepts Flint's offer. It's settled, then.

Jackson hassles Ernie to get the next round in; noises of breaking wind and the counting of money. Roane wants more mysterious talk of mad men and Tookesbury Hall. Pissed out of his brains, he recalls the nine painted strait jackets, their story and journey. Intent sat up straight, inviting Jackson to, "Tell us about the Bastard Isles, again."

In the far corner, grim old merchantmen look up, angered, growling in recognition of the named Isles. The phrase *Tip tod* passed round like a burning stick. They calm, eventually, chewing on gristly pints.

"Not much to tell." Words like biting lemon; bitter. "Not on any map. Has no flag, but trees like impaled spiders. Only good for one thing, an' that's burial."

He has heard, but struggles to *know*. Raking around for words of his own and a handkerchief, Roane with hand in pocket pulls out the ebony key. Key of the second floor of secrets. It begins to flake, crumbling in his hand. Ashes. The ledger is open on the table. It is opened randomly at a faint grey brown line in a medical hand: *The Librarian, she is logophobic with hatred,* and the remark, *A world of books gone flat.* Roane's shirt turns from red to black. The others ignore this, are too drowned in drink, calling for another bottle.

An old man in drab NHS glasses stoops over Roane, nods his acquaintance, takes his spectacles off, breathes on the lenses, holds them to his face and stares at him through them, telling him, "Sometimes you can only see the view by misting up the window." He puts them back on, unpolished, smeared. He wanders off.

"Bloody saddle-sniffers, the lot of 'em!" louds Jackson. "Look at 'em all, stupid bastads waiting ta die. By taste of ale 'ere, they ain't got much longer ta wait." He burps, a bruised mouth widening.

And in their corner, the effigies of Old in long woollen coats, damp as chicken bones. One of the old men is handling a vintage photograph, carefully turning it over, reading all the faded words long-handed on its back. Stroking sepia. The second hand contact - time by proxy. Another old man with half a Guinness, laboriously weaves pencil thin thoughts of unfinished regret: frail moments with a Fiona Cooper video, the memory of forgetting. Dry hearts and a pocketful of moths.

Old men who shit once a year.

Their souvenirs of minds, gone by.

Reality smothers Roane like dank peeling wallpaper. In fact it *is* the pub's wallpaper that is smothering him. Great sweeps of it unroll off onto him. Only he laughs.

"Ooooooouh," grunts Jackson, spinning in his seat. "I feel like Princess Margaret..."

"I do 'ope that weren't a Freudian slip," mocks Flint.

"Fuck off," drawled.

Suddenly music starts up. The *Marseillaise* cranked, rumbling through scratchy speakers.

"...Do what?"

The barmaid appears in a French maid's outfit. Fishnets and a beret. She's doubling as the stripper this particular lunchtime.

Mr Jackson is clearly terrified. Bloody eyes coiled about themselves, strangling sight. **"Oh God, she's takin' 'er clothes off!"**

They stampede, scattering tables, glasses. The mad ledger and biography taken up, pocketed. Ernie, unconscious, is dragged dribbling from the imminent *horror*.

"Brazen!" screams Jackson as they make good their laughing escape out into rain, to scatter, to Wimbledon and beyond.

***

It was a mile to the cemetery. Drunken, Roane walked to it in the rain. It was where they bury and burn the dead, dump the husk. Doctor Goldflame is buried here.

The cemetery is where General Gordon's mausoleum stands. Strangely enough, there is also a marker to Howard Carter of tatty stone. And the men who work here are paid *not* to tend it. Mystery money. The Egyptian debt.

Engagement rings and boyhood wooden swords lie discarded in the long grass. There are cypress and yew trees, green as when the snow goes.

Masonic graves of sinister symmetry. Alabaster shadows. Death and dirt.

He had walked through a cemetery like this, on childhood Sundays with his mother. They would stop, stare, read names on gravestones. *Mary Jane, wife of...* They laughed at the strange names, pointing to the dates. Bowed over a tomb now, seeing double, *laughing* at the name he cannot see through whiskey beer eyes. Cannot decipher the rain razed inscription. Cannot understand the secret language of graves, *Born. Died.* Gone but forgotten. Moss and moth scarred, a rusted Christ nailed upon a corroded cross. The same old death scene - who *passed* away, who *fell asleep,* but never died, never rotting in a hole. And as he grew, so he believed the stone mason's truth, and death became a way of life: the black clothing, sombre skin. The walks in the rain. Mortuary employment. The pornography of death.

And now he too must die.

He had chosen to die in rain. He had come here to die.

He *knew* now about the rooms on the second floor. Floor of secrets. He had listened to Flint, Fish, Jackson in the pub, heard and read the words of Doctor William Miles, had *seen* the room of light and the room of *books gone flat.*

It was simple.

They had all been Mad men and women in a Mad house.

Truly Mad. Gone beyond. They had *become* their madness, grown into it.

Rooms that were once men and women. Mad men. Mad women.

They had succumbed.

Become

Now he, Roane, thinking himself an old spirit of rain, (probably some tragic Cree tribe incarnate), would also become. He'd dump the inferior husk of his 'consciousness', bin the Ego and *be* the ego, the truest *self.* He would be a man without shadow; it was as easy as that, the enigma of eternity. (He'd read *all* about it in a second hand parapsychology booklet once.) Come to a cemetery and dig a grave for your illusionary self: *Burying the Shadow!* It sounds like the title of a 'gothic' horror paperback.

He'd passed a workman's hut when he came in the gates, there was sure to be a shovel in it. They sometimes hid them in the bushes. He looks around, sees a scrub of wild rowan, stumbles forward with predictable arrogance, slips, falling face down into wet webby bracken.

A start of birds go kniving by.

Someone coughing in the distance.

Giggling, on hands and knees, like praying. He needs no shovel; he will dig his own shadow's grave with his own hands.

Digging. Like a dog.

He unearths worms, nails, and spangles of shimmering silver: an unbequeathed pocket watch, shattered, scattered around a tombstone. Pieces of old broken time shining in the mud and shit. Dead time.

He digs. He remembers - Francis Bacon buried a chicken in snow on Highgate Heath; *it* remained fresh, but *he* caught a chill and died. Ha! *The least of all evils…* Roane chuckling to himself, rotten soil under fingernails. Dark clumps of hilarity. Silly *sod!* Cackling, snorting. An abandoned hiccup, then a wave of nausea. A pain in his chest like something stuck there, struggling, *spreading* through him.

His vomit is thick and heavy. It comes in waves.

Like the sea

Black sick, dark and greasy as a shadow.

Heaving black bile, he pukes in the space he has dug. *Psy-sick.*

He looks up, seeing for the first time an adjacent gravestone, awaiting planting, before him. The name on the tablet is:

DOCTOR JUDITH ANNA GOLDFLAME

and beneath her name, a carved palm tree and the inscription:

LIFE IS SPENT IN A FEAR OF KNOWING
DEATH, UNLIKE AUTUMN,
KNOWS NO WINTER

Hallucinating, he thinks he can see an ocean aflame, burning churches and *the skull of a horse sailing by.* He looks up and one word thunders into thought. The word - *Spoiled*

Lurking in the bushes, there is an old man watching the last funeral of the day. He likes to see the women weep, watches the coffin lowered Hellward - down. Likes to think of the big hard wooden item entering the juicy open hole. The ultimate hard-on. His black tie is stiff with spilled sperm. He likes to recall that death is only a lifetime away. Later, he will enjoy the fragrance of stolen grave flowers as he's dripping hot remembrance candle wax onto himself. He moves on, holds back. There's a danger in watching too long.

He lives for your goodbyes.

An icy breeze jolts bones of webs snagged in a broken masonry angel's wing. The budding of grey trees goes unseen. A cuckoo bleats among the generations of the dead.

Round the back, where no one sees, lie the wreaths and

floral tributes picked from unattended graves now nobody comes. The decrepit long stems are left here to rot and to wait for the sexton in cloth cap and canvas movement to rake them to pile and put them to match. The debris of the dead house, disembodied, immobile, save for the dancing leaves that char, flicker and ash jolly on the air. Cinders of time.

Flowers to burn.

10

They had drunk themselves honest and separated *to Wimbledon and beyond.* Alone now, holding the book of madness, the leather bound ledger of names, dates and manias. Mayflies snagged in the hair on his arms, he moves from room to room with Maudsley the parrot at his side. He is on the second floor of the madhouse. Floor of secrets. He *knew.*

He knows.

He had wanted to see the rooms for himself, no audience. The bird was OK, he at least talked sense. It was now impossible to tell if there were ever any other rooms or secret cubbies - the original Hall blueprint hidden forever under Trojan Blue spray paint.

He had wondered at the time why Judith would leave them and *him,* of all people, an asylum. Of course, he had had it checked out: a favour for a favour - some Doom Town historian called 'Faiths', who turned up little more than nothing, who turned up two days later, strung up in a Bromsgrove backroom wearing his mother's clothes, his teeth heaped in a tea cup, psyche scratched. Strange shit. Self-inflicted weirdness. Tosser.

There are patients' names in the ledger scored out, defaced. What happened to them?

He stands on the threshold of the room of right angles. The room gives an impression of movement. Steel shining on steel. Silver shudders. He flicks through the pages, finds an entry with no name, but the date 1915 and a scribbled afterthought – *"10 days".* He reads the words *"too dangerous for war"* and learns of a toe-less 'maniac' who fed the birds ten pink treats and had his danger burnt out of him by science. Some poor bugger living a life of night, caught, padded and clamped, swabbed, enucleated, his temples strapped, a bit of wire to bite on. An on 'On' switch and a delayed blue light. Eyes falling and the last thing heard. *"...too dry, do you?"* The heart cancelling five beats. Sleep. Tears. A life of night, and this room - a knife blade bookmark alongside that thought.

He proceeds to the room where a light bulb drips from the ceiling and grows into the walls. He recalls with casual fear, the name 'Wires' and 1899 - a parson's son struck by lightning. Apocalyptic visions of snakes and angels, an electric religion. *Plugged himself in...*

The bulb hangs there, an electric web. The circuit of glass glowing grey. A sound: reverberation –

ohmmmmmmmmmmmmmmmmmm

A sudden galvanic heat, raw dry...

He closes the door, moves on.

The name on this page is *Xavier Wake.* The room is rock. Jurassic. He reads and knows. Little truths, simple infinities. There is a fossil man, jumping. Shadow fossil. A feather-winged insect frozen in stone: a quarter thought caught in limestone. There's an enormous barrelled head poking through rock. *Something jawed, fanged.* **Fulgivorasaurus Rex Regum.** An unknown specimen. Something the Geological Society once laughed at the idea of: continental drift? In Northampton! *...no significant dinosaur fossils have ever been discovered in the county.* Didn't want to get their spats dirty crossing the north/south divide, favouring the sunnier climbs of Lyme Regis. No one had believed him, but he'd found it, had unearthed the God of all Lizards on a (Oolitic ironstone) Northampton allotment, 1907. Their laughter hurt him, drove him out, and out of his skull. Mind exile. Tookesbury candidate.

The floor is powder; greeny-grey purple. Sharp with the stink of seas. Shells, fossils from the upper chalk, trodden down by years.

He remembers the name 'ammonite' derives from the ancient Egyptian god, Amon: inspiral horned, Jupiter prototype. But then, did that matter?

Maudsley takes a closer look at the fossil man - and there, there in a fold of stone skin, *there*, an appendix scar.

little truths

They move on.

This fourth room, upturned tree. A room of roots. Roots of the Terebinth tree. In a locked room below, the branches of the tree, spread out, waiting. Like an open hand. There are sketches of tree roots in the ledger. Words. A name - *Mr Eke.* His history is read: shocking. The walls and ceiling, brown as burnt maps. Autumn only a cold breath away. He touches a root, *touch wood,* as an offering of respect. He knows it will do no good.

On to -

Captain Sydney Erickson Welles, committed 1891, an 'explorer'. Floor of soft sand. Cave paintings, thick air, scattered ancient ornaments, skins, dry grass. Soot from the base of the mountain. At the window, stretched across - a chart. He examines it, flinches at the name of the rumoured land.

So it *was* true.

He laughs, leaves.

A room of ribbed beams and ever-burning hearth. Crude, sour white walls. A name in the book, *Morris Bacon.* A Welsh hill peasant.

There is something... almost frightening to the vacancy of this room.

Another room, now. This room, he had seen it before and had not *quite* believed it. A room of bad blood. The floor, sticky as a seven sugar tea. A clock, a mirror, a picture on the wall, *swallowed,* drowned in blood. According to the ledger the occupant of this room was *Sister Phaedra,* an orphan out of Venice, taken in, rescued by the Sisterhood of

Our Lady of Sorrows. Stigmatic, she was, and found in bed with Padre. They called her The Angel of Maggots, God's Harlot, and wanted her burnt. Instead, she ended up here, a scarlet woman in a red room. The rest of her history has been torn out, like a heart.

More rooms: a library of dusts. Somewhere in the ledger there is bound to be word of a twisted librarian or bibliomaniac. A guilty Egyptologist's room - confession in predynastic hieroglyphs. A room of lace. A *locked* room, no keyhole, just the door of black wood. A room of broken clocks.

The terrible room which once housed the mathematician Sir Septimus Weems...

A tiled room. Turquoise blue tiles. Perfect Moorish ceramic, seven inches by seven inches. Damascene. Dark blackened blues: a room of Peacock darkness. He had seen the sumptuous temple at La Zisa, had seen the spaces where these original tiles had once filled.

A room whose walls are seeped in deepest purple flock wallpaper but, poking out as if through saturated velvet, there are bones beneath the paper. A wallpapered grave.

A room, much smaller than all the others - walls and ceiling running with clear fluids, virginal juices pooling, feeding the wild pansies, *loves-ease,* curling up through the pristine bones of a mule.

Onto a room in which there is only a butler sink, corroded tap dripping, within the sink a silver sheriff's badge knocked and nudged by every single drip drip drip.

Room after room after room.

A room stacked floor to ceiling with plain delft. A room full of twilight. A room full of candlelight. The room that once housed the wife of an artist, she hated him and his art. Best not look in that one *particular* room...

He steps into the room where the walls have slouched. Baggy brown canvas. Inhuman sepia of deflated, dead flesh.

Wall jowls, moulding. Stale. A dead room. A killed room - bullets had torn through it in the Blitz. There is a small stone face behind the door, a gargoyle. Golem. There is the faint greasy stink of clinker. *Dennis Poulting,* a transient pyromaniac, who they used to let go and watch over the furnaces. A date, *November 31st 1919.*

Puddles soop in canvas pocks.

Maudsley has wandered away; maybe he has the right idea. Too many rooms. Too many histories. It's like theft, picking at the wounds of other people's minds. Blasphemy, once removed.

He takes himself off, rests. Maudsley crooning somewhere in the background. The ledger, words and drawings in a medical hand, Dr William Miles' words. He'd been *given* the post of head doctor in 1910, no one else wanted it; two doctors before him had drunk themselves dead, another packed case and set off overseas, a sudden missionary. One dropped dead upon entering the room of blood. One just disappeared.

Miles wanted compassion as treatment. No ice-pick lobotomies. He was fascinated by the rooms and their rumours. Years slowed by, the mad came and were mad and died, and then one day, a little something occurred. The obvious enigma: a patient, a pathological voyeur, vanished, and in his place, a room of doors and keyholes appeared. The grounds were searched, but nothing found.

One month later, the Russian countess was gone, leaving no trace, but there, where she had been, a cell adorned in perfect doll's house furnishings. (And the schizophrenic mask maker of Wapping who was no longer there, a room of plain white walls, not even a window, sprung up.) It was then that he thought he *knew.* He dismissed all the other staff, and those patients not *truly* mad, (Odysseans feigning lunacy to cheat the war), were shipped off to lesser asylums, leaving him to observe his select few. But the Hall was losing money, the owners curious as to why there had been no recent admittants. So Miles *allowed* two new cases in. One, a whore, whose incarceration would be settled by an eminent politician. The other, a shellshock case, John Fairford, fresh from the trenches of a Gloucestershire insane asylum. John had dreams of drowning, suffocating. He had been gassed at Ypres, made deaf by mortar fire and bumpkins in a bughouse had cremated his brain.

The whore was named for a lake. Rydal was her name. Rydal Bowtell. A Baker Street girl. Some sodomite's minx. *Melancholic,* she was 'lovesick'. She was diseased, crawling with syphilis she had acquired off a judge. She was pretty enough with her red hair and white grey eyes. Soft brain, hard heart. Paid off. Left to rot.

Miles had made sketches, took samples, photographs. He even had tombstones erected in the grounds for those who had not died: *the Basil Valentine Jnrs* the *Mordachi Scarrats.*

Freud was approached by telegram, concerning the ideals of alchemical metaphysics and the mechanics of wish-fulfilment. He replied by letter; sealed with wax. Upon opening, his reply was four sheets of paper, all blank. Empty. Another truth.

John Fairford changed into a room of poppies and gasmasks on the twelfth night of May, 1919. He suddenly wasn't there. Miles had woken, he had heard screaming, or thought he had. And there, in Fairford's soft cell - mud and mud on the floor, a red devil in stained glass on a wall where gas-masks *grew*. Poppies all around like slain velvet. And vapour, clinging to breath, burning. Once, and only once, he thought he heard a voice within the room; curious, scared - *"it smells of onion."*

Impossible. He had not believed it: A man and his thoughts *becoming* a room, replacing bricks and mortar. No, it couldn't possibly *be*. Miles had fallen from the pinnacle of sanity, or thought he had. (Not mad, but greedy, tiny in comparison.)

He howled, he cried, he whooped with joy. He ran to Rydal's cell and stuck himself inside her. She did not look at his pink burnt face, did not feel his stub of skin.

Bats were at a high leaden window, frothing. Scratching. Re-spoiling night.

He had not thought of the consequences.

Bitter brown, his thoughts; like some fever thrown off in childhood. Best not think about it, occupy the mind with another matter - the Hall, think about the Hall. Tookesbury Hall, the mad zoo, and he, the curator. Master of the beast, a tiger tamer in a travelling show, for he knew it was conceivable that at any moment the Hall might yawn and shift itself, *stretch its many hallways and pounce away*. Walk out on him. It was a living *thing*.

Rooms which were once men.

A *mad* house.

If he listened carefully, he was sure he could hear the walls breathing.

The bats were inside the Hall now. He saw them sometimes in mirrors.

He had the whore daily. Took her from behind, like a wolf.

Irma Katpooks turned into a room of pastel sounds.

On Christmas day, Calloed Smitts, the cannibal whom Miles had encouraged with art, escaped. Miles found him in the cellar, locked him in there over night. By morning Smitts *was* the cellar.

Miles was thick with the infection now. Syphilis. Chancres deepening. His vision - hellish. He was convinced that the bats nibbled at his ears whilst he slept.

The whore came close to death, sweating out her time, the medicine was delivered, silver nitrate for his eyes, a concoction of muck to spoon on the sores. The arsenic to be taken orally.

He had seen syphilis in pamphlets only: diagrams of sailor's teeth, fever charts. *Skin.*

They would re-infect one another, the whore, the doctor, pass the flame from mouth to mouth.

He dreamed he saw his mother giving birth to a bird.

The bats ate all his waist-coats.

Once, he had the revelation that the skin of the Earth was peeling slowly off.

He dreamt that he dreamt that his dead father was being buried alive by ghosts.

It was Sunday, a dark Sunday when the politician called. He had taken a Hackney to the Hall and walked up the drive. The door was open. He entered slowly, looking for an attendant or doctor. He had come to visit the whore, to pay the forthcoming year's bill and his *respects.* He did not see the man with burnt pink face and silver in his eyes come limping up behind him with an axe.

Miles put the politician's carcass in the furnace.

He climbed the tree that was Mr Eke. Sharpened his pencils on the room of right angles. He took ice from the room of ice and put it in his brandy and soda. He tried to read the books of dust in the library of dust. He succeeded in performing a blood transfusion between the room of blood and himself. He partook of the rooms, leisurely. *Used* them.

Betrayed them?

He had no conception of what he thought. Was it jealousy or paranoia? Miles was not mad, but he had 'caught' a madness off the whore. Her disease and its significance: softening of the brain, blindness cured only by silver, the pain which came in waves (like the sea). He **knew** she had plotted his insanity with her filthy ways. Well, he would not be bested by a bloody woman! He bound her and beat her. He kicked her until the strait-jacket was pink with blood. He unbuckled her and took her from behind. Dry discharge. Wet eyes.

It had taken him two years, but he had written it, his tome: **The New Laws of Madness.** Freud would be forgotten, but *he* would live forever. Immortal. He had finally *discovered* madness and called it 'Evil'. Impure. The Devil himself would stand outside his door at night and wait and whistle and quote Faust and…

His mind was breaking.

Now he did not know. Was it real? Did any of it *actually* exist? He stayed away from the whore for two nights, two days. Her food pushed through a slot in the wall. And then.

The night was thunder. A storm shook the Earth and Tookesbury Hall. He had drunk down a bottle, decisions swam within. Who would he allow to publish his marvel? Were *they* even ready for such colossal insight? Already the bats had grown to disproportionate dimensions. Where must he go to escape this heathen pit, this Tookesbury Hell. He would settle in Rome and be blessed. He had adsorbed enough sin.

He had the whore's food on a wooden tray. He knelt, bent back, eye to her keyhole. Some Penny Dreadful Peeping Tom, peering in. *And then it happened…*

He *saw* her.

She was *changing.*

Stretching out, through, down, around. The Room. She. Her. **It.**

Miles stared, an icicle with burnt silver eyes. The whore had changed into a room, she had *become* like the others. The true mad! And there, there in her centre, no, *its* centre, was a smaller 'room', a secondary. Its features slowly forming, a face, eyes half open, a twisting thing of a shape, half live, lifting -

Familiar. Embryonic. *His face*. It was *his* face.

She had been with his child, his, and had changed, both of them, her and it into a bare blankness. Sterilised. Clean.

Safe.

He could hear heartbeats.

The sound of breathing.

The sanest sensation that it was *he* who was being spied upon.

His world passed swiftly then, like a pantomime dream. Another bottle. Lightning tearing out his bloody hair, tearing up the blank correspondence from Freud. Scratching *Mystery* on a wall of hieroglyphic truth. Leaving poppies outside Her room. *Their* room.

He drew a heart on a broken mirror and hanged himself with silk.

The authorities eventually discovered his body and the bodies of three others; patients who had starved to death whilst he hung there.

There is only the faintest of shadows now, a stain, nothing more of the poppies Doctor William Miles laid at the door of Rydal Bowtell. A shadow, pink as lychee peelings.

So now he had read the book, knew the history of Tookesbury and all its forsaken. Poor bastards, what did they know?

Or care?

Tookesbury was a victim of its own space and time. Built on disbelief, *carved by an atheist mason* and left in the hands of respectability and men of science. It was the year *1888*, and the mad were rife as always, and freaks belonged in a sideshow or in a cell. With Tookesbury, it's as if all the mad were wrapped up in stiff white coats and piled in, one on top of the another, built up like bricks, like acrobats. Layers of white time. Frozen strata. So many, that they were built into a big white house. A mad house of Mad men. (Unthinkable!) Bricks in the establishment wall: solid citizens, locked away, forgotten, out of sight and out of their minds. It became what it was. **Itself.**

He knew now, but did not care. Doctor Judith had left the four of them her home, Tookesbury Hall, for them to find the secret, to believe and become.

A final keepsake - Themselves.

Mr Jackson lights his lighter, touches flame to paper and burns the history of lunatics past. Brown flames curling in on blue. He drops the ledger to the floor where it creases, breaks. Crumbles to dust.

He moves off, calling after Maudsley. Wants nothing more to do with other people's cinders. Has had his fill of joyless ashes.

11

Life is an incurable disease.
***Abraham Cowley* - To Dr. Scarborough**

Face down and floating. In darkness. The crucified man, his body a black cross slipping down river. At the shore, a washerwoman bent double, washing flags and shrouds. Fires flutter in the distance: lanterns of burning towns.

His father was an American: the local air force base. Metal birds, black machines. The mother had been no good. Saturday night, up on the kitchen table, towel in mouth, legs spread. A drunken pair of hands pushing metal in her womb - pulling - pulling out a monster with a crack in its head. They popped it in a bucket, covered it with a cloth. His mother, dead in a dug hole cradling a pail. Mother and shun.

These were his 'makers', their nothingness of myth and race passed down through the blood and belly.

The father - shipped off - liberating fishing towns. 1975. Shot down. Missing in action, hiding in the jungle, curled in a cave afraid of the dark. Swallowing the soil of Asia. Heat. Leeches. Ghosts with guns chasing through the long grass. His last thoughts were that - the Devil is a monkey sitting in a tree and green is the colour of Hell. Dead and mad in Vietnam.

The mother, a Celt, and all *that* made her, and all she had been told. Her father's father under the sod in France. Bones stretched out: a map of mankind. White poppies, black crows.

The crucified man has been beached, feet stuck in sand,

the body upright, a scarecrow now. The god of ghosts hung up in a field of vivid grey corn; a battlefield. Swords, axes, stakes of iron scattered on all sides. The wake of war. A consequence. Horses and men turned inside out. There are body-bags piled in the field; they are full, but moving. Curiously twitching.

Helicopters swarm overhead, ghostly silver light shining off them. They approach, swoop, downing their missiles, scorching a path, making a new sun. Napalm.

The battlefield has become molten. Swords melt, shields of a dragon design combust. The body-bags are frying, kicking. Helldancing. The fire is liquid, stubborn. The fire is red, black as boiling blood. The scarecrow is swept away on carrion seas - a ship now, the crucifixion is the mainmast, shroud for sails, the figurehead is a skull with eyes and hair. The hair curls around itself and is the rigging, tangled and greasy. Sailing the black ship of self.

In inferno seas, churches have become shells of burnt basalt. Cathedrals drown in fire. White asylums brown with burning. The skull of a horse sailing by.

There are waves in the sea of blood, waves of white poppies breaking as the sea screams. The scarecrow-ship-crucifixion is tossed about fiercely as the sea *rises* and stands upright.

Black. She who *was* the sea, stands surveying night. She is giant, the height of a mountain and black with crows. Cloaked. A slay of heads hang at her neck, heads with mouths open, speaking. Bodiless voices, though now *She* is their body, the Mother of Mourning, black-boned, fire-haired: black fire.

Life, death and in-between, She speaks, the sweetest sound of Banshee song. Her tongue, long scarlet, coiling down to tear the word **'LIFE'** on to the scarecrow's heart.

She - the sea - fire - Mother of Darkness, spreads her wings of arms and one by one, the crows take flight - away -

specking the dawn horizon. Gone. She has gone. Nothing. Nowhere. No more darkness.

Only light.

Dead. He is dead, the mad man - Jerusalem.

He had been dreaming. Fever dreams of the ghost that had been life. An odyssey through birth, birds, fire and darkness. It was an insect that killed him. A black mosquito: some leftover from an hallucinogenic nightmare of 1922. It had bitten him, communicated the given disease - the psychic message of death. He had fallen forward into darkness and stagnation of the madhouse cellar, (now a cannibal), was swept away, off, out into the world of water beneath London and its lost.

Washed through buried rivers, pushed along the subterranean flow, swift down streams of forgotten distance, the mad man dreaming he was a ship, plotting a course - *on* - through the abyss, siphoned into deeper archaic gullies, sweated out between cracks five fists big, to be plunged among tunnels flooded with the nights' rain. All the time dreaming, dying, moving on. The roar of tube trains one wall away. He was sucked into sewers, spewed out on a tidal rush of shit into pipes thick with wires, reeled in, *shocked,* stung by the current and discharged in spits of sparks. Dreaming, thick with clay and death. He became stuck, lodged between two water pipes, flimsy things of old corrosion, they soon burst. The pressure smashed him up through the earth, stone and plastic cable.

He was no longer underground. The eruption had pushed him up through flagstone floor, squeezed him out as if pus from a wound. His body was stretched out, crucified without a cross. Telecom wires tangled in his hands and mouth. Clay in his eyes. Gallons of water glugging out around him christening his corpse. Brown waters seeped out, staining the edges of broken burnt pews. Torn Bible pages lay swamped in ash and deluge. A defaced bronze Christ hung from the wooden nave roof, a black Bakelite telephone coiled at its base. The remains of the mad man had been returned, given back by night to the Church of Rust.

Moths lay in eaves, listening.

Maggots held their breath…

A brave spider scurried out, skimming the water, settling on the mad man's hand.

No pulse.

No breathing.

It hurried up his arm, crossed to the chest, up to his face. It crept along his cheek, loitered at his lips… and shat in his mouth.

Nothing.

Nothing

The spider scooted, *wheeled,* threw itself off, caught itself mid-air in web.

A shout went up. Insectoid rejoice: **"THE LAMB IS DEAD!"**

Vinegar Flies looped the loop. Bacon Beetles died laughing.

The Lamb was dead. And killed by one of their own. Just look at the signs! Hawk-Moths came closer to investigate.

Dry white black vomits stained his jaundiced yellow face. Pus remnants scummed up swollen eyelids. Old blood on his lips, eyes, tongue and gums. There would have been blood 'below', but they didn't want to look there. Some Silverfish, however made a feature out of scuttling around the caked-on anal haemorrhage.

Ladybirds tittered. Glow Worms guffawed.

An Assassin Fly settled on the dead man's stomach. There were small red blotches on the hot, dry skin.

Strange that the skin was so dry after being wrenched through water for two nights. But then, what did a fly know?

Soon they had smothered him, old dead mad Lamb. Headlice nested in scars. Ants in his muscles. Apple worms lolled where there once were ears. Bees flew above, ghostly green pupae minced below.

They looked and *saw* and **knew**.

Knew how it would have been, the infection spreading slow, the pulse like stone, the fever, they could smell it on him. They laughed at the confusion he must have felt, and at the terror in his stomach; like eating fire. The pain in his brain like being trod on. Like God's mouse trap.

They knew. They passed the words from mouth to mouth: *"Yellow Fever!" "Mosquito!" "Dead!" "Dead!"*

Spiders spun candy cotton, maggoty cherubim chanted devotions. Stag beetles spread wings, wearing obese horned haloes. Flies in adoration. Fleas in the pulpit.

He lay there, the mad man, the dead man: bitten by dream, dead by choice. The ghost of a life not wanted.

And then the telephone rang…

For a second there was silence. Between the *thwuuunnggs* of the rusty phone, no thing stirred, shadows frozen. And then the eye, the left eye of the mad man…

twitches.

A bell is ringing in his mouth.

The eyes crack open, loose grey, gone beyond. Eyes holding no exit.

His body snaps up, arm of twisted burns snatching up receiver, *listening…*

A voice: "…Hello, I wonder if I could have a minute of your time. Have you ever thought what an improvement it would be to your life to have replacement double glazing fitted…"

The mad man, no longer dead, replaces the receiver.

Dull thick pain weighs in his head. He hears lift music. There is plastic and wire in his blood dry mouth. He spits it out. He lifts his head, slows it right, then the other way. He has returned, the prince of the abyss, to the Church of Rust. Prodigal revenant resurrected by wrong number.

Somewhere, sometime - not quite now, he knows there is a fifth voice, a Flame of Gold to be snuffed out…

But for now, there's just the scattering of invertebrates. The fading echoes of a centipede's "Ha Ha's"

Encores of hatred. Flies, in hiding.

The laughter soon stops.

IV

Gooba Gabba

got~ist~tot?

The deed is all, and not the glory.
Goethe - **Hochebirg**

"How often have I said to you that when you have eliminated the impossible, whatever remains, however improbable, must be the truth?"
Sir Arthur Conan Doyle **- Sign of Four**

1

Life's little day.

They had spent the morning watching the 'build up' of the big top. The tent canvas splayed out in sections; a blank Tarot laced together, gathered up by a dozen or so big lads. An elephant was used. Side ropes around its neck, strolling backward, tugging, raising the canopy. King poles sledge-hammered in. The tent suspended: smaller ropes passed through quarter poles, knotted, tied tight, guyed off with heavy wire. Hammered. The men slope off for a quick cough and a drag. The elephant is fed a bag of onions; it has a chill.

The side wallings of the tent and the box office are hung in place. The 'punters' entrance is a small tent adjoining the big top. It is designed in the shape of a laughing clown's face. The painted smiley mouth is parted wide, inviting. They watch now as the seating, bandstand, and ring itself are ushered carelessly in through the open mouth. Eaten up.

The morning is grey with gull: a skeletal sky, rattling, mocking on wings of feathered bone. A Bedlam sky with its first rain falling.

"What's that?" points Ernie, full of wonder.

"A llama," explains Flint.

They watch as it is walked around and groomed.

To the side of the tent are cages, animal wagons, the big diesels and a flash chromey Mobile Home.

Fish is sketching in a blank dream diary.

Flint though, is uneasy. He can hear a sound like the sea, far away, coming in. It is a noise like roaring, but it could be that of a tiger. The wind blows hard, pulls his clothes around. His cropped hair, tousled. He calls through the wind: "Norman, me an' Ernie's off home now. I don't like this wind..."

Fish does not hear. He sketches. A Rizla paper hanging from his lower lip. He had begun to roll a roll-up, but had been distracted, the search for the tobacco tin forgotten. The rain hits the Rizla, sticking it to his chin. It dissolves and is washed away. Fish has not noticed. Sketching, he rubs rain around the page. He watches white boys splashing their piss against the side of a rusty generator. Piss prophets divining by urine. And the future does not look good.

There's a mean wind getting up.

And the circus is in town.

2

...to make an end is to make a beginning.
T.S. Eliot

The end has begun.

Ernie is meeting only dead ends: Flint is on the phone, shouting at the Weather Centre. He doesn't like 'this' wind. "I was bloody *there* in '87, mate. It blew two of me front teeth out!"

Mr Jackson, too, has his mind on other things. He needs an alibi: This evening he intends breaking the bones of one of the two young policemen who worked him over, a week previous. Flint said that he would get it sorted, but there's nothing like doing the job yourself. Satisfaction guaranteed. He has since found out that the other pig is history - some nigger with a Luger, Lewisham way, had seen to it. It made all the newspapers, even the Guardian.

Maudsley as usual, is nowhere to be found. Norman's still out and young Roane's wandering around the ground sniffing flowers. No one wants to know. But Ernie persists.

Had they forgotten already?

Jackson remembers: he's still to pick up his winnings, £12,000. Flush, raking in pocket, pulling out and throwing to Ernie, a fifty pence piece; *his* winnings. Paid off. Being told to "Go play in the traffic."

Flint bangs the phone down. "Fuckers!" Shivering, a mug of Bovril cupped, slopped to his mouth. Something weird is going down, something *very* weird. He slips his gloves on, dials a new number, dives headlong into the cupboard under the stairs. Shouting, cannot hear for the wind rattling the windows: "...Yeah, 'allo, is Mr Jabbs there?"

Ernie, shaking with futility, looking around, seeing only space. Closed doors, brick walls. Hearing only secrets on the phone. *He* couldn't hear the wind, no trees being blown about, no noise down the chimneys. Just excuses. Obstructions so that he couldn't go to the circus tonight. Lies.

Fist in hand, grinding teeth of rust together, like two iron minds straining for thought. He will go on his own. He will run away. To Hastings. To the sea. He will live in the dunes and sleep in a deckchair. Thin tears begin and suddenly the back door is rattling, violent, maybe there *is* a wind coming, pushing this way. Ernie looks for something to duck behind as the door crashes open -

It's Roane.

Ernie goes rushing up to him: "We saw a bald funny horse with ears!"

Roane laughs. Benign. "A what?"

"Bloody llama." Jackson sails by, angry, turning alibis in his mind. Looking for pearls, finding only stone.

"A llama and a 'nelephant and a big tent wi' a smiley face on and..."

Jackson cutting Ernie's monologue short with, "Bloody circus..."

"A circus?" asks Roane.

"Aye, circus, tonight. Will ya come? I got tickets, look." Ernie rakes out the tickets, waves them about.

"Bloody crows," curses Jackson, stalking off.

Just then, Fish strolls in. A lightning-blasted weather vane under one arm. The four points of the compass fused together. Ernie jumps on him, "Are ya coming ta circus tonight, Norman?"

Fish nods, resting the weather vane. "Yeah, alright."

"And what about you?" Ernie asks Roane, who agrees.

Strange sounds are coming from the general direction of Mr Jackson. *Words?* 'Bloody Henri Bergson' followed by 'Ointment?' and 'No' as afterthoughts. He looks up guilty, as if overheard.

Ernie braves: "Will ya come to the circus, Mr Jackson?"

He thunders forward, raising a hand as if to strike, but still: Michelangelo's Adam. Hand reaching out to possibilities, finger pointing. Mouth open. Thoughts sliding into place: "Circus, ya say?"

Lots of people at a circus. Lots of memories to remember him by. *Even* at a circus he'd be obvious. Just cause a scene for the audience already there - pick a fight with the knife-throwing act or kick in a clown - **Nobody** would forget that. A perfect alibi, he was nowhere near the scene of the crime, *he* was at the circus all night long, he's even got the scars to prove it. See?

And then he's back again, licking lips, smiling, teeth like a loaded deck. Slapping Ernie on the back - "Nice one, lad!" He looks to his watch. "I'll meet ya all there, at what, say, seven tonight?"

Ernie triumphant. Leaping. "Wheee! Circus! Circus!"

Flint emerges from the understairs cupboard. A woollen scarf wrapped around his top-most. "Circus?" he shivers.

"We're all off to the jolly old circus!" heavies Jackson.

"That's just as well," explains Flint, "I'm to meet some associates there myself."

"Anyone we know?" from Jackson.

Flint sneezes, wipes it on his cuff. "No, not unless you know any Aborigines."

Roane pipes up, "I found these in the garden just now. Down by the greenhouse. I thought you may know what they are, being a gardener..." He breaks off, unsure of speaking too long. He throws a small packet of seeds to Flint.

Caught. There's a name on the packet - *Xochipilla.* Flint,

edgy, watching out the window, looking at trees bent back by the wind, clouds pushed from the tableau. He's twitching the packet between his fingers.

"What does the name mean?" asks Roane, not knowing if the word was the seeds' *genus*, or indeed, their *owner*.

Flint stares at the packet, he tries to open it, his hands shaking. He rips the packet, unconsciously rapid and malign, and the black seeds scatter everywhere.

Scattering the seeds of *Xochipilla.*

Flint, nervy: "Sorry, sorry."

Seeds everywhere.

And the four winds fused together.

3

Language is fossil poetry
Ralph Waldo Emerson

"*It's all right,*" say the Voices.

Watching, looking through dust motes, thunder in his skull. Dead thoughts. An inclement mind greasy with dirt. A bit of broken bone sticking out through polythene all burnt and lurid. The ground around him, split, rent, pushed up and out. Muck from a water pipe glopping about his black-wrapped feet.

The Voices gab, "*...just sheep.*"

Out in the world there is rain in the afternoon. Children splash in puddles, dogs chase raindrops. There is the soft smell of damp soil and wet stinging nettles. The laughing sound of rain on lakes. Shadows of seagulls on walls no longer used.

"*No,*" cackle the Voices, "*Cinders there instead.*"

Jerusalem, choking, lurches forward, coughing. He spits out something red. It is a rosebud. Petals on his tongue. Thorns in his throat. Should this mean something?

"*The machine function,*" inform the Voices.

He must go north again to a mad-house and kill the fifth voice. Goldflame. The flame of gold. The philosophy is forgotten. The sorcery, decayed.

Rain sweeps through the walls. Strong winds rattle the Church door.

"*Tunzi,*" say the Voices. "*Tunzi,*" and "*toast.*"

***

Years ago Mr Jackson had his fortune told by a bird in a Tlemcen bazaar - a performing macaw that would turn over Tarot cards with its beak. For Jackson, it turned the death card. He was none too pleased - striking the vendor and pissing on his figs. Now it was time for death, not dying, but change. He needs a disguise. In four hours time he is to cripple a young policeman, pour bleach in his eyes and set him on fire. He already has his alibi and two litres of Domestos waiting. With any luck the newly-reported serial killer would be suspected.

With Maudsley perched on his shoulder, he rakes through a wardrobe which has mirrors on its inner doors. Some antique of Doctor Judith's. He pulls out a floral pink dress. Perfect! Just his size, twelve sizes too small. A Laura Ashley GBH.

"Bollocks," comments Maudsley.

He bins the dress, takes out a hat box. In it is a floppy black fedora. Hanging on the rail is a man's long grey overcoat, its pockets full of mothballs. He likes their smell, sniffing them, asking Maudsley, "Now, what about me face?"

"Aawk, coon!" suggests the bird.

"A nig-nog?" nods Jackson. "Bootpolish, eh?" He rubs his chin, looking up, seeing his face in the mirror, he cannot recognise himself. **That** would be the perfect disguise. If *he* couldn't identify himself, who else could? It *is* him, only he no longer *knows* the face that peers back. It's as if he's taken on some involuntary emotion.

He has become an incomplete stranger.

Touching the face, he can no longer see the memory there. Memories of steaming bananas in Papua New Guinea, or snogging with a split lip. This face wasn't one that had touched at more ports than any wave or was burnt from the fever in the Small Church of St. Anne's, Trebizond, the church on the sea sands... No, now he looks like an October man, a coffin full of autumn. Brute brown his colour, age raw. A face of bruises and eyes. An aged thug. A scar-crow.

He pushes the mirrored door to. Puts Maudsley on a chair-back, pulls on the long coat and picks up the bleach. Match boxes rattling in his newly found pockets.

He will need the hat, it is raining. He had a son somewhere, a piece of history thrown away. A waste. Must be nearly thirty by now. Ah, well.

Fish is painting onto broken glass. Black and yellow ochre. Not looking, he rinses turpsy brushes in a cup of black coffee, wipes them on his old pyjamas.

Ernie dives into the scene, asks, "What ya doing?"

"Not doing," says Fish, "Done." He holds an oil wet shard up to the light. His thumb leaving a print of whorls in one tacky corner. No need for a signature. He places it alongside several others. "I'll call it, 'The New Meat'," he says. Suddenly he *sees* Ernie, a new canvas. "How'd you like to look like a clown, then?"

"What d'you mean? Paint me face?"

"Yeah." Fish looks in at his coffee cup, thinks better of it. "Sit yaself down 'ere."

Ernie rushes forward but reality trips him. A voice born of doom: "But it's raining, Norman, it'll all wash off."

"No probs," Fish rakes out a palette knife. " Now then, sit *very* still…"

Rain makes a labyrinth of the window's pane.

Roane stands staring out through the glass. Not taking part in the world, just watching. Dark clouds and darker gulls.

The warmth of the old iron radiator reminds him of a safer time before all this happened. He strokes the wool of his black jumper, it smells faintly of Lenor. He feels he should cry, but all that comes is a soft laugh of joy.

Tonight he will go, along with the others, to the circus, where he will cheer on the clowns and applaud the tiger-tamer. He will be gladdened and walk home in the rain. It is to be a celebration of life, before death.

Tonight, he will **become** a room. He has decided.

He had discovered the secrets of the mad house. He *knows,* but doesn't know what to expect.

He opens the window, reaches out, touches rain. Black hair spilling round his pale fine face. A water colour ghost. Calm, happy. Not knowing of the danger in watching for too long, of seeing *too* much.

The labyrinth has run away.

Things are looking worse. Flint had called up Mad Flo, the Maori psychic, and even *she* had left town. He can't get through to anyone else; the *Wind* must have brought down the telephone wires. This is no ordinary gale. It *knows* what it's doing. It had been called up, summoned, the Aborigines had told him. They had been following it for months now. A psychic hurricane: it started small in the Gibson desert then headed north-west to Indonesia, then on and on, changing course, dying down only to resurface, bigger and wilder. In Apache Junction, Arizona, the local clairvoyant *discovered that by tuning her TV to channel 13 and darkening the screen it was possible to register the approach of the hurricane as a strong white light on the screen.* She had been watching the channel when *it* tore through her apartment. They're still picking bits of her out of the neighbourhood. Nowhere else was effected, no one saw or heard a thing. All instruments set in its path to measure the speed of the Wind have been destroyed, blown away like straw buildings.

He's going to have to make a dash to his shed in the garden. At least there he can fill his pockets with esoterica, weigh himself down with hope.

He opens the back door, darting out into rain and cold

air. Into the Thinking Wind.

Standing about; waiting. Bloody cold as another pigeon shits on his shadow. The coat Jackson wears is not long enough to hide his crutches. His hat and coat, heavy with rain. Looks like a vaudevillian, feels a right twat.

He can't be seen here, by the corner of the block, but he can see the policeman, out of uniform, skulking down in the underground car park. He can see him smoking a cigarette, waiting. Jackson arranged for an assignation between the cop and his snout, but the snout wouldn't be showing, Jackson had seen to that. He will give it a little while longer, let him get onto his second fag, then just as he's lighting up, that's when he'll do it.

He doesn't look round; best just to stare into puddles. Once you've seen one ghost town, you've seen them all - dogs running wild, the metal smell of tinned soup cooking. Soap operas whining: Australian voices in the afternoon.

Right - the cop's just flipped away his fag, is rooting for another. Jackson moves in -

The first blow lands hard in the spine. The cop is down, the titanium crutch smashing into his head, chest and legs. Long ago, Jackson had learnt to balance on just the one crutch. He *hops* savage now around the fallen man, hammering him, repaying in kind. And the young man is screaming, saying "sorry, sorry," and not knowing why. But 'sorry' is a useful word and Jackson has heard it before. He slams the crutch into air, missing but not caring. Too quick in vengeance, is he getting too old for all this? Nah. The bravado is too much for him. This is old business with a young man. All the *really* good violence was left years ago, propped up in a rubber sack somewhere. Death isn't funny. And this means nothing.

The cop lies creased in on himself. Clothes, face and hand black with blood. Three of his teeth broken in a puddle. His ribs loosened. He makes a thin noise. Fuck him, stupid bastard.

Jackson walks away, off to Sidcup to the Moghul for a curry and a drink. He'll still make the circus by seven.

4

Outside in the rain, the Thinking Wind blows hard, rakes lead off the Church roof, pushes in the windows. The Voices drip like water, whimpering of *"Sausage meat"* and *"sufficient larks..."* A stained glass window depicting the Burning Bush is blown in out of its leaden surround. It falls to Jerusalem's feet, shattering on sandstone floor. Red and orange smithereens.

Jerusalem picks up the fallen window, tatters of scarlet lacerate his thumbs. Red sound of scalded gulls screeching. He presses it to his face, folds lead and glass about his head. Makes a mask of broken stained glass. He breathes slow, heavy, misting up the view. He stands and considers. There is no explanation for his action.

He had been dragged into the world, given away, tutored by maniacs, beaten and chained, prayed *at,* driven on by the Voices, chewed on by bugs, drugged, experimented and spied on by men of 'knowledge'. He had escaped by choice. He had been called to the Church of Rust to be its champion. He has been blown up by a gas blast, near drowned in the Thames, *awarded* yellow fever by drug dream mosquito. He died in underground streams, hallucinating, but Earth did not want him, spitting him out. He has even been cheated of death. Reborn by wrong number. Yet he is just a man, (in reality, still a boy. Seventeen years old), a burnt-out case going through the motions. In another life he might have been an artist or a gardener, or a face in the crowd. Loved. Jerusalem Lamb: burnt black. Broken glass and muscle. Just mad. Just a man.

Jerusalem **going**. Walking from the Church of Rust, out

into Thinking Wind and rain and its laughter. Leaving the door wide -

open

Wind has its own noise. Like that of a pig in pain. The Thinking Wind, however, is ten thousand sties awash with acid. The Voices comment, screaming, **"DEAD! DEAD ELECTRIC!"**

Jerusalem walks through streets against wind. Thunder and Lightning in a sky of fried Guinness. Passers-by pass by, not seeing, eyes full of rain. And through cacophony of pig pain, laughter, gulls and Voices, he can hear salvation.

At the traffic lights, an old transit van waits on red. Unseen, Jerusalem opens its back doors and climbs in. He is greeted with warm soft sounds: *Coooooooo cooooo cooooooooo.* The van's cargo is thirty cages of homing pigeons.

The van drives off. Heading north.

Through the open door it comes. Through pushed-in windows, through cracks in the west wall: the Thinking Wind

It rages round the Church, rattling in the rafters, tearing up the font. Ripping down Christ, tears away his face of magpie bones and maggots. Shakes foundations, crumbles walls down onto what's left of Anastasia's carcass. Its maelstrom stirring up the last embers of the pews' ash bonfire. Thin flames spark up. It snatches fire and throws it. The confessional catches, is soon devoured. It whips up blaze and Bible and slams away, out through the roof. Gone.

The south aisle is ablaze, roof lead is molten, hot as Hell. *Stewing,* windows split and explode. The nave blisters. Sandstone bubbles, ignites. The Bakelite telephone has baked. Christ has melted. The walls come crashing down.

Wasp nests combust. Spiders scald. Insects run in tiny circles until they are nothing more than clinker.

The ground trembles *upward,* breaking gas and water mains. Air explodes. All is furnace. Through roaring timbers it is possible to glimpse terrible faces in the fire: burning gargoyles. Fiery angels.

The falling rain is roasted.

Soon all is ash and the Thinking Wind returns, scattering embers in the atmosphere, blowing away the ruin until nothing is left of the Church of Rust.

5

...hurricanes were described on Beaufort's original scale as 'winds such that no canvas can withstand.'

From: An Index of Possibilities - Energy and Power

Ernie wears the skull of summer. Crimson and canary yellow: Norman had painted his face with oils and a knife. Smears of verdigris in his tufty hair. As the paint dries, it feels funny, tight. Rain runs down off his face, it tickles and he laughs. Rotting metal in a mouth of old smiles. Cracks form around his lips. Rain cannot wash his colours away. An immortal Grim-mouldy.

Flint, Fish, Roane, Ernie *and* Maudsley have walked through mud and rain to arrive at the circus. Flint in a big coat, weighed down - effigies of iron in every pocket. He won't speak for fear the Thinking Wind will hear him. He looks everywhere, looking for Aborigines, but catches sight of a drunken clown - white face, pink wig, lipstick smudged in phocine whiskers, steaming with purpose towards them, bawling, "Maudsley!"

"Oh shit," says the bird.

The clown is Mr Shyte, Hubert Shyte. One time partner of "Maudsley the Magnificent!" He ushers them away into a very large, flash Mobile Home. They are greeted by a small girl in tight sequins. Shyte's 'niece'. She brings glasses, two bottles. Vodka is poured, Maudsley given a double. Flint feeling safe under a soundproof roof.

Between gulps, Shyte breaks into sloppy recollection. "'Maudsley the Magnificent and the Gabbling Dommerar!'

Talk of the town we was... Plymouth, Penzance... We played 'em all... Supported Vince Hill once, didn't we?"

Maudsley, clearly embarrassed, head buried in empty glass.

"Bexhill, Hastings..."

Ernie is impressed.

"Rhyl, Skegness..." Shyte can suddenly hear himself. "Eastbourne? Bognor?" It's not until he gets to "Bridlington!" that he really breaks down. Head in hands. Vodka-teared. "My God! What have I done with my life?"

"Cheer up," says the girl, handing him a pug glove-puppet. Maudlin, he slips it on, goes 'oink oink' and laughs. The others escape, seems he has forgotten them, as he's pushing the pig face between young sequined legs. "Oink oink!" The girl only giggling.

Experience all the Treasures of the Orient At Schrent's Circus

That's what it says on all the posters, but no one can read them. Rain has washed the words away: a watercolour job-lot off a receivership-wrecked printer, Limehouse way. The posters, fallen, have been trod down, trodden into mud and puddles. A painted tiger's face fades to the touch of raindrops, has been crushed beneath feet of careless people rushing to the big top.

Lightning shatters sky. Darkness falls, bringing headlights speeding to the scene.

The car is a Mercedes Benz, it pulls up outside the tent. Mr Jackson gets out. His crutches, inch thick into mud. It's like a battlefield. He stalks in, waves the driver off.

A passing boy asks his mother, "Mummy, is that man on stilts?"

Jackson slaps the child around the head. No one seems to notice.

Fish and the others loom up. Wet shadows. Flint asking,

"Where you been?"

"Sidcup," from Mr J.

"Oh," as response.

Ernie hands in their free front row tickets; they are taken, franked and returned. They have been *accepted*, now there is no turning back.

Maudsley wants some popcorn, he and Ernie wander off. Flint is already **gone**, searching for Aborigine mystics. Roane, Fish and Mr J left all alone together. Three strangers, all different now. The weeks they have been at Tookesbury have transformed them, turned them, like previous mad men, into themselves. All of them, all changed - Roane wants to be a room, but in his own way he already is; a waiting room. No man is an island, yet we still float. Fish had fried, given a mind and art. Ernie's face is hidden beneath oil paint, a work of heart. Mr Flint is scared now, feary of weather that could shatter his stony name and self. Maudsley has changed by *not* changing. A blank chameleon. And Jackson has grown tired of life and the living of life. It's like an out-lived view. A postcard faded from the looking at.

All different. These four weeks have seemed four years. All their scenes eaten up. Time on a full stomach.

Jackson conjures a carafe of Indian wine. Fish also produces a bottle: two litres of Smirnoff pilfered from Shyte the clown. Bottles, not words, pass from mouth to mouth. A new prologue made.

Behind them, the audience is already applauding the first act.

Roane is 'merry', his cheeks tingling red.

"By God," Jackson swoops, scoops up a tatty piece of poster, "now there's a name I've no' seen in a long while." He hawks and gobs, "Kenny Schrent."

"You know him, then?" asks Fish.

Jackson steams into a tirade of injustice and filth: "Lent 'im money in 1950 so he could start a business, ain't seen nor smelled 'im since. Looks like Buster Keaton, long dead, dug up and brushed down. Face of old kettle scrapings, wanky eyes, leer like a melon rind. I 'eard he dyed his hair, left the Grecian 2000 on too long, rusty snags at his eyebrows and scalp. Has 'unnatural desires' for all things foreign. Masturbates over maps. Had a collection of stained Freya Starks when I knew 'im. He used to lick navigational compasses, y'know, 'til he got poisoned by radium salts, made 'em glow in the dark. Cancer of the tongue and gums now, hee hee, most of the mouth gone. Talks like a broken thing. Won't use a voice box, no. Last I 'eard, he were getting through five or six mail order brides a year, Filipino girls, pretty lasses. But he's rough with 'em, uses 'em 'down below' as ashtrays. Left seven or so limping round Bradford. The bastad. Must be worth a few bob though, if 'e owns this outfit." Jackson looks up, hears a sound like the sea. It is wind billowing around the canvas of the big top. He finishes the spicy wine, the vodka all gone, and remembers there's an alibi to be had, damage to be done.

Fish has taken a handful of mud out of the ground, rolled and shaped it. He holds it in his hand and closes his finger firm around it, *reshaping* the uninvented.

The bewigged Madame Taru and buxom Mama Cocha stroll by with their four swans, each one dyed a different colour. Blue, black, off-white and yellow. They are the next act on. They are smiling, over-embalmed in razzmatazz. Cocha farts. Out in the ring, the little Italian lads are juggling flaming wands. The audience grunts out its appreciation.

"My, but they're all on the ugly pills tonight," says Madame Taru.

"Quite awful," agrees Cocha, casting an eye over the audience. "The usual nellies and drears, they're all here tonight."

Daft old lasses and old, old men, coughing and

wheezing through the best bits of the show. Glugging down the laxative, spooning in the linctus. If it's not on prescription they don't want it. Every cough and sneeze, sticky punctuation in the sick note of life.

And there in the cheap seats, sit the shop-soiled girls with builder boyfriends. (Wasteground lovebites. Gravel Valentine.) Over by the exit, sit some bright young things, all *too* serious. Smiles thin as gravy. Lank laughter in a manmade cardigan. Amnesty International chic.

The back row: an Australian female impersonator sitting on a stack of muscle men magazines, straining for a better view. She's with a little man with a little moustache. Both of them have prying eyes and inquisitive nostrils. Seems they're looking for some new sensation. And in front of them, another 'couple'. Some mouthy Gnostic and his red-haired partner, who's fidgeting, not really wanting to be there. She's passed up the chance of an affair tonight, for *this*.

The day releasers are in the front row, sitting in their Pac-a-Macs and shower caps, rain dripping on them even through the tent. Two of them have umbrellas up. Others are strapped into shiny chrome wheelchairs and soft foam rubber booties. Puddles gather in minds. One wants his mother. Their skins smell of milk. Mental mosaics quietly dying.

The jugglers swallow fire. Their act and flames quenched.

The audience, in their role, applaud.

In the centre of the ring steps a leggy Filipino, black hair spilling down her back. She's dressed as the Ring Master: top hat, red coat and spangles. She introduces Madame Taru and Mama Cocha into the ring, four colourful swans also attend. The lights dim.

Ernie, his painted face assuring access to all areas, is backstage. Clowns commend him on his make-up, ask if he's new to the troupe. An elephant strolls by, and Ernie is invited to feed him popcorn.

There are Palomino horses wearing plumes. A yak being plaited. All around, the sound of generators humming.

The animal trainers are fourth generation, all inbred. Sons of sons, their daughter's daughters. Sometimes twins. Two beautiful acrobats flirt with Ernie; he can't tell which is which. One gives him a red balloon, the other, a wink.

He is shown the caged animals by Bob. There is a lion, two rhinos, a python, a Bald American Eagle and a tigress called Penelope.

"'allo, Pussy Cat," says Ernie.

Penelope purrs.

Bob is called away to dress the chimpanzees, he "won't be long." Penelope rubs against the bars of her cage and Ernie strokes a finger across her fur, feeling muscle and strength through sleekness. She is marmalade and Marmite. Eyes like two skies. She yawns and licks Ernie's hand.

It is only then that he sees her cage door is open.

The *Karadji* were late.

Flint had arranged to meet them here at seven. It was now eight-fifteen, where were they?

The Thinking Wind is filling up his mind, making his ears pop and teeth shiver. He sees the big top canvas billowing, dipping in. The guy ropes vibrating. It must be stopped; it has taken too many lives already. The Aborigines know it, have followed it. But he fears the worst, then behind him, a voice, shouting -

"G'day, Flint. How's it hanging?"

He turns, and there are Huey and Dabbs, brown as earth in their long wax jackets and cowboy hats. They too are weighed down. Lumps of Ayres Rock in every pocket.

"It's getting worse!" shouts Flint.

"What?" yells Huey.

The three huddle together, calling through the howling Wind. "How we gonna stop this?"

"Think we need a sacrifice, mate."

"Human?" screams Flint.

"Something big!"

"How big?"

"Dunno yet," hollers Dabbs.

"'ere," calls Flint, thumb toward the big top, "d'you reckon there's any virgins in there?"

"I like it!" roars Huey. "A bloody virgin sacrifice! Whooo!"

A 'woman' is chosen from the audience to sing a song. She wears a long brown skirt, hob-nail boots and a colourful yellow scarf over an obvious platinum wig. Her bosom defies gravity. The make-up she wears is painted an inch thick. Grubby stubble showing through foundation. Clutching her handbag, she is asked her name by the Ring Mistress, and in a rough falsetto, introduces herself as "Mrs Abram Mort!"

Supposedly unbeknown to her, four chimpanzees dressed as ghosts in white sheets sneak up behind her. The audience roar.

The band strikes up a cheesy tune and Mrs Mort in spotlight, powers into a scraggy rendering of 'My Way'. The chimps cavort and prance, lifting her skirt, sticking their head beneath. Not *noticing*, she carries on. A man in the band blows his nose, losing his hanky down his trumpet, getting his hand stuck retrieving, banging into the drums. Cymbals crashing, a foot through the tom toms. The audience in epileptic throes of rejoice. Grown men pissing themselves from the spectacle. Mothers simpering with joy into chapped, cold hands.

One chimp clambers up Mort's skirt, up past the waistband and out, head poking through cleavage, and to cheers, pops one of the false breasts. A blown balloon. The other 'breast' is taken, left to float away.

The audience applauding mock mastectomy.

Finally, the song is finished. She bows in the spotlight and by ghostly paws, her skirt is whipped away, revealing hairy legs and a pair of Union Jack bloomers. Howls of laughter as 'she' is chased, shamed, from the ring by apes dressed as dead men.

Roane claps. Fish sketches.

Maudsley is in conversation with a Russian acrobat.

Jackson stalks the circus, serving as the scar to others faces. He is waiting for the big one. Already he has loosened the cages of lion and tiger, frayed the tightrope and spiked the knife thrower's tea. But it's not enough. He must get *himself* remembered, not the chaos. There's only one thing for it...

Round the back, where the animals are kept, that's where he finds her. By God, she's bonny. Hair like molasses, face like the young Vivien Leigh, but skinny, there's nothing of her. Her tells her so - "Eeeee, I've seen more meat on an abortionist's coat hanger."

The Ring Mistress looks up - "Sorry, can I help you?" - a broad Filipino Bradford twang.

"As it 'appens, lass, ya can. Me name's Jackson. Mr Jackson. I work for *immigrations...*"

He need say no more. Within seconds, she's slung off her red stage coat and top hat and is out, fleeing into night and rain.

Shyte the clown throws a bucket of confetti over Roane. The young girl in sequins rides a unicycle. There are more chimpanzees, this time on horseback, dressed as cowboys. Elephants parade. The Strong Man lifts a bench full of nubiles. The Snake Lady dances. And the audience laps it up, needing the unreality of it all.

There is an interval, a strange overlong quiet ensues. Nothing but a few seconds, but long enough. Something is not right in the circus. No one performs. No music plays. A nervous rustling from the crowd, rain banging down on the roof of the tent, and then through the crackling loudspeakers...

"Ladies and gentlemen," there is no mistaking the voice, "for your delectation and delight," Roane and Fish share a look of mock horror, "we proudly present the proprietor of tonight's show…" From out of the shadows *strides* Mr Jackson in a tight red coat and torn top hat. Clip-on lapel microphone. In spotlight, it can be seen he holds a runt of a man by the throat. The man is tied and gagged in his vest and soiled pants. The crowd hoot, not knowing. Jackson ties him to a post in the centre of the ring. "Ladies and gentlemen, boys and girls, I give you… the one and only, Kenny Schrent, otherwise known as The Amazing Mr Indestructible!"

Hurrahs of adulation from the audience.

Schrent *remembers* Jackson, had thought him dead.

Schrent's wanky eyes popping terror. Terror in his tummy. Nothing in his throat but butcher's velvet. Scars.

It continues -

Jackson at his most manic, shouting: "Put ya hands together an' give a nice warm London town welcome to the atrocious Captain Cutlass and the lovely Janet!"

Cutlass staggers out, pissed, thanks to Jackson. He *wears* a Mexican bandito outfit and a second-hand toupee. Janet, five inch heels, hair Brylcreemed down to her arse, is squeezed into something mauve, resembling distressed tin-foil. She wheels a trolley laden with swords, knives and axes. Clowns roll in a twenty foot dartboard and arrange it to the post Schrent is tied to. Looks like he's the bullseye.

Jackson *explains* the act. "Big dartboard, right! You lot," indicating the audience, "call out number ya want 'im to hit! Right."

Excited ripple of nervous applause.

"Thirteen!" shouts Roane.

"Nice one!" Jackson, thumbs up, grinning dangerous to Roane. "The man wants THIRTEEN!"

Cheers from the crowd.

Janet takes a switchblade from the trolley, holds it high, twirling it. Light catches the blade; she tilts her head back, lowers the knife, slow, into her open mouth, swallows the blade to its very hilt and slowly removes it. Handing it to Cutlass.

Jackson, impressed. Asking her - loud speaker voiced - "D'you take it in the mouth then, luv?"

There's a commotion backstage. The Strong Man, Janet's boyfriend, comes tearing out.

Cutlass throws the first knife.

Schrent, gagged - weeping. People think he's laughing.

Thirteen! A direct hit. The crowd cheering. Someone calls out, "Forty seven!"

Eddie, the Strong Man explodes into the scene, looking like he's just evolved. The first fist thrown. Jackson ducking it.

Janet swallows a sword blade.

Crutches and knuckles flying in the spotlight.

"I've 'ad 'er!" taunts Jackson. "Cunt like a corn circle!"

Cutlass lobs the sword. Schrent shrinks. A warm puddle of piss trickling down his leg.

KERCHUNK!

The blade misses, embedding itself in double-top. The audience aren't fussed. They're watching the scuffle.

Maudsley calls out - "One hundred and eighty!"

Janet with a trio of rapiers to her lips.

Jackson smacks the Strong Man in the cobblers. Leans to Cutlass with the promise - "I'll give ya fifty quid if ya get 'im in the face…"

"Done!" accepts Cutlass, throwing.

Amidst amok, Flint and the Aborigines have stolen into the big top, out of the teeth of the Thinking Wind. They search with little luck through the audience for a sacrifice, a possible virgin. Dabbs shouts through the noise of the Wind. The audience though, cannot hear it - "Oi, Flint, had any luck?"

"None mate, how 'bout you?"

Dabbs shrugs. "They're all a bunch of old tarts, mate. This lot wouldn't know purity if it bit 'em."

"Ain't seen a crowd this rough since Adelaide!" yells Huey.

And then, three as one, they see in the middle of the ring - tied, helpless, haloed in switchblades, the ugliest, nastiest specimen of life imaginable. **Kenny Schrent.** If *that* wasn't a virgin, they didn't know what was. They bundle down, through spectators, heading for the trolley laid out with sharp, shiny knives…

The second rapier is thrown, slicing into treble twenty. Cutlass burps and up pours bile. His head spins. Had someone spiked his drink?

Jackson cracks The Strongman in the face with the tip of one crutch. He goes down, howling. Blood spattering his bronzed, oily chest.

Norman sketches. Roane only laughs, happy, enjoying the show.

Janet takes the third rapier and pops it in her mouth. She's professional enough. She can carry on. Two years at Butlins had taught her that.

Cutlass suddenly pukes.

Jackson gets in a few more rights to Eddie's bloodied head.

She can take no more. Janet, breaking down, begins crying. Thick tears, runny mascara. The third sword wobbly in her little hand.

Outside, the storm ranges on. Blue lightning. Brown thunder. Noise of life's scenery shifting. The Thinking Wind, boiling, brewing something bad.

The audience goes wild with the arrival in the ring of Flint and his strange black friends. "Must be the cabaret…" - shouts heard through the standing ovation.

Just as Janet faints, Flint swoops by, intent on swiping her rapier. But he's too late, it goes down with her. So he grabs an axe off the trolley instead -

Schrent can't believe it: the show's been hijacked. Cutlass vomits gin, liquid paraffin and Earl Grey, it looks like Janet and Eddie are dead, and now there's a madman steaming toward him with a bloody great battleaxe. But the punters love it! Now, he thinks, seems like a good time to start screaming.

And then it happens.

Popcorn vibrates.

Balloons burst.

Outside, the guy ropes are torn up and out.

Suddenly the world is on fast forward.

The big top ripped away by the Thinking Wind.

The noise is deafening. A shadow lifts and covers the sky. A deluge of mud and dust rains down all around. King poles collapse, crash. Thick ropes slam into Mr Flint. He is lifted high, but holds on. Huey and Dabbs sling themselves at other flailing ropes, grabbing on, screaming, they too, swept up and away.

The audience are only witness. They watch as the big top and three shouting men are taken starward, carried off into night by the Thinking Wind: a kite in Hell's tempest. Curious, the painted design of the clown's mouth on the side of the big top, flaps down and up, giving the impression of laughter. Flights of yellow and red balloons float away also. Lesser suns.

Cold air whips about the circus. All are looking up, the hurricane, tent and three men, gone. Only stars and darkness now. Silence sits upon every lip. Raindrops gently echo. The droning of generators. Clouds gather and part. The sky turning *unsympathetic yellow*. Dry pink white lights flash in the distance. Static air. And then, a crack of slow lightning and thunder booming, rolling in from outside night.

The clouds burst.

Like a cloud castle, the bricks and mortar of rain and hail come smashing down. Like coins, like silver fever, the stalactites of night, coming down, washing away the scene. Scratching out the night's events: swilling Eddie's spilled blood, sluicing away the knife thrower's sick. Rain has rusted the thrown swords and blades, has scrubbed Shyte the clown of his drunken make-up and robbed his 'niece' of her sequins.

The ice of rain has woken Janet from her swoon.

Schrent has drowned. And rain has made pulp of his giant dartboard.

The ground is mush when the rain stops. Swampy. The wild animals roam freely, their fur and skins drenched. Cages lie empty. Penelope the tiger has vanished. So has Ernie. Circus colour is leeched. Washed away.

A string of carnival lights, yellow, pink, drip with rain. They are spinking on and fizzing out. Ping.

The audience is scattered. Knocked over, sunk down in their seats. Some clap wildly. Others are crying. A few just sit and stare. Thick with mud, fragile and stupid in their little hats; looking like gnomes on the Somme.

Rain has razed the evening, deleted it, as if it had never happened.

Maybe it never did.

6

He shall defend thee under his wings, and thou shalt be safe under his feathers: his faithfulness and truth...
Prayer Book

Fleas in the mind. Thoughts scratching, hopping. He hears the birds, they are purring. He kicks out the van's back door and is off.

The van swerves away. Thirty cages of homing pigeons take flight from it. Escape. They do not feel the rain; the harsh wind does not ruffle their feathers.

He had sat with them, released them, shared their space and time. They had flapped about him, rubbed into him, shat on him. He knew where they were going. They were going home, leaving Jerusalem adrift in the cold sea of night. Rain laughs at him. He is pawed at from all sides by a Wind that thinks. Pig apocalypse, laughter and the screaming view of scalded gulls - red leaded glass bent in at his head. Feathers and shit snagged on his burnt black self: Wicca Man after cremation. Icarus post-fall.

A car passed, too quick. Foot down.

Rain blows in through cracks in the stained glass, seeps down his face. He remembers and breathes, misting up vision. Hell in a hand mirror.

The Voices tell him, *"Dumb without the place where the flesh fell off!"* and he knows they are right. No church, no mother but nightmares, no death. He roars: a furious instinct identified. He will eat the Goldflame, devour the bright burning voice and evolve from fire, become the walking flame to cleanse, heal, condemn and destroy. But these are trivial killings - the taking of sounds. Any maniac's trade.

He is not responsible, the mad man. For his mind has gone, washed away by rain - a space there instead. A dreadful shabby hole thick with strange heat, lonely time. A man no more, not living, not quite dead. Loreless. Unbeing. A never man.

The Wind shifts the stars.

He spreads his thick, torn arms, and is taken, lifted, snatched into air, weak in the fist of night. Winged shadow, tumbling, twisting, carried away by the Thinking Wind. Soaring above life and the living. Below, the World. Noise of moths drowned in cats' milk, the rusting of bridges and skin. The regrets of men.

Flying. He is a savage angel. King of Birds, vulture god. Wakonda, Rangi, Seth. He is none of these things. A stone in air. A mad man in the sky.

In the distance, the white mountain, the white house of madness. Tookesbury Hall.

"Coooeee! Inch blood! No, no! Nailed bacon said I!" reveal the Voices.

The Thinking Wind subsides, dropping Jerusalem onto Tookesbury roof. Given. He watches the Wind depart. Faraways off, toward midnight, he sees a whale beneath the moon with three men chained to it. It means nothing. (Flint, the Aborigines and big top, swept deeper into night.)

Up on the madhouse roof. A human figure, faceless but for scarlet glass. Terrifying.

Descension to horror. Lamb smashes through the roof into the Hall's attic. His fall is broken by a bench full of test tubes.

Through darkness, he can see it is a vast room. Sounds of emptiness, white screaming walls dumb from age, choked with dirt. The brown of coughing. Old air, dead paint. Shelves of books wait, medicinal tomes gross from quackery. Huge glass jars stand row after row. Things preserved within. It is a Victorian laboratory.

On a table, the skull of a man? Bone wrong, sunk in on itself, furrowed at jaw and eye sockets.

There are brains in bottles. Slices of brain sealed in amber. Segments. Madmen's eyes in brine. A heart in a grey glass jar. And there - a face pressed to a glass pane. The preserved body of a young woman, naked, floating in mucky fluids in an immense glass tank. Little pickled mad girl. After death, her hair had continued to grow. Auburn thickets rotting on the scummy surface of the formaldehyde. There are other things also. Experiments. Noises Jerusalem has never heard. Lingering distortions, sad secrets.

A laboratory of death theft. The room at the top of the madhouse. A skull encasing other minds' mistakes. Victorian science. Affordable damnations, malicious errors.

In darkness - the fragility of glass and thought - he moves, overturning tables, tearing up benches, pushing over bottles, smashing jars that imprison time. The wrong-skull he shatters underfoot. The photographs, books and wax recordings are torn. Their lies and screams dissolve in chemical relics. The *research* stinks and withers. Old bones gone to jelly. Imprisoned madness freed to die.

Jerusalem hauls up a rusted contraption of steel seat, manacles, skull-bolts and wires and rages it through a wall of wood and stone.

He pushes out and through, dropping to the topmost corridor. He finds steps.

Moving on into the darkness down the stairs.

Roane had left on chaos - laughing.

The circus had drowned. The big top blown away. He had seen clowns and coloured swans. He is tipsy in the night, following straight paths, leaving behind, moving on. Clown confetti caught in his hair and dark fashion. Black bride walking the aisle of night. He is going home, to Tookesbury Hall, going home to die and be reborn, Self mother, the egg that lays itself. He is going to become a room. He has decided.

He sings to himself and whistles, celebrating life in the darkness. Brittle moon, no clouds now, tall trees all around, taller stars. He cannot help but laugh.

What will he become? What *design* will his room/self take?

He can envisage black stained glass windows, dark as thought. Walls and floor of smooth marble, pale as skin. A veiled mirror. A yew tree would be nice, or sprigs of rosemary growing from the skull of some horned, mountain animal. He wants the room to have the mood of forgotten flowers and remembered rain. He is only thinking.

He comes upon a church, the lych-gate creaking. He jumps over a low stone wall and makes for the tall stone cross that dominates the façade. And he knows not why, but he walks around it three times, clockwise. The direction of the sun.

He comes away feeling foolish.

Walking off, dizzy. In spirals.

The labyrinth is simple. He has been here before. He had died here, in the white abyss, locked in the cellar by a bird that talked, bitten by fever dream insect, and lived through the journey of death with ease. He stops now, on the third floor, listening *without* ears -

Through screeching gullish red, Jerusalem catches scent of Goldflame's room: yellow chalk hangman eroding on a wall of white. Straitjackets, ancient and painted. Moth decay. Webs.

He stoops and wrenches up a bare floorboard. It snaps. Long old nails stick from it. Woodworm prance. He will batter the Golden Flame, snuff out its song and heat. He stalks on. Down.

All about, the loose din of madness. Gasmasks, books of

dust, bare white walls: paintings the tide of time has washed away. He knows the noisesss, but rejects them. He has gone beyond insanity, his is an almighty madness. The sacred Lamb.

Jerusalem follows the sounds of 'Goldflame'. (A playtime whistle, a dead girl, bones, roses. The laughter of rain. Roane's noise, not Doctor Judith's.) The Voices, clamorous with the announcement, *"Forsook feathered fiddle de dee fucked fat foe."*

He is outside the room. The door, off its hinges, rests against its frame.

Lamb is in the room, the wood of hurting, raised. But the fifth voice is absent. He can hear the void.

under his wings…

Somewhere in the world, a bell tolling. Clocks killing time.

From the broken floorboard that he holds, a single flake of rust drops from one of its nails. He hears the molecule plummeting, hears the explosion its shadow makes as it crashes to the floor.

Exempt from reality.

He will wait in this empty room. He will outlive this bloody dross of darkness.

Keep going little night.

Roane stumbles up the gravel driveway of the asylum. The white Hall waiting as it would always wait. It suddenly occurs to him that soon, he will be *part* of the Hall. There is something strangely sexual about that, it makes him hard. He likes it.

Jerusalem can hear the Fifth Voice, *Goldflame.* Hears the crunch of drunken gravel walking. Oily chatter: loose change in a pocket. He hears one more thing also, the sound of destiny.

Shadows gather in the room. Hidden, impossible ghosts.

Roane is at the front door, but it is already open. A thin light burns inside. He shrugs and enters.

Jerusalem tenses. Teeth of rottenness scrape together, broken sinews popping. Fists, fists…

Roane climbs the stairs -

Jerusalem becomes warm.

So unbearably hot. So hot that the nine gaudy strait-jackets of the room begin to melt. Mad art slooping down the walls.

Roane misses his footing, steadies himself, laughs dry, continues.

The game of Hangman combusts.

Roane can hear movement upstairs, breathing.

The chunk of floorboard is no longer in Lamb's grasp. He hears the Voices, they are rejoicing, teary, saying: *"One of us! One of us!"*

Roane sways in the dark of the corridor, one hand flat to the wall. Balanced. He starts up the second flight of thirteen steps.

The room is thick with night, dark as what has gone before. *Close your eyes and there's the darkness; waiting.* Lamb is pressed to a wall, stretched out, watching. Watching himself - he cannot move, *but is moving.* Spreading out, spilling like black ink into corners of himself. Consuming, rejecting. He hears the rustle of black polythene shifting…

His vision is no longer scarred by screaming red gull glass; there is *only* this room in a madhouse in London. Through the quiet darkness he finally hears a purr.

It is only when Roane reaches the top of the stairs that he sees her eyes. Shining summer blue. Confused, he barely feels her breath and the massive sudden paw that cuffs him.

"C'mon Pussy Cat, time we were off. Let's go out back way." It is Ernie calling. Penelope, the tiger, follows after in the darkness. Ernie had returned to Tookesbury Hall to pack a bag, to **go**. Off to Hastings with his new friend, Penelope.

In the dark, he does not see the tiger break young Roane's neck, has no knowledge of his crooked body at the base of thirteen steps.

The back door closes and a hush fills the Hall.

The Angel of Rain is dead.

Jerusalem had heard the noises, something dying, then falling. He did not hear it land. Empty, open. There is nothing now, no sound, no madman with Hell inside his head, no room to speak of, but a *nest* of black polythene, warm and silent, spread out from wall to wall. Shadows standing sentinel. At the heart of the nest there rests an egg of pitted grey, solid stone.

A Lamb egg.

A fossil is a hidden thing. The remains of past life preserved in rock. But the artefact, a bone or invertebrate, that has *become* the fossil, no longer exists. It is long dead. **Gone.** The soft parts, the muscles and organs are stripped free, eaten, decay. What remains are the workings of what lay beneath. A leftover of death, left open to impregnation: a soft shroud of sediment, a gradual crystallisation by calcite or azurite.

A replica preserved in time.

Occasionally a fossil is found, *dug up*, cracked open, the shape of ages within/without, revealed. Cast and mould. Mirror of stone no longer hidden. Twice discarded, moved on.

And what are we? The mind a mould, the body, the cast. What lies beneath? What is hidden? Should it be poked about, excavated? Cracked open.

From actuality, to being, through becoming. A fish into a fossil exhibit. A mind into a Bedlam aviary. A man into a room. But some minds have already 'moved on'. Gone. And what remains?

7

...bid the company farewell.
Sir Walter Raleigh

Norman found Roane's body. He had been sketching his way toward the moment for weeks. He spent two hours drawing and painting the corpse before he thought to call the police. Sculptures of a dead man. A steel life.

The police could see no signs of foul play, the body taken in a black van. The inquest announced death caused by a fall whilst in an intoxicated state. Death being instantaneous. He was cremated a week later. (Simon, the social worker, could not make it, sent a wreath of carnations instead.)

A month later: a private exhibition of Fish's work, organised by a Jew operating from St Leonards on Sea; someone Mr Jackson knows. Jackson now being Fish's 'manager'. Strictly sixty/forty split on all works sold.

The Fleshers Exhibition is held in an annexe of the British Museum not open to the public. Four figure entry fees. Californians and Kuwaitis parting with a years' alimony for a 'Jupiter S Earthborn' original.

Boxes of welded kebab-brown steel with holes bored in them; peer through the holes and you're looking through telescopes at eggcups full of toe-nail clippings, at concealed mirrors coated in sugar. You're staring back at yourself. Look again and you could be gone. There are ants in there eating your sugary reflection.

Industrial cave paintings. Sketches on pages torn from a blank dream diary.

Stacks of hundred dollar bills soaked in water, seeds planted between each sheet. Thin green shoots growing there.

A carpeted skeleton. Rusty iron vaginas.

Fish is around somewhere, with roll-up and can of Tennant's Extra, *peeling* Victorian turquoise tiles from the VIP ladies lavatory, third floor of the museum. He has plans for them.

Sea dawn.

Fallen morning over Hastings beach. Ghosts of boats and the pier in the distance. Misty hotels. Night fishermen and their driftwood bonfires. Seaside streetlights dying for the day. The last star shining in a too vivid sky. A trawler two miles out. The *lost* sound of a fog horn. And Ernie on his seat of stones watching the gulls gliding, smooth as water, dropping mussel shells onto rocks, ripping out breakfast.

Penelope rolls in the water, splashing through the Fairy Liquid foam. She sleeps in the day in their rented room up on the cliffs, but likes a run at night, along the beach or through the Old Town.

Ernie's oilpaint face has peeled in the salt air, faint traces of crimson and green left. He eats hotdogs, chips, drinks fizzy pop and takes tea at the Regal, now. He likes it here; playing at the sea's edge, waves rolling out, biscuit grey shells and tiger paw prints in the damp shiny sand. He found a starfish last week.

The sun rises and meets his smile.

He doesn't mind the chattering sarcasm of gulls, or the beer brown of the sea. The dead birds that are washed up no longer need to fly. They can swim now.

The stones and pebbles on the beach remind him of the gravel driveway at Tookesbury Hall - *that* went out into the main road, but where does this path lead? And where does all this sea come from? It's so big. Big as looking.

A curious gannet hovers too close over Penelope and she roars. Ernie chuckles. Kid Canute smiling at sea and sky. Laughing at life.

The water goes out now, but it will be back. The sea always returns.

Maudsley has been penning his memoirs; a deal struck a drunken fortnight since at the Groucho Club. Contracts signed. Miramax have already bought the exclusive rights on *all* film and multimedia options. Apparently, Spielberg has made interested noises.

Maudsley has found the new room of silent black polythene and is respectful of it. He sometimes sleeps there, curled against the warm stony egg. At the moment he's working on Chapter Seven: **An Erroneous Pelican.** He writes with a plucked tail feather bitten to a point. Indian ink.

"Awkk, hubble, bubble," says Maudsley with the appearance of Mr Jackson.

"Mornin' laddie." Jackson is cowed, stooping slow, a bull on Librium. Pours himself a six sugar tea, doesn't want it. Too uncertain to smoke. Hand to face, grey stubble, facing the window without seeing out. A black crow flaps there. He has spent whole days sleeping since the circus. Waiting in silence. Woke this morning from a dream that he had armed himself with a scythe, castrated his father and cast the bloody bits into the sea. The dream unsettled him, as dreams do.

There is still no sign of Mr Flint.

He looks and suddenly sees a large cardboard box has arrived for him, been there days. Roehampton postmark: artificial legs.

On top of the box, a postcard. Twelfth Tarot design and the legend - *Eluctor fatum nec demoro in prep*. On the other side of the card, GREETINGS FROM THE GOLDEN AGE

BAR, Hungary. It's from the Reverend Dacy and Imram Poones: the news that Nelson Browne is dead. Pneumonia caught from standing in a puddle of chilled Double Diamond. The heavy hint of Alzheimer's. There is also the promise of 'adventure' in Istanbul.

Jackson's on his last legs here. King of Scars too long in dry dock, homesick for anywhere. He's been in two minds forever, and out of both of them. Nowhere is big enough for him, except the past. A land misplaced by cartographers. His thoughts are compassed: shadow maps. The knowledge of all that is forgotten.

the promise of 'adventure' in Istanbul

What to do?

Play it by ear. Kick off the cargo. Slip away.

"Err, I'm just off out, laddie," he calls to the bird. "You take care now."

And Mr Jackson is out the door, gone to stand watch on the deck of the World.

"Awkk, God bless," says Maudsley the parrot. "God bless."

Glossary

(By popular international request. No really.)

Adie, Kate – UK Television war correspondent
Aedes Aegypti – yellow fever-carrying mosquito
Anorchid – one without testicles
Axminster – expensive carpeting
Baker Street Girl – a prostitute
Balatronic – unintentional clown
Balor – Celtic god of death
Balthazar - one of the Three Wise Men
Bedlam Aviary – caged birds kept for the stimulation of inamates of Bedlam Asylum
Black-in-the-Green – Jack in the Green: Pagan character symbolising the advent of summer
"Bloody there in 1987..." – referring to the hurricane in England at that time
Blue Tac – Sticky Tac
Brass Monkeys – cold, i.e. cold enough to freeze the nuts off a brass monkey
Brasso – liquid metal polish (UK)
Butlins – a holiday camp (UK)
Cafard – French slang for the madness produced by terminal boredom
Call My Bluff – UK television 'guess the meaning of the obscure word' game, watched by the housebound, bedridden and students
Cayman - alligator
Chromophobe – colour phobic

Cooper, Fiona – producer of soft porn videos
Crombie – short for Abercrombie, a brand of black coat
Dangerous Saracen Magic – the priesthood originally termed the concept of zero as this. *Nothing will come of nothing.*
Deerstalker and Inverness – hat and cloak famously depicted as worn by Sherlock Holmes
Dementia Peacocks – *dementia praecox:* schizophrenia
Dewsbury – Yorkshire town
Dilly – Piccadilly Circus, London
DK – directoire knickers. Bloomers
Double Diamond – canned ale
Eluctor Fatum Nec Demoro In Prep – Struggle Will Not Stop Time
Flat Foot – a policeman
Frangible – easily broken
Fulgivorasaurus Rex Regum – Lightning Eater, King of Kings
Galloways – a strong cough remedy
Gazza – Paul Gascoigne, an English soccer player
GBH – Grievous Bodily Harm
Golden Lane, Prague – alchemical capital
Gooba Gabba – see Todd Browning's film *'Freaks'*
Green Line - a coach transport company
Grim-Mouldy – Grimaldi – the clown
The Guardian – UK newspaper
Hackney – a horse drawn cab
Hedonophobia – fear of pleasure
Heliophobia – fear of the sun
Hindley, Myra – a UK child killer
HK Semi Auto Heckler and Koch rifle
Homo Diluvii Testis – fossil of a giant salamander in 1735, which became known as the Diluvian Man

Humors – the four chief fluids of the body: blood, phlegm, yellow bile, black bile
Hush Puppy – a brand of shoe
Hysteresis - the influence of previous actions on subsequent events
Inanna – Sumerian fertility goddess
The Independent – a newspaper
Ithyphallic – penilely erect
Ixtab – Mayan suicide god
Karadji - aborigines
Knackers' Yard – originally an equine slaughter house
Liggerati – self-important non-creative freeloaders found at any artistic occasion. Buy your own fucking drinks.
Light and Mild – a mixture of light and dark ales
Luger – Germand hand pistol
M&S – Marks and Spencer (UK department store)
Mackeson – strong, dark beer
Marasmic – withering, wasting away
McKewans Export – a strong lager
Meccano – metal construction kit, popular since the 1950s
Meths – methylated spirit
Monkey - £500
Morecombe & Wise – UK comedy double act
Motley and Slap – full clown make-up
Narranschiff – ship of fools
NHS – the UK National Health Service
North-Man – origin of the name Norman
Norton – a brand of English motorcycle
November 6th – the day after Guy Fawkes' Night
Number 4 Iron – a type of gold club
Nutty Slack – cheap coal
O and O – over and out
The Old Barker and Johnson Routine – M R James and

his brother took the roles of these humorous shop-keepers
Ouroboros – Gnostic tail-swallowing snake
Ouzelem – apocryphal bird that flew around and around in ever decreasing circles, until it vanished up its own behind
Pacamac - emergency rainwear
Palimpsest – paper or parchment from which previous writing has been erased
Papist! – many thanks to Steve Alton!
Parousiamania – fear of the second coming of Christ
Pasul – appertaining to Kosher slaughter
Pebbledash – mortar with pebbles in it used as a coating for external walls
Phocine – pertaining to seals or walruses
Pinguid – full of fat, greasy
Pools coupons – soccer-related weekly gambling game
Pyknic – short, broad and muscular
RADA – the Royal Academy of Dramatic Arts
Rampton – a psychiatric 'hospital'
Rizla – a cigarette paper, for hand-rolling cigarettes
Roehampton – home of the limb-fitting centre
Rosinante – Don Quixote's scrawny horse
Rozzer - policeman
Saddle Sniffers – popular unsavoury pastime involving the saddles of girls' bicycles
The Saint and Greavesie Show – UK soccer pundits' television show
Sakarabru – African god of retribution
Scars on Sunday – a play on the title of a religious TV programme, Stars on Sunday
Scumbered – fouled with dog excrement
Snout – a police informant

The South Bank Show UK television arts show
Spam – tinned meat
Stark, Freya – explorer/travel writer
St Trinians' – Fictitious, riotous girls' school, depicted in English films c 1950s
Stride, Elizabeth – 1888, a victim of Jack the Ripper
Stump Sock – protective garment commonly worn at the end of a limb, favoured by amputees. (Author note: I've worn one. No, really.)
Sudatory – sweaty
The Sun – a tabloid newspaper
Sutcliffe – Peter Sutcliffe, the Yorkshire Ripper
Tab-ends – the remains of hand-rolled cigarettes
Tip Tod – the Devil
The Tube/The Word – crap 'yoof' TV programmes (1980s)
Tunzi – Zulu word for shadow
Twin Set – knitted cardigan and matching jumper
Untergehen – going under, psychological terminology
Woodbine – an extremely strong, filterless cigarette
Xochipilli – Aztec god of flowers
Zimmer Frame – walking frame

HYPERION ELE
ME.
PH COGOR INTERIRE.
NATVS SVM EX HERMOGENE.

JOHN KAIINE: WRITER, ARTIST, PHOTOGRAPHER.
EX-LONDON GRAVE DIGGER.
MARRIED TO WRITER TANITH LEE
AND TWO BLACK AND WHITE (FEMALE) CATS...
'FLOWERS' ON-LINE COMIC STRIP COMING SEPTEMBER 2013.
WWW.ACESWEEKLY.CO.UK
SACRIFICIAL LAMBS T SHIRTS COMING SUMMER 2013.
WWW.SACRIFICIALLAMBS.CO.UK
DOLLY SODOM - SHORT STORY - SHORT FILM (A DARKER SILENCE).
WWW.BRANDONDEXTER.COM
KAIINE.COM COMING WHENEVER...

CPSIA information can be obtained at www.ICGtesting.com
Printed in the USA
LVOW06s1921110813

347339LV00002B/89/P